Mother of Exiles

The Epic Fantasy Adventure of a Prodigal Son Returning to the Exile Forest

Joel C. Flanagan-Grannemann

https://www.ServantsoftheMoonandSun.com

© 2024 by Joel C. Flanagan-Grannemann Joel@ServantsoftheMoonandSun.com

Version 1.0 Published November 2024 in Seattle, WA

Edited by Jay-Jay Flanagan-Grannemann

TheHyphenatedEditor@ServantsoftheMoonandSun.com

Cover Design by 100covers contact@100covers.com

DDC: 816.3 Flanagan-Grannemann

Suggested LC subject headings:

Interpersonal relations — Fiction

Women soldiers — Fiction

Interpersonal relations and culture — Fiction

Forest people — Fiction

Forests in literature

Forgiveness — Fiction

Library of Congress Control Number: 2024921610

Please sign up for announcements and updates at **www.ServantsoftheMoonandSun.com**

ISBN: 978-1-966000-00-6 E-Book

ISBN: 978-1-966000-01-3 Trade Paperback

ISBN: 978-1-966000-02-0 Hardcover

Contents

Dedication

This book is dedicated to my parents, Anita and Bruce,
to all those at the Farm who helped raise me,
and to Tony Rice and Gordon Lightfoot, whose music inspires me.

Author's Note

For your protection, all Fairy names have been translated into your language.

Prologue: What Has Come Before

Aurora is having an extraordinary effect on the Realms.

She's barely a month old, and she's already provoked renewed hostilities between the Humans and the Fairies and caused a civil war in the Fairy Realm. (Her effect on Elen will be wide-ranging and complex, and is unknown, as of yet, to most of the Humans, Fairies, and Elenites living there.)

A little history: The brief love affair (between Talia, Heir to the Fairy Realm — now absent Queen — and Bastile, then Prince — now King — of the Human Realm) that produced Aurora has caused ripples of conflict and change all across the Realms, and even within the Exile Forest.

After an attack on Talia and her companions (8 Ladies, 9 soldiers, and Flora, a supplemental mother to them all) by Wingless, a Blood Cult leader and sometime ally of the Queen's sinister Three Sisters, Talia is exiled from the Fairy Court. In her time of exile, she discovers a vast conspiracy to reawaken foul, blood-fueled Magical practices of the past. After freeing one outpost of evil, Talia decides that her only path forward is to investigate the past, seeking answers about her ancestor, the almost universally reviled (though some say unfairly) Exile Queen. Pursued by agents of her treacherous aunts, Talia takes refuge in the last stronghold of the Exile Queen, a mountain deep in the Fairy Realm.

Hounded even there by terrible men with poisonous weapons, Talia flees to the far edges of the Realm, on the Sea of the First

Fairies, where — for a time — she and her company find refuge and peace.

There, on the shore of the sea, Aurora (then known as Sunrise) is born. She is proclaimed Talia's Heir and, despite her half-Human heritage, future Queen of the Fairies. Talia and her Ladies plan to return to their home in the palace at the capital city of Fae-Treval and forge a path toward peace between the simmering Realms before war erupts.

But it is not to be. Acting on behalf of both King Bastile and the Three Sisters, Wingless sends Elenite assassins to Talia's cliff-side sanctuary. In the attack, many of Talia's Ladies and soldiers are killed, and the survivors are left scarred in both mind and spirit. Acting on his own agenda, and contrary to the instructions of the Three Sisters — who want her killed — Wingless abducts baby Aurora, leaving the body of a dead child for Talia to find and mourn in her place.

Manipulated by both the Three Sisters and Wingless, King Bastile accepts the baby as a replacement for his stillborn son. Strong Fairy Magic is used to conceal Aurora's Elenite nature, and hide from Bastile's wife — Rose of the Briar Clan — the true parentage of the girl she believes to be her daughter.

Seeking bloody revenge on Bastile for the death of their child, Talia and her surviving Faries attack the official presentation of his newborn daughter to the Human Realm. Talia casts a curse on the baby: her unavoidable death will come after just sixteen short years.

Unbeknownst to Talia, Aurora is her daughter, and ancient Fairy protections respond to this unforgivable treachery with a devastating backlash, damaging Talia's wings and cutting her off from her magical Power. Chaos reigns as some of her Fairy companions and protectors are captured. Talia and her Lady Elanor escape, but they find themselves trapped in the Exile Queen's secret sanctuary. Completely cut off from her Power, the only exit through a Ring she can no longer operate, Talia is impelled to face her grief over the death of her daughter.

Forced to accelerate their plan to take over the Fairy Realm, on what becomes known as the Night of Black Wings, the Three Sisters and their followers stage a violent coup using Fairy-killing, blood- and corruption-forged blackblades, occupying Fae-Treval and killing Queen Zellandine.

Upon her escape from the Exile Queen's hideout, Talia is once again overcome with a lust for vengeance, and uses forbidden Blood Magic to access her Power to infiltrate the palace, now held by her aunts. She attacks her youngest aunt, Gren, in revenge for her mother's death. As Gren bargains for her life, however, she reveals that Talia's daughter is not dead, but merely stolen and hidden from her. But controls implanted in Gren's mind kill her before she can reveal where the baby is.

Meanwhile, Captain Shatterstaff and the remaining Ladies and soldiers escape an attempt to execute them and proceed to help as many loyal Fairies as possible escape Fae-Treval for the sanctuary of the Exile Queen's mountain.

Determined to find her daughter, Talia names the Queen's Justice, Titania, as Regent and leaves her new post as Queen behind. Her former Lady and novice Shrinekeeper, Goldberry, and the soldier Raven go with her, seeking missing members of their company. This is not their story, though.

So, where is Aurora in all of this?

In the chaos after the casting of the curse, while trying to escape using faulty Fairy Ring Magic, the Fairy soldier Spearhead and the Thorn Brother Canin rescue (abduct, really) baby Aurora, seizing her from the arms of her father, King Bastile. Spear claims the baby as her own, seeing her as a replacement for her lost son.

That's why Aurora is the reason (via a source of help as yet unknown to them) that Canin and Spear are where they are right now.

On the edge of the Exile Forest.

Chapter 1
Homecoming

"It'll be dark soon."

Silence.

Canin tried again. "There might be a storm coming. Can you sense anything?"

"I'm not a weather Fairy," Spearhead snapped. "I can't sense the weather like. . . . I can't sense the weather." Relenting, she pointed to the east. "But those dark clouds and flashes might be a storm." She had fastened her shirt again. Earlier, she had demanded Canin's cloak, using it as a basket to carry baby Aurora. She stared at Canin expectantly.

When he didn't answer, she snapped, "This is your home. I've never been here. You must be the one to lead us to shelter and safety." Then her expression changed, as she looked down at the sleeping Aurora. "I told you he isn't too bright."

He wanted to snap back at her, but she was right. Canin corralled all his prior thoughts and locked them away. If he thought about Min and the others, or the Blood Ring, and the horrible eyes of Wingless, or Spear's broken wings, he would curl up in a ball and cry till the end of the Realms.

They needed him. Spear and Aurora. Both of them.

"Yes, this is my home. There should be watchers near." A thought occurred to him. It had been buried under everything else that had happened, but was now rising to the surface. "There should be watchers near," he said with more certainty. "I know there's a Treetower here."

4

"Treetower?"

"Yes, a guard or watch tower."

"Then take us there."

Canin looked at the setting sun. He raised his hand and walked it over the line of the forest before him. "There," he said. "Follow me."

Walking briskly toward the forest, Canin felt a surge of confidence. He knew where he was. His eyes, adapting to the dim light, picked out the proper tree. After a few steps, his ears noted that Spear wasn't following. Turning, he was blinded by a flash of fire.

Spear hadn't moved. At her feet lay a small, bright fire. She held Aurora's basket tight in one hand. Her other hand was raised, fist clenched over the fire.

"Spear!" Canin called, running back. "What are you doing?"

She turned to look at him and he stopped dead. Her eyes shone in the firelight; the slits of her pupils filled with flames. It was a fire he had seen before. The memory of her slaughter of the cultists filled him with horror and revulsion. As he reached for the wooden knife on his belt — the only weapon he had — Canin realized with great uneasiness that Spear still had her sword.

"I couldn't leave them," Spear said, her voice far away.

Canin now understood; she was burning the broken shards of her wings.

"Spear," he said softly, stepping closer and reaching out to her.

She opened her fist and made a flinging gesture. The fire went out.

"Spear," Canin said again more strongly. She waved him away, not letting him touch her.

"There is nothing to be done," she said. Pushing past him, she began walking in the direction he had been going.

Canin stared down at the charred spot in the grass. "Mother's mercy," he muttered. "What have you led me to?"

"Come on," Spear called lightly. "A storm is coming, and we must find the Treetower."

"Coming," he called. Taking one last look at the ashes of her destroyed wings, Canin turned and followed.

5

☾ 〰 ☼

The trees of the forest loomed up before them, dark in the coming gloom of the storm. They moved in the wind, clacking, their thorn-studded branches shaking. Long dagger-like thorns and wickedly hooked ones shone in the dying light. Weapons of both defense and assault, they eagerly sought more visitors to rip and tear apart with their wooden stilettos and sabers.

The Exile Forest was a living rampart against the cruelty of the Realms.

To Spear it was a foreboding wall of green and brown sentinels, fierce guards in thorn-studded armor. She had faced walls of armored Humans with only small sparks of anxiety, but these wooden warriors gave her pause.

But she was a Fairy soldier. She would not show them any fear.

Canin had been forced to run to catch up with Spear, or she would have plunged right into the underbrush. Right into the sharp arms of the thorn trees of the Exile Forest. Calmly, he showed her how to find the path that led safely under and around the thorns.

"I can see them," she told him impatiently. She hovered her hand over one of the thorns, which was as long as her hand. She started forward, then stopped, passing Aurora, who was still sleeping, to Canin. Then she put on her ringmail. Canin started to ask if she needed help, but it seemed her Power was back. The shirt slipped smoothly around her damaged wings and the ties fastened without his help. She then turned and held out her hands for Aurora.

Canin handed the wrapped baby back. Spear brushed her sleeping face.

"There's a path this way," he said after she didn't move. "It would be better for me to lead."

"This is your home," Spear agreed.

Canin eased by her and led them on to the forest path. Old habits awoke, and memories flooded back as he led her through the darkening forest. He ducked, avoiding a branch covered in short thorns, glancing back to make sure Spear did, too. A sapling, its long thorns on spindly branches, waved at him, forcing him to step to the left, then back, then forward, his feet remembering the dance.

Behind him he could hear Spear grunting and huffing, muttering either to herself or to the trees. Smiling to himself, he caught a branch in just the right place so Spear could duck underneath. With a proud gait, he followed her out of the trees into a clearing.

The Treetower was right where he remembered. It sat in the center of a glade near the edge of the forest. It was a large oak tree that shared the coloring and leaves of the other, smaller trees, but did not have the long thorns of its smaller siblings. The grass around it was short and matted down, showing a long history of regular traffic.

Canin frowned.

"What's wrong?" Spearhead, ever the wary soldier, asked, catching his mood. She shifted Aurora to free her sword hand.

'How could she draw her sword and fight with a baby in her arms?' a part of Canin's mind wondered. 'With absolutely no trouble at all,' he answered himself.

"There should be someone here," Canin finally admitted. He gestured up. "We shouldn't have been able to walk to the edge of the forest and into this clearing without being challenged."

"Maybe your Thorn Brothers aren't as diligent as you remember them being," Spear taunted him.

"No." Canin ignored her tone. "There's something off here. I can feel it." He stepped warily to the base of the tree, expecting a shout or an arrow at any moment. He ran his hand over the rough bark. He moved to the left, searching for something.

The close crack of thunder made Spear jump and woke Aurora. Spear shushed the baby and glared at Canin.

"It there shelter here or not?"

"Just a moment," Canin said. He buried his fears of what had become of his Thorn Brothers. The notches should be here. Finally, halfway around the tree, his fingers found a dent deep enough for his fingers.

"Found it," he said, turning, but Spear was right behind him. He started back. He hadn't heard her following him. Her face was full of barely contained fear. Rain had begun to fall. Most of it caught in the canopy above, but a few drops hit his head.

"These form a ladder," Canin explained. He reached up and pulled himself up. Muscles he hadn't used in a long time roared back to life and he was up the side of the tree in a moment. He pushed through the concealing branches and came to the closed trap door of the Treetower.

Here he stopped again. His instincts were screaming at him. There was an itching around his eyes, imagining an arrow aimed there. 'Mother, guide me,' he beseeched, then banged on the trap door.

The sound echoed in the space above, and died away. Canin strained his ears, but couldn't hear anyone moving around above him. Taking another breath, he grabbed the handle and pushed up. The door moved slightly, but did not open. He pressed up with more effort, to no effect.

"The bar must have fallen closed," Canin said. Glancing down, he called, "Spear, do you have something I can slip through the crack? The bar must be closed. My knife is too thick." As the words left his mouth, a thrown blade hit the wood of the trap door by his hand with a thunk. Startled, Canin almost lost his grip on the handle and the improvised ladder.

"Hurry up!" Spear called. There was an edge to her voice. "It's raining harder!"

Canin pulled the knife free and worked it between the frame and the trap door. He moved it back and forth till he felt the blade catch on something. Hoping he remembered which direction the bar went, he pushed. He heard the bar slide across the floor above him. Relieved, he pushed up on the trap door slightly.

Through the crack, he could see only darkness. The air was musty, as though the door had been closed for several days. Hoping the Mother was with him, Canin pushed the trap door fully open and stuck his head inside.

Still nothing. There was no sense of presence in the small room. Canin climbed fully into the room and sat on the edge of the frame, his feet still dangling out the trap door. He reached to his left, feeling for the expected candle and flint. They were there, and by feel he struck a spark and lit the candle. When no one loomed out of the darkness at him, Canin relaxed and looked around.

The room was much as he remembered. It was small, big enough for just two or three people. In front of him was a window covered by a camouflaged and waxed curtain. Beside the window were a wardrobe and a chest. Another chest sat to his left. Moving the candle's light, Canin saw two bedrolls on the floor, with a box lined with blankets between them. There were also spare blankets folded at the foot of each bedroll.

Frowning at the appearance of the room, Canin climbed fully inside. The ceiling was as low as he remembered it, leaving him only a little space above his head. The rain on the roof beat louder, and more thunder rolled in as the storm grew closer.

"Canin!" Spear yelled from the ground.

Dropping to his belly on the floor, Canin stuck his head out the trap door. Below, he could see her, now illuminated from above by a floating Fairy Light. She had drawn her sword and was holding Aurora close with her other arm.

"It's safe!" Canin called down. "Looks like it might have been. . . ."

She cut him off. "Good. Take her." Spear gestured, and Aurora, still wrapped, began to float up beside the tree trunk. Canin could hear her begin to giggle and coo at the flight. When she floated through the trap door, he grabbed her and settled back. He unwound the damp cloak encasing her and gazed into her smiling eyes. Again, they grabbed on and would not let go of his spirit. There was no fear in Aurora's face, just happiness.

"It's like you fly all the time," Canin said, brushing a drop of water from her head. Her hand reached out and grabbed his. For the first time, he noticed that she had something on her arm. A tarnished button tied with a Fairysilk cord moved up and down her arm as she grabbed at him.

"What is that?" Canin started to ask.

"Move out of the way," Spear demanded, pushing her head through the trap door. "I need more space to get inside."

When Canin didn't move, she glared again. "Move back. If you make me catch my wing, you'll regret it." She nodded back to the healing, but still raw, edge of her wing.

Canin finally moved himself back and gave her enough space to climb into the Treetower. With a bang, she shut the trap door and drew the bar across to lock it. Then she seemed to relax.

"Not bad," she commented. Slightly taller than Canin, she had to stoop a bit to keep her head from hitting the ceiling. She took in the room with a quick glance.

"What's in the chests?" she asked.

Before Canin could reply, Aurora, who had been startled by the bang of the door, began to cry. Canin started, and could only stare down at the baby in his arms, having no idea what to do.

Spear lost all interest in anything else. "She must be hungry again." She gestured toward her back. "Curse! Gone again. Help me out of this?" she said, turning.

Canin had to duck, or her damaged wing would have smacked him in the head. "It's all right, Little Wing," Canin said. He placed her in the box between the bedrolls. She settled in, fitting perfectly. Her crying grew quieter.

"Motherless," he swore. "It's like this was made for us."

"Canin, my ringmail," Spear reminded him over her shoulder.

Faster this time, Canin eased her out of the ringmail and set it aside. Spear then pulled off her shirt, exposing her back to him. An unexpected surge of desire hit Canin as he watched the muscles of her back move and flex. Then he remembered Min and pushed the feelings savagely away. Oblivious, Spear sat down on the left-hand bedroll. She picked Aurora up and put the baby to her breast. Both sighed contentedly. Canin turned abruptly and went to the covered window.

The waxed cloth was fastened with bent nails all around the opening. He turned a few so he could pull the cloth aside. The feel of the waxed fabric on his fingers brought back a surge of memories. He thought, 'Niel might have treated this.' A jumbled blur of confused and somehow shameful emotions flooded him. Niel had raised him, but was not his father, but his real Fairy father hadn't been a true father to him either. Canin again shoved those emotions aside.

Through the gap, he could see that the rain was coming down harder. He could dimly see the clearing and the trees beyond. If there was anyone near, they would be kept away by the rain. Canin relaxed slightly.

"What's in the chests?" Spear asked again.

Not wanting to turn, Canin felt his way to the chest on the other side of the window, stubbing his toe on the way.

Spear giggled. "You're a fool," she said. "But a cute fool, like Min said." He heard the rustle of cloth. "There. Covered."

Canin turned and saw that she had draped one of the blankets lengthwise across herself, covering her breasts and the baby. Canin nodded in thanks. Indeed feeling the fool, but relieved for the restoration of Spear's decorum, Canin undid the latch and opened the chest. Spear's Fairy Light floated closer. There were two quivers of arrows on top. One set was fletched with black feathers, and the other — longer clothyard shafts — was fletched with blue feathers. Another surge of memory hit him. "Tymora," he muttered. "You're still making arrows."

"What did you say?" Spear asked. "What's in there?"

"Arrows," Canin told her, holding up one of the quivers. Underneath he saw two sheathed long knives and an axe. It was designed for cutting wood, but Canin could use it to defend himself if he had to.

"Arrows," Spear repeated. "Anything else?"

"Two knives and an axe," Canin said, putting the quiver back.

"Leave them out," Spear commanded. "We need to be armed."

"But this is my home," Canin disagreed. "We don't have anything to fear here."

"This is not my home," Spear replied. "And I'll feel better with more weapons around."

Canin tried to shut the chest, but Spear raised her hand and held it open.

"Bring them out," she ordered harshly.

Canin wanted to argue more, but the look in her eyes reminded him of what she was capable of. He set the quiver down and brought out the blades. One slid across the floor so Spear could pick it up.

"Good weight," she said, testing the heft. She held down the sheath with her knee and drew the blade. "Good metal. Not silk-steel, but good quality." She tested the edge. "Sharp." She thrust it into the floor at her side. Canin jumped slightly. Smiling, Spear said, "Keep the other one."

Canin nodded as he pulled out the axe and set it on the floor. Finally, he pulled out the blue feathered arrows.

Spear's eyes lit up. "Those are magnificent." She held out her hand.

Canin, feeling a surge of jealousy, pulled them closer. "These were made by a friend. They're mine."

"Who's the better archer?" Spear asked, but she dropped her hand.

"Raven was teaching me," Canin protested.

Spear lost her smile. She looked down at Aurora. "Useless without bows anyway," she muttered.

'Now I've stepped in it,' Canin commented to himself as he set down the quiver. He stood and opened the wardrobe. The door creaked and felt loose on its hinges. Inside hung several cloaks of green and brown. Canin brushed them aside and found what he had expected. He reached in. "Thank you," he breathed. He thought about not telling Spear for a moment, but rejected the idea quickly. She might be broken somehow, but she was still a soldier. And they were in this together.

Canin turned triumphantly and held up two bows. One short, the other long, both polished and strong, the best his old friend and teacher could make. Then he slumped.

Spear's eyes were closed. She was asleep.

Chapter 2
Fairy Eyes Crying in the Rain

A flash of lightning and a crack of thunder woke Spear, who flailed in the blankets that were draped over and around her. She tried to stand, but her coverings were tangled. Growling, she tore at the bindings, needing to get free. Movement to her left made her throw up that arm in defense.

"Spear," Canin called, as he somehow blocked her blow. "It's all right."

She didn't hear him, and continued thrashing.

Reacting on instinct, he remembered the actions of the woman who had raised him. When he was a child, a young woman who had recently come to the forest had reacted badly to something about one of the Thorn Brothers. That night, she had woken the house screaming. Young Canin had been scared, not knowing what to do. The sturdy, no-nonsense Elenite woman who was not his mother had calmly gone into the young woman's room, taken her hands, and spoken to her quietly. Slow and gentle, till the young woman was strong enough to fight off the darkness on her own.

Canin put his hands on both sides of Spear's head, holding her lightly.

"Spearhead," he told her, forcing calm into his voice. "You are safe. I'm here. You're safe. Spear, you're safe."

13

Her own instincts kicked in, and she put her hands on his shoulders and tried to push him away. Somehow Canin was able to keep his hold on her. All the while, he continued speaking in a low, calm tone. "Spear, you are safe. There are no enemies here. You're safe."

Her breathing began to regulate, to match his: slow and measured. Her hands stopped pushing at him and relaxed, settling on his shoulders.

"Spear," Canin kept saying, "you're safe."

Her eyes opened, and Canin saw the panic drain out, replaced by worry and embarrassment.

"Did I wake her?" Spear asked, her voice low. A dim Fairy Light bloomed above them.

Canin glanced down. The box where Aurora lay was beside them. In the dim light, he could see that she was still sleeping, wrapped tightly in her blankets.

"No," Canin reassured her. "She hasn't stirred."

Spear let go of him and laid her hand on the lip of the box. Canin moved one of his hands to cover hers. She started, but did not move.

"You are safe," Canin said again. "We are safe."

Spear tried to say something, but her emotions overwhelmed her, and she threw herself into his arms, pushing him back against the wall. She wrapped her arms around him, laid her head on his chest, and began to cry softly. Canin just held her, stroking her back and murmuring soft words.

Canin looked over and thought he saw the shine of Aurora's open eyes in the Fairy Light, but he blinked, and they were gone.

"Trillium," Spear muttered later, still enclosed in his arms.

"What?" Canin asked, confused. He had been dozing, and her voice woke him abruptly. The warm weight of her on him, the light patter of the rain, the familiar smells: they all combined to give him the strongest sense of security he had felt in a long time. Maybe since that night at the inn with Lady Min, when he had slept with her wings wrapped tightly around him.

"Trillium," Spear said again. She pulled away from him, settling into a cross-legged position and wiping her eyes. Canin felt suddenly cold, deprived of her warmth. "That was my name as a child. Maybe you can call me that when this happens again."

Not trusting his voice, Canin reached out. She took his hand.

"There's something broken in me," she admitted in a desperate whisper. "I thought being a soldier, a mother. . . ." Her voice broke. Canin squeezed her hand. She shook her head. "Fighting for my Queen. Winning a place in the Queen's Guard. Serving the Heir. Being one of the Nine. It thought it would all help me heal that broken part of myself." She smiled. "And for a time, it did. Gold kept me grounded. She helped me be a better sister and a better soldier." The tears came again, and she set her head in one hand. Canin held on tight to the other one. "Goddess, why didn't I go with her? I knew she spoke the truth, but I was too wrapped up in Talia's quest for justice. I thought I could make up for my mistakes."

"You did," Canin assured her. "If you hadn't been there, I might not have made it out. Aurora would still be in the hands of that horrible Wingless." He gave her arm a shake. "She led you to where you needed to be. Where we needed you to be."

"But I'm still broken," Spear argued. "I don't know if I can hold it inside. I'm afraid I'll hurt her." She looked up at him. "Or you." She shifted, and gripped his hand between hers. "She made me promise to keep you safe."

Canin felt tears in his eyes. He shifted so he was facing her head on. "I know. I'm broken, too. I was just beginning to heal. Now, she's gone. I may never see her again."

The strength Canin had been using to keep himself together shattered like ice. Nothing could hold in all the great losses he had suffered in his young life. The woman he loved was lost, maybe dead, or maybe on the other side of the vast Realm. He was back in a home he had left in shame, with a woman who was almost a stranger. A Fairy who balanced on the edge of a knife. And there was a baby. A baby he had helped steal from the Human King and his pet wingless, bloodthirsty Fairy. It was all too much. Canin let go of Spear's hands, burying his head in his own to cry freely. He cried more tears than he thought he had within him.

After a time, Canin felt a touch on his arm. "You are safe," Spear whispered. He felt her slide closer. He looked up. She slipped her left arm around him. In her other arm, she held Aurora. The baby's eyes were open and shining brightly.

"Don't cry, Papa," Spear whispered. "Your daughter is here and safe. I am here and safe. You saved us. We're home. The Goddess and the Mother led us here."

To Canin's tear-addled mind, her voice was not that of the soldier he had trained with, or the broken-winged Fairy he had led through the forest. It was a voice he had heard in his dreams. In a dim, hazy memory of the past, before the forest. Memories he was too young to have. A voice of the past.

Canin brushed the tears away. "My daughter?" he asked.

"Yes," Spear said. "Our daughter."

Clinging to the only thing he had, Canin put his head on Spear's shoulder. Together, they cried and listened to the rain. Aurora's arm somehow came out of her wrappings and she latched on to his hand. Completing the circle, they sat through the night.

"So I will be your partner, wife, woman.," Spear grimaced at the words, but moved on. "Whatever a committed relationship is called here. This is our child. We were cast out of the Realm for our love. I was wounded. You saved us. We came here to find a home." She began to gesture. "You can be a Thorn Brother again. I can train your people. Show them the Fairy way of killing those men who wrong them. We can build a house, or move into one. You can see your old friends again. You can make up for leaving them. Speak to those people who raised you, very well I should say; apologize for not treating them like the parents they were to you. And we can live together. We'll have to work on the intimacy. I know you still have feelings for Min, but she's not here, and I am. We can take it slow. I don't want to hurt you. Leather-wings are different in pleasure than others. You'll get used to it. I'm sure you will. It's been a while for me. I better work on my Silence Weave. I'm hungry. Is there food here? Producing all that milk has drained me. Did those Humans not feed her? She'll suck me dry." She paused to breathe and looked at Canin. He was staring wide eyed at her. She cocked her head. "Well, I'm hungry. It's morning. Aren't you?"

"Spear, I. . . ."

"I can go hunting." Spear stood up and grabbed the shorter bow. "I'm not as good as Raven, but I'm sure I can hit something." She opened the chest, letting the lid drop back with a bang.

Aurora, who had just gone to sleep, woke with a loud cry. Spear dropped the bow with another bang, making Aurora cry even harder. Spear scooped her up.

"I'm sorry," she cooed. "Oh, don't cry." She turned to Canin. "We're hungry. Get us food." She dipped her head and began to mutter into the baby's hair.

Canin took a deep breath. He approached the second chest, which held a few supplies. It was mostly dried meat and roots. There was also a sealed clay jar, which Canin suspected was wine. He picked up some of the meat and went to where Spear was rocking the crying baby on her bedroll.

"Spear," Canin said calmly over the cries. "Let me hold her."

Spear glared at him.

Canin tried again. "Trillium. Let me hold her. She's reacting to you. She'll calm down when you do." He held up the meat. "Or when you've eaten."

Spear, still glaring at him, surrendered the baby. "I regret telling you that already." She seized the dried meat from his hand.

Canin sat down and set Aurora in his lap. Still crying, she looked up at him. He waved his hand, trying to get her attention. Her young eyes didn't focus well, but she finally began to follow his motions and her crying slowed down, then stopped. She grabbed his hand and put a finger in her mouth.

Spear laughed around a mouthful of food. "You won't get anything from him," she told the baby. She offered him a bit of meat.

Canin took it and chewed, thinking.

"So what do you think?" she asked. "You know this place better than I do. Maybe another story would be best."

"I don't know if I can stay."

Spear sat back, a look of betrayal and fear rushing to her face. "I don't understand. You said so earlier. You held her and we promised each other. She's your daughter. You rescued us."

"Spear, I still love Min. I don't know if I can just forget her and make a new life with you here." He shook his head. "I just found her again. I feel like I'm betraying her by not going back."

"You don't even know if she's alive," Spear accused him. "She could be dead. All of them could be dead. The Humans might have killed them. The cultists. Maybe even the Fairies. She was using Blood Magic. If the Queen captured them. . . ." She stopped.

"They might also be alive. They might have made it safely back to the mountain."

"Do you know how far that is?" Spear waved her arms. "Very far. You could never walk it."

"I've walked it," Canin disagreed with a touch of anger.

"And she might not even be there. She could be on the run. You could just miss her every time." She put down the dried meat. "I need you. I can't do this alone. Not with her. Not broken." Her face became desperate. "You can't. I told you my name!"

Aurora was still gumming his finger. "I won't leave you right now. I don't even know if you'll be accepted here. Fairies are feared."

"But you told Min this is a place of exiles, of people who've been wronged and who need sanctuary." She pointed at him. "Your Mother of Exiles told you to help. Well, I need help." She pointed at Aurora. "She needs help. She needs the sanctuary of the Exile Forest." She frowned. "Or was all that just a story you told Min so she would take you to bed? Poor broken boy who needs the tender embrace of a beautiful Fairy."

His anger rose. Canin wanted to snap back at her. How dare she call him a liar who manipulated others for his own pleasure? Didn't she know what he had done? Here, and in the Fairy Realm, to survive and get back to Min?

"Ow," he said. Aurora was pulling his fingers apart. He pulled them out of her grasp. "Strong," he muttered.

"Yes, we are," Spear said defiantly. "We are strong. We don't need you." She held out her arms. "Give her back. If you don't want us, we'll leave. I will find my own way."

"I didn't mean that," Canin said. "I just don't know what my path is."

"Then go and ask your Mother," Spear said. "I know the Goddess has led me here. I will stay. With or without you."

Ignoring her gestures, Canin set Aurora down in the box. He laid his hand over the opening when Spear tried to pull her back out. Her fist clenched.

"She is my child," Spear hissed. "Do not get in my way."

Despite his tension, Canin stood his ground. "She needs to sleep. We all do."

"I need to eat," Spear contradicted him. She picked up the dried meat and began chewing on it with anger. "Is there more?"

Canin waited a moment. When she had settled back down, he removed his hand from the box and stood, returning to the chest and pulling out the box of provisions. Seeing it, Spear's eyes widened. She grabbed it from him and began to paw through it eagerly.

"Dried apples," she said happily. She stuffed a few slices into her mouth. "I haven't had these for a long time."

Canin sat down and began to eat. Slowly, so he could keep an eye on Spear. She devoured the dried fruits and most of the meat. Canin knew he had to act swiftly, or she would leave him nothing. He glanced down at Aurora. She was sleeping again.

"Spear," Canin said, trying to get her attention. She looked up, a piece of sausage stuck in her mouth.

Canin laughed. She glared and bit off a piece before offering him the rest. He took it with a smile.

"I need to think. I'll go and see if I can find anything fresh. There should be a spring near by."

"Good," Spear said. "I'm thirsty, too. Too much salt."

"Promise me you'll stay here. Hidden."

Spear nodded, not looking at him.

Canin reached out and cupped the side of her head. She put her hand on his.

"Promise me," he said with more intensity.

"I promise," Spear said, looking right into his eyes. "I will stay here with Aurora. I will not leave. I will wait for you to come back with water and fresh meat."

"Thank you." He tried to pull his hand away, but she held it.

"And you must promise to think. I need you. You need us. We're here for a reason." She pulled his hand up and kissed his palm. Another surge of desire shot through him. She must have sensed something, because she lingered on the kiss. Finally, he had to yank his hand away. She smiled slightly and went back to eating.

Chapter 3
Thorn Brothers

Canin knelt by the spring. He took in all the sensations: the feel of the cold air on his skin, the musty smell of the wet ground, the burbling of the water flowing over the rocks. He dipped his palm in and drew out a handful of water. He drank, and was overwhelmed by the memories that flooded up as he tasted the crystal clear liquid. He remembered standing at the side of Niel, the man who had raised him, as Niel showed him how to tell if the water was safe to drink. Niel had always smelled of good dirt and whatever crop was being harvested at the time.

Canin filled two water skins and sat back on his heels. So many memories inundated him, he was awestruck. Every step he had taken since he and Spear had arrived had brought back something from his past. He felt a twitch of anxiety about his return to the sanctuary village. Seeing the house he had grown up in. The people who had raised him. He wasn't sure it would be a happy reunion for anyone.

"My parents," he said out loud. "They were my parents in everything but blood. More than blood." He recalled Flora, who was a mother to all the Fairies in Talia's company, both the Ladies and the Nine. She had demanded their respect. Even Talia's, though the younger woman outranked her by a wide margin in Fairy society. Flora had kept them all together as a family. And she had accepted him without hesitation.

"I've been a bad son," he admitted to the rippling water.

Then, with the memories of Flora, came those of Min. Beautiful in the morning light. Her white hair and iridescent wings shining. Her hands: soft, but also strong and sure. Guiding him in every possible way. Her body against his, moving with passion or simply sleeping. Holding her as she told him of losing her Sisters. Her gentle arms around him as he realized he would never be able to ask his father all the questions he had for him. That last view of her as she climbed to the top of the tower in the Human Realm and flew out of his life.

Spear was right; Min was gone. On the other side of the Realm. Far away. Mother grant her safety. She was too far away. He was home, and he would remain there.

Canin began to put away the water skins. If he left Spear and Aurora now, he would be no better than his Fairy father. Abandoning them in a strange place, surrounded by strange people. He couldn't do that to them. He would not be his father, walking away from his family.

"Mother of Exiles," he said to the water, "help me on this path. Help me to be the father Aurora needs. Help me to be the partner Spear needs. Grant me the strength."

Canin stood and picked up the long bow. He ran his fingers along the curve again. The wood spoke to him. It vibrated, wanting to be used.

A rustle in the underbrush on the other side of the stream caught his attention. He pulled out an arrow and set it on the string. Concentrating, as Raven had taught him, he turned in the direction of the sound.

A large bird ambled out of the brush toward the water. It saw Canin and stopped, cocking its avian head at him.

'Turkey,' Canin thought. 'Thank you.' In a smooth motion, Canin pulled back, aimed, and released. The arrow leapt through the air, striking the bird with a thunk and releasing a small cloud of feathers. The turkey fell with only a small squawk.

"Thank you," Canin said again. He stepped over the stream and knelt by the dead bird. He pulled the arrow out, checked it for damage, and then cleaned it in the water.

"Dinner for our new family," he said proudly, slinging the bird over his shoulder and heading back to the Treetower.

☾ ⌇⌇⌇ ☼

Canin stopped near the edge of the clearing. He heard voices. Moving carefully, he approached the edge of the forest and peeked out.

Four men — all in brown and green — stood in an arc looking up at the tree, bows drawn. A line of black feathered arrows formed a fence in front of them.

"We don't want to hurt you," one of the men was calling. He pulled back his hood to expose his grey hair. Canin thought he recognized the voice and the double-headed axe on his back. "We just want to talk to you."

"Stay back!" Spear called. Another arrow flew from the window and struck the ground in front of the speaker. Canin saw the faint shimmer of a Shadow in the window, but didn't think the men had noticed.

The man on the far right raised his drawn bow, but the grey-haired man pushed it down. Canin finally got a good look at him. Recognition — along with hope — bloomed in his mind.

"Look." The grey-haired man gestured to the ground. "Perfect shots. Whoever is up there is an archer." He glared until the other man lowered his bow.

"She must be the one we were told to expect," the man on the left said.

"Tell us who you are!" the leader called again. "We want to help you. The Mother told us you were coming." He took a careful step. "You must be hungry."

"Stay back!" Spear called again, but she did not fire. Canin could hear her tension. He needed to do something before she broke and killed them.

"She'll run out of arrows soon," the man on the right said.

"You remember how many arrows are in that quiver?" the man on the left asked.

"She can't hit us all," the man who had been silent till now said. Canin remembered that voice, too. He frowned.

Four arrows hit the ground, in rapid succession, one in front of each of the men.

The grey-haired one laughed. "I don't want to risk it."

"I hear something," the one on the left said. "A baby crying?" The men looked at each other and then up to the window.

Canin could hear it, too. Aurora was starting to cry, and would soon be screaming. He carefully set down the dead turkey. He made sure his wooden knife was in plain sight on his belt. Setting an arrow on the string of his bow, he stood and stepped out into the clearing.

"You're scaring my wife and child," Canin announced. He raised the bow and drew back the string slightly.

The men turned, surprised by his sudden appearance. Their bows shot up. Canin glanced up and saw Spear, free of Shadow, at the window, an arrow drawn back.

"Hello, Wolf," Canin greeted the center man. "Hello, Brothers. I'm back."

Confusion colored the faces of the two younger men at either side of the leader. The fourth man looked hard at Canin and frowned. His fingers twitched on his bow string.

The grey-haired man, Wolf, squinted, then broke out into a wide grin. "Canin," he called happily. He motioned to the others to put down their bows. "Our Brother has come home. Mother of Exiles be praised."

The younger men lowered their bows. The other man did not. Canin kept his string taunt and adjusted his aim.

"Hello, Crow. It's been a long time," Canin said. He kept his eye on Crow's fingers, taut on his bowstring.

"I didn't think you had the courage to return," Crow said.

Canin did not reply. He aimed the point of his arrow at the middle of Crow's chest.

Tension crackled in the air.

"My wife will do anything to protect her child," Canin calmly advised him over the arrow. "She might even defend me. Put down your bow. She will not hesitate to shoot you in the back." He drew back a bit more.

Crow narrowed his eyes and also drew back.

"Crow!" Wolf snapped. "Put down your bow. This is no way to greet a returning Brother." He put his hand on the wooden knife on his belt.

Crow glanced at Wolf and saw that the others had moved away from him. With effort, he released the tension on the string and spread his arms. "Yes, Prime," he acquiesced.

"You, too, Canin," Wolf called.

Canin looked up and nodded to Spear. She lowered her bow and disappeared from the window. The cries of the baby began to subside. Canin lowered his bow and put away the arrow.

Wolf handed his bow to one of the younger men and strode across the clearing. Canin, not quite sure what would happen, moved his hand to his knife.

"Canin. Setab," Wolf said, spreading his arms and embracing Canin in a hug. His Elenite eyes danced with happiness and a line of tears ran down into his short grey beard. "I thought you were dead. Mother's mercy, you're back." He squeezed Canin again, so hard that Canin was forced to drop his bow. His other hand was crushed between them, the hilt of his knife digging into his wrist.

"Yes, Wolf," Canin said, his tears beginning to flow, too. "I'm home."

Wolf pulled away. He put his hands on Canin's shoulders. "Lily will be glad."

Canin put his hands on Wolf's arms. "Niel?" he asked and watched Wolf's eyes. The wrinkles there deepened as he frowned.

"I am sorry, Setab," Wolf said, his voice full of compassion. "He died two seasons ago."

Another loss. "I never told him," Canin replied, grief rising. "I've just begun to understand what he did for me. Now he's gone."

"He understood," Wolf assured him. "He knew what he meant to you."

Canin shook his head. Wolf's voice turned harder. "He's gone. He is at rest. Niel kept his family together. He took in so many children like you. More than he should have. You taint his memory to feel shame. We should celebrate his life."

Canin smiled. "He has Returned to the Cycle."

"Spent some time with the Fairies, I see," Wolf said with a grin. Then he turned Canin toward the others. "You know old Crow there."

Crow slung his bow over his shoulder and folded his arms. He was Elenite, and kept his black hair short. He gave a brisk nod to Wolf. His hand rested on the silksteel sword at his belt. "I'll make sure there are no other lost pets around." He glared at Canin again before walking off into the woods.

"Crows never forget," Wolf commented, "and he won't either."

"She chose me," Canin said, watching the man disappear into the woods. He had forgotten the anger and bitterness Crow bore him.

"Then she died," Wolf said. "So that makes her choice wrong to him, and since she's gone, he only has you to hate." He dropped his voice. "He loved her, too."

"I know. I will have to make peace with him."

Wolf cocked his head. "You've grown. The young Canin would have cursed him."

Canin spread his hands, but did not comment.

Wolf smiled again. "You'll have to tell me your tale. All of it. A wife. A child."

"Soon." Canin looked at the others, who were hovering a few feet away.

"This is Sam." Wolf motioned to the man on the left. Sam stepped forward and offered his hand to Canin. He was Human, with pale hair and an easy smile. The wooden knife on his belt looked new. Canin started to grip his arm as a Fairy soldier would, palm to arm, but remembered Human customs and shook hands with the Thorn Brother instead.

"Wolf has told us tales of you," Sam said. "Good to meet the real man."

Canin looked at Wolf in surprise. The old man shrugged.

The other young man, also Human, stepped forward. He was bald, with an ugly scar covering the left side of his head. "I'm called Granite," he said, taking Canin's hand. He gestured to his head. "My father tried to kill me with a rock when I was a child. Mother caved his head in with a piece of sandstone. And then we ran to the forest. Or it might have been granite. She gets the two confused." He looked at Wolf and Sam and shared a smile.

Canin frowned slightly at the joke shared between them that he didn't know. He settled on saying, "Well met, Thorn Brothers."

"These two just earned their knives. I've been training them," Wolf told Canin. "I use you as an example of what to do and what not to do."

Canin smiled. "I did make many mistakes." Canin's attention shifted up to the Treetower. Aurora's crying had ceased. Spear had pulled the cloth back, blocking the window again.

Wolf saw his gaze move. "Can we meet your wife and child?" he asked.

Canin sidestepped the question by asking one of his own. "Is Maggie still . . .?" He stopped, not quite knowing how to phrase his question.

Wolf understood. "Still in the forest? Alive? Yes, she is," Wolf told him, to Canin's great relief. "She's the Prime Thorn Maiden now." He looked at the other two. "I'm not sure where she is."

"She's by the Green," Sam said without hesitation.

Wolf raised his eyes, and Granite grinned. Sam smiled and shrugged.

"I should speak to her, or at least let her know," Canin said, looking at Wolf with slight embarrassment.

Wolf finished his thought. "Before Crow speaks with her. She deserves to hear the news that you're back from you, or at least from a friendly voice."

Canin nodded. "But the Green is a long run."

"I can take a message to her," Sam offered. "I can make it." He looked at the sky. "Before the sun has reached mid-day. That will give her time to get back here before dark."

Granite shared a look with Wolf. Wolf shook his head. "She's too old for you."

"I don't care," Sam said, folding his arms.

Wolf looked at Canin. After a moment, Canin realized he was being asked to approve of the run.

"If it won't take you away from your duties," Canin said slowly, watching Wolf's face. "I would be very grateful if you would go to her."

Wolf nodded, and Sam closed the cap on his quiver and slung his bow over his shoulder. He tightened his belt and stuck out his hand to Canin.

Canin took it. "Thank you, ... Setab." He hesitated at the word, unsure he should be using it, but Sam only smiled warmly.

"Do you want me to tell her anything other than that you're back?" Sam asked.

"Just tell her I would like to see her."

Sam nodded again before turning and running out of the clearing. He passed quickly into the forest and was gone.

"He won't listen," Granite said to Wolf. "We tell him she's not interested in him."

"She's not interested in anyone," Wolf stressed, "But the boy will have to find that out on his own." He turned back to Canin. "So." He returned to his earlier question. "Can we meet your wife and child?"

Canin looked back at the window in the Treetower. It was still closed.

"I don't know," Canin started. He looked at the arrows sticking in the ground. "She's been through a great deal of trauma in the last few days. I don't want to press her."

"I understand," Wolf said. "We'll treat this as a normal first meeting then. How about tomorrow morning? Lily, and a few others. All women. I'm sure she'll come anyway, regardless of what you want."

"And I need to speak to her," Canin told him. "I have some apologizing to do."

"I'm sure she doesn't see it that way. Regardless, she can bring Sekrine, so she can check the baby and your wife and make sure they're both in good health. A few Thorn Maidens. Nothing to make her feel closed in."

"Sekrine is still here?" Canin said with amazement. "She seemed so old when I was a child."

"She's Elenite," Wolf told him. "And too stubborn to get old."

"I just remember her voice. I always found it soothing," Canin said with a little honest embarrassment.

"It's still beautiful," Granite replied with a bit of wistfulness.

Wolf smiled and nudged Canin. "Do you think that will make her feel safe?"

Canin considered. He turned and looked back at the Treetower. "I think it will be for the best. We can't stay here forever." He put his hands on his hips. "I will prepare her. But make sure they understand she might be very touchy and skittish."

Wolf looked hard at Canin. "There's something you're not telling me, son . . . Brother. If she's a danger, then I need to tell them. I will not put our healer and midwife and others in a possible volatile situation."

"She is a danger," Canin admitted, "but with me by her side and a small group, she should feel safe enough."

Wolf frowned. "Maybe you both need more time. If rushing this welcome will end badly, then you can stay here by yourself. You can watch this part of the forest. We can provide you with anything you need." He put a hand on Canin's shoulder. "Whatever you need. Take time to make her feel safe. Those are the words of the Mother of Exiles."

"I understand, and I'll speak with her. If Maggie makes it here, I think I can introduce them. Maggie and she are cut from the same cloth. If she's still as I remember her."

"She is," Wolf agreed. "I will leave the judgment with her." He gestured to the turkey on the ground. "I'll send more provisions. Turkey is good, but you and your family need more. Lily still bakes bread."

Canin broke into a wide grin at the thought of Lily's bread. 'My mother's bread,' he corrected himself. It still felt odd, but his youthful determination not to call her mother was eroding quickly.

"I will make sure you have some," Wolf said, guessing some of the inner thoughts of the man he had trained to be a Thorn Brother. "Not to rush you, but we need all the knives we have. The King has grown harsh. The clans the old king held in check are seizing more and more power every day. They press us on all sides."

From what little Min and Flora had told him about Bastile, that did not surprise Canin. "I would be honored to fight alongside you again." His face dropped. "I must ask Her forgiveness. I disobeyed Her orders."

"She knows your heart, and I'm sure She will forgive you," Wolf replied with certainty. "You can go before her when you're ready."

"Thank you," Canin said sincerely, and shook hands with Wolf again. Granite handed him the turkey, and Canin nodded his thanks.

Granite nodded back, then followed Wolf back into the woods, but not without a backward glance up at the window of the Treetower. Canin turned, and saw Spear peering around the window frame.

Chapter 4
Feathers

"You didn't tell them," Spear accused. She stood in the middle of the room, Aurora on her hip.

"I didn't," Canin confirmed. He was sitting on the floor, with the turkey in front of him. He was carefully plucking its feathers, one by one. He did not look up.

"Why?" she demanded. "Are you ashamed of me, or is there something you're not telling me? Do the people here hate Fairies?" She knelt down and tried to look him in the eye, but he kept turning away.

"Curse you," she said. "Look at me!" Canin stopped and looked at her.

"I need to know if there is a danger here," Spear told him. "As a soldier, I need to know."

"No, they don't hate you," Canin said.

"I don't believe you."

"Fairies are distrusted," Canin admitted. "After all, there are many Elenites here, and many are products of. . . ." He stopped, not wanting to say the word.

"Rape," Spear stressed. "I'm a woman. They have nothing to fear from me in that way." She adjusted how Aurora sat on her hip. "I can feel that you're still not telling me everything."

Canin lowered his eyes.

Spear's anger grew. She started to yell at him, but Aurora suddenly cooed and kicked at her. Spear took a deep breath and pushed her feelings down. She reached out and cupped the side of his head.

"Look at me," she told him gently. He looked up, meeting her eyes. "If this is going to work, if we're going to find a place here, you need to be honest with me. Even if it's hard. Even if it hurts." She pressed her fingers into his hair. "I need the truth."

Canin wiped his hands on his pants, then pressed one over hers. "I promise. I will never lie to you."

Spear's eyes melted, and she leaned closer to him. She tried to kiss him, but he moved back.

"Please," he said. "I can't do that."

Spear let go of him and leaned back. She smiled. "Let me know when you can," she said with a smile. "Now, tell me everything you know about Fairies and the Exile Forest."

Canin looked down and resumed plucking the dead bird's feathers. "Of course, we remember the wars and their violence very well. Fairy men are feared, and soldiers most of all. Most of the women here were victimized by them. And many of the men are children of Fairies and hate them for what was done to their mothers."

"What about the love stories, like your mother?" Spear asked. She was becoming frustrated with his slow method of plucking the turkey. "Here," she said, handing him Aurora. "Hold her, and I'll do that. Keep telling your stories."

Canin wasn't given the option to protest, so he took Aurora and slid the partly plucked bird toward Spear.

"I don't remember many. There was one, but his was tragic." He cocked his head at her. "Most Fairy and Human love affairs end badly."

"Hmm," Spear said. She hadn't touched the bird, but was staring intently at it. She closed her eyes and held her hands around it. With a sudden popping sound, the outer feathers all flew off and started rising to the ceiling. Canin stopped speaking and just watched. The feathers flew off the bird in a haze and began to form a spinning circle above them. More feathers rose and joined their brethren. Soon the bird was bare, and a cloud of feathers swirled above them.

Aurora sensed the movement and reached out with her little hands, laughing.

Canin smiled and watched. Spear grinned and brought her hands together with a small clap. The feathers stopped, hanging motionless in the air. Spear snapped her fingers, and the feathers drifted to the ground, covering them all.

Canin smiled despite himself. Spear laughed with Aurora. Canin brushed a few feathers out of his hair, grinning at the silliness.

"Why do they end badly?" Spear asked, allowing the feathers to envelop her.

Canin picked up a feather and tickled Aurora with it. She smiled at him.

"Fairies live a long time," Canin said simply. "No matter how strong the love, the Fairy always has to come to the realization that they're doomed to watch their love grow old and die. And their children, too. For most, it's just easier to leave." He looked off into the distance, through the walls of the Treetower. "Some of their loves never understand this, and are still waiting for their winged love to return." He sighed. "And they never do."

Spear puffed out a breath to push a feather off her nose. She moved her hands in a sweeping motion, and her Power gathered up all the feathers, except for the one in Canin's hand. She made them into a pile at her side. "Soldiers killed and raped," she said matter-of-factly. "Depressing love stories. It's all sad, but it doesn't account for your anxiety, and why you didn't tell them who I am." She picked up a feather and pointed it at him. She waved it, prompting him to speak.

"You're right," he admitted. "It's not just that." He laid down his feather. "There's another reason Fairies are treated with utmost caution."

"If you don't tell me. . . ." Spear waved the feather at him. "I will tickle her until she pees all over you." She raised her eyes and floated a feather close to Aurora. Canin batted at it, but it danced out of range. Spear smiled and floated another one.

"I was a child," Canin began. Spear, knowing the tone, settled back. The feathers floated back to her, and she made them dance in front of her eyes.

"I was with my parents, my adopted parents," Canin stressed. Spear smiled brightly at this admission, the first time she had heard him say it aloud. "We traveled to one of the smaller villages outside of the forest. It was one of the few times they took me outside. Niel was bringing his crop of radishes. An old friend of his loved them, and they were going to trade for something. I don't remember what. We were walking toward the center of the village when Fairy soldiers appeared out of the air. A dozen, at least. Must have been out of Shadows, but I was young, and suddenly there were tall, winged soldiers grabbing people and holding them with blades and arrows at their throats. Lily pushed us into a store and closed the door. I don't think I ever saw them so afraid. She barred the door, and Niel began looking for weapons. I went to the small window and looked out. The people of the village had been herded together. Then an Iridescent appeared. He was tall, and his wings shone with light. I never saw anything so scary. He spoke, and everyone could hear him." Canin looked at Spear. "Now that I know more about your people, I understand this memory more. Then, I was scared, but also fascinated."

Spear, full of rapt attention, motioned him to go on.

"He called for someone to be brought to him. I don't remember the name. He knew she was there, and he would kill someone unless she came out. I saw a man try to intervene, but a soldier knocked him to the ground. The Iridescent became angrier when no one came forward. He yelled for his lieutenant to take aim." Canin paused. "Lily tried to pull me away from the window, but I wouldn't move. I guess I made a noise, because she stopped and stood behind me. I felt her hands on my shoulders.

"Then I heard someone calling. I looked, and saw an incredibly old woman, walking with an old man. He was supporting her. Her son. I remember her being one of the oldest people I had ever seen. She called out a name. It didn't make any sense to me. The Iridescent turned and looked at her. Even from far away, I could tell he was confused. She said his name again. Then she said, 'It was under the dome of the Tower of the Stars. That's why his name is Starfall.' She gestured to the man at her side.

"The Iridescent waved his soldiers to let the rest of the villagers go and walked up to the woman. He was very tall, and he towered over both of them. The man tried to stay strong, but soon wilted under the intense gaze of the Fairy.

"I remember what he said next, because Lily would repeat it all the time. 'How can it be you? You're so old.'"

Spear laughed. "I can hear one of those arrogant Iridescents saying that. I've probably met the bastard."

Canin nodded that she might have. "She replied, 'Time goes faster for me, Love. Faster for your son.' She gestured to the man beside her. He was older than Niel. The Iridescent just stared at her for a long moment. He did not move. His wings didn't even twitch. The old woman just stared at him. Somehow, she kept her eyes locked with his. Then, without a sound, or a gesture, the soldiers fired. Three or four arrows hit each of them. They hit the ground, already dead." Canin looked at Spear. "I think that was the first time I saw anyone killed." Spear just looked at him.

Canin continued. "I don't know why Lily didn't pull me away from the window. I just watched as the Iridescent stood over the dead bodies. I remember his voice. He said, 'It was a mistake,' then he waved his hand, and the bodies burst into flame. Then he disappeared, along with the soldiers." He shook his head. "Now I know they probably used their Torcs or Shadowed, but to young me, it was the most terrifying thing that I had ever seen."

Spear reached out and patted his leg. "He returned them to the Cycle," she explained. "If he had hated them, he would have left the bodies. In his mind, I guess he hoped they would meet again. Maybe even as Fairies. Goddess knows if that's possible."

Canin, shocked at her interpretation of the events, could only stare at her.

"A Fairy killed his lover and child. That sounds like Iridescents. Bloodline-obsessed bastards." She shrugged. "I am none of those things." She gestured to her wings. "My wings are damaged. I'm not here to kill anyone. I'm here to keep my child safe."

"I know," Canin said, trying to ease her mind. "I'm just telling you why some of the people here might hate and fear you."

"You'll protect me," Spear said simply. "Everyone loves you." She gestured to the plucked turkey. "How do we cook this?"

"Not everyone," Canin muttered, setting Aurora down in her box. He then rose and went to the window. With a flourish, he pulled back the curtain to let in the light. Then he worked his fingers into the floorboards and pulled up a section. He stepped back to reveal a stone-lined space in the floor. There was a small stack of kindling and a pile of charcoal inside. Spear clapped with surprise at the hidden cooking pit.

Smiling, Canin walked to the chest he had gotten the dried meat from the previous night. He pulled out three metal bars as long as his arm. Two he thrust into holes on either side of the pit. The other, he laid into the forks at the top.

"If you would be so kind, My Lady."

Spear smiled and, with a bow, lit a flame to the kindling.

"We should carve it into smaller pieces," Canin suggested. He drew the long knife. "It will cook faster."

Spear was already carving.

As their food cooked, Spear tried to get him to tell her more about the forest and its people: the Thorn Brothers, the Maidens, Wolf, his family. Anything so she could understand more about the place she now found herself in. But Canin stayed quiet. He turned the spit and tested the food. When a bit was done, he handed it to her, but he didn't speak.

Spear kept asking, but still he did not answer. Eventually, she decided he would tell her when he was ready, and started to play a game with the feathers. She picked one up with her Power and propelled it into the wall beside the window. It stuck, quivering in the wood. Canin started as the feather buzzed his ear, but went back to cooking. She kept zipping the feathers past him, trying to get him to react. Using his training from Steel, Canin ignored them. Spear, smiling, brushed his face and his hands. He never flinched. Then, using both hands, she sent a whole cloud of feathers at him. He absently batted away one that came too close to his face.

Finally, she had just one left. She picked it up in her hand and aimed it carefully at him.

"Canin," she called, a touch of seduction in her voice. He looked up. She threw it right at his face. Canin grabbed it out of the air. His expression neutral, he ran his fingers up the shaft, smoothing the feathers. Spear grinned. He stood and walked to her. He kissed the feather, then slipped it down between her breasts.

Spear caught his hand and held it to her chest. They locked eyes. "Moon and sun," he said. Pulling his hand free, he returned to the cooking pit. Spear pulled the feather out and pressed it to her face. She looked at the pattern of the moon and sun she had made in feathers on the wall. "I am a Servant of the Moon and Sun," she whispered.

Chapter 5
Maggie

It was twilight. The warm rays of the setting sun cast an otherworldly glow over the forest. Canin stood at the window, watching how the light hit the trees. He couldn't remember ever watching a sunset before. 'There was always something to be done. I never took the time to watch,' he thought sadly. He looked back into the room. Spear was nursing Aurora again. The subtle light of the setting sun glinted off her bald head and caught in Aurora's golden hair.

'How could I even think of leaving them?' he wondered.

The call of a briarrose hawk pierced the twilight. It rose at the end, then stopped.

Spear's eyes came up, her nursing trance falling away at the sound.

"She's here," Canin remarked. Spear frowned. Canin turned back to the window, his shoulders tensing. Behind him, Spear put Aurora down in her box and picked up her bow.

At the edge of the clearing, three forms emerged from the brush. Two carried baskets, while the third carried a bow. All of them were cloaked and hooded in dark green. The third raised three fingers to their hidden face and another call of the hawk filled the clearing.

Canin put two fingers in his mouth and made the same call, but let it fall at the end.

The third motioned to the others. They walked a few steps into the clearing and set down the baskets. Then they nodded to the third and slipped back into the forest. They made exaggerated noises in the underbrush and leaves as they moved off. The third slowly raised her arms, pulled off her quiver and bow, and set them on the ground. Then she unbuckled her sword belt and laid that on the ground as well. She cast back her hood and took five steps forward. Then she folded her arms and waited.

Canin turned back and was startled to find Spear at his shoulder. She had an arrow on the string, and a watchful look on her face.

"She'll probably hit me," Canin warned her. "I don't want you to do anything. Unless she pulls a weapon and tries to kill me."

"Then I will kill her."

"No," Canin contradicted. "Don't kill her. Just push her away. Nothing lethal."

Spear frowned at him.

"She's the equivalent of a captain here. She should be respected."

Spear narrowed her eyes at him, but then nodded. "Why would she hit you?"

"She's the older sister of my dead wife."

Spear continued to look at him. "I would welcome you back as a returning brother."

"If she hadn't been pregnant, the fever might not have killed her."

"And she blames you?" Spear asked.

Canin nodded.

"I would hit you, too," Spear agreed. "But I will watch her." She moved to the window. The woman below saw them, but did not move. She just watched and waited.

Canin sighed. "I'll go down and talk to her. If things go well, I'll bring her up. If that's all right?"

"She seems more like a soldier, so I will meet her," Spear agreed. "Make sure she knows who and what I am, though."

Canin nodded. He moved to the trap door. Spear caught his arm and pulled him into a kiss. Canin tried to pull away, but she was too strong. He relaxed and embraced her, carefully keeping his arms clear of her wings. She finally let him go.

"If she kills you before I can do anything," she said, caressing his face.

"Thank you," Canin said, off balance. He then reached down and brushed Aurora's sleeping face lightly with his fingertips. She reached out and grabbed his hand. Fighting back tears, Canin let her hold his finger for a moment. Then he pulled away.

"Goddess keep you safe," Spear said, then returned to the window.

Canin took one more look at the two of them and then started climbing down.

He reached the ground and walked around the base of the tree. As he came into view, the waiting woman unhooked her cloak and let it fall. She spread her arms to show that she had no other weapons.

Canin stopped a few paces away. She, of course, looked older than he remembered. Her red-blond hair only had a few strands of red left in it. But her arms still looked as strong as he remembered.

"Maggie," Canin said through a lump in his throat.

"Canin," she said, walking up to him. She was as tall as he was. Looking up over his shoulder, she nodded. She then balled her fist and hit the side of his face.

"That's for her," she said. She paused a moment, to let him recover and to make sure no arrows were flying at her. When he didn't move and Spear didn't shoot her, Maggie hit the other side of his face. "That's for my lost niece." Canin staggered back.

She stepped up and hit him again, in the stomach this time. "And that's for leaving me alone."

Canin fell to his knees. Maggie heard the creak of a bow string being pulled back and looked up. Canin, with effort, raised his hand in an 'I'm all right' gesture, and Spear lowered her bow and stepped back from the window.

Maggie went to her knees and gathered him into an embrace. "Brother," she said through tears, "I'm glad you're home."

"I am, too," Canin said into her shoulder. The tears he had been holding back since she had appeared came flooding out of him, and all the tethered pain of Brenna's death tumbled out behind them. He gripped her hard and cried jaggedly. She also released her pent-up agony, and together they cried for their mutual loss.

After a time, their acute grief subsided. Canin felt drained, but also free of some long-carried weight. He pulled out of her embrace and wiped his eyes. She did the same and settled into a sitting position on the ground. She wiped her eyes again and shook her head.

"Are you wearing armor?" she accused him.

"Just a ringmail shirt," he said, smiling slightly.

"You're learning," she congratulated him. "Thank you for making sure your archer wife didn't kill me."

"It took some convincing," Canin said with forced lightness. "But when I explained who you were, she said she would hit me, too."

Maggie smiled. "So, did you find what you were looking for?"

Canin looked up into the sky. The stars were starting to come out. The moon, just a sliver of white, was beginning to rise. Canin was back in the little room at the inn, Shatter across from him telling him his father was dead. Min holding his hand. "No, but I found what I needed."

"She guides us," Maggie said simply. "So, is she what you needed?"

"Yes," Canin answered, thinking of both Spear and Min.

"Good. I worried you would return more broken than when you left."

Canin reached out and took her hand. "Is your mother still here?" he asked carefully.

She pulled her hand out of his grip. "No. She died not long after you left. She took her grief and all the anger she had toward you and turned it inside." She shrugged. "She poisoned herself. She's better off now. She hated her life."

"I'm sorry," Canin told her.

She shrugged again. "She stopped being my mother a long time ago. All that was good in her disappeared after her rape. Mother's mercy! Brenna was all she had to cling to, and when she was gone." She stopped. "I don't blame you for leaving."

"There was nothing else I could do," Canin admitted. "I just needed to do something. Avenge her somehow. I lost myself. I'm sorry I left you alone."

"I've always been alone," Maggie admitted. "It wasn't too much different. I threw myself into being the best Thorn Maiden I could be. The Mother pronounced me Prime not long after my mother died."

"So, there's still no one?" Canin asked.

She shook her head. "I just don't have those feelings for anyone. Sam follows me around. He's a good man. There's much potential in him, but the thought of being close to him." She shrugged again. "I have none of the passion everyone talks about." She smiled.

"Maybe I'll let him one day, just to let him exhaust his passion. Maybe that will satisfy him."

Canin shook his head. "That will only attach him closer to you. You need to just tell him how you feel."

"He won't understand. None of them do." She folded her hands in her lap. "Only with Wolf, do I sense he understands. And even then only a bit."

"Is he still the wolf among the sheep?"

Maggie laughed. "He can't spend as much time outside the forest now as he used to. But he still has his rounds. Why do you think he was here?"

"The berry widow?"

"She has two of his sons," Maggie confirmed.

Canin looked at her. She was smiling. The pain he had seen earlier began to disappear into the reunion.

"You were at the Green? Is Bitter still with us?"

"He is. Very old now. We had to build a ramp to the Treetower. He still watches, staring in the direction of the Fairy Realm. Waiting for her to come home." Maggie shook her head in pity.

"His son?"

"He is the Prime spinner and makes most of the clothes for the Maidens." She offered her arm for him to feel. "Lightfoot still makes sure he has his tea every morning and night. When word came that the Fairy Realm was closing its borders, he spent all his silver on enough tea to keep his father happy."

Canin smiled sadly. "I don't understand. His Fairy wife told him she wasn't coming back. That he should forget her."

Maggie shook her head. "I was told she just left one day. After bringing them here." More sad shaking. "I've tried to get him to talk about it, but he won't." A thought occurred to her. "You went to the Fairy Realm looking for your father. He might speak to you."

A surge of fear or pity bit into Canin's belly. "Maybe. After we get settled. It's hard to talk about. There was much tragedy there."

"And good," she said. "You came back with a wife and a child. It couldn't have been that bad."

"It's hard to explain," Canin said. "I don't know if I can put it into words just now."

"Well." She patted his leg. "When you're ready."

"Sutab," Canin began.

"Prime," Maggie corrected. "I'm still mad at you. And you haven't earned the right to call me that again."

Canin nodded, understanding in his heart, but still aching at the distance he had put between them.

They sat in silence for a while. Canin struggled, trying to find the words to explain who Spear was to Maggie, but he had no idea how to start. Maggie simply watched him and the window above. Darkness began to fall. A clear light bloomed through the curtain. Maggie narrowed her eyes and looked harder at Canin, but he remained silent. She could see him thinking.

"There's something you want to tell me," she finally said. "But you can't find the right words."

Canin frowned at her. "Am I that easy to read?"

"Yes. You had that same expression when you came to ask me about Brenna." She folded her arms. "I can see a Fairy Light in the tree. And not the color that's usually sold to Humans. That fancy ringmail."

"She's a Fairy," Canin admitted. Maggie smiled. "A Leather-wing soldier." Maggie lost her smile. Suddenly afraid, she looked up at the window and then back to where her weapons lay on the ground.

"You should have told me that sooner," Maggie complained. She moved to stand. Canin grabbed her arm, but she twisted out of his grip.

"She comes here seeking sanctuary, like any other woman," Canin told her. "We couldn't stay in the Fairy Realm. Her liege turned against her."

After a moment, Maggie settled back to the ground. "I understand that. But others might not."

Canin took a deep breath. "She's been hurt, both physically and emotionally. Her wings were damaged in our escape."

"Fairies cut the wings off criminals and rapists," Maggie spat.

"They weren't cut off. She lost part of them when we escaped." He motioned behind him. "They were severed just past her shoulders. She can't fly." He reached out to her. "I'm not lying. Her wings weren't removed because of a crime. Evil men, evil wingless Fairies, pursued us. We escaped, but she paid a high price."

Maggie let him take her hand. "I believe you. This changes things. You say you were driven from the Fairy Realm. By evil Fairies." She shook her head. "The Human Realm is in chaos. The King is weak, and the clans are seizing more power. Men come here trying to recruit Elenites into the Lions of the Sword." She made a disgusted face. "The Elen towns are torn between. There are rumors of a Fairy civil war. Now you come home with a Fairy soldier as your wife." She pulled her hand away. "It will be hard for others to accept her. Soldiers are feared. They're hated for what they've done."

"I understand. I remember. I grew up thinking I was a child of rape. But she didn't serve with any of that type of soldier. She served with honor."

"That won't matter to many. I believe you, but others might not. And if something happens, an insult, an attack, a misunderstanding. Someone could attack her."

"And she will strike back," Canin said with determination. "I will defend her. I will defend my child."

"Against me? Against Wolf?"

"Anyone."

Maggie sat back on her heels. "I would do the same. But I am Prime. I protect the people of this forest. It is my responsibility to keep them safe. If you and your Fairy bring danger, then I don't know if she can stay."

"She's not my Fairy," he said, more to himself than to her. "I'm her Elenite. We were brought here," Canin stated. "I can't explain it, because I don't understand it myself. All I know is that the Mother brought us here. Saved us. Wolf said you were told to expect someone." He gestured back at the tree. "There were two beds and a place for a baby. She knew. She brought us here. For a purpose. I left another behind." He lowered his voice. "I lost. Someone I love. I might never see her again." Canin's voice broke and he had to stop.

Maggie slid closer and embraced him.

"I made a decision to stay," Canin said into her shoulder. "Spear believes she was guided here, too. Her Goddess set her on a path to bring our child here. A place of safety. Please don't turn us away."

Maggie pulled slightly away from him so she could look him in the eye. "Spear?" she asked with a smile.

Canin chuckled despite himself. "Her full name is Spearhead."

"Fairies are strange."

"I just spoke with Wolf and Crow," Canin replied. "Our names are strange, too."

"Yes, they are," Maggie admitted, breaking fully from the embrace. "This is a delicate decision. I understand she . . . Spear," she said, the name odd in her mouth, "has been hurt. No one who has come here hasn't been hurt in some way. It would be a betrayal of all we are to turn you away."

"It would be," Canin agreed. "I understand there might be danger with her, but she understands that, too. She's a soldier. She will obey you as her captain. Just speak with her."

"I will." Maggie stood and gestured back. "I also brought food and more blankets for you."

"Thank you," Canin said, also standing.

"I will leave my sword here."

"No," Canin disagreed. "Wear it. She'll respond better if you're armed. It will prove your strength."

"I thought I already showed her that."

Canin rubbed his jaw. "You did. Please don't do it again. She protects me. And never, ever threaten our child."

"I would never," Maggie said, shocked at his implication.

"I know, but be careful with your words. And tell everyone. Aurora is her life now. She would do anything to protect her."

Maggie started to make light, but saw the darkness in Canin's eyes and heard the seriousness in his voice. She nodded instead. "Aurora, eh? Beautiful name."

"For a beautiful baby."

"So, let's go meet your powerful Fairy wife."

Canin walked over and picked up the two baskets. Maggie put her sword back on and picked up her bow. Canin looked up and saw Spear watching them. He signaled her and she disappeared from the window. Maggie followed him around the tree.

Canin set the baskets down at the base of the ladder. "I'll go up first. Then I'll pull up the baskets."

"To prove our good intentions, and that I'm not holding the provisions hostage," Maggie said with a nod of understanding. "I'm a leader of prickly women, too."

Canin nodded, then went up the ladder. Spear already had the trap door open and pulled him inside. Her face was tense.

"What did she say? You spoke a long time, and I can sense that she's worried. You said we would have a place here. Is it because I'm a Fairy? I won't run away. You said this was a place of safety." She finally stopped to take a breath.

"This is a place of safety, and she's concerned. There's never been a Fairy who's come here looking for sanctuary." Canin put his hand lightly on her arm. "Trillium, she's worried for her people. I don't blame her. We must show her we can be a benefit to the forest. You must prove you won't be a danger."

"We accepted you," Spear shot back. "Even when we found you in that Cultist house."

"I know you did, and I'm grateful." He looked hard at her. "Talia wasn't so accepting. She would have killed me if Min hadn't been there. Min persuaded her. I'm just doing the same thing."

Spear swallowed her next statement. "I will be humble and strong. We need to get this woman on our side." She smiled, though it was slightly off. "We must persuade her."

"Yes, we do. Now." He went to the wardrobe. "I need that hook. ..."He pulled a length of rope with a steel hook at the end off a peg. He went to the trap door and lowered the hook. After a moment, there was a tug on the rope, and Spear and Canin hauled up the basket. Spear took it and set it down, beginning to go through it.

Canin lowered the rope again. "Spear," he called after a moment. "I need your help. This one is heavier."

Spear looked up from her inventory of the first basket's contents. She did not move. Canin strained, pulling at the rope, hand over hand. Finally, she went over and added her strength to his. The basket thumped to the floor of the room.

"I smell something delicious," Spear said, opening the lid.

Canin sat down. He looked at Spear. "Are you ready? Is Aurora sleeping?"

Spear pulled herself away from the food. "Yes. I put a Sleep Weave on her after I fed her."

Canin looked confused.

"Her eyes aren't Elenite."

Canin hadn't thought of that. It was too late now to claim that this was his adopted daughter. Spear saw the conflict. "We'll just have to figure a way around," she said.

Canin sighed. "I guess we will." He looked through the trap door. "Come on up, Maggie, Prime Thorn Maiden!" he called.

Spear pushed the baskets toward the walls to clear the floor and put her sword back on. She stood at rest, her hands folded at her waist. Standing, Canin looked at her one more time, and whispered a hopeful word to the Mother. Maggie reached the top of the makeshift ladder and Canin helped her inside.

Maggie turned to face Spearhead. If she was surprised or shocked by Spear's readiness or by her damaged wings, she did not show it. She took up a similar stance.

"Spearhead. Greetings," she said with the voice of command. "I am Maggie, Prime Thorn Maiden of the Exile Forest. Canin tells me you come seeking sanctuary for yourself and your child."

Spear stood straighter, reacting to Maggie's voice. "I do, Ma'am. Canin and I were brought here by the Goddess and your Mother of Exiles. We seek a safe place to raise our baby." She gestured to the box. "I am a trained soldier. I served my Queen and the Heir with honor and loyalty. I will serve you and your people in any way I can. I will make any oath you require of me." A careful smile crept onto her face. "All we need is a place of safety. All we need is for you to give me a chance. If not for me, for my daughter."

Maggie looked her over for a long moment. Spear stayed at attention, never shifting her eyes, never fidgeting. Canin, however, fidgeted freely and clenched his teeth.

Maggie then took a step forward and reached out her hand. "I do not make the decision on who will stay and who must go, but I see you are a good soldier and a good mother. I will do my best to persuade the others to let you and your family remain here." Maggie took Spear's arm in a Fairy warrior's grip. "Do not make me regret this."

"I won't, Ma'am. I swear by the Goddess I won't."

Maggie pulled her arm away. "Now, can I see your baby? Canin swears she's the most beautiful thing since the sunrise."

"She's sleeping," Spear said. "She sleeps a lot. I just fed her."

"I won't wake her," Maggie said. "I would just like to look at her."

Spear started to say something, but Canin stepped in. "She's right over here," and motioned Maggie to the box where Aurora slept. Maggie went to her knee and peered in. Aurora was indeed sleeping, a peaceful look on her little face.

"She is beautiful," Maggie agreed. She looked from Canin to Spear. "She doesn't look like either of you," she said offhandedly.

Canin was caught flatfooted, but Spear spoke up. "She looks like my mother." She rubbed her bald head. "I had blond hair when I was young, too. Or so I was told."

Maggie smiled and turned back to them. "Well, I was told Lily put some bread in the baskets. Shall we see what else there is?" Spear relaxed, and Canin closed the trap door before pulling the second basket over to where Maggie and Spear had sat down.

They sat in a triangle, with the basket in the center. Canin began pulling items out. One particular bundle, still warm, drew his attention. He almost cried at the smell as he unwrapped it, finding two steaming loaves of fresh bread.

Maggie and Spear shared an understanding glance.

Chapter 6
A Night Under the Trees

"It'll take a little time for them to get here," Maggie explained. She was standing by the open trap door, getting ready to leave. "I wouldn't expect them before mid-day."

"That'll be fine," Canin assured her, but he began to feel anxious. Seeing Lily, after all this time. He wasn't sure she would welcome him.

"Don't worry," Maggie said, reading his mind. "She understands." She shifted into her Prime voice and faced Spear.

"Two of my Maidens are watching from a distance. I don't expect any trouble, but with the clans, you can never tell." She turned to Canin. "Call of the wood owl if there's trouble."

Canin nodded in understanding.

Maggie turned back to Spear. "I can come back at first light. You can show me some of your Patterns, and I can show you mine."

"I would like that, Ma'am," Spear replied.

"You can call me Maggie for now." Her voice dropped. "Maybe in the future you will earn the right to call me Prime."

Spear bowed in respect.

Maggie covered her discomfort at the gesture by turning to Canin and embracing him firmly. "It's good to have you back, Canin."

"I'm glad to be back."

"Mother guide your sleep," Maggie said in parting, and climbed down the tree. Canin watched her reach the ground, then closed the trap door. Spear went to the window and watched Maggie disappear into the night.

Sighing with relief, Canin began to put away the containers that had held their meal. He picked up the last piece of bread and began to chew.

"I understand why she's Prime," Spear remarked from the window. "She's strong and just. She reminds me of Shatter."

"That's a strong compliment," Canin said around the bread crust. "She worked hard to gain that position."

"We shall see if she can fight, too," Spear said. "What did you try to call her? Sutab?"

"Yes. Sutab," Canin said. "It's a name of honor. 'Trusted sister.'" Canin drew a deep breath. "Setab is 'trusted brother.' Maidens and Brothers call each other that."

"It sounds like old Fairy, but not." Spear frowned, looking out the window. "I wish Gold were here. She could tell me."

She turned back to him and began unlacing her shirt. "Now we have to make love."

Caught flatfooted again, Canin could only stare at her as she removed her top. Behind him, their bedrolls slid together.

Spear pushed him back into the blankets. Straddling him, she first pulled off his shirt, and then his ringmail. Canin was finally able to overcome his shock and grabbed her hands as she reached for his belt.

"I can't."

"Yes, you can." Spear looked down and noted his reaction to her nakedness and proximity. "We told them we're wife and husband. We have to make them believe it. Maggie doesn't have experience with passion, so she didn't see anything to question. The others will. Your mother certainly will. We need to make them believe we had a child together. That we've been intimate." She put her hands on his bare chest. "I haven't even seen you without your shirt yet. And you've hardly looked at me." She grabbed his chin and forced his eyes to hers. "I need you. I need you to be close to me. I need your passion."

She cupped his face. "Pretend I'm Min, if you have to. Just make love to me. We're going to be here a long time. There'll be time for other feelings to grow. I just need you now. It will help." She lowered her head. "I bond very fast. Too fast. I made the mistake of trusting another man once, and he betrayed me." She looked up. "I know you won't do that. And I need this intimacy. It will keep me grounded. Tomorrow will be hard. I can feel my broken mind coming out. This will help."

Canin wanted to push her away. His self-made vow to Min filled his mind with guilt, despite her having told him that Fairy relationships were different from those he was used to. She had shared before, and she'd implied that she would share him as well once they returned to Fairy society in Fae-Treval.

"She would," Spear told him. "She shows the true depth of her love by encouraging you to find passion and joy with another. She would happily sit by your bed as you made love to another, as long as she was next."

Despite his body responding to Spear's heat pressed against him, he frowned. "How'd you know what I was thinking?"

"It was obvious," Spear said offhandedly. "Of course you were thinking of her."

"And before. You said I needed to apologize to the woman who raised me." He caught her hand as it drifted to his belt again. "I never told you that. I was just thinking about it. I never said anything."

Spear looked ashamed. She took his hand and pressed it to her belly. The heat of her flesh almost melted his control.

"I'm sorry. Your thoughts are very strong sometimes, and I have trouble keeping them out. I know I'm not supposed to listen. Gold tried to teach me blocking, but I just can't keep you out sometimes." Her voice dropped. "Honestly, I don't want to keep you out. Let me in. This will be healing for both of us."

Canin freed his hand and began to run it up her chest between her breasts. She shivered at his touch. He moved closer, his lips brushing hers.

"It's you who have to let me in," he breathed. "Or are Leather-wings that different?"

"No," she breathed, "we're not."

Spear sat in his lap, her arms and legs wrapped around him. Their breathing was returning to normal, and the sweat of their passion was beginning to dry. It had been quick and primal. Each of them had needed something from the other, and each let the other take it.

Canin's mind was still, knowing only the heat of her surrounding him. This had felt different. Not full of passion, as with Min, or awkward and fumbling, as with Brenna. She fit differently with him. Maybe their brokenness meshed in a way he hadn't expected.

"No, I didn't expect you to fit me like that either." She moved her hips slightly. "No wonder Min was so happy when you returned."

Canin pulled back slightly to look at her. "I don't know what to say."

She kissed him, and her hands moved down to his hips, sending a sudden warmth surging through him. She broke the kiss with a gasp. "Fairy Magic," she muttered, moving her hips faster.

"Thank the Goddess," Canin whispered back, letting the passion take them again.

She had her head pillowed on his chest. She might have been asleep. As Canin listened to her slow breathing, the strangeness of his life overwhelmed him again. Only a few days ago he had been working for a group of murderous, cruel cultists. Then he'd been rescued by an angry Fairy seeking vengeance and had been reunited with his lost love. Now he was making love to yet another Fairy high up in a tree, with a baby sleeping in the same room. He wondered if he should laugh or cry.

"Neither," Spear muttered into his chest. "Kiss me."

He did. She began to move against him again, but Canin pulled his lips from hers.

"Please," he begged. "Not again. I need to rest."

She smiled. "I can help with that."

"No," Canin said. She frowned.

"I don't think I've ever had a man say no to me before." She propped herself on her elbows and looked at him. "I've definitely never said no to a man I liked, or a woman."

"I just need to be with you." Canin tried to explain. "You need intimacy. Well, I need to be in your arms. Just being here with you makes me feel closer."

She nuzzled back into his chest. "You're strange."

"I know."

Spear sat back up. "It's been a long time for me. You had all that bed play with Min, while the rest of us had nothing. I demand my share of your passion." She kissed him again. She took his hand and guided it between her legs.

"Show me what she taught you," Spear whispered, biting his ear.

☾ ⌇⌇ ☼

Under the dim Fairy Light, Canin stared at Spear, who sat cross-legged at his side. She made little movements with her arms and hands, bending and flexing. Her lower body stayed still.

"I wish I could be on my back," Spear said. "I prefer that way. But Steel says a soldier should never be on her back, unless she's dead. Only Feathers make love on their backs." She looked at Canin. "But I like it. Gets the right angle." Canin blushed. Spear shook her head. "We'll have to work on that."

Canin pushed his discomfort away. She was different, and he would have to get used to it. "You're good at moving things. Can't you float yourself?"

Spear smiled slyly at him. "Looking for a way to get on top of me? Didn't get enough?"

"No," he said with all sincerity, "I did not."

Spear shook her head sadly. "I can't concentrate for that long. And you're heavy."

"You'll have to work on that, then," Canin said flirtatiously and brushed her leg.

"I've tried. You think it's easy to sleep with these?" She gestured to her ruined wings. "It's hard."

"I'm sorry," Canin said again, the feel of the broken wings in his hands on their arrival day coming back to him. He would never forget the horrible sound of them shattering.

Spear pushed the thought away. "I'll just have to get used to it." She leaned over and began to kiss him again. Canin slipped his arm around her waist. She pushed him down and climbed on top. She was settling into a rhythm when her eyes flew open.

"That could work," she said, climbing off him abruptly.

Shocked out of his passion, Canin sat up and watched her as she grabbed one of the folded blankets Maggie had brought and spread it out on the floor.

"Feels like Fairy silk," she muttered, running her hand over the fabric. She looked at him. "Was this made here?"

Canin glanced at the corner and saw the spinner's mark. "I think that was made by Lightfoot."

"The son of the foolish Human," she remarked, remembering their conversation with Maggie earlier. Canin nodded, feeling offended for Bitter.

"Good." She began to carefully fold the blanket. Canin just watched. Moving with sharp intensity, still naked, she shaped a rectangle about as tall as she was and wide enough for two. Then she knelt at the edge of the blanket. "Goddess. Mother of Waves, grant me your Power." She cupped her hands together and held them over the fabric.

Canin saw a light begin to form between her fingers. She spread her hands slightly and a ball of silver light emerged. She frowned in concentration, pushing her Power into the Weave. A sharp smell filled the air and the hair on Canin's arms stood up. Spear frowned, her brows going down sharply as she concentrated. The Weave sparked and dimmed.

"You're trying too hard," Canin called, rising. He lightly placed his hand on her shoulder. "Let it flow. Don't fight it."

"Grant me some of your Power," Spear demanded.

Canin didn't know how to do that, but he imagined a light forming in his hands and offered it to her. She took his offering greedily and used it to feed her Weave. Canin began to feel lightheaded, and the hand he was using to touch Spear began to tingle.

The ball between her hands grew. Canin had to look away, but he kept feeding his light into her. Spear grunted, and then pushed down with her hands into the blanket. There was a snap and a sudden burst of a smell like rain. Canin let go and dropped to his knees.

"I took too much," Spear said, concerned. She helped Canin lie down with his head in her lap and flowed Healing into him. He felt its warmth drive the dizziness away. After a moment, he raised his head.

"Well, what did you do?"

"I think I made a bed I can lie on," Spear said with some confidence. "The silk was perfect for it. I was able to anchor the Weave to the cloth like Gold showed me. It should float me just enough that my wings aren't crushed."

Intrigued, Canin struggled to a sitting position. "Try it."

Spear sat down on the blanket and eased herself back. Wincing as her wings touched the cloth, she snapped her fingers. The Weave triggered, and she floated half a hand above the blanket. Smiling, she turned to Canin.

"It worked," she said, her face full of childlike glee. "I did it."

Canin smiled. "I knew you could." He grabbed another blanket. Wrapping it around himself, he snuggled up against her.

She looked surprised as he put his arm over her and closed his eyes. "I did this so we could make love."

"Wake me before sunrise," he muttered, falling asleep. "I'm too tired now."

"Canin," Spear said, but it was too late. He was already asleep. Smiling, she pulled his blanket over herself, then brushed his forehead. "Sleep well, Love." Then she was asleep, too.

As their breathing settled into a synchronized rhythm, a dim light began to form over Aurora's box. A whirlpool of red, blue, and black swirled over her. A flash of silver light from Canin and Spear's direction dimmed the blue aura. Aurora made a noise in her sleep, then the swirling colors disappeared.

Chapter 7
Mother's Milk

Canin woke with the bright sun in his face. Sitting up, he yawned, stretched, and looked around. Spear was gone. Beside him lay his folded shirt and pants. He picked up the shirt and pulled it over his head. As he did, a message was triggered.

"Canin, Maggie came early, and I didn't want to wake you after last night. You looked so peaceful asleep. I wanted to wake you with my hands, but I didn't think you'd want your forest sister to watch, so I fed Aurora instead. She's asleep for now, but will need to be fed again when she wakes. There's a bottle — strange thing! — staying warm in the fire pit. Maggie and I will be sparring till you wake up. Bring Aurora down after you feed her. I left you some bread and some kind of meat Maggie brought for breakfast. Hurry. Get up! They'll be here soon."

He didn't just hear her voice in his mind; he saw images of himself sleeping, and then felt what Spear had wanted to do to wake him up. Then she was feeding Aurora. Canin felt a slice of the joy she had felt as Aurora had taken nourishment from her. Shaking his head to clear the images, he pulled on his pants. Another series of vignettes piled into his mind.

"Get up. You're too slow! This might be a way we can make them believe we've been together longer than we actually have. I'll read your mind, and act on your thoughts." Canin saw her smiling face and felt her joy of discovery fill him. *"I wish Gold were here. She'd be fascinated by all this."*

"I'm getting up," Canin said to the air. Below, he could just make out the sound of wood hitting wood.

Under the window, the fire pit was open, and a pot with a lid sat on the banked coals. He recognized it as something from his old home. No wonder Spear was confused. Fairies never had to deal with mothers not being able to make enough milk, or babies without mothers. He recalled one season when the house had seemed to be filled with babies. Niel and Canin had done nothing, it seemed, but make, heat, and then make more Mother's Milk. He lifted the lid of the pot and found a bottle with a leather nipple resting in a pool of warm water.

"Let's see how you find our Mother's Milk," Canin said, as he reached into the box to pull Aurora out of her blankets. She yawned and opened her eyes.

Canin almost dropped the bottle when Aurora stared up at him. Her green eyes were clear and awake. Her oblong pupils and the swirl of silver and white of her outer eyes glinted in the morning light. They crinkled as Canin looked at her, bottle held just out of reach. They scrunched more as she reached for the bottle and began to cry. The sound jolted Canin out of his paralysis. He put the nipple in her mouth and she began to suck, her cries quieted. Canin looked around, expecting something or someone to be lurking in the shadows, but he was alone with the baby. She made happy noises and reached for his hand.

"I don't understand, Little Wing. I swear your eyes were blue," Canin told her. "Spear must have done something, but why wouldn't she warn me?" He sighed. Aurora kicked at him, and he had to tilt the bottle more so she could access its dwindling contents. "Mother's mercy." Canin spotted the breakfast Spear had promised and, with some difficulty, was able to pick it up without disturbing Aurora. He made his own happy sounds as he ate with one hand.

"Well, you seem to like that," Canin commented as they both finished their breakfasts. Aurora burped. Canin laughed and wrapped her back up. She smiled at him again.

"Now, how to get you safely to the ground." Canin began looking around the room. He saw the baskets from the prior night, but he couldn't carry her in one and climb safely down the tree. And Spear would skin him if he lowered her in a basket first, leaving her unprotected below. He blew out his breath in frustration. "Fairies," he swore to Aurora. "Your Mama didn't think about us."

Aurora only yawned and closed her eyes.

"At least you have faith in me," Canin said. "You might fit in the quiver," he mused for a moment, but quickly discarded the idea. He went to the wardrobe. Only the green cloaks hung inside. "I'll have to call her," Canin finally decided. "She'll have to float you down." But Canin frowned. He didn't want to do that, either. He needed to solve this problem on his own. He looked again at the contents of the room. "You can solve this," he encouraged himself.

He paced the room, looking for inspiration. Returning to the wardrobe, he examined the cloaks again. A thought struck him, as he remembered Spear covering herself with the blanket in a rare show of sympathy for his discomfort. He pulled a cloak out.

"This might work," he said. Setting Aurora down, he wound the cloak around his body like a bandoleer. He knotted it at his shoulder and tested its strength. The knot held. Then he settled Aurora in the folds of the cloak at his chest. She giggled again as he pulled her tight against him. Satisfied that she was secure, he carefully raised his arms to ensure that she stayed in the folds. She did. Canin took another deep breath, then opened the trap door and lowered himself gingerly through the opening. His feet found a notch in the tree and he slowly descended, stopping at each rung to make sure Aurora was still secure.

"You're holding back," Maggie accused.

"Yes, I am," Spear agreed amiably.

"You don't need to. I've been fighting Humans, Elenites, and Fairies since I was not much older than Aurora. I can hold my own."

"I don't doubt that, Ma'am, but you've never fought a Fairy soldier of the Queen's Guard."

"Why do you say that?"

"You're still alive."

That brought Maggie up short. The two of them were standing in the clearing. They faced each other with sword-length branches in their hands. Maggie hadn't had time to fetch proper training weapons, so they'd done the best they could with the wood around them. Maggie took a sip of water and tried to slow her breathing. Spear was calm and still.

"Soldier," Maggie said in her command voice, "don't you have the control to give me a good fight?"

Spear snapped to attention at the change in Maggie's voice. "I do. I'm holding back." She glanced over her shoulder at the Treetower. "I don't want to hurt you. Canin. . . ."

"Is not the Prime Thorn Maiden." Maggie brought her wooden weapon to a guard position. "I am. Just don't break any bones."

"As you wish," Spear replied with reluctance. She brought her own weapon up.

"Ready," Maggie called. "Now."

Three things happened almost simultaneously. Maggie's hands rung as Spear's blow shattered the branch she held. She felt a woosh of air, as the branch passed over her head, and a blow to her chest that drove her to the ground. Her breath exploded out of her as she hit the grass. Maggie recovered her vision to see Spear kneeling over her, branch at her throat.

"I see," Maggie said as she caught her breath. "But." She flicked her left wrist and a short blade appeared in her hand. She pressed it close to Spear's belly. "I would take you with me."

Spear started to knock the blade away, but caught herself. She released Maggie and sat down beside her.

Maggie pulled herself to a sitting position. She started to say more, but saw the look in Spear's eyes and stayed silent. Instead, she returned her blade to its hidden sheath and rubbed her stinging hands.

Spear calmed herself. "If this were a real blade, I would have taken your head off. You would have never even known you were dead." Spear threw the branch away.

Maggie started to argue, but decided better. "You'll have to teach me that."

Spear shook her head. "I can't. It was my Power. I moved faster than you could see. Only Fairies can do that. And then only for a short time."

"I will remember that."

Spear nodded. Then her head turned. Maggie followed her eyes and saw Canin come around the tree. Spear was on her feet so fast, it seemed to Maggie as though she'd sprung into the air. Spear took a few steps in Canin's direction, then returned to offer her hand to Maggie.

Maggie took it, and Spear levered her up. Then she turned and was instantly at Canin's side. He blinked at her sudden appearance.

"How is she?" Spear demanded, reaching into the cloak Canin had wrapped around himself to hold the baby. Maggie smiled at his discomfort as she pulled Aurora from his grasp.

"She's fine," Canin managed to say. Then he bent close to her. "We need to talk. Aurora. . . ."

"What's wrong?" Spear demanded, the worry and anger in her voice making him step back. Maggie, surprised, took an automatic step forward.

"Spear," Canin said, trying to calm her. "I just need to ask you something." He glanced at Maggie. "Over by the tree."

Spear, clutching the bundled baby to her chest, turned on her heel and headed around the tree.

Canin looked at Maggie, stopping her question. "I just want to ask her how Aurora was this morning."

Maggie smiled, still off balance from Spear's abrupt changes. "You just want a moment with your wife. I understand."

Canin smiled guiltily and turned to follow Spear.

Around the tree, out of sight, Spear waited. "What's wrong?" she demanded again.

"Her eyes," Canin told her. "They're Elenite now."

Spear visibly relaxed. "Of course they are. She's our daughter." She brushed Aurora's forehead. "They're even closer to Fairy eyes than oval. She's more Fairy than Human."

"But she's not," Canin started, but Spear stopped his words with a kiss.

"Silly, you were dreaming," Spear said after pulling away. "I must have made a mistake with my message. I'll have to be more careful."

Canin, caught between wondering if Spear truly didn't remember what Aurora's eyes had looked like or if she was just fully invested in playing her new role, stepped closer. "Did you do something? You were worried about her eyes last night."

"What would I have done?" Spear held the girl up and spun her around. "Look, Aurora. This is your new home." Aurora squealed as Spear spun her faster.

Canin tried to get her attention, but saw Maggie coming around the tree, a look of grand amusement filling her face.

"A runner just arrived. They'll be here soon."

Spear lowered Aurora with a concerned expression. She covered it by becoming serious. She handed the baby to Canin and turned. "You said you had blankets?" she reminded Maggie.

"Yes. I brought a few, and another runner is bringing water from the spring." Maggie looked at Canin with more amusement as Spear brushed by her. "She's nervous to meet them," she commented as Canin followed, more slowly.

Canin only nodded and made sure Aurora was bundled tightly.

"She changes so fast," Maggie noted, falling in beside him. "Has she always been that way?"

"Yes, but she's been worse lately," Canin had to admit. "I hoped your sparring would calm her."

Maggie rubbed her shoulder. "It did. She's a deadly fighter. I can understand your fear." She stopped and grabbed his arm. "She will be a great asset to us. Her style of fighting works very well with ours. Anything she can teach us will help."

Canin stayed silent.

"But," Maggie continued, "if she turns on us. . . ."

"She won't," Canin cut in.

"It will take the lives of many to stop her," Maggie finished.

"She will not turn on us," Canin said with determination. "I give you my word." He tried to walk away, but Maggie held him.

"If she does, you might be the only one who can stop her." Her eyes bored into his. "Are you prepared to do that?"

Canin bit down on an angry retort. Aurora began to whimper as he clutched her hard. Realizing what he was doing, Canin relaxed. "I am prepared to defend my wife from anyone." His voice dropped as he nuzzled Aurora's head. "Even herself." He gently pulled away from Maggie and went to join Spear.

Chapter 8
Reunion

Spear was directing a young, and very tall, Thorn Maiden to lay out the blankets on the grass.

"No," she said to the young Elenite in exasperation. "Can't you see that they clash? Switch them."

The young woman, caught between frustration and fear of the tall Fairy, seemed paralyzed. Spear stepped closer, her fists clenched. The Thorn Maiden stepped quickly back and put her hand on the hilt of her sword.

"Spearhead," Canin called, coming around the tree.

She turned, saw Canin and Aurora, and felt her anger fall away. "I just want it to be perfect, for your family."

"It is," Canin said calmly. He put a hand lightly on her arm. "Humans can't see as many colors are you do. To them, they match." He gestured to the blankets.

"Heron, please go and see what's keeping Sadie," Maggie called to the Maiden. With relief, the woman turned and ran off into the woods. Maggie took a moment to calm herself, then addressed Spear. "Do not speak to my Maidens so. I am their leader." Her voice softened. "They're young, and many have come here from difficult situations. You understand?"

Spear straightened at Maggie's tone. "I do, Captain. I will do better."

"You don't have to call me captain," Maggie tried to tell her, but Spear had already turned back to Canin. She sat down on the blankets and reached out for Aurora. Canin laid the baby in her arms and then sat down beside her. They leaned their heads close and whispered to each other.

"Mother's mercy," Maggie swore under her breath. "I'll watch from the edge of the clearing," she told Canin. He nodded, then went back to looking at Aurora with Spear. Maggie sighed again and went to stand at the edge of the woods.

☾ ∿ ☼

"When they get here, I want you to take her and greet them while holding her."

"But you're her mother," Canin disagreed. "They'll understand. Lily has raised many Elenite children, and Sekrine has delivered countless babies."

Spear shook her head. "No. You must hold her. I'll be at your shoulder. They must see her in your arms."

Canin began to argue, but Spear laid her hand on his arm. Images of Spear holding Aurora filled his mind. Then Spear was gone, and Aurora stood alone, sorrow filling her face. Then Canin was holding Aurora, and Spear was gone. The two of them were surrounded by others; their faces were hazy, but they were obviously people of the forest.

A pain grew in the back of Canin's head. He pulled away from Spear.

"You think they'll reject her if they see her as your daughter?" Canin asked in a whisper. Spear nodded.

"Spear, these are good people. Stop being so suspicious."

Her face went from angry to sad in a blink. "Do not fight me on this. You must do this for her."

Canin wanted to argue, but the memory of Crow, arrow on the string, came to him unbidden.

"See," Spear said. "They may be good people, but good people can still do horrible things."

Canin remembered Talia, blood-spattered and smelling of smoke, standing before him at the cultists' crafthouse, and could not disagree. He held out his hands and took Aurora without another word.

Across the clearing, Maggie stepped out of the trees and waved. Spear was on her feet in a blink. Canin, startled, was unable to stand while holding Aurora. Spear hauled him to his feet with one hand, her eyes never leaving Maggie.

"Trillium," Canin whispered, "you are safe."

Spear tried to smile, but her hands desperately reached for her sword belt, which she had left up in the tree. Remembering that, her hands began to fidget, clasping and unclasping. Moving in front of her to shield her from Maggie's view for a moment, Canin reached out and took her hand. She gripped it, holding on to him as if he were the only thing keeping her from falling.

Canin tried again. "Calm. You are a powerful Fairy soldier. You faced down knights at the Battle of Brine Hill. You've defended your Sisters from evil. This is nothing."

"But this is everything," Spear disagreed.

Canin smiled at her, his growing love flowing out of him and toward her. Spear finally smiled. The image of her naked on her back filled his mind.

"Stop it," Canin said, trying to push the image out. "My mother's coming."

Spear smiled again, gave his desire a pinch, and withdrew. Now Canin shifted uncomfortably.

"You are a strong Thorn Brother," Spear said with laughter in her voice. "You faced down Wingless and won your way into the beds of two powerful Fairies. This is nothing."

Canin's retort evaporated as a small group emerged from the trees.

Four women, all cloaked and hooded in the green and brown of the forest, stepped into the clearing. The woman in the lead carried a child, a boy. She took several steps into the clearing and then stopped. The others lined up alongside her. The boy began to fidget; it had been a long walk, and he didn't want to be carried any more.

The leader addressed the woman to her left. "Coltsfoot. Could you watch Alexander? He wants to run."

The boy slipped out of the leader's arms and took off running. With a glance at Maggie, Coltsfoot followed him.

Her hands freed, the leader pushed back her hood. Her hair was iron grey, with just a few strands of red remaining. Her kind face was freckled, and lines of concern and laughter creased it.

"Hello, Canin," she said. "I'm glad you're home."

At the first word she spoke, Canin was filled with a profound sense of both joy and shame. This woman had taught and scolded him. Laughed with him, and shared her profound worry for his future. Her voice had been the last thing he had heard as she had blown out the candle beside his bed each night of his youth. Most mornings, it had woken him as well. He had forgotten how much he missed that voice.

"Lily . . . Mother," he said through a lump in his throat. Spear squeezed his hand. "I'm glad to be home."

Lily closed the distance between them in just a few steps. "I never thought you'd call me that," she admitted, tears in her eyes. "Mother bless, I thought you were gone." She threw her arms around him and Aurora. She was a head shorter than him, but she filled his senses. She was everything he remembered and everything he now understood.

He let go of Spear's hand and embraced her. They stood as one, reunited. Mother and son.

The smell of her hair — roses — filled his nose. "I'm sorry," Canin muttered. "I'm so sorry."

They held their hug until Aurora began to squeak and kick. Lily laughed and pulled away, but still held him at arm's length.

"This must be my granddaughter." She tickled Aurora's chin. "And this must be my new daughter." She held out her hand. "Greetings, Spearhead. Welcome to the Exile Forest."

Spear took the offered hand without hesitation. "Greetings, Lily, Mother of Canin," she said formally, bowing slightly over the woman's hand. "You raised a wonderful son. I look forward to getting to know you."

If Lily was shocked by Spear and her manners, she didn't show it. "And I look forward to knowing the woman who healed his heart." She looked back at Canin. "I worried you would never get over her."

"I never will," Canin admitted. "But Spear has helped me find a way to let go of the sorrow and remember the happiness."

"That is a lesson we must all learn," Lily said wisely. She let go of Canin and fully embraced Spear. Canin saw the shock on Spear's face, quickly replaced by wonder at the openness and caring of this woman. Spear let go. Tears came to her eyes, and she hugged Lily with a fierce intensity. Then she tried to wrap her wings around her.

"Lily, Mother," Canin corrected himself. "Spear isn't used to such displays." Canin saw the pain in Spear's face, as she couldn't use her wings as she wished.

Lily pulled away. "Of course. Forgive me." Lily wiped her eyes.

Canin and Spear shared a look, giving Spear time to get control over her raw emotions. "Flora," Canin mouthed.

"No need," Spear said. "There was a woman who traveled with us. She was a second mother to me and all of my Sisters." She held out her hands, cupped, to Lily. "We called her Mum out of respect and admiration for all she did for us. Would you allow me the honor of calling you Mum as well?"

Profoundly moved, Lily put her hands in Spear's. "Of course you may." Her Elenite eyes danced with joy. "What would you like me to call you? Spear seems so. . . ." She lost her words.

"Jewel," Spear suggested. "My mother sometimes called me that. When I wasn't knocking things over with my clumsy wings." She realized what she had said, but pushed through. "I haven't been called that in a long time."

Lily saw the pain in Spear's eyes. She had known many women over the years who had come to her with similar pain in their eyes. Pain that went so deep, its foundations were long forgotten. It took time, but Lily always found a way to ease the impact of that pain. 'You will have a long walk with this one,' she thought. "Then Jewel it is," she said amiably. She gave Spear's hands another shake. "Now, I must hold that baby."

Before Canin could react, Lily was pulling Aurora out of his arms and settling her onto her chest. Spear moved to take Aurora back, but Canin caught her hand. Her grip was crushing, but Canin kept his face calm.

"Mother," Canin admonished her. "Please ask first. We're very protective of her."

Lily registered the contained anger and fear in Spear's eyes and felt a touch of anxiety and remorse. "I'm sorry." She offered Aurora back to Spear. "I've overstepped again. You've just met me."

"You may hold her, Mum," Spear said with forced calm. She eased her grip on Canin's hand. "It will be good for her to know the touch of others."

"Has the child been fed lately?" Another of the women had stepped up beside Lily. She was shorter than Canin's mother, with dark black hair and brown skin. Her voice held a lilt that Spear had never heard before. There was no indication of age in her, other than the wrinkles of her hands and the deep experience in her Elenite eyes and voice.

Spear frowned at the woman. Canin squeezed her hand again in support.

"Pardon," she said. "I am called Sekrine. I'm one of the midwives here." She sized up Spear with a glance. "I haven't been this close to a Fairy in a long time. Tell me, how is your Healing power?"

"I wasn't the Medic of our group, but I can stop bleeding and knit bones," Spear answered automatically. "As any soldier can."

"Splendid," Sekrine crowed. "The Mother has provided for us again. I have a little Healing ability. Together we can save many. How soon can you come to the sanctuary village? I have patients who need your Power."

Canin sensed Spear's panic. She wanted to back away from this intense older woman. Lily sensed it, too, and turned to Sekrine.

"Now, don't overwhelm her. This is her first day," Lily chided the other woman. "She must have time to get used to her new home. Then she can help you."

"Pardon again," Sekrine said with a bow of her head. "I walk too fast. When you are ready."

Spear nodded, but did not speak.

Sekrine looked at the baby. "May I examine her?" She didn't move to touch Aurora, but merely looked at Spear and Canin.

Spear glanced at Canin, looking for advice. "She's the best midwife in the forest," Canin told her. "Many mothers would have died if not for her knowledge and swift hands."

"And many children run and play because of Sekrine." Lily looked at Maggie. "Is that not right?"

Maggie nodded. "She's the only one I'll send my Maidens to when they have children."

Distrust pulled at Spear. To see another woman holding her baby made her itch. Spear wanted to pull her out of Lily's grasp and run.

"I trust her," Canin said simply.

Spear took a deep breath and nodded. Lily passed Aurora over, and Sekrine laid her on the blankets and began to unwrap her. Spear and Canin knelt on the far side of the blankets, watching intently. Lily stood behind Canin and put her hands on his shoulders.

Sekrine muttered as Aurora's little form was revealed to her. She gently touched her arms and legs, muttering more. Then she rubbed the baby's belly. Aurora cooed and all around smiled. Sekrine gently turned Aurora over and gasped at the two scars on her back, running down from her shoulder blades.

"Poor baby," Lily said.

"What are these scars?" Sekrine asked sharply, looking up at Canin and Spear. "A child this young should not bear the marks of such violence. Are these from her birth?"

Canin used all his strength to stay calm and keep Spear sitting beside him. He Sent, in his own poor way, a sense of calm to her. Otherwise, she might have snatched Aurora up and run.

"We were captured by Blood Cultists," Canin explained, "when we escaped the Fairy Realm. They held us for days. Spear gave birth in that horrible place. They took Aurora and were bleeding her." Canin stopped. He hoped his emotions were clear enough. He looked at Spear as if he could not go on.

"Canin saved us," Spear said flatly. "He got us out. He saved me."

"Oh, how horrible," Lily said, hugging Canin. She looked over at Spear. "Is that how you lost your wings?" she asked carefully.

"Mother," Canin cautioned.

"I'm sorry," Lily said, embarrassed. "Jewel, forgive me."

Spear folded her arms. "It's all right," she forced out, looking down at Aurora. "I don't remember much. They were very cruel."

"We were lucky to escape. The Mother guided us," Canin filled in when Spear went silent.

Sekrine frowned and ran her finger over the scars. She opened her mouth to speak, but Maggie spoke first.

"These are the same people who come trying to persuade our young men to follow them. Cajole them into joining the Lions." She looked at Canin. "On the full moon, when Wolf and I meet with the Children, you and Spear must join us. Tell us who these men with the fake smiles truly are."

"They slaughtered my Sisters," Spear said with cold intensity. "They will never hurt my family again." Aurora was beginning to fuss, the air on her skin and the intensity of the conversation disturbing her. "Give her back," she demanded of Sekrine.

"Please," Spear added at Canin's look. Sekrine nodded and began to wrap Aurora back in her swaddle. Spear held herself back from reaching over and pulling the baby away from the older woman.

The midwife passed the bundled child back with a smile. "She seems healthy. I would like to see her again in a few days. Make sure she doesn't pick up something in this new place."

As Spear pulled open her shirt and let Aurora nurse, Canin replied for her. "We will. She seems to have a healthy appetite. She took the Mother's Milk fine this morning. Thank you." He nodded to Maggie.

"I made sure she brought some," Lily put in. "We all know you know little of children," she teased Maggie, who smiled in understanding.

The Thorn Maidens were returning from the spring with two clay jugs. They set them on the ground and began to pass out cups. When everyone had one, Maggie filled them with clear water.

"The Mother of Exiles," she pronounced, raising her cup.

"The Mother of Exiles," the others responded, with Canin and Spear a beat behind.

The dark-haired boy reappeared and plopped down in Lily's lap. He grabbed for her cup and pulled it from her grip, spilling most of its water on himself. He then reached out a muddy hand toward Aurora's lightly kicking feet. "Baby," he said.

"Don't touch her!" Spear snapped, slapping his hand away.

"Alexander," Lily scolded, a moment after. She shifted him away from the glaring Spear. "You know not to touch without asking. Now, run and play. Go find Coltsfoot," she told him, looking for the Thorn Maiden she had sent with him earlier. He sniffed, rubbing his nose as he stood out of Lily's arms. Then he started to run, tripped on the grass, and fell sprawling. With obvious practice, he picked himself up and took off into the woods. A moment later, Coltsfoot appeared from the opposite direction, her hair full of leaves. Without a word, Maggie, Lily, and Sekrine pointed in the direction Alexander had gone. With a frustrated, "Thanks," she followed, yelling for him to slow down.

Lily turned to Spear. "I'm sorry, dear. He's full of energy." She tried to rub away the mud he had left on the blanket.

"It's all right," Spear said low. Her nursing trance broken, she looked around the clearing.

"Another child?" Canin asked when Spear didn't speak again.

"Yes," Lily said. "Poor thing was abandoned by his mother. Another midwife in one of the Elen towns sent him here about two seasons ago. I had decided not to take in any more children, but once I saw his beautiful Elenite eyes, I couldn't help myself." She glanced at Spear. "He has the same shape to his nose as you do. Is it possible he's from a distant part of your family?"

"I have no family left," Spear said shortly. "They all died in the war."

Lily moved to say more, but Canin stepped in. "That would have been . . .?"

"Yes, right after Niel died."

Canin knelt in front of her. "I'm sorry. I treated you both badly. Now, I can't make it up to him."

"There's nothing to be sorry for," Lily said, taking his hands. "We understood you. You needed to hold on to some hope of finding your family. By not calling us your parents, you protected that hope. Many of our children did that." She pointed to Heron, who was helping Maggie and the other Thorn Maidens set up some food. "Heron there was one of mine. She still just calls me Lily. There are others that call me many things. I accept them all. We're here to make sure you and all the others have a safe childhood and grow to be productive members of our forest family. It doesn't matter if I am called 'mother,' or 'aunt,' or just 'that woman.' I measure my success by how you've all turned out." She leaned in and kissed him on the cheek. "And you seem to have grown up to be a fine man. With a fine family. There's nothing to be sorry for."

Canin held on to her hands. "I still wish I could have told him."

Lily smiled sadly. "He knew. I think he saw himself in you. He was sad when you left, but he knew you needed to. He would look up into the sky at night and wonder where you were. He would pick out a star and imagine you were watching it, too."

"He taught me that," Canin said, his voice rough. "I always hoped my mother was looking up at the same star." He sat down. "I guess I was wrong. He was the one doing the looking."

"Fairies," Spear said cautiously, looking at him with shining eyes. "When we die, we Return to the Cycle to be born again. What did Niel believe?"

"Not much of anything," Lily replied. "He didn't hold any weight with the Father's Realm in the Sky. He thought this one was what was important. To him, his life would be over when he died, and he wanted to leave this realm better than he found it."

Aurora finished nursing and began to drift off to sleep. Spear fastened her shirt and shifted the sleeping baby to ease the ache in her arms.

"I'd be happy to hold her," Lily offered. "You must be hungry, and it's hard to eat with a baby in your arms." Spear hesitated, but then her eyes were drawn to the food being prepared. "I can tell you stories of Canin when he was a boy," Lily enticed.

Spear grinned and handed the baby to Lily. "Yes, Mum. I would very much like to hear some stories."

Canin looked betrayed, but stood and went to help Maggie.

Chapter 9
Little Wing

"She seems to be getting on well," Maggie commented. She and Canin were sitting apart. They had eaten, and Lily was still telling stories to a rapt Spear. Aurora was sleeping comfortably in her new grandmother's arms.

Sekrine had left with Heron, Coltsfoot, and Alexander to return to their village. Alexander had been making a nuisance of himself, and Lily had thought it better to send him home.

"I will be back before moonrise," Lily had assured him. "Listen to Sekrine and Coltsfoot. I'll tell you the next part of the little people tale when I return."

"Yes, Auntie," Alexander moped.

"I will make sure she gets home safe," Maggie assured Sekrine. "My Maidens will escort her."

Sekrine said her goodbyes to Canin and Spear. "I expect you in my house with the baby before the next moon."

"Yes, Midwife," Canin agreed. "We will bring her."

"I want to check both of you out, too. Walking all that distance." She shook her head. "I don't know how you young people do it."

Canin and Spear exchanged glances. "I promise," Canin said.

"So, what do you plan to do?" Maggie asked.

"We'll stay here another night. After that." He shrugged. "I must go before the Mother soon."

"One of the Children can come to you tomorrow." Canin frowned. "Or the next day," Maggie amended. "I have duties to return to, but Stonefoot and Sadie can stay. They'll watch from out of sight." An idea occurred to her. "I can ask Wolf to come and talk with you. He can tell you everything you've missed. And how things have changed. He should still be with the berry widow."

"That would be a help," Canin said with gratitude. "Thank you for all that you've done. I'm sure it hasn't been easy."

"I am not Crow or my mother," Maggie snapped at him. "I do not blame you for her death. She died when she was supposed to die. It was her time. It wouldn't have mattered if she had married Crow rather than you. She would still be dead."

Canin lowered his head.

Maggie took another breath. "I'm sorry. It's been hard. Your return has dredged up a lot of old memories. I try to honor my sister every day."

"I do, too."

"She would want you to be happy," Maggie said with certainty. She looked over to where Spear and Lily were laughing. "You'd better go. She'll tell the bath story next."

Canin stood. "It has been good to see you, Prime."

"I'm glad you're back, Canin." Maggie embraced him. "We need you, now more than ever. I'll make sure Wolf brings you some more weapons." She smiled. "I don't want Spear to be the only one with a sword."

"Thank you," Canin said again. He pulled away.

Maggie watched him walk over and sit down beside Spear, who put her arm around him and laid her head on his shoulder. Maggie felt a momentary tug of something. Maybe envy. She pushed it down, and went to inform her Maidens of their new assignment.

☾ ∿ ☼

"And then he jumped right into the pool outside the Mother's Sanctuary. With all the Children watching." Lily laughed at Canin's embarrassed look. "It took days to get all the leaves and petals out of the pool. Aieren was very angry. I had to bake my berry bread for all of them for the whole moon."

Spear kissed Canin on the cheek. "You must have been a cute child."

"He was," Lily agreed. "When he wanted to be. Other times he was a brat."

"I wasn't that bad!" Canin tried to defend himself, but Lily glared at him and he wilted.

Spear laughed, a sweet, honest laugh. "I must remember that look."

Lily smiled and patted Spear's leg. "There is much I can teach you, but every child is different. As mothers, we must find the proper way for our children. Sometimes it's hard. Sometimes we can't see the way until they show it to us."

Spear nodded with understanding.

Canin glanced over and noted that Maggie was looking up at the sky with increasing impatience. "I think it's time for you to head home, Mother."

Lily noted the darkening sky herself and sighed. "I guess it is." She handed Aurora back to Spear. "I could stay."

The look of panic on Spear's face made Lily laugh. "No. I see you two want your privacy. I remember when Niel and I were first married. I hated when his father wanted to stay with us." She stood, with Canin's help, and hugged him tightly. "I really missed you. And to hear you call me 'mother.'" She stopped and brushed her eyes. "I did not think it would affect me so."

"I love you, Mother," Canin said into her hair. "There's so much I need to tell you." He pulled away. "But for now you need to get home. Your other children need you. It will be dark soon, and Maggie has much to do."

Lily wiped her eyes again. "That one is a true brat. Yes, I must. I'll see you in a few days. You'll be coming to the Sanctuary soon?"

Canin looked at Maggie.

"I will speak with the Children," Maggie said. "I'll ask Wolf to come back, so Canin can understand all that has changed since he's been away. A few days."

Anxiety was clear on his face, but he pushed it away. "I must go before the Mother. I must ask her forgiveness."

"Do not worry," Lily counseled him. "She will hear you and forgive."

Canin wasn't so sure, but he hid his doubt with another embrace. He clung to her for a moment, then pulled away and put his arm around Spear.

Lily wanted to hug them both again, but Maggie laid a hand on her arm. "We must go."

"Yes," Lily admitted. "Mother watch over all of you." She then allowed Maggie to take her arm and lead her away, back into the forest. The two Maidens followed. At the edge of the trees, Lily turned back once again to wave. Canin returned the gesture, then the group disappeared into the greenery and the growing dark.

Spear held her breath, making sure they weren't coming back. When the rustling of their movement through the forest moved further away, Spear relaxed. She shot to her feet, grabbing Aurora from where she lay sleeping.

"Come on, before they turn around," she ordered Canin, hauling him to his feet. "Bring the basket they left us."

Canin picked up the basket, then noticed the blankets the Maidens had left. He bent to begin folding them.

"Leave them," Spear called from the other side of the tree. "Hurry up!"

Canin, still in a daze, followed the sound of her voice. She was standing impatiently at the foot of the tree, looking up. "Can you carry the basket up?"

Canin weighed the basket of provisions Lily had left. He nodded.

"Then get up there," Spear told him, making a shooing motion upward.

He climbed slowly, almost losing the basket when he had to open the trap door. Finally, he got inside and pushed the basket out of the way. Sitting down with a sigh, he looked down.

"She's coming up!" Spear called, and Aurora was flying again, giggling the whole way. Canin caught her and put her back in her box. Smiling, he brushed her happy face.

"You really do love that," he remarked. Aurora burbled at him in agreement.

Behind him, he heard Spear climb inside and shut the trap door. She didn't quite slam it shut, but she closed the bar with far more intensity than was needed. She sat down with another sigh, carefully leaning against the wall.

"I don't think she's hungry yet, but I am. What did they leave us?" She looked at Canin, expecting him to answer.

"I don't know."

"Well, look. She drains me, and all this with your mother and the rest has drained me even more."

Canin pulled the basket over and began looking through it.

"I should bathe her," Spear said. "The way that midwife looked at me. I could see it in her eyes. Bad mother. How could you let such a thing happen to your child?

"But you did," Spear answered herself. "You left him. Let him die. But now you have Returned, and I can finally be the mother you needed. I needed. Heat some water in that clever cooking pit. Not too hot, we don't want to boil her. What do we have to eat?"

Canin blinked at her, unable to follow her rapid speech and changing subjects. "There's a sealed pot of stew," Canin finally said.

Spear made a face. "No stew. Flora always made stew. Got tired of it. Still full of flavor, except when we ran out of meat and it was little more than water with some moonstems. I guess there wouldn't be any of those here. I have a sudden taste for them." She raised her eyebrows at Canin.

"No stew," Canin agreed. He pulled out another bundle. "Ham?"

"Any apples?" Spear asked. "I haven't had apples in so long."

"Apples aren't in season now," Canin told her. He dug deeper. Smiling, he pulled out a jar. "Not fresh, but pickled," he said, holding up a jar with apple slices floating in some liquid. Spear tilted her head, then gestured, and the jar floated to her hand. She broke the seal and fished one out. She took a careful bite. "Odd, but not horrible." She fished more out and ate them. "Is the water ready yet?"

Canin, who had not moved, could only admit, "No."

"Well, hurry up. I don't want that midwife to see Aurora dirty again. What a disgrace that would be."

"Her name is Sekrine," Canin reminded her. With effort, he went to the cooking pit. The pot was still there, but the water was gone. "I didn't bring the water up."

Spear waved at him. "Well, go get it then. I want to wash her and feed her, then she'll sleep." She pulled out another slice of apple and pointed it at him. "Then we can see if my Weave works." She grinned at him and popped the apple into her mouth.

Canin tried to smile, but his mental and emotional exhaustion turned it into more of a grimace.

"You're tired," Spear declared, climbing to her feet. "I'll go. I exhausted you, and then you finally see your family again. Stay here. I'll fetch the water." She motioned him to sit down. "Stay with her. I'll only be a moment."

Before Canin could reply, she'd opened the trap door and dropped through. He tried to call out, but it was too late. There was a surprised cry, then a thump. Canin pulled himself across the floor to look down through the opening.

Spear was lying on the ground, on her right side, her right arm pinned underneath her. She was pounding the grass with her left.

"Spear!" Canin called. "Are you hurt?"

"Curse!" she swore. "Cursed wings! Fool!" Her fingers dug into the dirt. She pulled out a clump of earth and grass. Throwing it, she swore, "Fool, fool, fool."

"Spear, are you hurt?" Canin called again. He swung his legs around, ready to climb down. "I'm coming down."

Spear fell back and moved to sit on the ground. She cradled her right arm in her lap. Canin could see that the back of her hand was almost touching her forearm. She held up her dirt-covered left arm to him.

"No. Stay there!" she called. "Fool forgot she has no wings. Fool, fool, fool." She wiped her left hand on the ground. Then she stopped moving and simply stared out into the forest.

"Spear!" Canin called again. Behind him, Aurora began to whimper.

"Stay there," Spear said so quietly that Canin didn't know if he had heard her with his ears or with his mind. "I just need a moment." She picked up her right hand with her left. "Look away," she instructed, but she didn't give him enough time to avert his eyes. With a twist of her left arm, she straightened the right. The sound of bones returning to their normal positions almost made Canin retch up his recent meals. He turned away from the opening and back to Aurora.

"I'll be up in a moment," Spear called out lightly.

Canin picked up Aurora, who was on the verge of tears. He pressed her to his chest and struggled to remember the song Lily had sung. He couldn't recall the words, so he told her softly, "Little one, Little Wing. The moon is rising. Little one, Little Wing. The forest is quiet."

After a moment, with him repeating these words, Aurora calmed down, and her eyes closed again. Canin held her tightly, feeling the warmth of her settle into his chest. Close to crying himself, about to shed tears he did not understand, he rocked her gently. The forest was truly quiet.

☾ ⌇⌇⌇ ☼

He must have fallen asleep, because the thump of a jug on the floor startled him. Spear was pouring water into the pot and blowing on the coals to bring them back to life.

"Sleepyhead," she teased him. "You look so cute with her in your arms. I hated to wake you."

"How's your arm?" Canin asked, shifting Aurora.

Spear held up her right hand, wiggling her fingers and twisting her wrist. "Better. Should be healed by morning." She sat down beside him. Her breath was hot on his face. "I'll have to use my left tonight," she teased, brushing her hand up his leg.

"Watch the water," Canin said, moving slightly back. "Here, help me unwrap her."

Spear's frown turned into a smile as they unwound Aurora's bindings. The sudden breeze woke her, but she didn't cry; she only looked up at Spear with bright eyes.

"You should hold her to your bare skin," Canin said, standing. He went to the pot. There had been some small pieces of cloth in the basket. He dipped them in the warm water.

"You won't be silly and look away?" Spear teased as she slipped out of her shirt.

Canin sat down across from them, the dripping cloth in his hand. "It's better for the baby. She needs to feel your heartbeat and warmth." He looked her right in the eye. "She seems fine," he said, and began to gently clean Aurora's legs. Spear smiled as the water ran over her skin. She moved to touch him, but she stopped, confused by his strange mood. She settled back and watched him gently wash Aurora's legs, then her arms. He went back to the pot for more water to clean her front and back. She marveled at his intent concentration. Throughout the whole bath, Aurora smiled and cooed. Canin ended it with a light touch to her head. He dried her with another cloth, then Spear let her nurse.

"You've done that before," Spear observed, her voice a bit dreamy. She was entering her usual nursing trance.

Canin sat back, putting the wet cloths down. "I always had to help with the babies. Lily said I had a light, calming touch. Time and loss made me forget, but I'm remembering now." He rubbed his hands together. He looked at Spear, not shying away from her nakedness.

She reached out her hand. After a moment's hesitation, he took it. "You do have a light touch," she said, only slightly flirting. "I don't know if I deserve it."

"You do," he told her. "You scared me when you fell out of the tree."

"I just forgot," she said, shrugging slightly. "I've been flying all my life. Not being able to will take some getting used to." Aurora began to kick, and Spear shifted her to the other breast.

"You could've been hurt."

"I was hurt," Spear countered, holding up her hand. "But I can Heal."

Canin opened his mouth, but Spear stopped him from speaking. "It's been a long day." Aurora was done. Spear gestured blankets over to them. "Come here, and let her feel your skin, too." She laid down on her side, her damaged wings behind her. Aurora settled into the crook of her arm. Canin rubbed his eyes, then removed his shirt. He gently laid down with her. Spear put her arm over him and pulled him closer. Aurora burbled as she fell asleep.

Both Spear's warmth and Aurora's settled into Canin. Memories of lying like this with Min brought a knot to his throat. Afraid to wake the baby, Canin pushed the tears down. Sadness covered him, wrapping him in warm wisps. He didn't understand why; he was home, and Lily had forgiven him. Spear and Aurora were safe. They would be accepted into the community of the forest. So why did he feel like he was on the edge of breaking down?

"To be here, you must give her up," Spear whispered. "To be with us, you must forget Min. Leave that part of your life behind. I'm leaving my life behind, too. I burned it. I can never go back." Her hand tightened on his shoulder. "We can never go back."

Canin understood. The only way for them was forward.

Spear began to sing softly.

"Little one, Little Wing. Sleep. Sleep. Wings around, you will not fall. Wings lift you, little one. Little Wing."

Canin dropped his defenses and let the sadness overtake him. He took it all in and made it a part of him. He would never forget his Lady of the Moonlight. He asked the Mother and her Goddess to keep her safe.

Misunderstanding, Spear sang, "They will, Little Wing. Your Mothers will keep you safe, Little Wing."

Chapter 10
The Perch

Spear waved her hand over Aurora's box, and a glowing globe formed around it. She felt pride as the Weave grew. Then the light flickered, and a spark jumped from the globe to Spear's hand. She jerked back, but Canin, standing behind her as a solid wall of confidence, kept her steady. She frowned and raised her other hand. The glow stabilized. Spear smiled and dropped her hand. The light faded for Canin, but the Weave was solid.

"Now she can't hear us, but we can still hear her," Spear said with pride. "Gold would be so proud of me."

Canin didn't respond, but rubbed her shoulders in congratulations.

Spear turned and tried to kiss him, but Canin backed away.

At her frown, he told her, "I can't. Not right now."

"I just put all my energy into that Weave," Spear argued. "So we could use the Weave I created last night. I need you. Don't you want me?"

"I do, but. . . ." Canin struggled for words, but didn't move further away. "I just need some time." He gestured to the roof. "I'm gonna go up to the perch. I need to think. I need to be alone."

"You're going to leave me," Spear accused. She grabbed his arm. "You're going to slip away, taking what you wanted all along. You bastard. I should never have trusted you. Never dropped my Ward for you."

"I am not leaving you," Canin assured her. He was momentarily startled by her reaction, but he quickly realized that she wasn't really talking to him, but rather to her past again. "I have no intention of leaving you, Trillium." She tried to turn away, but he lightly touched her face. "There is nothing I would take from you. Aurora is ours, and I would never leave her without a father."

She struggled, but began to relax at his touch.

"You were left without a father," she finally said. "You have to make up for his failing."

"I do."

"Then why don't you want to sleep with me? You enjoyed last night, I know. Or am I just a dark, clumsy substitute for her?"

Canin started to deny that, but he realized it wouldn't be the truth. She was, in a way, a substitute for Min. Last night had been purely physical. He might never love her the way he loved Min. And he felt shame for that.

Spear sensed his feelings and tried to pull away.

"You aren't clumsy," Canin told her, holding her tight.

"I fell out of the tree," Spear retorted. She raised her eyes to his.

Canin smiled. "I know. You'll get better. I feel ashamed. I used you last night. Used your need to keep my sorrow at bay. I don't want to use you like that again."

"You used me?" Spear said, slightly shocked. "I thought I was using you. I haven't been with a man since." She stopped. "Since a long time ago. You have nothing to be ashamed of. I wanted you. We can keep each other's sorrow at bay. This may not be what you had with Min. But we fit," she said, sliding closer. "I never had a man fit me like you do. In all ways." She replied to his slight grin. "You felt it, too. I know you did. We were brought here to be together. I know we were."

Canin let go of her hand and kissed her, long and passionately. She wrapped her arms around him and crushed him to her chest. Eventually she broke the kiss and pulled him back to their bedroll. He acquiesced to her desire and his, letting her pull him down on top of her. He felt their bodies rise, as the Weave supported them.

"Once," he murmured into her neck. "Then I must go up."

"Twice," she bargained back at him, wrapping her legs around his waist. Her lips and hands stopped any further protests.

"What are you going to do up there?"

"Think, and speak to the Mother."

Spear was tracing the letters of the Fairy alphabet on Canin's back. He tried to follow the motions, but quickly lost any sense of what she was spelling. He just relaxed and let the sensation of her finger on his skin connect them.

She stopped tracing. "I don't understand."

He shrugged his shoulder to prompt her to continue her attentions. As she started again, he said, "When I was little, and as I grew up, when I needed to make a decision or felt out of sorts with the realm, I would climb to the highest spot I could reach. There, I would talk to the Mother. I always felt she could hear me better, the higher I was." His voice dipped, lost in memory. Spear's finger traced languid patterns on his back. "When I first got here, I just cried a lot and asked her to bring my mother back. Then, as I got older, and my mother didn't return, I asked why she left me. The Mother never answered. Then, one night I was staying with Lightfoot's father. I'd been following him around for days. I wanted to be a spinner, and Lightfoot was the best. He tolerated me. Let me watch him and his group. I never had any skill, but he let me try. I think I ruined quite a few batches of silk, but he was kind and let me discover for myself that the spinner life would never be mine. Back then, Lightfoot would always spend the new moon with his father. So I went with him to Bitter's Treetower overlooking the Green. I listened to the old man tell tales of the Fairy Realm and his lost Fairy wife. I thought it was so romantic back then. He was still waiting, committed to the idea that she would come back one day, and they would be together again. No matter that she would still be young and he was already old. Now, I feel differently. I just feel sad for him."

Canin stopped as the sorrow rolled through him. Spear stopped tracing and hugged him hard. She tried to kiss him, but he turned his face away.

"I had never been in a Treetower before," Canin continued. "I was fascinated. I asked so many questions, and Bitter showed me every corner. He was so proud of his home. Then he took me up to the perch. Sitting up there, I could see all of the forest laid out before me. I remember being awed, and humbled by its vastness. I felt the Mother standing at my shoulder. I begged Bitter and Lightfoot to let me spend the night up there. Bitter agreed right away. I think he saw something in me. Something I was too young to understand. But Lightfoot was horrified. I don't know what promises he had made to Lily and Niel, but it took some serious begging from me to get Lightfoot to even consider the idea. Finally Bitter had to use the weight of his age and authority over his son to convince him to allow it. Bitter lashed me to the perch with so much rope, I could barely move, never mind fall. Then he left me alone with the forest."

The strength of his memory was so clear, Spear could see it. She watched the sun set into the trees and the darkness settle over him. She could feel the rope around his waist, and the chill rising in the air.

"I sat there for a long time. Then I asked Her why I didn't have the skill to spin, why I couldn't make useful things for others. Why, no matter how much it was explained and demonstrated, I couldn't make the silk. And there was only silence. I got angry. I wanted to rage and yell at her, throw things." Canin sat up, laughing. "Though what I would be throwing at, I don't know. She was far away." Spear also sat up, making no effort to cover her nakedness. Canin didn't notice his or hers, he was so wrapped up in his story and his memories.

"Then I remembered how Niel dealt with anger and frustration. He would step away, if he could, or take a deep breath. Then he would attack the problem, whatever it was. He never raised his voice. Never struck us. Sometimes he would be gone for hours, but he always came back with an answer to the problem." He smiled wistfully. "Why is it we never understand what someone means to us till they're gone?"

"What did Lily say?" Spear asked with a sad smile. "We must honor their memory and trust that he knew."

Canin nodded, hearing, but still not quite understanding. He shook away the grief and returned to his story. "I took a few deep breaths and concentrated on the sounds of the forest. The owls, the skittering of the bugs, the peepers singing. Then, like water flowing downhill, the anger and frustration drained away. It was just me and the forest. The night sky and the stars. I looked to the southwest and saw the Dancer rising. I traced her belt and sash with my finger. Marveled at the bright stars there. I must have fallen asleep, because the next thing I knew, I was standing at the edge of the forest. A woman in a red dress was standing in front of me. She was asking me to help her, to protect her. She grabbed my arm. There were tears in her eyes, and terror in her voice. Behind her came the thunder of hooves. I pushed her behind me, drew a wooden dagger from my belt, and held it up as a shield against the coming riders. There was a sound like thunder, and thorns grew from the ground, striking the men from their mounts. The horses galloped away, leaving the men on the ground. Before my eyes, they were drawn into the dirt and disappeared. The woman pulled me around and hugged me, thanking me for saving her. I held up the wooden dagger before my eyes. Then I heard a voice. 'That is why,' it said. Then I woke up. I was hanging over the edge of the perch, held only by the rope around my waist. But I didn't struggle. I pulled myself up and secured myself back in the seat. And I knew what my purpose was." Canin reached behind him, and without looking, grabbed his wooden knife. He held it up, blade parallel to the floor, between them. "She told me what I was meant to do. When the sun rose, Bitter and Lightfoot came to get me, and I asked Bitter how to become a Thorn Brother."

Spear put her hand over his. "You were called. I felt the same thing when my mother and father flew off to war. At his Return, I knew the Goddess meant for me to take their place as a defender of the Fairy Realm."

Canin set his knife on the floor between them, but kept her hand in his. "My parents" — that word was coming to his lips more easily now — "were concerned, and they tried to counsel me away from this path. But the next day, Wolf was at our door. He took me into the forest and began to teach me what it meant to be a Thorn Brother." He reached out to touch Aurora's box. "Despite everything that's happened, I don't regret becoming a Brother. It brought me to this place with both of you."

"Then what do you have to think about," Spear gestured, "up there? You're not leaving us. Not leaving your reunited family. Why spend a night in a cold tree when you could be here, warm, with me?" She brushed his arm, moving up his shoulder to his face.

"I can't explain it," Canin said. "I just need to. I need to talk to Her. I need that silence to explain why I left, and why I came back."

"She knows," Spear argued. "She knows your heart. Why?"

"Maybe I need to put it into words in my mind for when I stand before Her." Canin shook his head. "You won't understand till you stand before Her yourself."

Spear let go of him and settled back. She scowled at him. "If you must go, go. But if you leave me, I will hunt you down."

"Spear," he said earnestly, trying to convince her. "I am not leaving." She shook her head. "Here," he said, standing. Canin reached up. He pulled a hidden latch in the ceiling, and another trap door opened. Spear's eyes grew in surprise. "This is the only way up. You'll be sleeping right underneath it. I couldn't slip past you if I tried."

"You could climb down the tree, or jump," Spear argued.

"The tree is pruned in a way that makes that impossible. The only way up is the ladder cut into the trunk. And what happened when you fell out the door?"

Spear scowled at him so hard, he thought he had overstepped. "I broke my arm."

"And the perch is even higher. If I jumped, I would break more. If I survived." He knelt in front of her, taking her head in his hands. "I will never leave you or Aurora. I promise you."

"Men have promised me things before," she told him. "I promised — vowed, even — that I would never leave my Sisters. But I left her." She looked at him, with a child's fear in her eyes. "What if it storms again?"

"Trillium, you are a powerful Fairy soldier." He reached over and pulled her sword closer. "No lightning would dare come near." He offered her the sword, hilt first.

"You're right," she said, brightening. She took the hilt and stuck the blade into the floor. It quivered, and the metal sang. "Another kiss before you go," she demanded, opening her arms. He went to her, and she hugged him fiercely. Her kiss was almost savage; he felt all his breath being pulled out of him by her passion. Finally, Spear broke away and playfully bit his neck.

"Come back before dawn. She'll be hungry." She pushed him away. "I will be, too."

Canin, suddenly reconsidering a night alone, fumbled back, almost tripping over the basket. Recovering, he began to gather his scattered clothes. Spear stared at him as he struggled into his pants. She smiled so invitingly, Canin started to go to her, but she floated a blanket to cover herself and closed her eyes.

"Make sure the door is closed," she muttered, falling asleep. "It'll be drafty." And then, between one breath and the next, she was out.

Canin fastened his pants and picked up his shirt. Carefully, he reached through the globe covering Aurora. His fingers tingled, but nothing else happened as he brushed her thin hair. She sighed in her sleep. Canin wanted to pick her up and hold her, but decided that would be too much for Spear tonight. He settled for another brush of her cheek and withdrew his hand. Still feeling the tingle from the Weave, Canin brushed Spear's face. She muttered in her sleep and batted at him.

"Sleep well, Beautiful," he whispered, but immediately regretted it. He had called Min that. He worried Spear would wake up and hit him, but her breathing stayed even. After a moment, he buttoned his shirt and pulled himself through the trap door. Reaching back down, he realized he had left his knife behind. He started to retrace his steps, but the knife floated over and settled into Spear's hand. She gripped it to her chest and settled more firmly into the blankets. Canin saw her eyes glitter for a moment in the moonlight, then close again.

"I'm going to regret that," he muttered, pulling the door closed.

It took some time for his eyes to adapt to the moonlight. He used it to breathe in the scent of the forest and settle his passions. He didn't want that sort of distraction tonight. The Mother never frowned on relationships of any kind between the people of the forest, as long as there was no coercion or deception, but he still felt it might be disrespectful to speak with Her so soon after leaving Spear's arms. But then he could clearly hear Spear and Min call him foolish, but cute. Canin still needed to be clear of mind, regardless.

Walking carefully over the roof, he went toward the dark form of the tree. A combination of memory and luck guided his hand to the thick rope hanging down from the perch. Smiling — despite his conflicting emotions — Canin ran his hands up the rope. It felt strong. He gave it a tug to be sure. When it didn't tumble down on top of him, he began to climb. It was tougher than he remembered; his shoulders were burning by the time he reached the top. Breathing hard, he struggled onto the narrow platform there. Something skittered away under his hand, almost making him lose his grip. Taking a deep breath as the perch swayed a bit underneath him, Canin held on. After a moment, the movement stopped, and he looked around.

He was only slightly above the canopy. To the southwest, the Dancer was beginning to rise, her head just coming up over the trees. The silvery moon was bright above, and the stars seemed shinier than before. Another shattered piece of his heart settled back into place. He breathed in the scent of the trees and the old, solid wood underneath him deeply, then settled back and began tying himself into place. His fingers remembered, though his eyes were unable to see.

Confident that he wouldn't fall, Canin looked out over the vastness of the Exile Forest. In front of him, to the south, the edge of the forest met the grasslands and rolling hills of the lake lands of the Human Realm. He couldn't see them, but Canin knew the vineyards and towns there well. Their people traded with the forest, mostly in good faith. Their wines were very popular in the King's castle and even into Elen and the Fairy Realm. To his left, the forest stretched to the horizon. Canin knew the settlements beyond the forest there, too. That's where he had gone after his wife had died. Where he had failed a woman who had needed him.

His shame was colored with the knowledge that without that failure, he would never have found his birth mother, or gone into the Fairy Realm looking for his father. Never found Bell-Oak and a certain white-haired Fairy. Canin mourned the woman he had failed, but without her, he wouldn't be here, broken-hearted from one lost Fairy love and falling fast for another.

He felt a stab of guilt when he realized he had never known her name, this Human woman who had so shaped his life. A wave of shame hit him as he remembered that he had just left her body in the woods and fled after her husband had killed her. After a moment's remorse, he felt acceptance that she had led him to the path he now walked, and hoped that her spirit would forgive him.

"Mother," he whispered, "let her understand. Let her forgive me. I was a fool."

He bowed his head and let a tear fall for her. "But why did she have to die?" Canin asked. But he knew. He should have waited. Gained more experience and skill. Then he would have been ready to defend her and save her.

The knot of events tied his tired mind. If he had waited — just a season, or even a moon — Talia's people would have been gone from Bell-Oak by the time he arrived. She would never have stared across the table at him as he told his story. A proud Fairy soldier would never have called him nephew.

"You must accept it," he told himself sternly. "She's dead, and I'm still here. Honor her memory, and ensure she did not die in vain." He looked up at the moon and made a vow. He would find her family. Find her bastard husband and finally give her the justice she deserved.

He turned in his seat and looked to the north. The forest, green and dark, rolled on to the edge of his vision, where he could just barely see the rising of the land. There, he knew, stood the Sanctuary of the Mother, and the village he had grown up in. Beyond his vision lay the steeper mountains, where most of the forest's spinners lived. Under (and on the slopes of) Starlight's Shield, the precious fairysilk was made. He envied the spinners, making such beautiful things so the people of the Exile Forest could live and serve the Mother of Exiles. Afford to rescue women and children from horrible situations. Buy food and clothes for the babies left in the small shrines along the border of the forest. Arm themselves against the irate husbands and fathers who came looking for their runaways.

He thought he saw a glint of light through the trees. Those might be the lanterns lining the walkway to the Sanctuary.

"Or it might just be someone walking home," he said with humor. He bowed his head in reverence to the presence of the Mother.

Finally, with reluctance, he turned and looked to the west. The Fairy Realm was too far away to see. All that lay before him was more forest. He couldn't even see the drop of the land that marked the beginnings of Elen. But he knew it was there. He felt the broken piece of his heart cut deep, drawing more pain and grief. A small part of him wanted to climb down the Treetower and leave the forest. Run till he found the Diamond River. Somehow get across, and make his way beyond the border. There, he fantasized, Min would be waiting. Standing at the gate of a Fairy Embassy, waving to him as he turned a corner. She would fly to him, and they would be together again. That broken piece within him begged and cajoled, crying out to be healed. It called out to the other piece of itself that she held, begging to be made whole again.

It took more strength than he had ever used to turn his eyes from the west. He focused on the Dancer, now fully risen. He found the highest star on her belt and focused his eye on the distant point of light. He imagined her: Min, Lady of the Moonlight, sitting under the dome of the Exile Queen's mountain. She was looking up into the night sky. Her eye was drawn to that same star.

Canin showed that broken, bleeding piece of himself that star. 'She's there. I'm here. And that's all we can have. Our paths have turned away from each other again. We found each other once before. Goddess and Mother grant, we might again. For now, this is all we have.' With those thoughts, he gave the broken piece a place in his mind. It would always ache and bleed, but he surrounded it with a fence of memories and fed it all he could of Min. He would always remember her, but he had obligations to others now. Two other women needed him more. Min was a powerful Fairy; she would be safe. She would live long after he was gone. She would remember him. And he would go on here.

Above him, a star streaked across the sky.

Chapter 11
Broken Dreams

Spear slept. She dreamed.

"You must eat something other than apples. Your baby needs more nourishment. You need more nourishment."

"I'm sorry, Midwife, but everything else makes me sick."

"After this long? You're due in another moon." The midwife's concerned fingers ran over her belly. "The father? He wasn't . . . different?"

Spear shook her head.

"I can't. . . . It's hard to See the child."

"The father is gone," Spear said simply. She pulled her robe back around her belly.

The Fairy midwife started to say something, but changed her mind and helped Spear sit up. "Who will be with you for the birth?"

"I have no one. My squad left for the Human Realm."

"No family? Friends, other partners?"

Spear shook her head again.

"Well, Soldier, you must have someone with you. I will speak to your sergeant and lieutenant. You must have someone to ease your pain. I'll be busy with the birth."

Spear looked stricken.

The midwife made a deduction. "They're both men."

"Former members of Air."

She sighed. "I guess I can find someone for you. I have a friend who's helped with many births. She'll come. Now, I will see you at the quarter moon. Your child should come then."

A low cry broke into Spear's dream, pushing it further along.

"I told you to take off that ring. Your hands are too swollen. Look at your finger. You might lose it." Blurred, the midwife's face looked like a troll out of the old stories.

"It's all I have of him."

"I'm sorry, but I must remove it. Don't worry; my son is a master silksteel worker. He can repair it."

"No!"

"Luna, hold her."

"Please, no. He told me never to take it off. You can't!" Spear struggled against them, but the two women held her down.

There was a crack, then the ping of two pieces of metal hitting the floor.

"See, your finger is already getting better." The voice got dimmer as the midwife stooped. "My son will be able to fix this right up." She made a face. "Spear, was there some kind of Weave on this ring? It feels. . . . Spear? Spearhead?"

Blood and pain.

"Luna! She's bleeding! I need help! She might lose the baby."

More pain.

A stronger cry brought Spear awake. She sat up, blinking in disorientation. Aurora was bawling. Spear shook off the dream and reached into the box beside her.

"Oh, you need your wrapping changed," Spear tutted. "No wonder you woke up." She began to unwind Aurora's bundling. Spear looked up. "And he's being very loud. I wonder what he's dreaming of."

In short order, she had Aurora cleaned and wrapped in a fresh cloth. Spear sat back down and let Aurora nurse. Both of them sighed in contentment. Spear looked up, sensing, through the roof, that the sun would soon be up. She smiled.

"He's deep in sleep," she told Aurora. Mischief came to her mind. "I'm not as good as Gil was, but." She reached out with her Power. She found another mind nearby. "Yes, little sister. Help me wake him."

Aurora burbled what Spear thought was a laugh.

Canin woke with a start. A grey owl was sitting on the railing, a forearm's length from him. Her huge eyes stared at him, glanced down, then returned to him.

"Hoot," she said, then spread her wings and flew away silently into the pre-dawn light.

Canin shook the sleep from his head and began to untie himself. The rope was slippery with dew and the knots seemed to fight back. He tried to remember what he had been dreaming about, but it slipped away like the owl, leaving only a feeling. He gave up, and continued picking at the knots.

Finally, the ties came loose and he stood up. Stretching to the sky, he turned to the north and bowed in the Mother's direction, then turned and waved in the direction of the rising sun. Then he carefully made his way down the rope to the roof of the Treetower. As quietly as he could, he went to the trapdoor and pushed. It was stuck. He pushed harder. Still stuck.

"Motherless," he swore under his breath. He raised his fist to knock, but reconsidered. He might wake Aurora, and that would annoy Spear. 'Maybe I can climb in the window,' he thought, then rejected the idea. 'She'd spit me like that turkey.'

Then he heard a giggle from below. Pushing on the trapdoor again, he felt it fall open. Canin stuck his head through the opening.

"Good morning," Spear said brightly from her spot on the floor, where Aurora lay in her arms. A faint Fairy Light was shining over them. They were the perfect image of a mother and child. Their eyes were bright, looking up at him mischievously. Spear's right arm was wrapped protectively around the bundled Aurora, and the other was on the hilt of her sword, still upright in the floor beside her.

Canin felt a surge of love for the two of them. And amusement, and annoyance. And pride. Whatever the day brought, he would have these powerful women by his side.

Spear grinned as he climbed down. Canin leaned over and kissed her, then kissed the crown of Aurora's head.

"Did you dream?" Spear asked. "Did She speak to you?"

"I think so," Canin replied. He moved closer, planning to kiss her again.

"Good," Spear said, as she picked up a smelly bundle from the floor and dodged his approach. "Go wash this. By the time you come back, breakfast will be ready. She's already had hers. The Maidens will be up soon, and we must be good hosts. They dream loud, too."

Canin frowned at the bundle. His morning was not going as he had hoped, or how he had expected.

"There'll be time for that later," Spear told him. "Now go." She made a shooing motion.

"Can you pass me my knife?" he asked, resigned.

Grinning, she drew it out from between her breasts. She offered it to him hilt first. "It made me feel safe," she explained as he took it.

The hilt was warm from her body. He wanted to say more, but she turned away, toward the cooking pit. Canin went to the trap door down, slid the bar aside, and opened it. He dropped the smelly bundle to the ground.

"Minuet," he whispered, and the knife lit up with a pale silver light. With its guidance, he climbed down the tree and into the dawning light.

By the time Canin came back from the spring with the refilled jar, the Thorn Maidens were awake and preparing a cold breakfast. Stonefoot greeted him and took the water jar with thanks. She grinned, her brown Elenite eyes bright, as he hung up Aurora's clean wrappings to dry.

"Spear called down that she has some porridge cooking," Stonefoot informed him. She ran her hand over her short brown hair. "She wants you to wait at the foot of the tree, and she'll lower it down." She noticed Canin's slightly confused look. "I cut it all off last night."

"I thought you looked different, but I couldn't remember. It's been a long few days for me."

"I was inspired by Spear. It just makes so much more sense. No place for a man to get a hand hold." She glanced, pointedly, back at Sadie.

Sadie looked up from washing her face. She pulled her long blond braid forward and waved it at Stonefoot. "I will not give up my hair, no matter how much you pester me. I'll just have to be that much better."

Canin laughed. Stonefoot offered him a piece of sausage. Chewing, he walked around the tree. Looking up, he saw that the trap door was open, and Spear was looking down at him.

"If you're done flirting," she called down, "here comes the pot." She slowly lowered the pot of porridge using the hook and line.

"I wasn't flirting," Canin objected, grabbing the pot by the handle before she could hit him in the head with it.

"Why not?" Spear called back, pulling up the rope. "They're pretty."

Canin looked back, hoping the Maidens hadn't heard. By their smiles, though, he knew they had.

Spear yelled again. "She's coming down!" A basket came swinging through the door. Canin heard the now-familiar sounds of Aurora laughing. He caught the basket and smiled down at the baby.

"She was right," he told her. "You are the sun in our lives." She laughed again as he set her down.

"Coming down!" Spear yelled.

Canin looked up, startled, and worried that she was falling again. But Spear climbed swiftly down, her sword at her side and both bows slung over her shoulder. She reached the ground, kissed Canin, picked up Aurora's basket, and went to join the Thorn Maidens. Canin followed, carrying the pot.

Canin sat with his back to the tree, Aurora asleep in the basket at his elbow. He was cutting and shaping branches into mock swords and daggers. In the middle of the clearing, Spear was sparring with Stonefoot and Sadie. More correctly, Spear was blocking every blow the other women offered with a branch in one hand and the other tucked casually into her belt. Spear wasn't using her Power, either, simply her skill and experience to turn every thrust and jab the Maidens tried.

Canin smiled. He saw that the inexperienced women weren't working together. They were getting in each other's way more often than not, and Spear was using that against them. Spear pivoted and ducked behind Stonefoot, forcing her to block the blow that Sadie had aimed at Spear. Canin wanted to shout instructions at the women, but he remembered Steeltrap putting him through a similar dance, so he stayed silent.

Grinning happily, Spearhead brought the match to an end by disarming both of the Maidens with a smooth twist of her weapon, then knocking them to the ground with a simple sweep and Push. The Maidens lay on the ground, breathing hard and looking at Spear with a mix of admiration and betrayal. Spear stood over them, still. The branch rested lightly on her shoulder.

Feeling pity for them, Canin stood and walked over to them.

"Don't feel bad," he said, helping first Sadie then Stonefoot to her feet. "I never got a blow in the first time I sparred with her either."

"You barely hit me now," Spear said, breaking her stillness to grin.

Both women seemed stunned at how easily Spear had beaten them. After getting their breath back, they pressed her for an explanation.

"She has more experience than you do," Canin told them. "She's been a soldier longer than you two have been alive."

"I've picked up some tricks," Spear admitted. "And you two aren't used to fighting as a team. There were times I left myself open. If one of you had kept up the pressure on my left, the other could have slipped through on the right. But you kept getting in each other's way."

"It just takes time and experience," Canin told them, trying to take the sting from Spear's words. "I'm sure you'll be able to hit her after a few moons of practice."

Sadie glared at Canin, but Stonefoot smiled.

"Let's go again, ladies," Spear said, swinging her branch down off her shoulder to a ready position.

"How about we work with the bow for a while instead," Canin suggested, seeing the resignation on the women's faces.

Sadie agreed right away. "Yes."

"I'd like to see more of your Patterns," Stonefoot said. "I can see the similarities between yours and ours." After breakfast, the three of them had worked through the forest's four elemental patterns, while Spear watched. She was fascinated by the similarities and studied them intently.

Canin thought Spear was going to snap at them, but she put down her branch and gestured for Stonefoot to stand in front of her.

"You're quick," Spear noted. "Use your speed. First, just watch. This is the First Pattern." She began to move through the motions, slowly, so they could be followed.

"That's why they call me Stonefoot."

Spear stopped. She looked at the Maiden with confusion. "I am called Spearhead because I was always the Fairy on point. Why wouldn't they call you Swiftfoot?"

Canin tried to explain. "It's just a joke." Spear looked at him blankly.

"Wolf has an odd sense of humor," Stonefoot told her. Spear still looked baffled.

"It's a human tradition," Canin finally told her.

Spear nodded, not really understanding, but accepting that answer.

"Watch me," Spear told Stonefoot. "I will expect you to do this one perfectly before moving on to the Second."

Stonefoot looked like she had stuck her hand into a rabbit's hole and been bitten by a fox. Sighing, she followed each motion attentively.

Canin motioned Sadie away from Spear. "Do you have a bow?" he asked.

"I do," she replied. "We should go around the side, to ensure no wild shots hit them."

Canin agreed. He picked up his longbow and Aurora's basket.

"Even though she would just dodge them," Sadie said over her shoulder.

Canin couldn't disagree.

Chapter 12
Where Are the Apples?

"So, were you born here?" Canin asked after a few shots. Sadie was very good and was teaching him a great deal. Her bow had also been made by Tymora and showed long use.

"No," she said, lining up a shot at the target they had cut into the tree across the clearing. She released, hitting just shy of center, then lowered her bow. "My mother was a 'venal backworker,' as the Father's priests called her," she said with bitterness. "But they surely went behind the Father's back to see her. Always demanded services for free, too, or they would bring her before the Stones." She pushed her emotions down. "She was killed by one of them, and I had to run. I walked for two days from the vineyard lakes." She smiled. "In the wrong direction, before Maggie and a group of Maidens found me. Another of my mother's visitors had noticed I was missing and sent her a message." She lined up another shot. "He might have been my father." She fired, splitting her first arrow in two. "But it was probably the man who killed her." Her third shot split the second one. "It's his face I see when I shoot." She lowered her bow.

Canin sighed with understanding. "Have you seen him since?"

Sadie shook her head. "Maggie won't let me go anywhere near the Lakelands."

"I understand," Canin said. "One day," he said with promise in his eyes, "you can go with me to the east, and I will go with you to the south. We both have unfinished business."

Sadie looked at him with new eyes. "Maggie says we mustn't let our emotions cloud our judgment. That it just leads to more suffering."

"It does," Canin agreed. "We must never go out alone. But we won't be alone. She says there's a time and a place for everyone. Who's to say we won't be there when their time comes?"

Sadie held out her hand. "I will be by your side, Sutab."

"And I will be at your side, Setab." Canin shook her hand, then showed her the Fairy warriors' grip. She grinned at sharing this secret thing with him and stepped closer. Canin could smell her hair and feel the warmth coming off her.

"Then you will need to be better," she told him. "Pick up your bow, Canin. Your posture is good, but your breathing and release are off."

"Yes, ma'am," Canin replied, picking up the bow.

They had gone through most of a quiver when Aurora began to fuss. The clacking of wood, which had been a constant background noise, suddenly stopped. Sadie, who was returning from the target tree with a handful of arrows, heard both things and looked at Canin.

He had heard, too, and was reaching into the basket as Spear's voice called out. "She needs to be fed! Bring her here."

"Coming," Canin called back.

Sadie took his bow so he could carry Aurora more comfortably. "She has you on a short leash," Sadie commented.

"She does," Canin replied easily, settling Aurora over his shoulder.

Spear was already sitting, and took the baby with only a slightly demanding gesture. Aurora eagerly began to nurse. Sadie and Stonefoot tried — unsuccessfully — to hide their amusement.

Canin glared halfheartedly at them. "It's near midday. What do we have for a meal?"

"I need to bathe first," Stonefoot said. "Spear's worked me hard. There's a pool not too far. A quick dip to clean off the sweat should do it."

"That's a great idea," Sadie agreed.

"Go with them," Spear suggested, looking up at Canin. "Protect your forest sisters."

Canin turned slightly red and looked at the two Maidens.

"I don't mind," Sadie said, smiling and addressing Spear.

"I do," Stonefoot said emphatically. "No offense, Canin, but. . . ." She stopped, her whole head having gone crimson.

"This is not the Fairy Realm," Canin reminded Spear. "We're more. . . ." He fought for words, trying not to offend any of them. "Modest," he settled on.

Spear shrugged, settling back into her nursing trance. Her eyes focused on a faraway point, and her breathing slowed.

"I'll get some food together while you're gone," Canin told the Maidens. He went to the basket they had brought.

Stonefoot took Sadie's arm and led her away, but Sadie looked back and managed to catch Canin's eye. She smiled. Canin smiled back, but looked swiftly away. There was a bit more sway in Sadie's walk as the Maidens disappeared into the woods.

He heard a soft giggle from behind him.

"Don't say it," Canin warned, not looking back. Spear laughed a bit louder.

When they returned, Canin had a small meal laid out.

"No apples," Spear complained.

"They aren't in season," Sadie told her.

"When will they be in season?" Spear whined. She tore open a roll and stuffed ham into it. "Well?" she demanded around a full mouth.

Canin couldn't think of a reply and looked to Stonefoot and Sadie for help. Sadie only shrugged.

"There are orchards in the south," Stonefoot finally said. "But there's also that old man who lives up on the slopes of Starlight's Shield. He has a few trees. He starts coming down after the longest night. They're the strangest apples I've ever seen. Well prized by the Children."

"Manzanita," Canin said with shock. "He's still alive? He seemed ancient when I was a child. Always complaining he couldn't make enough silver to go home."

"Always talking about his home in the far south. Where some river emptied into the sea," Stonefoot agreed. "He's still alive, and still just as cranky. He's too old to make the journey now. He'll die on that mountain."

That made Canin unexpectedly sad.

"And then what will happen to his cider?" Sadie asked wistfully.

"We must meet this. . . ." Spear looked at Canin expectantly, still chewing.

"Manzanita," Canin supplied. "It means 'little apple' in the southern dialect."

"Manzanita," Spear repeated, the name feeling odd in her mouth.

"Why do you love apples so?" Sadie asked, but Spear had turned away. She was cutting more ham for the other half of her bread.

"I don't . . .," Canin started, but an image flashed into his mind. "Her grandparents had an orchard."

"I would climb the trees, stuff myself, and then fall out," Spear told them. "Mother would yell." She frowned. "She yelled at me right before she and father left." She gripped her food, crushing the bread. Canin laid a light hand on her arm. Aurora made a burbling sound from her basket.

"You should go to the pool," Stonefoot suggested, hoping to break the sudden tension. "It was very refreshing. We can watch her."

"No!" Spear snapped, almost yelling.

"Trillium," Canin whispered, taking the ruined bread from her hand. "I don't need to bathe. I'll stay here," Canin reassured her.

Spear blinked, and wiped the grease from her hand. "No," Spear said, her voice even. "You need to. Your hair smells. We'll take her. She needs to be bathed again." She made a face.

Fingering the end of his braid, Canin caught his smell and agreed. He stood and offered his hand to Spear. She took it and got to her feet. Her sword and belt leapt from the ground into her hand. She swung them over her shoulder, ignoring the shocked looks of the other two women.

Canin asked, "Where's the pool?"

"Just follow the stream from the spring," Sadie directed, pulling her gaze from Spear. "It's not far."

"Thank you," Canin said, picking up Aurora's basket. Spear took the other side.

"Practice your Patterns," Spear ordered them. "I expect you to be perfect when I return." She set off, pulling Canin with her. He flashed an apologetic smile at the Maidens. Sadie quickly covered her frown, while Stonefoot just sighed.

Chapter 13
The Bathing Pool

It was a short walk to the spring. A narrow stream flowed to the west and Canin and Spear followed it, moving easily through the underbrush. The thorn-covered trees loomed over them, forming a tunnel of green and brown. Canin breathed in the scent of the water. He pushed away his earlier tension and let his feet follow the stream.

"It's easier to move through the forest now," Spear remarked, glancing up at the canopy.

"The woods have accepted us," Canin told her.

Spear looked up at the trees, their thorns pointing down at her, but did not comment further. Then her mouth turned up in a sudden smile. "She seems to like you."

Canin wanted to deny noticing Sadie's interest, but the dancing joy in Spear's eyes pushed away that response. So he just shrugged.

"I wouldn't mind," Spear told him. "She seems like a good woman. Solid fighter. But you'll have to be careful. She's Human, and cannot ward her womb. Or do those of the forest have different ways? Does this Mother step in to prevent unwanted children?"

"There are certain herbs," he began to explain, then stopped at her grin. "I am your husband," Canin stated. "We agreed to that, and we have acted that way to them. Anything else would be awkward."

"Are the women here not allowed to choose their own partners? Are they bound to one man? Does you calling me your wife prohibit you from seeking out others for pleasure if the other is willing? Does it prohibit me?" She seemed shocked and set down the basket to look at Canin. "I thought everyone was free here to live their own lives. With or without a partner."

Canin shook his head. "We're free to be with whomever we want. We're just not as open about it as Fairies."

"You said that older man. . . ."

"Wolf," Canin supplied.

"That Wolf had women all over the forest, and in other places as well. Or did I mishear?"

"No, you didn't. He visits many women. I remember them being very accepting of his wandering ways."

"Then are only men allowed to be 'free,' as you say?" Spear jabbed a finger into his chest. "If so, then you're no better than the Humans they run from. Binding women to one man and never allowing them to leave."

"You misunderstand," Canin said, desperate to explain. "I don't mean the rest of the forest. For them, any relationship is fine, as long as the two agree. I was just saying I couldn't be with another. Certainly not so soon after coming here."

"So, after a few moons, you will go sleep with Sadie then."

Her abrupt change in tone, from what Canin had felt was a bit flirty and playful, to angry and accusatory, made Canin step back. Spear clenched her hands. She looked close to either tears or violence. With her, one could never tell.

"No," Canin said calmly. "I don't want to be with her. I want to be with you. I came here with you, and I will stay with you. No one else will tempt me away."

"Maybe you should be with her," Spear said. She looked down at the water and saw a distorted reflection of herself. "Who knows where your path will take you. I can't even see my own."

"My path is with you," Canin assured her. He put his hand gently on her arm. When she didn't pull away, he stepped closer. "I'm falling in love with you. I don't want anyone else."

"You might, one day," Spear said, her voice returning to normal. "Don't hurt her with a rejection." She looked into his eyes and smiled sadly. Then, as a cloud moved over the sun, she bantered back, "She's cute. I wonder if she'd care to share you with me?" She picked up Aurora's basket and continued along the stream bank.

Canin, left — again! — off balance, just watched her go.

'Is she teasing me, or is her mind fractured?' Canin wondered. He watched her hips sway — in an exaggerated fashion, in imitation of Sadie — as she walked. 'And how can I tell?'

"You'll have to be quicker on your feet," she called back. "Now, hurry. Aurora's going to start crying. And if she does, I won't be in the mood anymore."

Canin followed, feet swift on the springy grass.

As they walked, the bank on the right kept rising, but the left side was lower and easier to follow. Spear began to hum a tune unknown to Canin. The stream bent, then widened beside a clearing under a clump of short trees with wide canopies. Several large rocks had been moved to block the water at the far end, forming a shallow pool. The sound of the water flowing over the barrier rocks filled Canin's ears and soothed his jangled nerves. Spear also seemed calmer. She put down Aurora's basket and took in the clearing and the pool. Sunlight fell in small patches on the ground through the gently moving leaves.

She spun, raising her hands. "Goddess's wonder. She's brought us to a beautiful place." She picked up Aurora and spun her, too. "Look, Aurora. What beauty she shows us."

Aurora responded by throwing up. Spear dodged. "Oh, poor child. Canin, help me unwrap her. There, there. We'll get you clean."

Canin took the soiled wrappings stoically, as all fathers have, and went to the end of the pool, at the little waterfall, to clean them. The water was cold, but invigorating. Behind him, he could hear Aurora fuss, but not cry, as Spear made motherly sounds at her. Canin turned to see Spear taking small handfuls of water and dripping them over Aurora's legs. She kicked a little at the cold.

Spear held her up from under her arms and held her over the water.

"Wait," Canin called. "It's too cold for her."

Spear stopped. Canin splashed back to them. He pulled a cloth from his pocket and dipped it in the water. "Here, warm this."

Spear frowned, still holding Aurora with her feet dangling just above the surface of the water.

"With your Power," Canin clarified.

"Oh," Spear said, and reached for the wet cloth. Canin took Aurora from her and returned to the bank, sitting down on the soft grass. Spear looked at the cloth in her hands, and steam began to rise from it.

"That's enough," Canin said, reaching for the cloth. Spear handed it over and sat down, frowning.

"I was going to put her in the water. Fool. Too cold."

"It's all right," Canin soothed her. He gently wiped Aurora's legs and body. She stopped fussing and accepted the warm water. "Hand me the big cloth from the basket. There should be a softer one to dry her, too."

Spear continued to stare into the water.

"Spear," Canin said more loudly. "She needs to be wrapped up again."

His voice pulled Spear away from her thoughts. She rummaged in the basket and came back with the requested items. "I'm sorry. I don't know what I was thinking. Fool. Fool."

"It's all right, Trillium. Every new mother must learn. Lily used to tell me it was good I came along later, because she'd already gotten all her mistakes out on others."

Spear tried to smile, but let Canin dry Aurora and wrap her. Afterwards, she began pulling absently at the grass.

"She's hungry," Canin remarked after the baby was wrapped up snuggly again. Spear didn't respond.

Canin bent Aurora's face close to Spear's ear and whispered, "Mama, hungry," in a high-pitched voice. He used his other hand to make Aurora's legs kick Spear's arm. "Mama. Milk."

Spear tried not to smile as Canin kept tapping her with Aurora's leg and calling for milk. She finally broke and turned. She grinned and began to unlace her shirt. "Papa just wants to see my breasts."

Canin handed Aurora over. "Yes, I do," he admitted, and settled back in the grass to watch.

Spear became suddenly modest. She covered herself and Aurora with her shirt. "This is not for you to gawk at," she chided Canin. "I am feeding our daughter." She waved with her other hand. "Get in the water. When she's done, I'll help you wash your hair." When he didn't move, she ordered him to. "Get moving."

Canin, caught between frustration and amusement, sighed and began to take off his clothes. When he was naked, he turned to see her appraising eyes on his backside.

"I can gawk," she told him. He leaned in to kiss her, but she waved him away. "You stink. Water." She pointed. "Now."

"Yes, ma'am," Canin replied, settling for kissing the top of her head. He waded into the waist-deep water and began to shiver.

"It's cold," he complained.

"What kind of training do you Thorn Brothers have that you can't take a little cold water?" Something floated out of the basket and shot toward him. He caught it before it hit his chest. It was a rough bar of soap. Lily's, he knew by the smell of roses. "Clean up, and I'll be in to keep you warm in a few. She's hungry."

"Promise?" Canin asked back, but she had closed her eyes and dropped into her nursing trance. Canin shook his head in amusement and began to wash.

"You need to take this out more often," Spear complained as she struggled to unplait his braid. He winced as she pulled. "Did you use Flora's porridge to hold it together?"

They were sitting in the pool, close to the bank. The water was up to the middle of their chests and felt a little warmer now. Or maybe it was because Spear was pressed against his back with her legs wrapped around his waist. Aurora was asleep in her basket, under a dapple of sunlight.

"Ow," Canin complained as Spear tugged a whole section of his hair in a direction it was not meant to go.

"Hush," she said, slapping him lightly on the shoulder. "I've almost got it all free." More tugging. Canin swallowed his complaints. "There," she said with satisfaction. She began to comb through his hair with her fingers. Sighing, he relaxed under her light touch. She massaged his scalp, drawing more sounds of contentment. Canin was floating happily under her hands when she suddenly pulled back and tipped him back into the water, then just as quickly lifted him out.

Spluttering and rubbing at his eyes, he tried to twist out of her hands, but she held him firmly in place.

"Calm down," she told him. "I just needed to get it wet."

"I hate being underwater," Canin complained as he tried to rise.

"Sit down," Spear commanded, pushing his shoulders down. "It's just water. Stop complaining."

Canin settled back, still grumbling and rubbing at his eyes. "I just hate my head being underwater."

Spear wrapped her legs back around him. "Did your mother try to drown you?" she whispered into his ear, teasing.

This time, Canin wrenched himself out of her grip and glared back at her. His fury rose, and he wanted to push her even further away, but she reacted to his anger and brought her hands up in defense. Seeing the dark look in her eyes snapped Canin to his senses. Raising open hands, he slid back away from her.

"I'm sorry," Canin said. "I just hate having my head under water."

Spear relaxed as well. "I should have warned you. I guess I found something broken in you."

Canin could only nod as his hands continued to clench and unclench. Suddenly, he was hit by a surprising wave of affection from Spear. Closing his eyes and taking a deep breath, Canin pushed the terror of feeling the water over his head and the deep memories associated with this deep-seated fear away. After a few moments, he turned and slid back to her.

She wrapped her legs around him again, whispering, "I'm sorry," into his ear. Her hand moved down his chest, caressing. "Would you like me to. . . ." She left the rest unsaid, as her hand slipped lower.

"No," Canin said, catching her hand and pulling it back to rest on his heart. To her surprised huff, he added, "Not yet." He felt her smile and playfully bite his ear.

Spear moved back slightly, then summoned the soap and began to wash his hair.

"This will take several rinses," she warned him as her hands moved through his locks. "I'll have to tip you back."

"I know. Just don't push me under."

"I won't." She made more noises. "This really is awful. How did Min put up with it?"

"We had other things on our minds," Canin replied lightly, relaxing again under Spear's capable hands.

"She must have really loved you," Spear said with equal lightness, before realizing what she had said. She waited for Canin's emotions to spike, but he remained calm.

"She did," Canin muttered dreamily. Spear resumed her work.

It took several cycles of washing and rinsing before Spear was satisfied with the cleanliness of his hair. "I wish I had a comb," she muttered as she smoothed his hair and ran her fingers through it. She divided it into three parts and began to braid.

Canin laughed. "I never thought I'd hear that from a leather-wing."

"We have hair," Spear told him. "Soldiers just don't grow it."

Surprised, Canin tried to turn, but Spear kept his head forward. "I thought. . . ." He floundered.

"We can control our bodies," Spear reminded him, as she gave his hair a tug. "I could grow hair if I wanted to." She dropped the half-finished braid and turned him around. "How do you think I would look with hair? I don't know what color it would be. What do you think?"

"I don't know. I've gotten used to you as you are." He ran a light hand over her bald head. A drip of water ran down her nose. "But I could get used to you with hair, too. It doesn't matter to me." He stopped to consider. "It might offend Stonefoot, though. She just cut hers off to be more like you."

Spear captured his hand and pressed it to her lips. "I had to wash my grandmother's hair. She lost her right arm, and most of her left. She refused to grow them back. 'Cursed Iridescent war took 'em, and those highborn Fairies offered me nothing but a spit of silver in return,'" Spear imitated in a gravelly voice. "She was a stubborn old soldier. I miss her." She kissed his hand again. Canin leaned in for a real kiss, but she spun him back around instead.

"Hold still," she griped, tugging at his hair. "You're so sloppy with your braid. It always bothered me. I want it neat."

Canin leaned back into her with contentment as she undid the half-finished braid and started again.

Spear poked him in the shoulder. "You had a wife. Didn't she show you how to do this properly?'

"No. I figured it out on my own. Brenna didn't care. She just wanted it out of her face."

"I can understand that," Spear said and gave him a squeeze with her legs. Canin replied by tickling her knees. She gave him another squeeze.

"There," Spear said with a few more tugs. "All done." She turned him around again and kissed him. "Much better," she commented after breaking the kiss. Canin tried to kiss her again, but she turned.

"I need you to wash my back and wings," she told him, offering the soap. "Just. . . ." She stopped, her voice catching. "Be careful of the edges. They still ache."

Canin just stared. He had avoided looking at them all this time, as if that would keep their stark destruction from becoming real. But now, here they were before him, with all their terrible damage. They should have spread out to beyond where she could stretch her arms. Instead, they ended at her shoulders. The ragged edges were still red and scabbed in places. Canin tried to reach out, but couldn't bring himself to touch them. He bowed his head in shame.

"Canin," Spear said sharply, "I don't blame you. It happened. I lost my wings. There's nothing I can do about it. I don't have the Healing power to regrow them by myself. It would take a full circle of eighteen. We don't have that, so I must live with them as they are." Her head and her voice dropped. "It was my sacrifice to get her back." Her head came back up. "I would do it again. I would give all of my wings." She shook them at him. "Now stop hesitating. The scabs itch. Wash them off," she demanded. "And stop feeling sorry for me. I'm a powerful Fairy. This is nothing."

'But it is,' Canin thought, 'and I will never forgive myself for it. No matter that it wasn't my fault. I should have been more careful.'

"The longer you take," Spear said, annoyed, "the longer it will be before we can see if that grass is as soft as I think it is." She wiggled her hips back at him. "I promised you later."

Canin leaned in and kissed the back of her neck. "Yes, you did," he whispered. He pulled back and began to wash her wings. "You did promise."

Spear sighed, pushing the disturbing feeling of her phantom wings to a corner of her mind. "You keep me together," she whispered. "Your passion is the cord, keeping my darkness inside. It binds me with your love. Keeps me together. So I can be a mother to her. Be the thing I never was, and make up for all that I did back then."

Canin couldn't hear her, but he felt her desperate need and the tragedy of her guilt. He pushed his own guilt away and focused on what she needed. He washed her wings and eased her pain.

☾ ∿ ☼

"Bind me, hold me," she whispered over and over. Her arms and legs crushed him to her, limiting his movement, but she didn't care. She needed his touch, his warmth, on as much of her skin as possible.

"Bind me, hold me. Ow, wait." Spear pushed him up. "Wait, still. Be still."

It took a moment for her words to penetrate his passion-clouded mind, but then her nails dug into his shoulders. "Stop," she finally said, her voice rising.

His eyes finally focused on her face. "I'm sorry," he said. "Too hard?"

"This grass is not as soft as I thought." She pushed up to a sitting position, so her wings were off the ground. He tried to get off her, but she tightened her grip, not letting him go.

"Just a moment," she breathed, pushing the pain in her wings away. "There must be rocks under us. You're trying to dig them up through me." She breathed into his neck.

Canin tried to apologize again, but she stopped him with a kiss. "Just hold me for a moment."

Canin rested his chin on her shoulder and focused on his breathing. The sounds of the forest and the water were muted. His world had contracted to just her. Her warmth surrounding him, her breath hot on his shoulder. The beat of her heart against his chest.

"Should we be doing this, right beside the baby?" Canin suddenly asked, pulling back enough to look Spear in the eye.

"Why not?" Spear replied. "She's asleep." She glanced over at the basket, and Aurora's eyes were closed. Her little chest rose and fell in a slow, steady rhythm.

"But can't she sense us?" Canin asked.

Spear dismissed his worry. "She's just a baby. Fairy children can't use their Power till they're much older. And she isn't even fully Fairy." Spear shrugged. "And what if she could? We're sharing a wonderful thing. Pleasure with each other. Joy. What could be better to expose her to?"

Canin glanced over at Aurora. "I don't know. She seems to know more than other babies her age. And she isn't part Fairy."

"Don't say that!" Spear said fiercely, grabbing his head. "Do not even think that she isn't ours. She is. She has returned to me. She is our daughter." The intensity of her gaze burned into him. Her skin, pressed against him, seemed to grow even hotter.

"Now, where were we?" she said, and with a motion he could neither follow nor understand, he was suddenly on his back, with Spear on top of him. She sat up, and planted her hands on his chest, then sighed and shook herself. "That's better. I guess I'll have to get used to it." She started to move again, and he could only think of her.

Spear leaned back languidly, supported by her hands, still straddling him. She stared up at the mid-day light coming through the leaves. Canin took this moment to really look at her. Before, it had always been dark. Their passion had been overriding, and there had been no time for simply taking in all that she was. Her body was covered in scars. Some were light and short, others long and dark. The only unmarked skin was her breasts and the front of her chest. All the rest was crisscrossed with marks of violence.

"And my face," Spear muttered, still looking at the sky. "That is my only vanity." She returned her gaze to his. "She was unmarked because she chose to completely Heal any injury. Soldiers don't." She looked up again. "Well, most of us don't. Shield told me her classmate was a Medic in Air. Their captain always made sure his wounds were completely Healed. No scars. Except for his arms. Vain bastard."

"That's a little disturbing," Canin said with a small frown. He had been comparing Spear's body to Min's. She had been unmarked.

"She had one scar. Everyone does." Spear grinned down at him. "You must not have looked hard enough."

"Why can you read me now?" Canin asked, slightly annoyed. "In the tower, you couldn't. Now it seems easy for you."

Spear shrugged. "We had just met then. Who knows. Our closeness might be the reason," Spear teased, moving slowly back and forth. "Or I might have woken something in you."

"You definitely woke something," Canin growled, as he sat up and met her halfway for a kiss. She moaned into his urgency. Then she pushed him down.

"Someone is coming," she said, turning her head in the direction they had come from. Her sword leapt from its sheath and into her left hand. She held it ready, but didn't move to get off him or cover herself. Canin, feeling exposed, could only look in the direction Spear was staring. Aurora's basket was between them and whoever was coming through the woods.

"Aurora," Canin said urgently. Spear's right hand gestured, and the basket slid across the grass so it was behind them. His wooden knife settled into his hand.

He grunted in thanks and stared into the greenery, gripping the hilt.

After a tense moment, Stonefoot emerged from the underbrush. She stopped, startled by the naked Fairy, sword in hand, straddling Canin. Canin could see that she was caught between wanting to turn away in embarrassment and her duty to deliver whatever message had brought her here. He felt sorry for her.

"Well?" Spear asked, when Stonefoot didn't speak and simply stared at them.

Stonefoot finally decided it was pointless to turn away. "Heron just arrived. Wolf and Maggie will be here soon. They have news." She continued to stare, her face a deep pink.

Canin also began to feel uncomfortable, but he couldn't shift out from under Spear without showing more than he was willing to.

"Thank you," Spear said calmly, lowering her sword. She stared back at Stonefoot. "Would you like to join us?" Spear asked, only half joking.

"You were gone a while," Stonefoot stuttered. "We were worried."

"We've been busy," Spearhead told her. "His hair was very dirty. Now," she told the Maiden, putting her hands back on Canin's chest. "Unless you want to watch." She turned back to Canin.

Stonefoot turned and ran back into the woods.

"That was a little cruel," Canin said. "They'll be bringing important news." He moved to get up, but Spear pushed him back down.

"They'll wait. You have a task to finish."

Chapter 14
Together We Stand Firm

When Canin and Spear emerged from the woods, Heron, Stone-foot, and Sadie were sitting around a fire, roasting another turkey. The scent made Canin's stomach rumble after his exertions. Heron smiled openly and waved to the couple, but Stonefoot didn't look up from turning the spit. Sadie smiled slightly, but then got up and picked up one of the clay jugs.

"I'll fetch more water," she said, brushing past Canin and Spear without another word.

"Told you," Spear said in an aside to Canin. She didn't wait for his response, but took the basket — where Aurora was beginning to fret — and sat with her back against the tree. She undid her shirt, preparing to nurse.

Canin went up to Heron, holding out his hand. "Greetings, Sister." Heron took his arm in an awkward warrior's grip. Canin smiled and showed her the proper form.

Stonefoot grunted.

Canin sat on the ground across from her. "Smells good," he commented.

She only shrugged.

Canin knew he needed to address what had happened earlier. "Fairies are different when it comes to such things."

"I saw," Stonefoot replied. She would not meet his eyes.

"She wasn't embarrassed. I was, slightly. I understand how you feel, but what's done is done. There's no reason to dwell on it. We're all family here. Has privacy become more common now? Our house was always full."

"No," Heron replied with a smile. "Lily's house is still full. I always had to go off into the woods with my sweethearts." She looked directly at Canin. "I almost walked in on Lily and Niel once when I was young. They didn't fully close the bar on their door."

Now Canin blushed, and lowered his eyes to push the image out of his mind.

Stonefoot was shaking her head emphatically. "It wasn't like that in my house. My mother said those things were only to be done behind a locked and barred door and in the dark." Canin and Heron laughed awkwardly at her discomfort.

"Now I understand," Heron said, and reached out to touch Stonefoot's arm. She pulled back, but made it look like she was reaching for the spit. Canin noticed this and looked at Heron, a question in his eyes. Heron only smiled with one side of her mouth.

"I meant what I said earlier," Spear said, breaking into the conversation. "If you want. . . ." She left the thought unfinished, looking, slightly unfocused, at Stonefoot, with Canin sitting beside her.

Stonefoot almost swallowed her tongue coughing to cover how uncomfortable this was all making her. She stood up. "I'll go and see how far away Maggie and Wolf are," she offered, and without waiting for a reply, ran out of the clearing.

Canin turned to Spear in reproach, but her head was now bent, and she was gazing into Aurora's eyes. Canin sighed and took over turning the spit.

Heron prodded the coals and added more wood to the fire. Canin, despite his curiosity, remained silent. She would speak when she was ready.

"We trained together," Heron finally said. "I thought there was something between us. But." She shrugged. "You would think a woman who hates men like her mother does would welcome a woman as her daughter's partner. But she took in too much of the Father's teachings when she was young."

"Then why come here?" Canin asked.

"I don't know," Heron admitted. "Stonefoot won't talk about it. And her mother won't even let me in the door."

"She must follow her own path," Canin told the Maiden with sympathy. "You never know where yours will lead. They may yet bend together for a time."

"Or they may diverge and never cross again," Spear cut in. She stood up and handed Aurora to Canin. "She needs to be burped," she informed him. "I must go up into the tree. I'll be back."

Canin held Aurora awkwardly as Spear disappeared around the base of the tree. Heron was caught between reacting to Spear's cutting remark and the amusing sight of Canin fumbling with the baby. "Here. I can hold her for a moment," she offered.

"No," Canin said, adjusting Aurora on his chest so her head was on his shoulder. "I think I have it." He lightly patted Aurora's back until she made a liquid burping sound and he felt a warm wetness go down his back. Canin closed his eyes in resignation.

Heron laughed. "Here." She reached out. "Let me help. Alexander was always throwing up. I don't know how many shirts he ruined."

Canin passed the now-grinning baby over. He took the sleeve of his shirt and wiped Aurora's mouth. She looked up at the grinning Heron, smiled slightly, yawned, and dropped off to sleep. Heron looked down at the dozing infant, and a smile of wonder crossed her face.

"Just like her mother," Canin said, pulling off his wet shirt. "Falling asleep in a breath."

"She's a wonder," Heron said, brushing the baby's hair with a tentative finger. She looked at Canin. "I have held many babies, but she feels. . . ." She stopped, unable to find words for the emotions that were filling her. She wanted to cry, and laugh with joy. The baby in her arms felt like the calm spot in a storm. Everything else might be in chaos, but holding Aurora, all was calm and peaceful. She wanted to hold on to that singular feeling. Heron felt something tug at the part of her that wasn't bound to the ground, a part of her that wanted to fly. She sniffed back hot tears from a long-forgotten well.

"I feel the same," Canin admitted, laying his wet shirt on the ground. Heron, trying to master her flood of emotions, could only point her chin at the water jug.

Canin dipped out some water and tried to rub out the stain. He grimaced at the smell. Behind him, he heard a gasp and the sound of pottery hitting the ground. Turning, he saw Spear standing behind Heron. Aurora was still in her arms, and her head was bent close to the baby's. The wine jug from the Treetower's provisions lay broken at Spear's feet. The dark red wine was splashed on her boots. Over her shoulder, she had the long knives from the cupboard slung on their belts. Her left hand went to the hilt of her sword.

"What are you doing?" she asked, surprised, and with growing rage.

Canin jumped to his feet, putting himself between Heron and Spear. "It's my fault," he pleaded, trying to assuage her anger. "She spit up on me. Heron was just holding her while I got cleaned up."

Spear raised her right hand, pointing her palm toward Canin. He felt a pressure on his chest. Heron looked up, holding Aurora out to Spear. Her eyes were filled with unshed tears, glimmering in the setting sun.

"What am I seeing?" she asked Spear. "I see a woman, tall, with golden hair, before a river. She's calling for help. Colors swirl all around her. Red, black, green, blue, all a whirlpool. Thorns, long and purple, surround her. She needs my help."

Spear dropped to her knees, splashing the spilled wine. She took Aurora's bundled form in one arm and Heron's outstretched hand with the other.

"The colors fade," Heron whispered. "She fades." Canin stumbled to them and laid his hand next to Spear's. "It's gone," Heron said, her heart breaking.

"I only saw a flash of color," Canin said, looking at Spear.

Spear shook her head, and climbed to her feet. "I saw nothing. Don't touch my baby." She went back to the tree and sat down. Spear looked intently at Aurora's sleeping face. "I don't see anything." She pulled the belted knives from her shoulder and threw them at Canin. "I brought these for you. You forgot them."

Canin caught them. He was torn between his compassion for Heron, who was in some kind of emotional distress, and the need to placate Spear. Spear solved his dilemma by holding up her hand, warning Canin away. Spear closed her eyes and gripped Aurora to her breast. She began to mutter, so low that Canin couldn't hear. His heart ached with fear and concern for her.

Heron was still on the ground. She looked up at the sky, mouthing words Canin couldn't make out.

"Are you okay?" Canin asked. He started picking up the shards of the broken jug. It must have hit a rock, because the bottom was completely shattered. The wine was soaking into the ground. He hoped it wouldn't kill the grass.

Heron took a moment to process his words. Turning to face him, her eyes grew, and she grabbed at the spit. They had neglected the turkey, and it was burning on one side. She turned it and held the opposite side closer to the fire.

"I don't know. It's fading now," Heron admitted. "It was like a bolt of lightning struck me, and I was filled with all these feelings. I felt such sorrow and hope at the same time. Then I saw the woman, and she was crying for help. The colors. They blinded me." She stopped, unable to describe it more clearly.

"Don't mention lightning around Spear," Canin warned her. He glanced at Spear, but she was still muttering to Aurora. He began to make out a few words. "Little one, Little Wing," came through, but not much else. Canin found a place to sit that wasn't stained by the wine. He absently placed the shards of the jug in what remained of the vessel. He would have to take it back to whoever had made it and see if it could be repaired, or made into something new.

"Rebuild what is broken," Canin began.

"Make it stronger," Heron added.

"Together we will stand firm," they said together.

"Against all who would break us." They finished the mantra, and were joined by four more voices from across the clearing.

Canin and Heron looked up and saw Wolf and Maggie standing at the edge of the woods. Sadie and Stonefoot had joined them. Stonefoot stood at Maggie's elbow, and Sadie was beside Wolf.

"You remember," Wolf praised, striding across the grass. His beard split in a wide grin. "What is that smell?"

"I dropped the wine jug," Canin admitted. He met Wolf and was pulled into a quick embrace. Wolf was carrying a large pack, with a sword strapped to the side. He set his burden down by the fire. Maggie was carrying a similar one and set it down beside his.

Heron stood and joined Maggie and the other Thorn Maidens. Maggie held out her hands and the four joined in a circle. "Well met," Maggie told them. "I rejoice that we live another day to serve the Mother and the Forest."

"The Mother and the Forest," the others echoed.

"Thorn Brother, I'm glad you're not dead." Wolf grinned.

"And I am glad you're not dead," Canin replied.

Wolf looked over Canin's shoulder. "Is that?" He gestured to Spear, who was still sitting.

"It is."

"Something wrong with her?" Wolf asked, moving to go to her. Canin held him back.

"She had a moment earlier. She'll be fine in time."

Wolf's eyes narrowed as he took in Spearhead. Maggie had obviously described Spear to him, but the sight of a Fairy with damaged wings, sitting on the ground with a baby in her arms, was something he had not been completely prepared for. His wary eye took in everything about Spear, from her scars to her strong arms and legs. Her soldier's sword especially drew his attention.

"I would greet her," Wolf said, "if she is to be a member of our family. And if she is someone who can easily best Maggie," he smiled, "I need to make friends with her."

"Let me," Canin said. He walked over. Wolf watched, while Maggie's Maidens filled her in with urgent whispers. Wolf began absently turning the spit.

"Spear," Canin called, kneeling down. She blinked, but didn't respond.

"Spear," he called again. "Maggie and Wolf are here." She shook her head slightly.

"Spear," Canin pleaded. "Please. Wolf wants to meet you and Aurora."

"Soldier," Maggie called from across the clearing.

Spear's head shot up. She blinked away the fog, taking in the new faces.

"Yes, Captain," she affirmed. "I'm sorry, Captain."

Wolf glanced back at Maggie, mouthing an amused, 'Captain?' at her. Maggie kept her attention on Spear, ignoring him.

Spear climbed to her feet. Passing Aurora to Canin, she strode across the grass to Wolf. Stopping a few paces from him, she stood at attention and addressed him. "Captain, I am Spearhead of the Heir's Guard. Former member," she amended. "I am here to serve the Exile Forest, and to protect its people. All I ask is a place for my baby." She glanced back at Canin. He stepped up to her side. "I will swear any oath you require. Serve in any way needed."

"It is good to meet you, Spearhead," Wolf said. "I'm glad you didn't shoot me when we first met." He held out his hand. "Maggie says you're a soldier of rare skill. I trust her judgment. We need your knowledge and experience." Spear took his hand in an awkward human handshake but moved to grip his arm when he smiled.

"Now, let's see if this bird is cooked." He let go of Spear and pulled the turkey off the spit. The others gathered around to watch him carve the meat. Canin put his arm around Spear and felt her sigh in relief.

"It will be all right," he whispered.

Chapter 15
Aurora's Effect

It was a simple, but hearty, meal. Wolf had also brought a pot of boiled potatoes seasoned with a spice Spear had never tasted before. She was hesitant at first, but after one bite, she swiftly devoured her portion.

"Like moonstems," she told Canin. "But not," she corrected herself. He smiled, and blocked her from taking his last slice.

"I'm sorry," Maggie said, "but I couldn't find any apples in the short time I had."

"That's all right, Captain. These are delicious. Thank you."

"You don't have to call me Captain," Maggie said automatically, but Spear had moved on to snatching potatoes from the others' plates. Only Sadie actively evaded her efforts, glaring when Spear's knife darted in. Everyone else took her childlike enthusiasm in good grace.

Canin watched Wolf through most of the meal as he bantered good-naturedly with all of the Maidens. Jokes and insults flew between him and Maggie, showing their long association and comfort with each other. Heron joined in and threw a few barbs, always at Wolf. Stonefoot mostly stayed silent, concentrating on her food. Sadie sat deliberately by Wolf and offered to help him whenever she could. By Wolf's casual acceptance and Maggie's slight annoyance, Canin knew this was something she did often.

Throughout the meal, Wolf's gaze would drift toward Spear and Canin, watching them out of the corner of his eye. Canin kept trying to get Spear to hold Aurora, and she would, for a little bit. But then she would pass her back when she saw a choice bit of bird, or so she could take a drink of the wine, which Wolf had also brought. The women all smiled at him, but none of them offered to take the baby.

Wolf finally set his plate aside. "Let me hold her, Setab. Spear keeps stealing your food."

Canin glanced at Spear, who frowned.

"Come now," Wolf said lightly. "I've never dropped any of my children. And I have. . . ." He looked up, as though he were trying to remember.

"Four," Maggie supplied.

"That you know of," Heron added.

"Four, and never dropped one," Wolf said with triumph. He looked at Spear. He didn't reach out, but just sat with his hands in his lap. "I'm a good father, if I do say so." His eyes darted from Canin to Spear. "It's good for a baby to be held by many. It will make her feel loved."

Spear didn't reply, but just stared at him intently. The conflict was clear on her face. Canin wanted to urge her to agree, but he sensed that she had to make this decision on her own.

"It's all right, Sister," Wolf said. "You just met us. I'm sure I'll grow on you."

"Like a mushroom," Maggie said to laughter.

Spear took a deep breath. "You can hold her," she decided. "If you're trusted with the safety of this forest, I should trust you with my child." She took Aurora — who had just woken up — from Canin and passed her to Wolf.

He took her solemnly. "Thank you for your trust," he said, adjusting the baby in his arms. "I will not betray that trust."

"No, you won't," Spear agreed, sitting back down. She took Canin's hand.

Wolf looked down into Aurora's open eyes. "Hello, little one," he whispered. "You have gone through much to reach this place of safety. We are honored by your parents' trust in us. May you grow to join our family."

At Wolf's words, 'this place of safety,' Spear gripped Canin's hand with crushing strength. Images of fire and the sound of falling stones filled his mind. He had to close his eyes as he became dizzy. The images subsided and Spear let go of his hand. Canin opened his eyes to find Spear studying him.

"It will not end that way," he assured her.

"You cannot know," she whispered back.

"I have hope and faith in the Mother and this family."

"So did we," Spear replied, turning back to Wolf.

He was still looking down into Aurora's green eyes. His own narrowed into a frown. Then he smiled and said, "If we must." He glanced up to find Spear and Canin staring at him inquisitively. He smiled broadly and handed the baby back to Spear. She tried to pass her on to Canin, but Wolf stopped her, saying, "She wants you to hold her."

Spear blinked, letting the child settle into her arms. Canin, puzzled, looked at Wolf with a question.

Wolf only grinned wider and got up. He turned to Maggie. "Prime, can I have a word?"

Maggie, pulled suddenly out of her conversation with Heron, gaped at him in surprise.

"I need to tell you something," Wolf said, holding out his hand. "Privately."

Maggie frowned, noticing the confused Canin and the suspicious Spear. "Are you sure?" she asked. "I thought. . . ."

"Prime, we need to talk," he said with more intensity.

Maggie knew that tone, and so did Spear. Both of them focused on the Prime Thorn Brother. Tension filled the small space.

"Nothing to worry about," Wolf told Spear. "I just need to have a chat with you," he told Maggie.

Maggie finally stood, ignoring his offered hand. "Well, let's go to the edge of the woods then." He followed her rapid steps.

"What is that about?" Sadie asked, following them with her eyes.

"I don't know," Heron replied. She resumed her attempts to get Stonefoot to talk to her.

Canin was surprised that Spear wasn't showing more anxiety at Wolf's sudden strange behavior. She was looking down at Aurora and smiling, her mouth moving with whispered words. Canin put his hand on her arm.

"It will be all right," Spear promised him. She shifted Aurora so she could take his hand. "Goddess guides us."

Canin smiled, lifted by her unexpectedly positive words. He was bothered by Wolf's sudden need to speak with Maggie, but he trusted these people.

"But that is not the plan." Maggie was angry. "That is not what has been agreed on and prepared for."

Wolf waited.

"What the bloody thorns is going on?" Maggie demanded. "You hold that baby, and then you want to change everything." She gestured back in the direction of the clearing. "Heron is suddenly all emotional and crying. Stonefoot is going through some crisis I don't understand. Even Sadie is more flirty with you than usual, which I hardly thought possible!" Her eyes narrowed. "Is it that Fairy? Is she affecting all of you in some way?" Her hand twitched to her sword.

"No. Spear isn't doing anything."

"How would you know?" Maggie asked. "If she was in your mind, you would never know."

"It's not Spear," Wolf assured her. "You know our weapons protect us. The Mother guards her warriors." He tapped the hilt of his knife. "And why would Spear do this? It makes no sense."

"Then what? What is in your head?" Maggie's hands clenched. She wanted to grab his arms and shake him.

"Have you held Aurora?" Wolf asked.

"No," Maggie replied, put off balance by the strange question.

"You should."

Maggie almost screamed. "What does that baby have to do with anything? Why has everyone suddenly gone mad?" She moved to return to the clearing.

Wolf grabbed her arm.

"Don't touch me," she growled, twisting out of his grasp. "You must explain yourself, Prime. If we do what you want us to, I will have to explain everything to the Children." Her anger burned into him. "I will not be made a fool of. Is this your misplaced fatherly feeling for Canin?"

"No," Wolf said calmly. "I never intended to make a fool of you." He shook his head. "I cannot explain how, but when I held her, I saw what would happen if Canin and Spear were together when Aieren arrived." His face was grim. "It was bad."

"She has affected you," Maggie said with confidence. "She read your mind and is now manipulating you." She half drew her sword.

"No!" Wolf cried. "How could she know? And why would she want to be alone? She relies on him so much. Leans on him. Canin keeps her balanced. I've only been around them for a short time, but even I see it." He pointed at her. "You know this is true."

Her blade thunked back into its sheath. "Yes. They are better together." She folded her arms. "Then I don't understand. Why?"

"Something connected us." Wolf struggled to explain. "It's like when the Mother speaks to us. There were images in my head. I saw what Spear would do with Canin by her side. Then I saw her alone, with just Aurora. I wish I could show you. You must trust me. I must take him away."

Maggie was still unconvinced.

Wolf dug deep into his memory, looking for inspiration.

"Do you remember that bastard cur James? When we were in the swamp?"

"No one believed me," Maggie replied, frowning at the memory.

"Neither did I," Wolf returned, "but I trusted your judgment and supported you anyway."

"And I was right," Maggie told him with triumph.

"And you were right," Wolf agreed. "And we took him to the thorns."

"You did that for me, so now I must do this for you?" Maggie reasoned, glaring at him.

"No," Wolf disagreed. "I trusted your judgment and instincts then. Please, trust mine now."

"This is more important than one cruel uncle given to the forest," Maggie told him, her anger draining away. She blew out her breath. "You're sure?"

"I am."

"Then how will we do this?"

☾ 〰 ☼

"They've been gone a while," Spear remarked. Aurora had finished nursing and was now sleeping.

Canin heard the worry in her voice. The Maidens were also looking back and forth at each other and glancing furtively in the direction Wolf and Maggie had gone. He had just opened his mouth to ask Stonefoot what she knew when the two Primes reappeared, pushing through the branches. Wolf went directly to the large pack he had come with, picked it up, and came to stand before the group. Maggie stood beside him, hands behind her back. The Maidens quieted and looked to their leader. Spear squeezed Canin's hand.

"We have a journey to start," Wolf said to Canin. "We need to be at the Green by midday." He began pulling things out of his pack. "You won't need much. That long bow, and your knives. I brought you a sword. Not as good as your lady wife's, but quality steel." Wolf held up the sheathed blade, the belt wrapped around it. He looked at the darkening sky. "Lightfoot expects us."

"That will be a hard journey for a baby," Canin replied. He started to stand, but was held down by Spear.

Wolf turned slightly to look at Maggie, but she didn't break her eye lock with Spear.

"Just you, I'm afraid, son . . . Canin. Spear will stay here with Aurora and the Maidens. One of the Children will be here in the morning." He folded his arms over his chest.

Spear sprang to her feet, radiating hot fear. Two of the Maidens scrambled up and were motioned to stand behind Maggie. With fear rising in his chest, Canin stood and moved in front of Spear.

"What do you mean?" he demanded. "Why do I need to go there, and why would I leave Spear here alone?"

"She will not be alone," Maggie assured him. "We will be here, and Lily is coming with one of the Children. We will keep her safe."

Canin could feel Spear shake her head.

"I don't think that's a good idea," Canin told Wolf.

"It is not a request," Wolf told him. "This is how it must be. Another of the Children will meet us at Bitter's Treetower." He took a deep breath. "If you refuse, you must leave the Forest, never to return."

Canin's reply was knocked from his mouth by the harsh tone of Wolf's voice.

"Is that a command of the Mother?" Canin finally asked. Behind him, Spear shuffled her feet. Canin took a risk and stepped back to put his arm around her. She settled into his embrace.

Wolf did not reply, but kept his eyes locked on them. The Maidens were staring at Maggie, who was watching Spear with a hard eye, her hand on her hilt.

Spear swallowed. "Who are the Children?" she asked.

Canin waited a moment for Wolf or Maggie to answer her, but neither did. "They're like Lords to you," he tried to explain. "They relay the commands of the Mother. They speak with the voice of the Mother in all things of the forest."

"We follow their commands with only the most respectful questions," Maggie put in. She stared at Spearhead. "You must understand that, soldier."

"I do," Spear replied.

"I don't understand," Canin said.

"It is not your place to question," Wolf said. "We are to obey."

"I've seen what a leader who denies questions can do," Canin told him. "I need more. I fear to be separated from my wife."

"Do you fear for her or for us?" Maggie asked harshly.

"Yes," Canin replied.

Maggie looked at Wolf. 'I told you,' was unspoken in her eyes.

"Then we will. . .," Canin started.

"You must go," Spear interrupted. "I'll be fine." She turned to Canin. "I am a strong and powerful Fairy. This is nothing." She looked at Maggie. "You will be here, Captain?" Maggie nodded, not rejecting the title. "And Lily is on her way?"

Again, Maggie nodded. "Then I will feel safe." She looked at Wolf. "Could Sandstone also be here?"

The confused looks on all their faces almost made Canin laugh. He didn't understand either.

"Who?" Wolf finally asked.

"The Brother who was with you earlier. The one with the scar on his head," Spear explained, brushing the side of her head with her hand. "He understands what it's like to be stared at because of something you cannot help."

Wolf looking questioningly at the circle of women. Maggie shook her head in confusion.

Then Stonefoot gave a short laugh. "She means Granite," she realized. "His head scar."

Spear nodded with enthusiasm. Wolf shook his head in mild exasperation.

"He and Sam are watching a Mother's Shrine not far from here." He looked to Maggie for permission. "Stonefoot could make the run?" he suggested.

Maggie nodded assent. "Take Heron with you," she told Stonefoot.

Stonefoot took on a stricken look. "I can make the run by myself."

"I can keep up with you," Heron told her, partly joking. Stonefoot tried to hide her discomfort. Sadie sniffed with contempt, raising Maggie's eyes.

"On second thought," Maggie said, "Sadie, you go with her. Heron can stay with Spear and Aurora. I must meet the Children's group." She gave Wolf a pointed look. "I do not know if I will be back before dawn."

"We'll be fine, Ma'am," Heron told her. She looked at Spear with friendship. "I would love to hear stories of the Fairy Realm. I never knew my father."

"I don't tell stories well," Spear warned her, "but I can try."

Maggie looked pointedly at Sadie, who was still sitting. She got up with effort.

"Tell Sam to stay," Wolf told the two women as they got ready to leave. "There's always more children about this time. And I suspect the red woman will be back."

Canin's eyes came up at the mention, but Spear grabbed him, pulling him back toward the tree.

"Get moving, ladies," Maggie ordered the still dawdling Sadie. Stonefoot had already shed her unneeded gear and was waiting at the edge of the woods. Sadie put her sword on and tightened her belt. Under Maggie's glare, she joined Stonefoot and the two of them took off into the woods.

Maggie went up to Heron. "Suggest to her that it would be better to sleep down here tonight. Offer to bring Aurora's box down. The others should be back before long. Use some Morning Leaves if you have to to stay awake." She bent closer. "Do not let her leave."

"Yes, Prime," Heron responded. "But I don't know if I can stop her." She left the rest unsaid.

"Do your best," Maggie counseled. "Keep her talking. I know she can talk. Ask her questions." Maggie smiled. "Flirt if you have to." Heron turned slightly red. "You know how Fairies are."

"I thought I did," Heron said, glancing at Spear and Canin, deep in conversation.

Maggie patted her arm. "The Mother will be with you." She turned to Wolf. He had prepared a small pack for each of them. "Old man."

"Old woman," Wolf replied. He scratched his beard as she continued to glare at him. "I know. I will regret this if anything goes amiss."

"We will all regret it," Maggie shot back. She waved to catch Canin and Spear's attention, but they stood face to face, with their foreheads pressed together, and didn't see her. She gave Heron one more supportive look and then took off into the woods.

Wolf took his sword from his side and attached it to one of the straps that ran over his chest. He made sure the hilt was in the right place, over his right shoulder. Then he made sure the cap was tight on his quiver and slung that over his shoulder as well. His short bow followed. The axe was too heavy, so he left it. Running out of ways to delay, he made sure his knife was secure on his left hip, then called, "It's time."

$$\text{☾ 〰 ☼}$$

"I don't understand," Canin whispered. They stood close, their foreheads touching. Aurora was awake and looking up at them both.

"We need to be accepted here," Spear said. "If this is what is required, then we must do this."

"I'm worried."

"So am I, but I've done many things that worried me. I've always survived, and I will again."

There was nothing else Canin could say. "I love you," he whispered. He looked down and met Aurora's eyes. "I love you, too."

"And I love you," Spear told him. She pulled her head away as Wolf spoke.

"It's time."

Canin sighed and let go of Spear. He walked over, accepted the sword Wolf offered, and, with the older man's help, put it on so that it sat comfortably on his back.

"It will be easier to run that way," Wolf commented. Then he handed Canin his bow and arrows, followed by the small pack of provisions. Canin secured the long knives on one side and his wooden knife on the other. Taking a deep breath, he looked up. Spear stood before him. She held out her hand.

He drew his wooden knife and presented it to her, hilt first. She took it, pressing the handle to Aurora's forehead, then her own. She then kissed the blade and presented it back to him.

"Bring this blade — and yourself — back to me."

"I will," Canin swore, pressing the hilt to his own forehead before kissing the blade and snapping it back into its sheath. He kissed Spear lightly, then brushed his lips over Aurora's head. "Keep her safe, Little Wing," he instructed her. Aurora cooed.

"Watch over her," he ordered Heron.

"I will, Setab," Heron vowed, taking his arm. "Mother guide you."

"Come, Canin," Wolf urged. "We have a long way to go."

Canin took one more look back at Spear, then followed Wolf into the woods.

Chapter 16
Running the Forest

"It will be easier if we run the edge of the forest," Wolf suggested as they trotted side by side down the trail leading away from the Treetower. "Or we could take the inner trails. They're faster."

Canin glanced at the sun. It would be dark soon, and running the trails would be tricky with the moon almost gone.

"You think I can't keep up with you?" Canin joked, attempting to push away his fear of leaving Spear.

"You've been gone a while, so I wanted to give you the option."

"I can run the trails."

"Good." Wolf smiled. "You remember the marks?"

"Yes," Canin confirmed.

"Then follow me!" Wolf cried, as he darted off into the growing dark under the thorn trees. Canin followed, his feet pounding on the ground as he sped up to stay at Wolf's heels. He left his worries behind, concentrating solely on his running. Leaves and branches slipped by his face; he dodged the occasional stone thrown up by Wolf's feet deftly. The daylight slipped away. His eyes shifted, looking to the guidefire mushrooms on the trees marking the trail. More memories crowded into his mind as he passed the star-shaped, glowing blue mushrooms. He could almost feel Brenna at his side as they tried to make it home before moonrise. Her laughter as they blocked Crow from passing them on the narrow path. More laughter as Crow slipped in the mud and slid into the thorns.

Wolf whooped as he grabbed a sapling, turning down a switch-back toward a swift stream.

"The bridge will be slippery," he called back in warning as Canin made the turn.

"Then don't fall into the river," Canin shot back.

Wolf laughed, taking the next switchback faster. He kicked up leaves and dust, forcing Canin to slow, dodging and sliding on the dirt.

The low roar of running water got louder, but Canin slowed as he noticed that Wolf's dim form had stopped. The 'bridge' before them was a large fallen tree, the bark on the top worn away by many seasons of crossing feet. Wolf took a swig from his bottle and passed it to Canin. Barely breathing hard, he took a drink with a nod.

"After the crossing, the path gets narrower," Wolf warned. "And some of the underbrush is becoming thick. Crow was supposed to bring a group down here to clear it, but I don't know if he did." Wolf frowned at the thought. Then he shrugged. "What's a few more scratches?"

"It's like he knew I was coming," Canin joked, passing the bottle back.

"The two of you will have to resolve this," Wolf reminded him. "I heard he might be setting up house with Wren. And you have your Fairy lady. Time to bury the past."

"I'm not the one standing in the way. You saw his reaction to my return."

"That was surprise." Wolf shrugged, putting the bottle away. "But I will speak with him."

"Let's keep going," Canin suggested. His anxiety was beginning to return.

Wolf nodded and crossed swiftly with experienced steps. Canin was a few strides behind, his feet remembering what they had to do. Wolf smiled and clapped him on the shoulder as he made the bank.

"Swiftly now, Setab," he urged, darting off into the forest with Canin behind.

The dark trees rushed past; his eyes focused on the guidefires' bright marks. Canin had never been the fastest, but he knew the forest. This was his home. He trusted the Mother and his own feet to keep him on the path. Deep in his spirit, he knew the shifting, sometimes chaotic, always kinetic mood of the forest. In his youth, he had surprised his teachers and many more experienced forest runners by finding new paths through the thorn trees. He knew when to trust and when to avoid.

When to push ahead, and when to. . . .

Duck!

Canin threw his head to the side and felt a branch pass right by his cheek. He took a few more steps, still right behind Wolf, but his pace faltered as he pressed his hand to his face. Canin felt wetness, and assumed it was water from the recent rain. After a few more steps, though, he felt a bright pain that brought back memories. He got out of step with himself and stumbled, sliding on the wet ground.

Hearing the break in rhythm, Wolf turned, then stopped and backtracked to Canin. He caught the younger man's arm, steadying him.

"I'm okay," Canin said, his hand still pressed to his face. "Keep going."

"Something caught you," Wolf noted. "Stop a moment."

Canin resisted for an instant, but the growing pain in his cheek made him acquiesce. Wolf sat him down against a tree trunk. By the light of one of the glowing mushrooms, he examined Canin's face.

"Hold still," Wolf urged. He pressed a cloth to Canin's face. "It just missed your eye. Good reflexes." He sat back. "I would hate to face your lady wife if you lost an eye." He pulled a small vial from his pack, then removed the cloth from Canin's face and smeared a clear paste on the wound. Canin's cheek burned for a moment before the pain subsided into numbness.

Canin leaned back, feeling the rough bark of the tree against his back. "She would kill me first, and then you."

Wolf smiled and sat down beside him. He looked around. "We're close. Why don't we stay here, and go the rest of the way in the morning? We don't want to get there too early."

Canin nodded in agreement. His legs burned from the long run. 'Out of practice,' he chided himself. 'I'll have to work on that.'

Wolf was beginning to pull some food out of his pack. Canin hovered his hand over the wound.

"It smells different," he commented.

"Aieren keeps adjusting the recipe. Shouldn't leave a scar." Wolf handed him a length of dried meat. "But then, Spearhead might like you with a scar."

"I don't know," Canin muttered, tearing into the food. Potent spices bit into his tongue. He turned to Wolf, who was ready with the water bottle.

"Still using too much rue, I taste," Canin said after a deep drink. He took a smaller bite the next time.

"I'm a man of habit," Wolf conceded.

They sat quietly, listening to the forest. To their left, they heard a squeak and the sound of something hitting the leaves.

"Owl," Wolf surmised as the forest went silent. Canin grunted in agreement.

They chewed and drank. Canin's eyes were beginning to drift closed when Wolf spoke.

"What do you feel when you hold Aurora?"

Surprised out of his drowsiness by the strangeness of the question, Canin didn't reply right away. He looked at Wolf. He could just barely see the man. The narrow moonlight didn't penetrate very far into the trees. He could only see Wolf's eyes reflecting the dim light.

"What any father feels holding his child," Canin said slowly. "Love, dedication to keeping her safe and happy. Worry that she'll throw up on me." Wolf chuckled. "Worry for her future. Fear I might not be able to protect her. Fear I will fail her as a father."

"You won't, son," Wolf assured him. "Never that. Just because your father was a bastard and left your mother doesn't mean you'll fail Aurora. And you have the example of Niel."

"And you," Canin told him.

Wolf shrugged. "I'm not there for my children like I should be. Lilac chides me every time, but I must serve the Mother. She pulls me away. They understand, but I fear."

"So that's her name," Canin said brightly. "I don't think I ever knew that. I just always knew her as the berry widow."

"That's what I call her," Wolf told him. "You, youngster, can keep calling her the berry widow." His voice turned serious. "That's a name between us only."

Canin smiled, thinking of Trillium. "I understand."

"Beyond the normal fatherly emotions," Wolf pressed.

Canin thought of the first time he had held Aurora and looked into her eyes. How he had felt his path change. But how to articulate that to Wolf? Canin also felt a stab of suspicion.

"What do you mean?"

Wolf struggled for words. "I just felt something when I held her. Something like when I. . . ." He stopped and shook his head. "There's something special about her. I just wondered if you felt it, too."

Fear spiked in Canin, and he was glad for the dark, hiding his face. "Of course she's special," Canin replied, sounding exaggeratedly offended. "She is my daughter. Spear and I endured much to escape with her and get her here. She went through a Mother-cursed ordeal."

"I understand," Wolf said, trying to appease Canin. "Everyone here has. I'm sorry if I offended you. It's just. . . ." He stopped. "I'm sorry. Asking you such questions, so soon. I apologize, Setab."

Canin wanted to say that it was nothing, but he held back. He was still angry at being pulled away from Spear, and worried about how she would react to meeting one of the Children. He wished he had had time to explain everything about them. Warn her.

"Who will be meeting us at Bitter's?" Canin asked, wanting to change the subject.

"I'm not sure," Wolf replied. He took a big bite of dried meat. Canin narrowed his eyes in suspicion.

"They always have clear plans," Canin said. "Always tell us exactly what they need done and when. But you don't know?"

"You and Spear were dropped into our laps," Wolf defended.

'More than you know,' Canin thought.

"This was put together quickly," Wolf continued. 'More than you know,' he thought. "And when I left to come to you, it had not been decided who would make the journey." Wolf considered. "Might be Cobalt. He and Lightfoot are close."

Canin grimaced. He and Cobalt had history. "And who will be meeting with Spear?"

"Aieren," Wolf replied without hesitation.

Canin clenched his fists in fear. "She rarely left her house and the sanctuary when I was younger. Now. . . . If anything happens to Spear," he warned Wolf.

"That is why we are here, Thorn Brother."

The steel in Wolf's voice brought Canin up short. He had forgotten the power of the Prime's command voice.

"Get some sleep," Wolf said, softening. "I'll sit watch. We'll leave at dawn."

"You need some sleep, too," Canin objected.

"If I get sleepy, I will wake you," Wolf assured him. He passed Canin a folded cloak for a blanket. "That's an order, Brother. Get some sleep. As you said, she is a powerful Fairy soldier. She can take care of herself."

Canin took the cloak and covered himself. 'He's right,' he thought. 'And Aieren is probably the best choice.' He gripped his wooden knife, searching for confidence in its strength. He closed his eyes.

"How did she know?" Wolf asked suddenly.

"Know about what?" Canin replied, his eyes still closed.

"Passing the knife. How did she know?"

Canin opened his eyes. "I thought it was a Fairy ceremony, or a soldier thing."

"No. It's a Thorn Brother goodbye." His voice sounded confused. "Brenna didn't do that when you left?"

A sudden memory brought grief. Canin saw his first wife on the threshold as she passed the blade back to him. Behind her, her mother glared. "I don't know," Canin mumbled. "I had forgotten." Canin closed his eyes tightly, pushing back the memories.

"You've brought more mysteries back with you," Wolf said, patting his leg. "Sleep, son. I will watch."

Canin summoned memories of Spear sitting with Aurora in her lap. He held them close as he reminded himself, 'She is a powerful

Fairy.' In his mind, she smiled at him. Confidence in her pushed his fear away, and sleep came easily.

Chapter 17
Bitter by the Green

They stopped at the edge of the forest to take in the whole of the Green. Canin smiled, gazing out over the vast field of waist-high bushes.

Remembering Aieren's lesson from his childhood, Canin thought about the history of these fields. Long ago, a Fairy Lord had come here. He — or more likely, his servants — had planted these vast rows of bushes. He had made his fortune in the Fairy Realm distilling a liqueur from their berries. But, despite his wealth, he hadn't had enough land to grow them in the quantities he wanted. Here, he had the blessing of space, planting acres upon acres of bushes.

Unfortunately, the soil of the forest was different, and produced berries too bitter for use in the lord's liqueur. You could still see the overgrown mounds of rubble from the houses and distillery the ruined Fairy had destroyed in his anger, upon realizing all his investment had come to nothing but cartfuls of cursed, bitter berries.

The Fairies left, but the bushes flourished, growing and spreading beyond their neat, Fairy-forced rows. Every spring the fields outside the western portion of the Exile Forest were aflame with purple and red flowers, full of buzzing bees and huge flocks of colorful butterflies, all coming for the bushes' sweet nectar. Deer and elk ate both the leaves and the purple berries, as did the smaller creatures of the forest, not bothered by their bitter taste. The people of the forest hunted those creatures, and the cycle of the realm continued on.

When Aieren told this story to the young children of the forest, she went on to explain how this act of a greedy and arrogant Fairy, who couldn't be bothered to plant a few bushes and wait to see how they turned out, was a primary contributor to the success of their forest community. She pointed to the bearskin blanket over her chair. "This came from a bear the first Thorn Brother killed for food and warmth during the first dark and cold winter here. The skull is still in the Sanctuary, one of the talismans passed from Brother to Brother down the seasons. The animals that come to the Green sustain us still, and they allowed those first exiles to survive the winter, and then to thrive. We set up beehives and gathered their honey, discovering its healing and soothing properties, in addition to its sweet taste. So don't hate the Fairies. Pity them. Pity their arrogance and shortsightedness. We picked up what they'd cast off. We took something broken and made it whole again. Because, 'Together we will stand firm against all who would break us.'" She quoted the well-known mantra with an accompanying recitation by the children.

"When I first held that skull," Wolf mused into the silence. He knew that Canin was thinking about the history of the Green; it had always been his favorite story as a child. "I was amazed at its size and the sharpness of its teeth. And the claws that beast must have had." He whistled in admiration. "You know what I thought?"

"What?" Canin asked, his eyes still focused on the landscape ahead of him.

"That the first Thorn Brother was one brave bastard to take on such a monster."

"He was probably cold and hungry," Canin commented. "And desperate to feed and clothe his family."

"Desperation makes us brave," Wolf agreed.

"It also makes us foolish." Canin still looked to the west. The bushes of the Green stretched to the horizon, but he knew Elen and the Fairy Realm both lay beyond. A flash of his own desperation almost made him do something foolish himself. He drew his wooden knife and pressed the hilt to his lips. "I will return to you," he whispered.

"Come now," Wolf told him, trying to stay light. "You loved the story of the First Thorn Brother when you were young. Begged me and the others to tell it every chance you got."

"I was young, and amazed by all the different ways it was told." Canin put his knife away. He turned to Wolf, smiling. "Old Hawthorn used to go on and on about how good the bear meat would have tasted."

"And he was killed by one on a hunt. Foolish bastard. Stay in cover!" He shook his head at the memory.

"Sometimes the bear eats you," Canin joked. "Let's go." He pointed to the right. "I can see Bitter's tower from here."

"Wait," Wolf said urgently, grabbing his arm. "I need to tell you something."

Canin, surprised by Wolf's sudden shift in mood, stared at him.

"Lightfoot might not be ready for us," he said slowly. "And I'm not sure one of the Children will be here yet. It's too early, and the journey is long."

"We ran it in a night," Canin disagreed. He moved back from Wolf. "And if they left the day before, there should have been plenty of time for them to get here. The Children pride themselves on being strong and swift." Something began to dawn on Canin as he noted the pained look on Wolf's face, the frown that distorted his beard.

Wolf made a disagreeing noise.

"What aren't you telling me, old man?" Canin demanded. "Why did you bring me here?"

"You and Spear were supposed to meet the Children together, back at the tower," Wolf admitted. He waved his hands as Canin grew angry at his betrayal. "But I saw something when I held Aurora." He desperately tried to explain. "I saw a vision of what would happen if you were together. I saw. . . ." He hesitated. "Horrible things. I needed to separate you two."

"That's why you went away," Canin said, now understanding. "Why Maggie acted as she did." He stepped up to Wolf and grabbed him by the belt across his chest. "What happened? What would we have done? What would she have done?"

Wolf let Canin hold him for a moment, anger blazing in his eyes, but then stepped back, breaking Canin's grip. His hand itched to draw his knife, but he held back.

"I don't know. I just saw the aftermath. Then I saw Spear alone meeting one of the Children."

"Aieren," Canin surmised, lowering his hands.

"And Cobalt," Wolf filled in. "You know how he feels about Fairies. I couldn't risk it. Please, Setab, I didn't want to lie to you, but I had no choice. I needed to protect the forest."

Canin clenched his fists, then folded his arms tight over his chest. It was too late; too far to go back. 'That's why he told me now,' he realized. He took a deep breath. The fear and anxiety were still there, but Wolf's words and confidence made him feel better.

"So, you're sure everything will be all right, now that she'll be meeting them alone?" Canin finally asked.

Wolf nodded. "I only know what I saw, but I believe she'll be fine."

"She is a powerful Fairy," Canin muttered. He let the tension go out of his fists. Something occurred to him. "So how did you persuade Maggie?"

"A lot of arguing and bargaining," Wolf admitted, also relaxing. "I reminded her of all the times I supported her when others did not."

"Those must have been few," Canin joked. "I don't remember a time when she hasn't been right. I do remember many times when you were wrong, though." Canin frowned at his own banter. What if Wolf was wrong about this?

"I am not wrong," Wolf asserted. "She is strong, as you say. And Maggie and Lily will be there. Spear trusts Maggie. They will keep her balanced."

Some of Canin's certainty had eroded, but the core of who Spear was remained. She was a soldier, and a soldier did her duty. Her duty now was to keep Aurora safe.

"Did she try to stab you?" Canin asked, letting the tension out of the air.

"No, but she wanted to," Wolf admitted. "And that is not the proper way to speak to your Prime, Thorn Brother. Or of another Prime."

"You're not my Prime," Canin shot back.

"But I will be again," Wolf promised. He tapped his head. "And I remember."

"The same way you remember how many children you have?"

Wolf glared lightheartedly at him. "Come on." He gestured. "The sun has been up for a while. Bitter is an early riser, and Lightfoot only sleeps a few hours."

Canin nodded and followed the older man. A burst of blackbirds erupted from a bush as they passed by, squawking at them in protest for disturbing their meal.

They knocked on the door of the cabin at the foot of the Treetower. Lightfoot opened it, sleepy-eyed and holding a steaming cup. He waved them inside. Lightfoot was a tall Elenite with short, greying blond hair and arms covered in the short white scars of a spinner.

"I didn't expect you both so soon," he told them, sitting down at the table. He offered them a cup of the bitter-smelling drink he held.

Both Canin and Wolf shook their heads. Lightfoot shrugged and took another drink. The berries of the Green were useful for something. Once dried, shelled, ground, and roasted, they made a potent drink for either driving sleep away in the morning or keeping it at bay at night.

"I didn't make enough anyway," he said. "A runner woke me to tell me you would be here today." He looked at Wolf for an explanation.

"I did what I thought was right," Wolf said, folding his arms.

"No matter." Lightfoot shrugged. "I wanted to speak with Canin as soon as I could anyway. This is as good a time as ever." He handed a note to Wolf.

"'I expect your chicken stew,'" Wolf read.

"For making Cobalt walk all this way," Lightfoot explained. He gestured to a large cairn at the back of the room. On top were two pots that steamed and bubbled. The stones directly under them glowed with a red light. Canin recognized the light and heat of Fairy Power.

"I put them on after I got the note. They should be ready to de-bone in a few hours. I have some vegetables, but the potatoes will have to be dug up from the garden." Lightfoot smiled at Wolf. "I assume you have your spices."

146

"I do."

"Good." Lightfoot gestured to two more covered pans. "I was getting ready to take my father his breakfast. I made enough for all of us." He took Canin's arm. "I need to speak with Canin privately."

Canin allowed himself to be led back outside and around the cabin. The Treetower seemed taller than he remembered. A ramp wound around the trunk now, going up to the building set in the arms of the tree. A circular deck had been built all around the tower, and a door cut into the side.

"My father can no longer climb the ladder," Lightfoot explained. He stopped before the little garden. "Take everything off but your knife," Lightfoot commanded.

Canin complied, stacking his weapons by the back door of the cabin. When he was done, he stood straight, hand on his knife, and waited for Lightfoot to speak.

"So the renegade Thorn Brother returns," Lightfoot said, looking him up and down. "Did you find what you were looking for?"

"Yes. I found the truth about my mother and father," Canin said to Lightfoot's frown.

"So, you spoke to them?" he asked with surprise, his eyebrows shooting up.

"No," Canin replied. "She was dead. But I read her letters. She loved my father, but she couldn't keep me."

"And your father?" Lightfoot asked around clenched teeth.

"He was dead as well. But I was told he loved her, too." Canin folded his arms. "I found love. It wasn't what I was looking for, but it is what I needed."

"In the Fairy Realm?" Lightfoot asked incredulously, not really hearing Canin.

"Yes," Canin replied simply. He was getting angry at Lightfoot, but he knew he had to remain civil.

Lightfoot nodded. "You will tell my father that you met his wife, and that she sent a message that she will never return, and he is to forget her."

Canin narrowed his eyes. "I won't lie to him. I was lied to all my childhood. I thought I was a child of rape. Bitter treated me like a son, and I will not betray that trust by lying to him. I will not destroy his hope."

Lightfoot waved away the objection. "What hope does he have? It's a delusion. A fantasy, that his Fairy bride will fly in one day and make everything better. You will tell him what I require you to tell him."

Canin set his feet firmly on the ground and faced Lightfoot squarely. "I will not lie to him." Inwardly, he grinned. 'That's why he made me disarm.'

"I can make it very hard for you here," Lightfoot said in a low menacing voice. "I am the Prime Spinner, and I have the ear of the Children. You're just a renegade Thorn Brother. One who defied the Mother's orders, and came back with a Fairy wife." He sneered. "And a half-breed daughter."

"You're a half-breed yourself," Canin pointed out, his anger growing at the insult not only to him, but to his family as well.

"And if I could, I would pluck my eyes out," Lightfoot snarled. "I would drain my blood. Expel everything that is Fairy in me. I hate them."

Canin wanted to say, 'Your Fairy blood is what makes you an exceptional spinner,' but instead, he remarked, "You hate your mother, not every Fairy. We're here for sanctuary, a home, a place of safety. Don't project your hate onto me and my family."

Lightfoot's hands clenched. "Do you know how many Thorn Maidens and Brothers went looking for you?" Without stopping to allow Canin to answer, he snarled, "Six. Only one came back. A man I grew up with led them. They were ambushed at the edge of that village you went to. Shot full of arrows, their bodies left to rot in the sun." He stamped his foot. "Ask Maggie who survived."

Canin didn't respond. His shame rose. No one had told him this. His foolishness had cost even more lives than he'd realized.

"One of the Maidens she trained," Lightfoot told him. "They let her go. After doing unspeakable things to her. Took her thumbs and first two fingers, so she could never wield a sword or draw a bow again. And what does she do now?" Lightfoot asked with a hiss.

Canin only stared at him.

"She washes clothes," Lightfoot said coldly. "A brave Maiden destroyed, forced to live the rest of her life with the memory of what you caused." He pointed an accusing finger at Canin.

"If you need me to admit I was wrong and say that I'm sorry," Canin offered, "I was, and I am. I was a fool, and should have waited. I was too young and inexperienced. I thought I only got one woman killed." He blew out a sigh. "Now I know there are many more lost lives I have to make up for. And more men I must bring to justice."

"Justice?" Lightfoot sneered. "What is justice? There's none of that here. Just survival. You destroyed the work of seasons. I lost one of the few dependable markets I had for my silk. You put the entire forest in peril! Now you stand here, wanting to come back home. I wish I had been the one to find you. I would have turned you back around and refused you entry to the forest."

"But you weren't," Canin said. "And you do not have that power."

"You don't know what I have," Lightfoot told him heatedly as he took a step forward. Canin stood his ground. "But I need you," Lightfoot said low. "I need you to tell my father what he needs to hear. Do that, and I will support your return to the forest."

"Only the Mother can say if I stay or go," Canin reminded him, but inside, fear crawled up his belly. He began to sweat.

"Believe that if you will," Lightfoot said, stepping back. He made a dismissive gesture. "I don't care." He gestured again. "Go have breakfast with my father. I'll be waiting."

"What changed you?" Canin asked. "I admired you. I looked up to you. I wanted to be you."

"But you didn't have the skill," Lightfoot taunted. "And I grew older. Now I understand."

"Your hate has colored everything."

"Yes," Lightfoot cried. "Yes, I hate her. Hate that she left me here. Left without telling my father she was never coming back. Left him with that foolish hope of his and those damn glowing rocks. I hate the damn tea he makes me find. I hate all those arrogant Fairies who look down on me. Who sneer and call me 'half-breed filth.' I hate you for believing there's anything good in the Fairy Realm. I hate your naivete. It's a good thing you didn't find your father, because he might have killed you."

Canin almost drew his knife at that, but Lightfoot's smile stopped him. That was what he wanted. Strike a Prime, and it wouldn't matter what the Children said.

"It's a good thing she isn't here," Canin told him calmly. "She would be disappointed and sad to see how her son treats his father."

"Disappointed?" Lightfoot almost screamed. "I do everything for that man. I built that ramp when he could no longer climb the ladder. I make him food on those damn glowing rocks of his. I bring him everything he needs. I should be back at the mountain, leading my spinners, but instead, I'm here. I hope he dies soon." Lightfoot turned and stomped off into the garden. He began pulling potatoes out of the ground and throwing them in Canin's direction.

Canin watched for a moment, letting the clods of dirt and vegetables hit him. "You're ruining your garden," Canin remarked, too low to be heard.

Lightfoot finally stopped and sat back on his heels. "Why are you still here?" he asked.

Canin turned away and returned to the front of the cabin. Wolf met him at the door, Bitter's tray in his hand. By the look on his face, he had heard every word. How could he not? Canin shook his head, not wanting to talk about it. He took the tray and turned to climb the ramp to the Treetower.

Chapter 18
Waiting Through the Seasons

"Come in, son," Bitter said, gesturing Canin inside. "I was wondering what was keeping my breakfast. Then I heard my son shouting, and I knew."

They sat down at a small table. Bitter was even taller than his son, but age was bending him. The dark hair Canin remembered was mostly gone, except for a well-trimmed ring around the back of his head. The room was bigger than Canin remembered. There was a real bed in the corner now, under the large window. Lightfoot had obviously expanded the room for his father. A soft fairysilk carpet covered the floor. Canin looked around a bit, but always returned his eyes to Bitter.

"You thought I looked old when you were young," Bitter commented, lifting the lid. "Now what do you think of me?"

"You're older now," Canin said. "Sir," he added, not knowing how to end his sentence.

"Call me Brother," Bitter insisted. He touched the knife at his belt. "I am still a Thorn Brother. Though." He stopped and looked up. "Others have to sit in the perch now. My old arms can no longer climb."

"I'm sure you could," Canin told him. "You're just resting and letting the younger ones do the work."

Bitter laughed and took a sip of his tea. "Is that how you got a Fairy wife, that flattering tongue?"

"No. I was just where I needed to be," Canin replied honestly, keeping his own bitterness to himself.

Bitter nodded with understanding. "I'm sorry I can't offer you some tea, but Lightfoot goes through such trouble to find it. He won't let me waste it. Or so he says."

"That's fine, sir . . . Brother. Just smelling it is enough."

"You know this?" Bitter said, amazed. "So, you have been there. I thought you might be like those strangers my son pays to lie to me." He sat back in his chair. "What do you remember? I was never far past the border."

"It's a lot like here, but with more Fairies," Canin joked.

Bitter smiled and motioned for Canin to eat. "I eat little now," he said, pushing his eggs around. "I wish I could have some of your sausage."

Canin offered him a slice.

"No. I'd be hours on the pot, and my son. . . ." He let the thought trail off. He took small careful bites of his eggs and occasional sips of tea. Canin devoured his meal. Despite Lightfoot's other qualities, he was a good cook. There were eggs, and thick bread with jam, and sausage, which was not over-spiced. Canin kept glancing up, knowing Bitter was eager to question him. Bitter noted the looks and kept waving the younger man to keep eating.

When Canin had finished his meal, Bitter took the last bites of his eggs and began nibbling on his bread. Canin tried to speak, but couldn't find the words.

"What did my son want you to tell me?" Bitter asked into the silence.

Respect for the old Thorn Brother made Canin answer without hesitation. "He wanted me to tell you I met her, and that she sent a message that she'll never be back."

Canin's direct words and the depth of his son's betrayal shook Bitter. He took a deep breath and drank some more tea.

"And did you?" Bitter finally asked.

"No. At least, I don't think so. She was Feather-wing, right?" Canin asked. Bitter nodded. "I met very few Fairies. Mostly Iridescents and Leather-wings. Two Feather-wings I met were very young, and the other was the maid of one of the Ladies. A very highborn lady," Canin said, still honor bound to protect Talia's identity. "What was her name?"

"Plumaria," Bitter replied. "But Fairies change their names like the weather."

"No, that wasn't her name," Canin said, sorry to put another crack in the old man's battered heart. "But maybe she knows of her. If I ever. . . ."

Bitter shook his head. "She hated the Iridescents and would never have worked for one. Her mother served them, and she was used and abused. Plumaria told me she would never be like her mother." Bitter took a moment to consider. "Did she have hair the color of sunshine? A voice to rival the sweetest songbirds?"

Canin shook his head. "It was iron grey. I always got the impression she was much older than she looked. She did have a sweet voice, though. A voice like your mother has in your dreams."

Bitter nodded in agreement. "Did she have a scar on her upper thigh?"

Canin blushed. "I never got that close."

Bitter smiled. "She was a wonder. I first saw her dancing on a little hill. Waving her arms and kicking her feet to some music only she could hear. Never had I seen such beauty, her hair shimmering in the setting sun. She must have seen me watching. When the half-moon rose, she gestured at me. I never hesitated. I joined her, and we danced all night long. I asked her name, but she said it didn't matter. In the morning, she was gone." Bitter looked at Canin. "I can see that you've felt the touch of wings wrapped around you."

"Yes," Canin whispered.

"I searched and searched." He smiled bitterly. "I watched that hill for three full cycles of the moon, waiting for her to come back. Then." He grinned, slapping his thigh. "I ran into her in the market. She dropped a basket of vegetables, and I rescued her potatoes from rolling under a stall. After that, we were happy."

He lost his smile. "I don't understand why she left us. I knew she would live longer than me. Longer than our son. I accepted that. I thought that's why we came here. I told her it would be enough." He banged on the table. "It would have been enough."

Canin steadied the plates. "My mother said the same things in her letters. She accepted it. But he could not." A tear slid down Bitter's wrinkled face. "Maybe she didn't want to see you and her son grow old and die."

"She told me that," Bitter argued. "And I accepted it. I loved her. With all my heart. Why wasn't that enough? I've been faithful. I've waited. . . ."

Canin reached across the table and took the broken-hearted old man's hand. "I don't know. Sometimes love isn't enough. She couldn't bear to watch you wither away. She thought it was better to leave and have the memory of you as you were."

"You've had your own heartbreak," Bitter noted suddenly, looking up. "I can hear it in your voice."

Canin couldn't speak. He nodded.

"One of her mother's friends gave me some advice. She was a scarred Leather. Tough and strong. No-nonsense. Her bodyguard, and probably her lover. You know how Fairies are. She told me, 'You'd better enjoy this, because she will break your heart.'"

Canin felt tears coming, but laughed through them. "I was told something similar."

Bitter's eyes lit up. "Then this wife you have, was not. There was another?"

'He may be old, but he's still sharp,' Canin thought with admiration. "Yes, but I cannot. Please. . . ."

"Don't worry, son," Bitter said, patting his hand. "It's just between two men who have both lost. I will keep your secret."

"It's not a secret," Canin started, but stopped. Why try to explain it all to him? Canin accepted the sympathy.

"Why don't you go on up to the perch for a while. You found clarity there once."

"Yes, but. . . ."

"Go," Bitter shooed him. "I have to think. And I can't do that with you here. Go. On a clear day, I can just see the Diamond River."

Canin rose, and bowed with great respect to the old Thorn Brother. He found the latch to the upper trap door and climbed through.

The sun was at mid-day when Canin returned below. He hadn't been able to see the Diamond River, but he had heard commotion from the forest and knew their other visitors were about to arrive.

The breakfast tray had been taken away and replaced with bread, cheese, and a dark red wine. Bitter was chewing on a slice of bread. He offered a tray to Canin.

"Wolf brought this up. He knew you would be hungry."

"Thank you," Canin said, taking the bread and cheese but ignoring the wine.

"Need your wits," Bitter observed. Canin nodded, chewing.

"Wolf is a good Prime. Better than any before."

"Yes, he is," Canin agreed.

"I am so proud of this Treetower. I've made it my home for these long seasons. I know it's foolish, but I needed to be as close to the Fairy Realm as I could. Someday she would be flying over the Green, and I would see her. I didn't want to miss that first sight of her."

"You understand," Canin started.

"I understand nothing," Bitter told him. "She will be back. She told me so. She promised. I will wait."

Canin could do nothing but smile at the old man. His own hope mirrored Bitter's. Bitter couldn't let it go, any more than Canin could.

"I want you to make me a promise, Thorn Brother to Thorn Brother." Bitter held out his hand and Canin took it without hesitation.

"When I die, I want you to make sure my body is burned. If Humans are allowed, I want to Return to the Cycle, so I will see her again." Bitter's hand was strong in Canin's.

Canin didn't know how he would fulfill that wish, but he nodded. "I will do my best."

"Maybe I'll be reborn a Fairy, and she'll find me," Bitter said, full of dreams.

"And you'll be young, while she's old," Canin said, risking a small grin.

Bitter smiled and clapped Canin on the shoulder. "That would be fair. Now." He pulled out a piece of paper. He took his knife and cut his thumb. After he pressed the bloody fingerprint to the paper, he looked Canin straight in the eye.

"When Cobalt is here, I will speak with him. I want you to have this place when I'm gone. Keep a watch for her. For both our lost loves."

"Setab . . . Brother, I cannot. Lightfoot will never allow it."

"I spoke with Wolf. He agrees." He waved his hands, taking in the whole room. "This and the cabin below are the perfect place to raise a family. You'll need the space, with a daughter and a wife. And maybe more children to have, or to adopt."

Canin tried to protest, but Bitter held his hand firmly. "This is what I want. Lightfoot hates this place. He'll rage, but the Treetowers are the responsibility of the Thorn Brothers to man. That's not something he can change. Lightfoot will be reminded of that." A wily smile creased his face.

"And this is the perfect place for the future Prime to live."

Canin held up his hands in denial "No, sir. I don't want that responsibility. I'm the renegade Brother. They would never put me forward. No one would vote for me."

Bitter grinned. "Not today. And maybe not tomorrow, but one day. She guided you back." He patted Canin on the arm. "One day." He took a deep breath. "Are you ready?"

"Yes, Brother."

☾ ⌇ ☼

The call of the wood crow brought Wolf and Lightfoot out of the cabin. They looked across the clearing to see people emerging from the forest. Three Thorn Maidens came out first, scanning the area with wary eyes. Wolf waved at them, and the third called back into the woods. A moment later, the Thorn Brother Crow emerged. By his side was an older man, dressed all in blue. The older man looked across the clearing and saw Lightfoot. He waved in a friendly manner.

"You bastard," Wolf swore under his breath, while smiling and waving. "That's why he was called back."

Lightfoot smiled.

"Interfere with my Brothers again," Wolf began.

"And you will what, Prime?" Lightfoot said with good nature. "I have the ear of the Children. Who makes them all they desire? Who supports this forest with our art? What will you do?"

"We shall see," Wolf said through gritted teeth.

Crow and the older man had stopped. The older man was holding himself up on Crow's arm. Behind them, two more Thorn Brothers emerged from the forest, their bows out. At a word from Crow, they began scanning the area, bows raised.

Wolf took a step forward, his voice ringing across the clearing. "Put down your bows! There are no enemies here."

The two looked to Crow, prompting Wolf to call out again.

"Brothers." Wolf's Prime voice penetrated, and they returned their arrows to their quivers.

"Good to see you, Wolf," the older man called. He began to walk across the clearing, his arm still on Crow's. "Now, where is he?"

"Hello, Cobalt," Wolf called back. Lightfoot began looking around.

The sound of a door opening above them drew all their eyes. Canin walked to the edge of the deck around the Treetower. Behind him, Bitter stood in the doorway, clutching the frame.

"Get off my tree!" he yelled. "I don't believe you! She's coming back. Take your lies away, you Motherless bastard!" Bitter turned and slammed the door. The creaks of the stressed wood echoed off the trees. Canin turned, noted the audience, and nodded in respect, then began his slow walk down the ramp.

Wolf met him at the bottom, a grin on his face. Lightfoot stayed behind, with a look like he was stuck between a skunk and a bear. Or more correctly, a wolf and his brother.

"I told you he wouldn't believe me," Canin told Lightfoot.

Lightfoot sputtered, his expression caught between a sneer and a frown. "You told him," he finally got out.

"You heard him," Wolf answered.

Canin tried to speak, but Cobalt was there, waiting. "Greetings, Cobalt," Canin said with a bow of his head.

"So, Bitter is still stubborn," Cobalt commented.

"Yes, he is," Lightfoot finally said.

The seasons had not been kind to Cobalt. Canin remembered him as a healthy man, but now his Elenite eyes were almost hidden by wrinkles and drooping skin. Sweat ran down through more wrinkles on his bald head. Canin reached out and took the man's hand. He felt old strength there, but the hand shook.

"I could never get him to listen. How could a youngster like this succeed?" Cobalt remarked. He raised his nose. "I smell something."

"As you requested," Wolf said.

"Good." Cobalt had not let go of Canin's hand. "Take my escort down to the pool. They need to clean up before dinner." Cobalt's look was stern. "You remember the way?"

"I do," Canin assured him. Despite being ready to defend his return to Cobalt, the dark look in the older man's eyes gave him pause. He remembered him as a terse and arrogant man. One who liked his days the same and hated any interruptions. By the look of him, he hadn't left the Sanctuary in seasons. Canin's heart beat faster in worry. This man, a descendant of the Mother, held both his life and the lives of Spear and Aurora in his hands.

"I know this place," Crow complained. "I can take them."

"Yes, go with them, Crow," Cobalt agreed. "I have business with Wolf and Lightfoot." He looked to the sky. "Keep them away till the sun has passed a handspan. That should give me enough time." He released Canin's hand and entered the cabin, helped over the threshold by Wolf.

Crow stared at Lightfoot, looking for aid. But Lightfoot couldn't offer any, so he turned away, entering his home and closing the door firmly.

"Come, Brothers and Sisters," Canin called, turning to those milling about in the clearing. "As I remember, the pool is quite deep and refreshing." Putting on a smile, he set out across the clearing. The Maidens fell in right behind him, with the Brothers a few steps behind. After one more look at the closed door of the cabin, Crow brought up the rear.

Canin found the trail with no trouble. Behind him he could hear the whispering of the Maidens. They were all young, and he didn't recognize any of them. He kept his head high and his steps sure. Soon he could hear the flowing water. Running feet from behind made him turn.

"Wait," Crow said, grabbing his arm.

Canin smoothly stepped back, breaking Crow's grip without being obvious. The Maidens and Brothers stopped, too, looking at them: the Maidens with interest, and the Brothers with only slightly veiled anger.

Crow felt their eyes on him. Gesturing angrily, he ordered them, "Go down to the pool."

The Brothers complied without a word, sliding smoothly around the Maidens. The Maidens looked to Canin first. When he nodded, they followed the Brothers.

"Well met again, Brother," Canin said mildly, resting his hand lightly on his knife.

"You are not my Brother," Crow snarled. "You are a renegade who has come crawling back to us. A defier of the Mother." He ran a hand over his close-shorn black hair. He held his fist in front of his mouth, the knuckles going white. "I don't understand why Wolf and Maggie have taken you back. You left us."

"I did," Canin conceded. "I defied the Mother, and I will pay. I have paid."

"Paid," Crow said, anger bubbling over. "What do you know of it? Five died. They all volunteered to look for you. All of them."

Canin bowed his head. The guilt weighed heavily on him. It was his burden. Crow was breathing hard in front of him. "What were their names?"

Crow blinked at him.

"I have a right to know who died because of what I did," Canin insisted. "I have the right to know who I must seek justice for."

"Justice," Crow sneered. "What justice? Are you going to find those men? Kill them? Your time away has made you a fool."

"Maybe, but I will give them the justice they deserve." Canin's voice turned to steel. He projected everything he had learned watching Shatter and Steel lead their soldiers and Talia's Ladies. "What were their names, Crow?"

Crow unconsciously reacted to his tone of command and stood up straighter. "Airlo, Phebee, Haon, Samual, and Cinna. Jessamine was the survivor."

"I knew them all," Canin whispered. "Samual taught me to pick locks. Haon taught me to swim. Cinna was my first guide around the thorns." He shook his head. Airlo and Phebee had been Brenna's friends. "Jessamine . . . ." He looked at Crow. "We will get justice for them."

"You think that will bring them back? Take away the terrors that haunt Jessamine every night?" Crow mocked.

"No. But it is the only thing I can do."

"You're a fool."

"Yes, I am. A determined fool." Canin held Crow's eyes with a hard gaze. "I served with a woman who was obsessed with justice. It is a dangerous pursuit. If you aren't brave enough." Canin broke Crow's stare, then turned and followed the others toward the pool. He knew it was foolish to turn his back on Crow, but he walked tall and steady anyway. When Crow didn't put an arrow in his back, Canin relaxed his grip on his knife. Soon, he heard splashing from around the bend in the trail, and quickened his pace.

Chapter 19
Stories Around a Fire

When they returned from the bathing pool, a table had been moved into the clearing by the Treetower. With ill grace, Lightfoot served each of them a small portion of the fragrant chicken stew, then sat down.

Cobalt raised his arms.

"Rebuild what is broken.

"Make it stronger.

"Together we will stand firm.

"Against all who would break us."

"Mother guide us," the others intoned.

Canin felt close to tears. Hearing those words spoken again, after so long away, brought a flood of emotions. Despite the dark eyes on him and the suspicion he felt from all around the table, he felt at home again. Wolf nudged him.

Leaving the tears in his eyes, Canin addressed the group. "Thank you all for making this journey. I hope this will not be the last meal I have with my Brothers and Sisters of the forest."

Cobalt raised his cup in salute but did not say anything. Crow only glared, and began to eat.

"I hope so, too, Brother," one of the Maidens spoke up. She ran a hand through her newly shorn pale hair. "Maggie has told us stories of you. I'm glad to meet you."

Canin smiled and thanked her. Red Miriam had been the first to talk to him at the pool, and had demanded he help her cut her hair like Spear's. Somehow it was already spreading. Canin wondered how Spear would react to these young women imitating her.

"Why are you named Red, when you have pale hair?" Canin asked, ignoring the dark looks from Crow and the other Brothers.

"She makes all her foes bleed," Wolf answered for her. He reached across the table. "She is my eldest," he said with pride. Miriam glowed. "And the best Maiden to walk the forest since maybe Victoria, granddaughter of Aconite."

"I am nowhere close to her," Miriam said with a modest nod of her head. Then her mouth went up in a teasing smile. "But thank you, Papa. Even if you don't remember my mother's name."

"It was a long time ago that Poppy and I were together," Wolf said, smiling triumphantly when he remembered the name. "She's a weaver in the Lakelands. She sent Red here when she came of age and the boys started harassing her. She knew I would teach her how to defend herself."

"And you did," Red Miriam agreed.

"Too well," one of the Brothers — a very handsome fellow — said lightly, glancing at her.

Miriam smiled at him, and Wolf glared.

The handsome Thorn Brother had finished his portion of stew and was reaching for the pot, but Canin was quicker. He ladled out a larger portion to the surprised Brother.

"Thank you," he said grudgingly.

"You're welcome, Brother," Canin said, already filling the bowl of another Brother. Then he filled the Maidens' bowls, to their smiles and thanks.

Cobalt demurred. "None for me. I love this stew, but it does not love me," he said with regret.

"I made a small pot with less spice for Bitter," Wolf said. "I'll get you some." He rose to do so.

Cobalt waved him back down "No. It wouldn't be the same." Cobalt glanced at Lightfoot. "Did you take dinner to your father?"

"I will later," he said sullenly.

"No," Cobalt tutted. "He must have some while it is fresh."

Lightfoot motioned at one of the Maidens. "Polly, take some up to my father."

"No, stay here," Cobalt contradicted, as the woman was rising. "You should take it up to him," he told Lightfoot. "You owe your father an apology, too."

At first, Lightfoot looked like he was going to refuse, but eventually he stood and trudged into the cabin. He came back out with a bowl on a tray.

"And tell your father you will be returning to the Sanctuary with me in the morning," Cobalt called out as Lightfoot was climbing the ramp. Lightfoot nodded.

"Crow." Cobalt turned to the Brother. "You will stay with these two fine men. Four more Thorn Brothers will be arriving by sunset tomorrow."

Wolf raised his eye. "I was not told of this. Is there a threat?"

"The Mother is nervous," Cobalt admitted. "We are to increase the force at each of the Treetowers. Uneasy rumors are coming from both Realms. The clans are gathering power. The Fairies are silent. She feels a storm is close. I want warning when it strikes."

Canin frowned. He had some information about that, but he wasn't sure yet how best to reveal it. He was still unsure of Cobalt. He would talk to Wolf in private.

"The rest of you will escort me back to the Sanctuary. There, Canin will go before the Mother and answer for what he has done." Cobalt's eyes focused on Canin.

"I understand," Canin said, bowing his head. "I have caused much suffering. I must make up for it."

"You shall," Cobalt agreed. "But you have also brought much back to us. Wolf tells me your wife is a powerful warrior. I can see she has already begun to effect some of us." He frowned at Miriam. "But she's a Fairy. There haven't been Fairies living here in numbers since Aieren was a child." He shook his head. Canin stole a glace up at the Treetower, thinking of Bitter's long pined-for wife. "Both of you will have to prove you are worthy of our trust."

"I understand, and I'm sure Spear does, too." Canin looked over the faces around the table. "We were led here. This is a place of safety for our daughter. I feel it deep down within me. Both of us are broken. We need a place to heal."

"We rebuild what is broken," Wolf stated.

"Yes, we do," Cobalt conceded with a frown. "But only the Mother can say if you two are worth the risk."

The last of a pitcher of highly watered wine was passed to Canin. He shook his head and passed it to the third Thorn Maiden, River, an Elenite with black hair and a careful smile.

"How did you get your name?" Canin asked. "Spear will bother you about it," he explained quickly. "She seems interested in our names."

River smiled just a little more. "It's in tribute to my mother. When I was a baby, she tried to cross the Diamond River. The current took us. Wolf," she glanced up at the Treetower, "fished me out. Other Brothers tried to save my mother, but . . . ." She looked down.

"I'm sorry," Canin said, feeling ashamed. "I've forgotten my manners. So long away. Forgive me."

"No," River said with a shake of her head. "I honor her sacrifice and strive to help other women like her. It is good to remember her. Or at least the stories I'm told."

"I can dimly remember when that happened," Canin said. He also remembered the whispers that had said the woman was fleeing something terrible. After all Min had told him of the Blood Cult, Canin wondered if River's tragic history was part of something larger.

River poured a swallow of wine into her cup and passed the dregs to Miriam. She laughed, theatrically trying to pour out the last drop to the amusement of the others. Crow and the other Thorn Brothers sat around their own fire, though one of them kept glancing at Miriam.

Canin knew he should be sitting with them, speaking to the younger ones and mending his relationships with them. But he just felt more comfortable with the Maidens. After the meal was done, Wolf and Cobalt had climbed to the Treetower to sit with Bitter, while the Maidens had pulled him to their fire and asked him endless questions about Spear. They were amazed that Spear had defeated Maggie with one strike. Maggie was their Prime, and to hear that she had been so handily beaten had amazed and humbled them. Polly kept tugging at her brown braid, and looking at Miriam's short hair.

"She used her Power," Canin tried to explain. "If she hadn't, it wouldn't have been such a quick fight." He wasn't sure, but he thought Spear would be embarrassed to have these women hold her so high above their Prime.

Canin glanced back at the Brothers' fire again. One of them held a wine jug and was looking at Miriam. She was still trying to get the last drop out of hers. Smiling, Canin gestured the handsome Thorn Brother over. Crow frowned, but the young man stood and came to their fire.

"I am sorry, Brother," Canin told him, "but I don't remember your name."

"Jacobella," he replied, sitting in the place Canin had made for him. He passed his jug to Miriam. "It was my mother's name. Tradition says I should be named for my father, but since he was a bastard Fairy rapist, she said, 'Damn tradition!'" He grinned at Canin, then realized who he was speaking to. His Elenite eyes widened. "I am sorry, sir. I . . . ."

Canin waved it away. "No matter. I can say with some certainty that my wife is not your father." He paused, watching the others' reactions. "But, with Fairies, you never know."

Miriam was the first to break the awkward silence with a loud laugh. She passed the jug back to Jacobella, who smiled brightly at her as the others joined in her laughter.

"You took our wine," another Brother complained to Jacobella, sitting down beside Canin.

"I brought it to the ladies," Jacobella corrected.

"I am Trailrunner," the newcomer told Canin, shaking his hand. He was Elenite also, with fair hair and a beard. "Is it true you walked the whole length of the Fairy Realm looking for your father?"

"No," Canin told him. "Just a small portion of it. And I rode for some of that time."

"And did you find him?"

"No," Canin replied. "He was dead. But in the end, I discovered it wasn't finding him that was important, it was my journey."

"Hear, hear," Polly said, slightly tipsy. She passed the wine to Trailrunner, who took it and drank with a smile.

"I don't care who my father was," Jacobella told him. "Who I am is the important thing." He thumped the hilt of his wooden knife.

"I discovered that, too," Canin agreed, and passed the wine on again.

They sat in silence for a while, with most watching the flames, but Canin was studying them. Jacobella's eyes kept going to Miriam, and sometimes she watched him as well. Trailrunner kept his head down, digging in the dirt with a piece of kindling.

Canin was watching River and Polly banter back and forth when he felt someone staring at him. He turned to find Trailrunner looking at him.

"What is it, Setab?" Canin asked quietly.

Startled, the other man did not reply right away. Finally, he drew a deep breath. "How did it feel when you knew?"

"When I knew my father was dead?" Canin guessed.

"Yes," Trailrunner replied. The rest of the group had fallen silent, everyone staring at Canin and Trailrunner.

"Well," Canin started. "Frustrating that I never got to meet him and ask him about my mother. Sad that I would never really know their story."

Trailrunner looked at the ground. His hands clenched.

"Brother," Canin started, wanting to give him sympathy, but Crow suddenly appeared behind them.

"It will be an early day," he noted. "Jacobella, Trailrunner, you will take the first watch. River, Polly, the middle one. Miriam and Canin can take the third."

"But we have to leave in the morning," Miriam protested. "They will get very little sleep. It would be better for your men to take the middle watch. They're staying here."

"Those are my orders," Crow told her. "I am in command here."

"You command your Brothers," Miriam contradicted.

"And I also command you until another Maiden of higher rank appears." He looked around the clearing. "I don't see any. So you will do as I say."

"She's right," Canin said. "We have a long journey, and first watch will allow them to get more rest."

"You have no authority here, renegade," Crow spat.

Canin stood. Over Crow's shoulder, he could see Wolf, Lightfoot, and Cobalt watching. None of them moved to intervene. Lightfoot was smiling.

"Then you have no authority to order me to take a watch," Canin told him.

Crow's eyes narrowed in anger. The two Thorn Brothers stood and moved closer to Crow. Behind him, the Maidens also rose to their feet. Red Miriam stood firmly on Canin's left, the others further back.

"And if you remember, I earned my knife before you. So I am of higher rank," Canin said, his hands hooked casually in his belt.

Crow took a step forward. "You Motherless bastard," he swore.

Canin stood his ground.

"We will take the middle watch," Miriam offered into the tense silence. "We can run faster and longer with less rest. Let the boys sleep. They'll need their energy for all the climbing of the Treetower to bring Bitter his meals." She grinned at Jacobella. "And empty his chamber pot."

Jacobella tried to stay stern, but he began to smile and quickly covered it with his hand. River and Polly laughed openly. Crow's face turned red.

"And what watch will you take?" Canin asked Crow.

With a wordless cry, Crow lunged at Canin. With an economy of motion, Canin slipped around the blow. Crow turned, sliding in the grass. Canin gracefully evaded him again. The young men and women just watched, moving out of the way as Crow tried to hit Canin, who evaded every blow, without ever raising his hands.

"Stand and fight," Crow snarled.

"I have no reason to fight you," Canin told him calmly.

"Stop running!" Crow yelled.

"You can hit him," Wolf called out. "You are a renegade, after all."

"No," Canin said. "I think he needs to hit me." Canin suddenly stopped moving. Crow's fist hit him in the side of the face, snapping his head to the side and bloodying his nose. He stepped back, rubbing the blood away.

Crow stopped, registering the hissing coming from the Maidens and the complete lack of reaction from the Brothers. He looked around the circle. Wolf and Cobalt were standing behind Canin.

"Maggie got three," Canin said, moving his jaw carefully. "She deserved them. You deserved one." He wiped his hands on his shirt. "Try to take more, and you'll see what I've learned while I was away." He brought his hands up in defense. "Brother."

Crow looked around the circle again. He saw open hostility on the Maidens' faces, and only neutral looks on those of the Brothers. He rubbed his knuckles.

"Not worth my time," Crow said, and pushed his way out of the circle.

"You heard him," Wolf spoke up. "Jacobella, Trailrunner, decide who will sit the perch and who will stay below." He looked at the Maidens. "Same for you two. Be ready when the moon is high." He looked at Miriam. "I will sit the perch for third watch. Miriam, stay below with Canin. I expect you to be ready to go at dawn. And that includes breakfast for all of us."

"Yes, Prime," Miriam agreed. She knew they would have a conversation later, in private. She took the other two Maidens off to find their sleeping gear.

"And since you seem to have mastered them," Wolf said to Canin, "you can lead us in the Four Steps."

"Yes, Prime," Canin said with a short bow.

Wolf turned to the Brothers. "Your watch has started," he reminded them. They ran off to take their posts.

Chapter 20
Actions or
Reactions

Cobalt was smiling slightly as he approached to Canin. "Come, I want to talk to you." He led Canin up the Treetower ramp, and together they stood looking out over the Green. Behind them, they could hear Bitter snoring.

"I don't want to wake him," Canin said in a whisper.

"You can't wake Bitter," Cobalt said at a normal volume. "I would have to roll him out of his bed. And put him on a night watch." He shook his head in amusement.

Canin smiled warily and looked at him with expectation. Cobalt folded his hands in front of his chest and Canin took a few deep breaths, waiting, using all his Fairy training to regulate his breathing and emotions.

"Why did you come back?" Cobalt finally asked. Both his voice and his face were stern, but not unyielding. Canin knew that his answer would, if not fully determine, at least strongly effect, his fate.

After another deep breath, he said, "I came back because I have an obligation to the people of the forest I left behind. To my fellow Thorn Brothers, to my Sisters in the Maidens, and to the memory of those who died searching for me, though I didn't know about them when I came. That is a shame I do not know how I can make up for."

Cobalt nodded in agreement.

"I have an obligation to my mother, Lily," Canin continued. He saw one of Cobalt's eyebrows go up at the mention of Lily. "I left her to mourn a daughter. I left Maggie to mourn alone for her sister. I have much to atone for."

"Yes, you do," Cobalt agreed. "You put all of us in danger with your rash actions. You defied the Mother, but you also defied me. I brought Her answer to your request." He thumped his chest. "I may not be directly in charge of the Thorn Brothers, but my brief covers those who break our laws. I've thought long and hard about what your fate should be."

"And what did you decide?" Canin asked, clenching his fists, preparing for the worst.

"But making up for your failings was not the only reason you came back, now was it?" Cobalt asked, looking at him intently and delaying his proclamation of punishment.

"No," Canin admitted, jumping in with hope. "I — we — came here looking for a safe place to raise our daughter. We have been through much sorrow and pain. Escaping from the Blood Cult scarred my wife, both in body and in spirit. We need a place to heal. A place of sanctuary. I took an oath as a Thorn Brother to seek out those in need. Now we are in need."

"Yes, you and your Fairy wife," Cobalt noted, leaning on the railing. The wood squeaked in protest, and Canin feared it might break under his weight.

"I know how you feel about Fairies, sir, and I can assure you. . . ."

Cobalt made a chopping motion and Canin fell silent.

"You know nothing of how I feel," Cobalt said in a harsh, controlled voice. "I've seen loved ones abused, assaulted, and killed by those motherless bastards. The King and the Queen think the war ended after Brine Hill, but the war on our people yet goes on. It never ended."

"We're caught between the hammer and the anvil. We're always between foes. They name us that, when they aren't calling us 'filth' and 'half-breeds,'" Canin agreed, looking at Cobalt with a strong, resolute face.

Cobalt drew a breath to snap at him, then stopped. "And we took their slur and made it a word of honor. At least between us."

Canin smiled, wondering if he was actually getting through to Cobalt.

Out over the trees, the pale light of the moon was growing. Canin saw it reflected in Cobalt's eye — the oblong pupil, the swirl of white and silver — so much like his own. Elenite eyes, eyes Canin saw everywhere in the forest. And — unlike in the Fairy or Human Realms — here they held pride and strength.

Cobalt looked up at the moon. "I was angry. Then the five were killed looking for you. For a long time, I was like Crow, nursing a deep hatred for you. Then, I realized you could not have done anything else. You were young and hurt. She wanted you to stay and grow, but I wonder. Did She tell you that, knowing you would leave anyway? All of this," he took in all of the forest with his gesture, "may have been the way she wanted it to happen."

Canin was amazed. He just stared at Cobalt for a moment, absorbing the words.

"If I hadn't gone, I would never have found Spear, and never had my daughter." Pain twisted Canin's words. "And those others would not have died."

"Yes, those others," Cobalt said, his voice becoming harsher. "Were they fated to die? And Jessamine. Traumatized, brutalized. Was that her fate, too?"

"I certainly hope not," Canin remarked, tears in his eyes. "I can barely remember their faces, but I know I caused their suffering. I did not mean to. Believe me, Cobalt: I never wanted any of this to happen."

"Maybe we aren't meant to understand," Cobalt said with some sympathy. "We do not have the ability to see the whole, as a spinner cannot see the whole shirt from just one thread."

"Is that all we are to Her? Threads?"

"Your words make me doubt you," Cobalt warned.

"I'm sorry. I knew I caused suffering, but I never realized it went so far."

"None of us ever do." Cobalt took a breath. "Remember the story of Her striding into Her stronghold after a battle, full of confidence because they had beaten off another attack? How they had killed many of the enemy? 'They will be a long time returning,' She crowed. And then She saw the dead, and the maimed, and all those who were simply exhausted from the endless fighting. All of them lay before Her. All of them dedicated to Her service, the wounded trying to stand on single legs and raising weapons with single arms. 'Like cursed lightning it me hit,' She said. 'I had done this. I had killed and maimed my people. They followed me, and I led them to their deaths.' That was the day She decided it was better to surrender and spare their suffering rather than fight on."

"I always heard that story as an example of Her great compassion for Her people," Canin said, half to himself. "Now I see that She saw the suffering She had brought, and took action to stop it."

"There are some things we need to fight for," Cobalt said. "And there are other things we must live with."

"But who says what things we must let pass, and what we must fight?"

"She does," Cobalt said simply.

"I don't understand. I've seen how the quest for justice can pervert a person, but. . . ." Canin stopped.

"It is not our way," Cobalt said firmly. "Yes," he said, catching Canin's surprised look. "Crow told me of your desire to get justice for those killed. It is not our way," he repeated.

"Maybe it should be," Canin countered. "Maybe we should stop the blow before it lands, instead of binding the wound after."

"Others have suggested that. I sympathize with your feelings, but we cannot risk our delicate balance here," Cobalt lectured. "The clans and the King see us as a minor annoyance. A convenient place to send their unwanted. Those fathers and husbands we kill, they write off as fools for not letting a wayward woman go. But if we did more, attacked in force. . . ." He shook his head. "They might consider us a threat. They might join together against us, and despite all we have here, we would not survive that."

"But," Canin started, but Cobalt held up his hand, stopping him.

"Not all think it is so dire," he noted. "More I cannot say just now. But I think things are moving, and you might be at the center of them. Others of the Children have hinted so."

Canin came up short at the implication. Was there more to his path than simply finding a place of safety for Aurora? More than getting her out of that house of blood and terror? More than saving Spear from herself?

"Not that I am not angry," Cobalt continued. "When Maggie found us and told us of the change in plans and said that Wolf had already brought you here, I was furious. Then I saw Crow's grin, and heard him stress — again — how untrustworthy you were, and how allowing you back in would poison us. He was practically crowing." Cobalt smiled just a bit at his pun. "And I began to think. As Maggie argued passionately for both of you, all these thoughts crowded into my head. All these questions. I trust Wolf. Trust his judgment. I spoke for his election to Prime over older, more experienced men. And Maggie did, too. I watched Aieren. You can never see where she stands, but I know she trusts Wolf and Maggie." He smiled again, wider. "And when Crow began to yell, I knew Maggie had won. With a simple motion, Aieren silenced the debate. 'Well, then, that is the way it must be,' she said. Then she sent us here and continued on." He shrugged at Canin's look. "And the whole way, Crow bent my ear. I didn't make up my mind till I saw Lightfoot and the look of triumph on his face. He's always pushing Crow forward. And then Wolf told me what Lightfoot commanded you to do.

"Now, Lightfoot is a great spinner, and a good leader of his men, but he lacks other qualities. And this becomes apparent in situations like this. And I saw how you handled yourself. Unlike the young man I remembered, you were humble, but strong. Respectful, but you knew what was right. You've grown, son. Excuse me, Brother. I cannot imagine the things you and your wife went through."

"Thank you," Canin said sincerely. He took the older man's hand. "I will be worthy of your trust."

"Yes, you will be," Cobalt agreed. "I trust Wolf and Maggie, but you still have to stand before the Mother. Her voice will be the one that decides." His gaze became more of a glare. "And if you betray me, or any of our Brothers and Sisters, I will take you to the Traitor's Pool myself."

"I understand," Canin said, bowing his head. "I will not betray you or the forest. I've come through too much, learned too much, to throw away what we have here."

"See that you don't," Cobalt commanded.

The silence stretched. Canin felt cautious hope. Despite Cobalt's antagonism, he would keep an open mind.

"What about Spear?" Canin asked.

"The Fairy," Cobalt said with a twist of his mouth. "She will be watched, too. And I cannot speak for all, but I doubt she will have a warm welcome." Then, with a begrudging shrug, he went on. "She is a trained warrior. If she is everything Maggie and the others think she is, then she will be a great asset. Her talk with Aieren will go well, and we will meet her at the Sanctuary."

'And if something goes wrong,' Canin thought, 'a runner will come in the night. And all our fates will be sealed.'

"Go," Cobalt urged. "It will be an early day."

Canin knew he was being dismissed. With a nod of his head, he turned and walked down the ramp. Wolf was waiting for him at the bottom.

"I heard some of what you said," Wolf said as he walked beside Canin. "I understand your feelings, but I do not know if it is the right time."

"We'll have to take action soon," Canin told him. "It's better to act first, than to wait for your enemy to force you to react." Wolf looked at him, raising his eyes in surprise. "There are things I haven't told you yet." He took a deep breath. "Things that may shed new light on what's happening with the King and the clans."

"And you want to speak to me about them first."

Canin nodded.

"Well, let's find a place where we can talk then."

Chapter 21
More Stories

They found a place close to where the Maidens were sleeping. Red Miriam raised her head when they walked by, but Wolf waved her back to sleep. By the look on her face, Canin knew he would be questioned when they went on watch later. He and Wolf sat close, knees touching. Trailrunner would pass nearby on his circuits around the clearing, but always stayed out of earshot.

"You know what happened after I left," Canin started. "I couldn't return. I felt so much shame."

Wolf wanted to disagree, but Canin didn't notice; he was lost in his own memories.

"So I went in search of my mother. Lily had always told me where she was, so her family wasn't hard to find. She was dead, and my aunt was living in her house. I found her letters and keepsakes of my father. They convinced me he wasn't a rapist, and they had truly been in love. So, I went in search of him. It took me a long time to gather all the clues that led me into the Fairy Realm. It was taxing beyond anything I'd ever done before. Being an Elenite among the Humans is hard enough." Wolf nodded in understanding. "But among the Fairies, it was almost impossible." Canin suppressed a laugh. "It's a good thing most of them are arrogant and just looked right through me. They assumed I was a servant, or some Fairy's toy."

"You are very handsome," Wolf noted.

Canin nodded in good humor. "I eventually found the castle my father had trained in. She must have guided me, because I met a group of Fairies there, led by a high-born lady and her Leather-wing soldier escorts. All women. They took me in. Their captain knew the company my father had served in, and was able to speak to a former member, who was now the lord of the castle. She discovered that my father was dead, and confirmed that he had truly loved my mother. The lady and her company were on their own journey, and I had been commanded to leave the Realm by the lord, so we parted, and I set my path back to Elen."

"Wait," Wolf interrupted. "You just happened to meet a high-born Fairy lady? An Iridescent, I assume. And they took you in. Like a lost puppy. And helped you. And then you left them. This company of beautiful Fairy women?" He chided Canin. "Son, I did not teach you well enough." He sounded very disbelieving of the whole thing.

"Very much like a lost puppy," Canin confirmed with a smile. He had definitely felt that way under Steel's gaze. "I had to leave them. She never told me much then, but they were traveling in secret, protecting something. I would come to understand more later. And I felt that I had to go off and find my own way, now that I knew the truth about my father."

"So, 'she' is Spear?"

"Yes," Canin lied, forging ahead. "We had a connection. I didn't understand it then. Why would she take up with me? A broken, lost Elenite? But she did. She did."

"We can never understand what brings two people together," Wolf said in his most fatherly voice. "I never understood any of it. I just knew." He tilted his head. "Or she made me understand."

Canin smiled, but bowed his head. "I left. Maybe I should have stayed. Been braver. Been more.... Maybe we would have had more time."

"You'll have plenty of time now," Wolf told him. "You're together again."

"Yes," Canin agreed, low, thinking of Min. "We will." He raised his head, looking into Wolf's eyes. "But then, I wandered, looking for a place to belong."

"You should have come home," Wolf scolded. "We were waiting for you."

"I see that now, but I didn't then. I fell in with some very evil people. Elenites and Humans who hated who they were. Wingless

Fairies who used foul arts to give themselves power. Maggie told me others like them have come to the forest, recruiting our youth into the Lions of the Sword. Whatever they've told you, they are foul in all ways. Nothing is beyond them. They use blood to gain Fairy-like power. And they'll take that blood from anyone, including children."

Wolf narrowed his eyes. "I have always had my suspicions about those men. They always smell."

"That's the blood," Canin explained. "They think it gives them power. It does for the wingless ones, but the Elenites." He shrugged. "It varies. A few gain power, but the others, it just rots."

"How could you have been drawn into such a group?" Wolf asked, disappointment in his voice. "I knew you were hurt, but so hurt that you'd join this. . . ?" He lost the words.

"They didn't reveal who they truly were at first. And I had other plans." Canin smiled. "I knew Spear and the other Fairies were somehow wrapped up with this Blood Cult. If I waited, and kept my head down, I knew I would see her again."

"You joined this foul cult," Wolf said, shocked, "just on the hope that your lost love would appear? You're crazy! Moon-touched." He barked a quick laugh. Trailrunner, who was close, turned at the sound, but Wolf waved him on, and turned back to Canin. "What did she do? Break down the door of a secret house and announce she was there to rescue you?" He shook his head at the absurdity of it all.

"Yes, she did," Canin confirmed with a grin, watching his reaction. "But I was waiting for her. After I shot the man who had been guarding me. Then they burned the whole place to the ground."

"Motherless," Wolf swore after a moment. "You're telling the truth," he marveled. "You are crazy. All of this is crazy."

'And most of it's true,' Canin thought. He was beginning to enjoy shocking the usually unflappable Wolf. "This Blood Cult and its cruel leader were allies of the King. Or maybe they were using him, and he was too dim to realize it. But this high-born Iridescent's company had been attacked by members of the Lions, and half had been killed. Including the lady's newborn daughter."

"Mother mercy," Wolf breathed. His eyes drifted to where Miriam was sleeping. "And this was part of her quest for justice?" Canin nodded. "She believed the King gave the orders?" Canin nodded again. "Then why can't we see the smoke from here? The Fairies should be taking apart the King's castle stone by stone."

"She was a renegade — exiled — and couldn't get help from the Queen's court. They were going it alone." Canin struggled to explain. It didn't help that he knew very few of the details. "I was reunited with Spear, and pulled into their plan to attack the King. On the day his newborn daughter was being presented to the Realm. She saw it as a fair trade: his daughter's life for hers."

The look of shock and betrayal on Wolf's face made Canin lower his eyes. "How could you?" Wolf asked, anger coloring his voice. "How could you? An innocent. His actions don't matter; she was innocent!"

"I didn't have a choice," Canin snapped. "She had already killed one of her own for being coerced into betraying her. Another killed herself because of the trauma of her injuries. And those were Fairies who had been with her for a long time, and who she had sworn to protect. What would she have done to me if I refused? I wasn't given a choice. I was never even asked."

"There is always a choice," Wolf said quietly. "Even if it means death. There is always a choice."

"I needed to protect Spear." Canin tried to explain, close to tears. "She was close to giving birth. I saw no path that didn't lead to tragedy. I did the best I could."

Wolf started to berate him again, but stopped. "Would I do the same thing?" he asked, low and almost to himself. "With the lives of my love and our child in the balance? I don't know." He took a deep breath. "I'm sorry you had to make those decisions."

Canin continued, "Since the baby was close, we were assigned to hold the escape route." He smiled. "There was never any thought that she would stay behind."

"That I can understand," Wolf told him.

"I don't know what happened with the King, but it must have gone badly. We were attacked and overwhelmed. Captured." Canin lowered his eyes. He did not want to face Wolf as he lied. He hoped the story he and Spear had formulated would be enough to keep Wolf from examining him too closely. "She gave birth in a cell. They took Aurora. Bled her. One of my guards made a mistake, and I got loose and freed them. Spear lost her wings using their horrible Blood Ring." He took a deep breath. "And then we came here."

Wolf was silent. "That explains the recent activities of the King and the clans, but not the silence from the Fairies. They closed their borders, and have let nothing in or out since."

"I think there's a power struggle going on," Canin said slowly. "I only overheard a little, but the more moderate supporters of the Queen are fighting the hateful ones. Who happen to be led by the Queen's sisters."

Wolf whistled. "Civil war. None of this is good. We'll be caught in the middle."

"Like Elen is," Canin agreed. "The people there simply want to live, but are trapped between two stones."

"We just want to be left alone, to protect those who cannot protect themselves. I've always been suspicious of those Lion bastards, but now I know who they are. I must bring this to the full council of the Children." Wolf got up, full of energy and ready to run.

Canin yawned.

"Sleep," Wolf urged. "I'll wake you for your watch. Mother guard your sleep," he said, rising.

"And yours," Canin replied. He rolled himself into his blanket. The stress of the day overrode his fear for Spear and he drifted off quickly. His dreams were full of wings, over and around him. Holding him, and buzzing by his head. He settled into their embrace and slept soundly till Miriam woke him for their watch.

Chapter 22
Sisters and Brothers of the Forest

Heron finally fell asleep.

She had been asking Spear questions — and telling her about the forest, its people, and some of its history — since Canin and Wolf had left.

Spear wanted to be annoyed, and a small part of her was, but she knew Heron was doing it to keep her attention away from the coming morning. Even though she hadn't answered most of the young woman's questions, her constant flow of them had been enough to keep the darkness at bay. Spear almost felt like she was back on the road with her Sisters, sitting around a fire and listening to Min and Raven banter about who had had the most bed partners, while Flora looked on in a mix of fascination and discomfort.

Aurora started to cry after Canin left. She wouldn't nurse, and her wrappings seemed clean. Frustrated, Spear first rocked her while sitting, then walked her around the clearing. She was still crying when Heron returned from the Treetower with Aurora's sleeping box and Spear's bedding. Spear was turning in small circles, angry and scared.

Heron approached her carefully. "Let me hold her for a bit?" she asked.

"She won't stop crying," Spear replied. "She won't nurse, and she's clean. I don't understand." Spear walked back to the tree, kicked at a stone, and almost slipped in the grass.

Heron followed, keeping her voice calm. "Alexander was like that. He would cry for nothing. Just to cry. It almost drove Lily crazy. Sing to her," she suggested, sitting down beside Spear's feet. "That was the only thing that would calm him."

"I can't sing," Spear said. She held Aurora at arm's length and glared at her. "What do you want?" she demanded. "He's gone away. He'll be back. Soon. He'll be back. What do you want?!" Her voice was getting louder. Aurora just kept crying.

Heron wanted to take the baby from her, but good sense stopped her. "You can sing," Heron told Spear over the rising cries. "I've heard you. You have a beautiful voice. You're just too frustrated."

Spear shook her head and pulled Aurora back to her chest.

Heron decided to try something else. "Spear," she said in her best imitation of Maggie's commands. "Let me hold her." She held out her hands expectantly.

Spear blinked and passed the baby down to Heron. She tried to pull her back, but Heron was already cradling the crying infant.

"There, Aurora," Heron said in a low voice. "I know, your father isn't here. He'll be back. My father flew away long ago. He never came back. But yours will. He loves you." She began to sing in a low voice, sweet, but untrained.

"Baby, the Mother is here.
"Quiet, the darkness is near.
"The Mother will shield you.
"The Mother will protect you.
"But hush little one, the storm is near.
"Hush little one, the lightning is near.
"Baby, the Mother is here.
"She wraps you in Her arms.
"She holds in you in Her wings.
"Hush little one, you're safe.
"Hush little one, your mother needs to rest."

As the words of the song tumbled out of Heron, Spear watched Aurora's eyes begin to open, as her crying lessened. Heron started over, and Aurora's hand came loose from her wrappings and reached out to touch the singing woman's face. Spear felt a moment of jealousy, but as Aurora finally stopped crying, she sighed with relief and sat down.

Heron glanced over at Spear. She smiled, a smile of sisterly bonds and happiness.

"Thank you," Spear whispered.

Heron kept singing, as Aurora began to smile and burble along with her. She gestured with her chin to one of the baskets of provisions. "Mother's Milk," she said between verses. "There's more in there."

Spear went to the basket and, after rooting around, found one of the bottles. The liquid had settled and was a pale, almost blue color.

"Give it a shake," Heron told her.

Confused, but willing to go along, Spear gave it a quick shake, and the liquid turned bright white again. In Spear's Sight, it still glowed slightly blue. Shrugging at the strangeness of this forest, Spear warmed the Mother's Milk and went back to Heron.

"I'll feed her," Heron said, reaching for the bottle. "She'll cry if I let her go now."

"She's my child," Spear told the Maiden, her jealousy and fear springing back to life. What if Aurora never wanted her to hold her again? What if she only wanted this woman to sing to her and rock her?

"We're here to help," Heron assured Spear, low and calm. "You've been caring for her alone. Allow us to help you. This is what the forest is for. To help those in need. That's what the Mother commands us to do." She held out her hand for the bottle, not demanding, but just reaching.

"My arms are getting tired," Spear conceded, giving her the bottle.

Aurora eagerly took the nipple and began to nurse. Spear sat down across from Heron. "What if she likes that better than mine?" Spear worried.

"She won't. This doesn't replace your milk. It's for when you can't make enough, or when you want Canin to feed her." Heron smiled.

"It allows him to bond with her like you do. It doesn't replace you. It helps you." Her face darkened. "She's lucky. Many never have their real mother's milk. This is all they have." She bent down and kissed Aurora's forehead. "I will guide you. I will protect you," she whispered.

An understanding of what Heron and the rest of the people of the forest offered, beyond Spear's ability to articulate, grew within her. She relaxed. "Thank you," Spear said. "I've been alone. And I've been through so much."

"You're welcome," Heron said.

After Aurora finished eating, they washed her and changed her wrappings. They shared smiles, and Heron showed Spear the best way to wash Aurora without making her cry.

'Sister,' Spear thought.

"We must get you more wrappings," Heron said. "Lightfoot makes the best, and they're so soft and strong. He knows their quality and charges mightily for it, but. . . ." She got a sly smile. "He and his spinners always need things. Perhaps you could trade, or your knowledge of the Fairy Realm might be useful to him for something."

Aurora's eyes were closing, and Heron urged Spear to put her in her box. "She'll sleep better now." Spear knew she was right, but she still wanted to hold the baby more. But Aurora began to fuss, and Spear quickly laid her in the bed of blankets. Contented, Aurora closed her eyes and went to sleep.

Sighing with relief, Spear settled back down against the tree.

"See?" Heron said with triumph. "Together we can keep her safe. And quiet."

Just then, noise arose across the clearing. Spear's sword leapt into her hand and she jumped to her feet. Heron stumbled, but recovered quickly to rise and stand beside Spear.

Stonefoot and Granite emerged from the woods, speaking loudly.

"Quiet," Heron snapped.

Seeing first Heron and then Spear, sword in hand, brought Granite up short. Stonefoot had described Spear to him, but he wasn't ready for a tall Fairy soldier, ready sword in hand, facing him down across the grass. His hand went to his own sword.

"If you wake her," Spear growled.

"We just got her to sleep," Heron explained, walking across the clearing. She motioned Spear to stay. "Where's Sadie?" she asked, looking the newcomers over.

Granite didn't relax till Heron was right in front of him. She stood, arms folded, glaring at him till he removed his hand from his hilt.

"She stayed with Sam. Said something about not leaving him alone." He grinned. "We did see some lights in the distance, but she just wants to try her wiles on him. Not that it will work." He started forward, but Heron stopped him.

"I thought she wanted me here?" he asked, annoyed.

"She did," Heron said. "But then you came thundering in here, yelling, and almost woke the baby. She's been crying ever since Canin left," Heron said in an aside to Stonefoot. "We just got her to quiet down. And you will not disturb her." She poked him in the chest.

"I'm sorry," he said. "But how was I to know the baby was sleeping?"

"She's a baby," Stonefoot snapped. "Of course she'll be asleep. That's all babies do, eat and sleep."

Facing the annoyance of these two strong women, Granite stepped back, raising his arms. "I surrender. I'll be good. And quiet. I swear."

"Good," Heron said, before pulling him forward. "Now, come and meet Spear and Aurora."

Smiling, Granite walked up to Spear. He took in her ready stance and obvious strength. He also noticed her damaged wings. Unconsciously, he touched his own scar in understanding, then held out his hand.

"Greetings," he said low. "I'm glad you didn't shoot me that first time."

Spear transferred her sword to her other hand and took his in a warrior's grip. "I hope I won't be sorry either."

Wincing in admiration at the strength of her grip, Granite nodded and then looked down. "Is that her?"

"It is," Spear told him. "My daughter. Aurora."

"It's an honor, Spear, Aurora." He knelt. He wanted to touch her, but resisted the urge. "I've been on the borders for a while." He looked up at Spear. "I'm sorry if I startled you."

Nodding to him in acknowledgment and appreciation of his apology, Spear put her sword away and sat back down. Granite knelt, not knowing what to do till Stonefoot pulled him to his feet and led him away, pushing food into his hands.

"Thank you," he said and began to chew on a piece of dried meat. "Any wine?"

Stonefoot smiled and shared a glance with Heron. "No," she replied.

Granite, deciding he was never going to understand any of this, shrugged and sat down and ate.

Heron sat back down by Spear and started talking again.

"No," Spear said, holding up her hands. "Please. I know what you're doing, and I appreciate it. But please, no more questions. Let's just sit." Heron nodded and fed the fire keeping back the night.

Stonefoot ate a little with Granite, then got her bedroll and sat down beside Heron. "Tired," she muttered, laying down. "Wake me before dawn." Then she was asleep.

Heron pulled the blanket higher up on Stonefoot's shoulders and rested her hand there. Stonefoot grunted and shifted. Heron took her hand away, but Stonefoot grunted again, and Heron put it back. With a contented sigh, Stonefoot settled back down.

Spear took in Heron's slight smile and body language.

"Are relationships between women frowned on or prohibited?" Spear asked after a while.

"No," Heron said wistfully. "As long as both agree, any relationship is accepted." She looked down at Stonefoot. "But those who come here, those who weren't born in the forest, bring with them the beliefs of Father Church. The priests tell them the only proper relationship is between a man and a woman. Anything else — even any thought of anything thing else — is prohibited." Heron pushed back the strands of her brown hair that had escaped from her braid to keep them out of her face. "Lily thinks that when women love each other, it takes men out of the circle and loosens their control on us. And the Priests of the Father want control above all else. But," she looked down at Stonefoot again, "it would be . . . tolerated. You know how men are, with their fantasies and cruel jokes. 'She'll grow out of it. She just needs the right man.'" Her face twisted. "'I'll show her,'" she imitated harshly.

Spear sensed a hidden pain, maybe not the girl's own, but still sharp and deep. She put her hand on Heron's shoulder. "Fairies hold no such beliefs, but I understand. The minds of our men are the same."

Heron smiled in thanks. "Despite being in this accepting place, their beliefs remain strong. And they pass them down. Teach them to their children."

"Then we must teach them the proper way," Spear said. "Pleasure and love are good. It doesn't matter where or who it comes from."

"I try," Heron said quietly. "And it's worse for the men," she said with a glance at Granite. "That is prohibited. On pain of mockery, and the repudiation of your family. Exile. Torture, and even death." She shook her head. "'You must not plant your seed in unfertile land,'" she imitated again. "The clans are obsessed with having children. The more the better. 'More to fight the Fairy hordes,' they say." Horrified by what she'd just said, she looked at Spear.

"We aren't hordes," she said in mock irritation. "We're more like flocks," she said with a smile that quickly dropped from her face. "That's how the Humans almost won at Brine Hill. They over-whelmed us with numbers. Threw the flower of their youth into our swords and tried to bury us in bodies."

"It's the Father Church that calls for all men to have sons. Any man who doesn't have at least two betrays the whole Realm and the Father himself." Heron glared off into the dark.

"Then why do you have so many abandoned babies?" Spear asked. "If they want children, why not keep them all?"

"Because they're the wrong kinds of babies," Heron informed her. "Girls, and Elenites, and those born of the wrong fathers."

"I don't understand," Spear said. She gripped the side of Aurora's box. "Why would you abandon your children?"

"I don't know," Heron said honestly. "I do not know. I could never give up something I carried under my heart for so long. Even if her eyes were the wrong shape. I would run. Bring her somewhere safe."

"Here," Spear said. She looked up at the stars. A tear ran down her face. 'I am sorry. Forgive me,' she begged in her mind. 'Mother of Waves, forgive me, and thank you for giving me another chance.'

Heron saw the tear and began to say something, but Spear re-turned her gaze to the Maiden.

"So, he?" She gestured at Granite.

"No." Heron giggled. "He loves both men and women. I guess he's more like you. Pleasure is pleasure, and love is love, as you say. I don't know how he does it. They call him ugly, but he never sleeps alone unless he wants to."

"Big or long?" Spear asked.

"Skillfully used," Heron replied without thinking, but then she turned red. "Or so I'm told."

Spear smiled. "No shame, Sister," she told her. "No shame at all." She glanced down at Stonefoot. "It's not my favorite thing, but I could show her, get her more comfortable with herself. More comfortable with the best ways."

Heron's eyes got wide. "I don't think. . . . She's not. . . . I'm not. . . .," she stuttered. Finally, she dropped her eyes. "Maybe one day, when her mother is gone."

"I'm here," Spear told her, patting her on the leg. "But you shouldn't wait that long. You don't want to regret things not said." Her voice dropped. "Things not done."

Heron got up. "I'll go and check the perimeter, and see if Maggie's returning yet." She moved quickly off into the woods. Granite watched her go with a strange look, then turned back to Spear.

"Is she going to stand watch?" he asked.

"You can go to sleep," Spear told him. "I won't be able to rest."

"You don't want to talk," he surmised. After a few moments, he stood. He waited patiently till Spear glanced in his direction. "I do have some questions for you, though."

"In the morning," Spear told him. "I need to meditate. That's the closest I'll get to sleep tonight."

Granite shrugged and laid down by the fire. He was snoring in a few breaths.

Spear smiled. 'They're true soldiers,' she thought. 'Able to sleep whenever the opportunity arises.' She glanced down at Aurora. The baby glowed with life in her Sight.

"Goddess," she asked. "Please guide me. Guide us. Don't let me be a fool before these Children. Let them see my true spirit. Aurora needs someplace to grow up safely. We don't have anywhere else to go."

The Goddess' only response came via the hoot of an owl and the brush of leaves as Heron walked around the clearing.

Chapter 23
Watching Stars Fall

Heron finally walked off what she needed to and returned to the fire. She glanced at Spear and then rolled herself into a blanket beside Stonefoot. After listening to their breathing even out, Spear used her Power to pull another blanket over and covered both of them with it before turning back to watching the sky. At least three stars had fallen since Granite had gone to sleep.

"Is that my fallen Sisters Returning?" she asked the darkness.

Time passed. Spear returned her eyes to the ground when she heard movement. Maggie ran into the clearing. She scanned, counting. Spear poked the embers of the fire and sent up a little more light. Maggie walked over carefully and quietly.

"Where's Sadie?" she asked.

"Stayed with Sam, or so Stonefoot said," Spear told her.

"That girl needs to learn how to listen," Maggie said sourly. She threw another stick into the fire. "You should sleep," Maggie told her. "It'll be light soon. They stopped a few miles back. Should be here not long after dawn. I came ahead to make sure you were okay."

"Worried that I had fled?" Spear said. "I wouldn't do that, Captain."

Maggie sighed. "If I ordered you to stop calling me that, would you?"

"I've been a soldier all my life. That's what I've always called my leader. It's a habit." She sat up straighter. "If I must, Cap. . . ." She smiled. "I will try harder."

"No," Maggie said, knowing she couldn't win. "No matter. Call me what you will. Just follow my orders."

"I will." Spear's eyes drifted up to the sky again. Maggie followed them to another falling star.

"You should sleep," Maggie suggested.

"I cannot," Spear said, not taking her eyes from the sky. "I meditate. It relaxes me, as much as anything can. Gold taught me, and I try to follow her teachings. I will be rested when the Children arrive."

Maggie knew she could press her no harder. "I will sit with you then."

Spear nodded, never taking her eyes from the stars.

Aurora's cries greeted the sun, pulling the Maidens rudely out of sleep. Heron sat up, puzzled by the blanket on her shoulders that she didn't remember pulling on. She looked down at Stonefoot, who was also blinking in the new light.

"Up!" Maggie called. She stood by the embers of the fire. "Aieren and the others will be here soon. Granite! Get your lazy feet moving. There should be enough water for porridge with the supplies. Heron, go gather more wood. Stonefoot." She aimed a kick at the still prone woman. "Get up and down the path. See where they are." She turned to Spear. "And you." She gestured at Spear, who was pulling Aurora out of her box. "Feed her."

"Yes, Captain," Spear agreed, unbuttoning her shirt.

Granite, startled by the brazen Fairy, watched with wide eyes, till Maggie hit him with a thrown piece of kindling.

"Never seen a woman nurse?" She fixed him with a steel eye. "And you never will again if you don't get breakfast going." She turned. "I gave you all orders. Get moving!"

Stonefoot grabbed her weapons and was off. Heron waved at Spear before darting away on her own task.

"Pardon, ma'am," Granite said to Spear with a wink, as he hauled a pot over to the fire. He poured dry porridge out of a bag and added water. He kept glancing back at Spear. She caught him looking and waved his eyes back to his task.

"If that porridge burns," Maggie snapped, leaving the threat unspoken.

"Yes, Ma'am," he said meekly, returning to his task properly chastised, making breakfast for them all.

Spear sat with her back to the tree. Aurora lay in her arms, fed and changed. She watched everyone go by with wide eyes and a smile. For once, she was quiet. Spear thanked the Goddess for that. Everyone else was on edge. Multiple people had brought her bowls of porridge for breakfast, despite her assertion that she could not eat. Finally, she snapped at Stonefoot, "I can't eat now! Go away!" Spear regretted the words immediately as the young woman looked down on her with hurt eyes.

"I cut my hair for you," Stonefoot said angrily.

"I never asked you to," Spear shot back. Aurora began to fuss.

"Stonefoot, go back down the trail," Maggie ordered, cutting off any further conversation. "They should be here by now."

"Yes, Prime," Stonefoot agreed, turning, but not without one more dark glance at Spear.

"That was uncalled for, despite your nerves," Maggie chided Spear.

"I know. I'm sorry," Spear said, shifting Aurora to her other arm. "I'll make it up to her. The best way to cut a throat without getting blood all over yourself, or maybe the best up under the ribs thrust." She mimed both motions.

Maggie sat down beside her. "Whatever you think is best. Can I . . ." She hesitated. "Can I hold her?"

Spear's face shifted from thoughts of the best ways to kill, to worry and fear, then to resignation, accompanied by a loud sigh. Maggie was getting used to these shifts, and waited for her to settle.

"I have little experience with children," Maggie tried to explain. "And I want none of my own. But Wolf seems to think there's something special about her. I just wondered...."

"Of course she's special," Spear said brightly. She handed Aurora over. Maggie took her, awkwardly, not expecting Spear to agree so fast.

"Hold her head," Spear instructed. "And put the other arm under her. There." Spear settled back. "You have her. She's beautiful. I think she looks best in the morning light."

Maggie looked down at Aurora's golden hair and wide, happy green eyes. She smiled, waiting for something. Aurora cooed and smiled back. Maggie didn't feel anything beyond a normal care for this little life in her arms. She had carried babies before. She always worried about dropping them. She didn't feel that worry now with Aurora. This little baby was supposed to be in her arms at this very moment. Beyond that, she knew that Aurora was now one of the people she needed to defend because she was a Prime. That was it. No bolt out of the sky telling her of some bright and terrible destiny, like Wolf and Heron had experienced. No wide-eyed, silly expression like Canin wore every time he held her. She was a baby — a fragile new life — but still just another member of the forest family. No more special than any other.

Maggie sighed. "She smells good," she told Spear, lacking anything else to say.

"She does," Spear agreed.

A commotion from the tree line drew their eyes. Stonefoot stumbled out of the forest, supporting another smaller woman. Stonefoot eased her to her knees.

Maggie passed Aurora back to Spear and ran forward. Spear clutched the baby to her breast, and summoned her sword to her other hand.

Heron and Granite were already running to help. The woman raised her head.

"Lily!" Heron cried, full of concern. Spear set Aurora in her box and stood, sword ready.

"What's wrong?" Maggie called, scanning the woods for danger. "You were supposed to come with the others."

Lily shook her head, swallowing a quick sip of water from Heron. "No danger," she said. "I just wanted to get here before them. I forgot." She drew a deep breath and began to cough. She took another drink. "Running is for the young." She patted the hand of a concerned Heron. "It's all right, child. I'll be fine. After a moment."

"Lily," Heron said full of exasperated concern and love. "They let you come alone?"

"Yes."

Maggie questioned her. "Who's in command? I will have their sword."

Lily tried to answer, but she was still trying to catch her breath. "If I could just sit down," she finally gasped out. Heron led her over to the tree and helped her sit down beside Spear. Lily took a longer drink of water. Spear offered her an untouched bowl of porridge, but Lily waved it away.

"Stonefoot," Maggie said, "better run and tell them she's here. I don't want them to worry." Stonefoot nodded and ran off.

"It's not Brandywine's fault," Lily finally said. "I got up before the others. Slipped away." She nodded at Maggie's dark look. "I know. It was foolish, but I wanted to be here with Spear." She patted Spear on the shoulder. "Not part of Aieren's entrance. You know how she can be."

She turned to face Spear. "Since my son," she said that word with a more than a trace of pride, "could not be here, I wanted to be. Jewel," she said, bending over so only Spear could hear, "I remember the first time I faced one of the Children. I wanted to be at your side."

"For Canin," Spear replied with a frown.

"No, for you. You are now my daughter," she stressed. "Unless you've cast him off already." She sat back. "I don't blame you; he's so moody. You can find someone better." She patted Spear's hand. "Don't worry, dear, I know all the best men. Or maybe women." She tilted her head. "My neighbor's daughter is a spinner. Rising high. If it wasn't for Lightfoot, she would be Prime. Very stable. Very solid."

Lily took another drink of water. "Heron, could I have something stronger?" she requested, holding up the water bottle. Heron took it with one hand, while holding the other in front of her mouth, trying not to laugh. Spear looked from face to face.

"I'm sorry, Lily. Someone broke the wine jug, and we drank all Wolf brought."

"That's what that smell is," Lily commented. "Well, at least the grass won't be sad." She turned back to Spear. "So, my dear, have you made a decision, or do you need to hear more about the people of the forest? Or are you looking for just someone to romp with? From what I hear, you and Canin have plenty of that."

Spear, still unsure of all of this, looked blankly at Lily. A bit of red began at the top of her head and crept down her forehead. "I have not left Canin. He just went elsewhere to meet with one of the Children. Or so I was told. Has he left me?" Spear began to stand up.

Lily grabbed her hand, realizing her joke had gone too far. "No, child. No. I was just joking." Spear sat back down, still puzzled. "I was trying to lighten the mood. Get you to laugh."

"So, he did go to meet one of your leaders?" Spear's whole body was twisting in confusion and worry.

"Yes, dear. Yes. I'm sorry. That was wrong of me." Lily hugged Spear awkwardly. "I just saw so much fear in you. Mother mercy." She laughed. "You two are well matched. He was always too serious."

"Well, then," Spear said, smiling. "I prefer men. Strong, with an above average manhood. A girl wants to be taken sometimes, and he isn't that kind of bedmate. Or, if the mood strikes, a slender girl, so I can take her." She looked from Lily to Heron.

Heron had stopped laughing and was staring wide-eyed at Spear. "I think I'll see how Granite is doing," she said awkwardly and left.

Lily was shocked, holding her hand in front of her mouth.

"I was joking, too," Spear assured her. "Canin is quite capable in bed, or on the grass, or in the water. I have to take his hand and guide him sometimes, but you know how that is, Mum." Spear patted Lily's leg.

"How are you going to get yourself out of this one, Mum?" Maggie asked with a wry smile. "I will still have words with Brandywine. She should have posted a better guard. To let you slip away like that!" Maggie walked away, shaking her head.

"I. . . . You are. . . ." Lily sputtered and then folded her arms in front of her. "I may have met my match with you, Spear. I wonder if Canin is prepared for you."

"Not usually," Spear said with a shake of her head. "I usually just grab him, and. . . ."

Lily held up her hands to interrupt Spear's explanation. "There are things a mother must not know. Is Aurora sleeping?"

"No," Spear said, leaning over and picking up the baby. She held her out to Lily without any hesitation. Lily almost cried as she took her. After the first time, she had wondered if it would take a while for Spear to trust her. And there was also what the other Maidens had told her.

"Mother's grace," Lily said, sniffing back tears. "I think she's even more beautiful today." She brushed back a strand of Aurora's pale hair. "Is it true she looks like your mother? She must have been a beautiful woman."

"I don't really remember her. She and my father were gone so much. They were soldiers. When she was home, she was always yelling at me for knocking things over." Spear looked down. "I was clumsy. Broke everything. My grandmother and her sisters raised me, mostly."

"Alexander is clumsy, too, but all children are," Lily reassured her. "They break things. Oh, Mother, if he had wings, I would have no plates or cups left." He patted Spear's arm. "It's just childhood. You'll see. She'll break everything, too."

"No, she won't," Spear said with a faraway voice. "She will be as graceful as a bird darting through the branches."

"Yes, she will be," Lily said, the same lilt in her voice. The image of a tall woman in a blue-green dress floated across her vision. Lily heard water. She shook her head to clear it. Aurora quivered with laughter in her arms.

"They're close," Maggie called out.

Spear leapt to her feet and reached down for her sword.

"Best leave it there," Maggie counseled.

"You should hold her," Lily said. Heron had helped her stand. "I will take her when it is time." Spear took Aurora back without a thought.

Anxiety clenched her belly as she watched a group of Thorn Maidens emerge from the forest and form a semicircle facing Spear and the others.

"You are a strong soldier," Lily whispered from Spear's side.

Thorn Brothers came out of the woods next, each standing behind one of the Maidens. Out of habit, Spear counted. There were seven Maidens and six of the Brothers. Maggie came to stand at Spear's right hand. Heron and Granite had moved behind Lily.

The line of Maidens and Brothers parted, and a great light burst across the clearing. Spear shielded her eyes, her Sight falling away.

A strong voice spoke from the light. "Spearhead. And your baby, Aurora. Welcome to the Exile Forest. I am Aieren, one of the Children of the Mother of Exiles. Tell me, why do you come here? And why should we allow you to stay?"

Chapter 24
What Do You Hide?

Feathered wings of iridescent flame surrounded Aieren. She stood tall, armored all in silver, from head to foot. The fire from her wings reflected in the breastplate, casting a bright aura all around her. Before her she held a sheathed sword, one hand resting casually on the pommel. Her face was stern and strong, but also open and welcoming.

"There are no lies here," Aieren told her in a voice as strong as the oak trees encircling them.

Spear was surrounded by light; the weight of Aurora was gone from her arms. She didn't know if she had set her down, or if Lily had taken her. She stood at attention, body stiff and ready for the next order this commander — this Lady of the forest — would give her. Only standing before the Queen on the day she was given her sword and tabard as a member of the Queen's Guard had she felt so awed by another person. She felt not just awe, but also respect and trust. Like the trust she gave to Captain Shatterstaff and her Sisters in the Nine.

A sliver of fear pricked her fingers.

"She is safe," the warrior-leader Aieren assured her. "Lily holds her. She is a mother to so many. Your baby is peaceful in her arms."

"If I cannot stay, please, let him stay with her," Spear asked, just short of begging.

"Why do you fear I will cast you out?"

"I am a Fairy, and my people have done horrible things to yours. I hear fear and distrust around you."

"Have you given us reason to distrust you?"

"No. But I slip sometimes. I'm broken, and I fear what is inside me."

"You cannot control yourself?" Aieren asked, her hand tightening on her sword. "Even for the sake of a home for your child? Even for the man you love?"

"I am strong," Spear replied, standing even straighter. If her wings had been whole, they would have stretched out in pride. Then her voice dropped. "But sometimes. . . ."

"We take what is broken, and make it new. You are not the first to come here with fear of the future."

"Then let her stay. Let him stay. I will go if you command it. Just let her stay."

"You would give up your child?" Aieren asked, looking down at Spear with a cautious eye. "Abandon her?"

"No, I will not. Tell me what I must say. What words will convince you?"

Spear looked boldly into Aieren's eyes. She projected everything she was and had learned into her gaze.

Aieren paused for a moment, fingers tapping on the hilt of her sword.

"How did you lose your wings, Fairy?" she asked.

"When we fled the Blood Cult, I was hurt and couldn't use the Ring. Canin took us through. We were trapped in between Rings. It was cold. So cold. I wrapped Aurora in my arms and wings to keep her safe. When we arrived, my wings were frozen, and they broke when I moved them. My wings! I still feel them, but I cannot use them. Pain!"

Spear might have stumbled, but Aieren's commanding gaze kept her back straight and her eyes up.

"But you paid the price."

"And I would pay it again!" Spear swore, bringing her fists together. "All of me, to keep her safe. I failed once. I will not fail again. He died; I will keep her safe."

Her voice still level, Aieren said, "I must keep my people safe. I must not fail. Are you a danger?"

"Yes, I am a danger. I am a powerful Fairy soldier. I've killed many, and I will kill again. My sword is swift. My arrows never miss. I am a terror in the night. I see when others cannot. Make light to blind my enemies. I will be your terror. I am yours to command." Spear dropped to one knee, offering up her hands as if she held her sword. "I was a soldier of the Queen. Now I will be a soldier of the Mother. I will protect my child, and protect your people. None will dare come near."

Aieren shook her head. "We are not the sword. We are the shield."

"A shield is useless without a blade in the other hand. One enemy will hit the wall and fall, but others will slip through. A swift blade will keep them from overrunning us." Spear looked up, strong as silksteel. "I will be your sword," she swore confidently.

"A sword will bring other swords. Those who live with a blade in their hands usually die by one."

"That is my duty. 'Brother, I am glad you are not dead.' Your Thorn Brothers understand death. They both bring death, and take others to it. Your Maidens kill to keep you safe. I am no different. I'm just a fiercer Maiden. And not a maiden. But so few of them are. Why do you call them that anyway?"

The sudden question made Aieren smile. "Men underestimate them. Lower their guard."

"Yes, they do. They underestimate all of us."

"Do I underestimate you, Spearhead? Warrior, mother, wife. What do you hide?"

"I hide my rage. I hide the pain of losing my Sisters to cruel men. I hide the rage to run from here and bury my sword in the breast of the man who commanded her death. We were bound to defend her, and we failed. I will not let another child die. I will die first."

"You just might."

"That is my duty."

"Sometimes it is your duty to live and keep protecting your family."

Spear just looked at her in silence.

"You have nothing to say to that, Fairy?" Aieren asked after a long moment.

"I do my duty," Spear said evenly. "She told us once, that she would not send us to our deaths needlessly. But then she did. I will not sell my life cheap."

"Who is 'she'?"

"She once was my realm. Everything I lived for. Now," Spear said with a glance to her right, "that is Aurora."

"And Canin?"

"He understands."

"I hope he does."

Aieren stepped forward, taking Spear's hands.

"Rise. I am not the Mother, just Her child and Her servant."

Spear looked up into the face of the tall woman. Her wings of iridescent feathers cast rainbows all around her. Spear struggled to unbend her knees and stand. Strength like mountain stone pulled her up. The light of Aieren's wings enfolded her.

"Welcome to the Exile Forest, Soldier Spearhead. May you serve Her well."

Aieren stepped back and took the bright light of her armor with her. The line of Maidens and Brothers closed, blocking her from Spear's view.

Aieren spoke. "I am told a beautiful pool is near. Please take me there."

"Yes, Aieren," a woman's voice answered.

Spear looked around the clearing. The sun had hardly moved. She swore she had been speaking with Aieren for longer.

"Oh," a voice called from the edge of the wood. "I forgot. The baby."

Spear turned. Lily was still holding Aurora.

"Lily, could you bring her here?"

Spear expected a spike of anxiety, but there wasn't any. Lily glanced at her for permission.

"Yes, Mum," Spear told her. "I trust you."

Lily smiled and kissed Spear on the cheek. She turned and walked quickly through the line of Maidens.

"Hello, Aurora," Aieren said.

A giant pillar of light rose into the sky. Its wings spread over the woods, and the soft light of dawn filled the clearing. A gasp rose as another, smaller, pillar rose beside it, casting the light of just before twilight, and was embraced by the larger one. The bright light burst, blinding everyone but Spear. With her Sight, Spear saw the two lights merge and swirl above them. Then they sank down, as gentle mist, covering everyone in the clearing. Spear couldn't tear her eyes from the light as she was surrounded by the sound of joyful weeping.

Then Spear's Sight left her, and she was blind, too.

Chapter 25
The Return Home

The group stopped well before dark. They were moving slowly, with Cobalt setting the pace and Lightfoot dragging his feet. Canin was impatient to be back with Spear, but Cobalt would not be rushed. And Wolf wouldn't let him run ahead. Most of the journey, Wolf asked him endless questions and requested clarifications about his journey through the Fairy Realm and his experiences with the Blood Cult. Cobalt listened intently, but didn't speak much. At night, he and Wolf sat apart, talking. Canin could easily guess the subjects they were discussing.

Red Miriam and the other Maidens took up the rest of Canin's time with their own questions and the demonstrations they demanded of his Fairy-learned skills. He felt the fool, demonstrating the Patterns he had learned from Spear and the other Fairy soldiers for them. He was unsure of some of the movements, and had to adapt what he remembered. Miriam and River picked them up quickly, with Polly lagging a bit behind. Soon, they were all moving gracefully together under the trees. Cobalt was coldly impressed, and Wolf was amused. Even Lightfoot had to admit the new motions worked with the old.

Canin was cleaning a rabbit for stew when a bird call from Polly, who was on watch, brought all their heads up. A moment later, Stonefoot bounded into the camp. She paused only a breath before she finding Canin with her eyes and running up to him. She engulfed him in a hug, panting.

"She and Aurora are fine," she gasped out. "They're a day or so behind."

Canin gave a whoop and hugged her tighter, spinning her around in happiness. Cobalt looked up from his nap and smiled at the interruption.

"They passed Aieren's test," Stonefoot said after he set her down and she had regained her breath. "I can't tell you the story of what happened. She'll have to do that," Stonefoot told him, a strange look on her face.

"No matter," Canin told her. He was used to people being unable to articulate things that happened around Spear and Aurora.

"I was sent ahead to tell you. They're going slow because of Aieren and Aurora. Maggie thinks another day to the Sanctuary."

Wolf looked up from stirring the stew. "I told you. She's strong."

"You were right," Canin admitted. "I should have trusted you."

Wolf grunted and turned back to their dinner.

"What trail are they taking?" Canin asked Stonefoot.

"The Pine Haven trail," she answered around a bit of dried meat.

Canin sat back, folding his hands in front of his face. "If I remember correctly, if we take the Black Thorn trail, we could be at the overlook ahead of them."

"Too overgrown this time of year," Wolf disagreed. "And too rough, up and down creek beds." He looked back at Cobalt, who smiled and nodded.

"I ran it a moon ago," Stonefoot told them. "Still have to watch your head, but it's pretty clear. Fools' Creek might be high, but we can cross higher up."

"Not something to run at night," Wolf told Canin. "And not for someone who just ran their first trail in a few seasons."

"I can guide him," Stonefoot offered, standing. "That is, if he can keep up with me."

"Want to get back to your wife," Wolf mocked. "Taking foolish risks. Fools' Creek is well named. You'll slide right into some of the longest thorns."

"I can guide them," Miriam volunteered. "I've run that trail recently. Even with the rain, the creek should be low. I can keep our Brother from falling into the water."

Wolf narrowed his eyes at the betrayal of his daughter. "That will leave only two Maidens as escort." He shook his head. "Too few."

Cobalt spoke up. "Let them go. Then I won't have to feel his eyes on the back of my head with every step I take. You're protection enough for me. And we're deep in the forest. We're as safe as we can be."

"Hawthorn thought that, too," Wolf said sourly. "And you know what happened to him."

"Stop worrying, old man," Miriam shot back. "He needs to be reunited with his family. And I want to meet Spear." She grinned with eagerness.

Canin thought he heard a bit of hurt in Wolf's reply. "Then go." He waved them away. "More stew for me."

Canin moved his sword to his back and strapped on his bow and quiver. Miriam was doing the same with her own gear.

"No provisions," Miriam told him. "Just some water. We'll be there for breakfast."

Canin walked up to Wolf. "Thank you, Prime."

Wolf shrugged off the title. "Hug Spear, and give Lily a kiss for me. We'll be along. Tell Aieren the council should be assembled by the time we get there."

"A whole council," Canin said with amazement. "For me and Spear?"

"Not just you," Cobalt corrected. "All the information you've brought with you. And yes, about your return to the forest as well."

"I thought I just had to stand before the Mother?" Canin asked, worried.

"You do," Wolf stressed. "But there is much to talk about. I thought you were leaving?"

Canin wanted to say more, but Miriam grabbed his arm. "Come on. It's getting dark." Stonefoot was already waiting at the edge of the woods.

"Run swiftly, Setab," Cobalt called. "Run swiftly, Sutab."

Canin glanced back once more, then followed Miriam into the woods.

Behind him, he heard Lightfoot, returning from relieving himself, call out, "Where are they going?"

"Well," Canin said, sitting down. "That wasn't my best idea."

"It was all our idea," Miriam told him. "Hold her arm so I can change the wrappings."

They sat at the top of a sloping hill. Canin was on Stonefoot's left, and Miriam was kneeling in front of her. Canin held her arm, one hand on her wrist, and the other on her shoulder. Miriam began to carefully unwind the bloodstained cloth binding Stonefoot's left arm. In her other hand, Stonefoot gripped a piece of wood, her knuckles white.

As the arm emerged, Stonefoot paled and looked away. "Do we have more root?" she asked.

"No," Miriam said. "But Aieren or Lily will have more. You did well, coming all this way. We'll get you to Sekrine, and she'll fix you right up."

Miriam looked over Stonefoot's arm at Canin. She looked less confident than her voice conveyed. She finished unwinding the cloth and looked closely at the arm. It was covered in red scratches, some closed, and some weeping clear liquid. A long black thorn was stuck completely through the forearm, a fist's length sticking out on each side. The entrance and exit wounds were red and bled slightly.

"Don't look," Miriam snapped as Stonefoot turned to peek.

"Feeling a little lightheaded," she reported.

"We drained the sap," Canin said to Miriam with worry.

"There will still be some inside. Don't worry," she said, addressing Stonefoot. "Sekrine will be able to remove it."

Stonefoot smiled slightly. She gazed down the hill. "No one on the trail yet."

Canin's concern was clear as Miriam rubbed a clear paste on the wounds and began to wind more cloth around the treated arm. "She will be fine," Miriam asserted.

"Wolf will fall all over himself crowing that he was right," Canin remarked, holding Stonefoot's arm still. "Then he'll fall all over me."

"He said you would slide into the thorns," Stonefoot remembered, wincing as the thorn shifted. "But it was me."

"He'll still rake me over the coals," Canin told them.

Miriam finished and motioned for Canin to let go. Stonefoot gently pulled the arm to her chest. She swayed, and Canin grabbed her shoulders.

"Nice view," Stonefoot said.

"Yes," Canin had to agree.

Before them, the hill sloped down into the woods. The trail head was clearly marked with two large pine trees swaying in the light breeze. Beyond that, trees in many shades of green filled the land. But Canin knew there were hidden watchposts and way stations in the shadows of the branches.

Behind them, and down the hill in a wide valley, stood the Sanctuary village. In concentric circles around the central mound of the Mother's Sanctuary stood a few hundred houses with thatched and grassy roofs. A hardpacked dirt road ran up the middle, directly to the green mound in the center. If Canin had been looking in that direction, he would have been able to see the strong oak- and steel-bound doors. They were closed for the night, but would soon be opened for the morning. Smoke rose from most of the houses, and a few people were moving about. Many were heading out of the valley and up the gentle slope of Starlight's Shield, the low mountain at the far end of the valley. Spinners, heading to the hidden places under the mountain where the Fairysilk was made. He might also have seen others heading to the east to the fields, where it would soon be time to harvest. Along the slopes of the hill, Canin saw goldenrod waving in the wind, a sure sign summer was almost over. Soon the bells would ring, and two large buildings by the Sanctuary would erupt with children and young adults beginning their day, laughing and yawning through the Four Steps under the watchful and patient eyes of the Children of the Mother. Squads of Brothers and Maidens would be moving out for morning patrols and greeting those returning from the night watch.

But Canin saw none of that. He was focused on the trail head. Watching for any movement signaling that Aieren's group was returning.

"Maybe we were too quick," Miriam said, waving to a group of Maidens approaching the hill. The leader recognized Miriam and waved back.

"Need aid, Sister?" she called.

"We're waiting for Aieren. Have you seen her and the others?" Miriam asked.

"We passed their camp by the falls. Should be here before second bell," came the reply. "She seemed eager to return home."

"Thank you," Miriam called back. The leader waved again and led her group toward the village for food and rest.

"Maybe you should take her to Sekrine now," Canin suggested. "I'll wait for them."

"I'm fine," Stonefoot protested. "I want to see Heron and tell her I'm fine. She'll worry if you tell her I fell into the thorns."

"She'll worry more when she sees you like this," Miriam told her.

"I want to see their reunion," Stonefoot said stubbornly. "And Dougal had one stuck through his leg for days. And he's fine. Sort of."

"That was an old one from a dead tree," Miriam told her. "Not one from a live tree." She stood. "Canin, help me get her up."

"Wait," Canin said, standing. "I think I see something."

A group of three Maidens emerged from the woods and looked around with a wary eye. The one on the left saw them and, after a moment, waved. The one in the middle called back down the trail.

Canin pulled Stonefoot to her feet and helped her down the hill, with Miriam holding her other arm. He kept his excitement tamped down and managed to remember to move slowly.

By the time they had reached the bottom, more Maidens and Brothers were emerging from the woods. To a person, they saw Canin and began to grin silly expectant grins. At an unspoken command, they parted, revealing three forms coming out of the shadows of the forest. The one in the center shone red, the red Canin remembered from his earliest memories. A white star shone in her lap. On the right walked Lily, smiling. And to the left was Spear.

Canin's heart leapt, but he could not move. He was held to the spot, overcome by relief. Spear seemed different. Her face shone in the red light coming off Aieren. She seemed calmer, or at least not balanced on the edge of a knife, as she had seemed to be since the tower. Spear glanced down at Aieren.

"Go ahead. She's asleep in my lap. Nice and comfortable."

Spear walked up to Canin, took his head in her hands and touched her forehead to his. "Greetings, husband. I am glad you are not dead." Her voice broke only slightly.

"I rejoice that we live another day to see each other," Canin replied, his voice breaking completely. Then he kissed her, to the cheers of the Maidens and Brothers. Lily wiped away a tear.

Maggie's stern voice broke through the moment. "What happened to you?"

"We took the Black Thorn trail, and she slipped into some thorns," Miriam reported to her Prime. "One is stuck in her arm."

"Then we must get her to Sekrine," Lily decreed. "Bring her over here. There's room behind Aieren in the cart."

"I can walk," Stonefoot protested, but she stumbled as Miriam led her forward. Heron, who had been in the rearguard, came running up and almost tripped trying to get to Stonefoot's side.

"Foolish," she said, fretting as she led Stonefoot toward Aieren. "Taking that trail."

"It was my fault," Canin admitted, as he broke his kiss with Spear, but remained in her arms. "I was eager to return, and made them risk the trail."

"And I supported him," Miriam said.

"But I was the one who suggested it," Stonefoot added, as she settled into the back of the cart. "We're all to blame."

"You came over Wolf's protests, I would guess." Maggie fixed both of her Maidens with a steel eye. "We will have words about this."

"It does not matter now," Lily put in, before either of the young women could speak. "What's done is done. We need to get her to Sekrine's ward."

"It's through her arm," Spear said, letting go of Canin. "I've seen many arrow wounds like that. I can remove it easily and stop the bleeding." She reached out her hand at Stonefoot.

"No!" Canin, Lily, and Maggie all yelled together. Spear looked at them, puzzled, her hand still raised.

"No," Canin said more softly. "It's a black thorn. There are barbs along the length, and there's a sap inside that's released if you try to pull it out." He watched Spear's face. "Either way," he told her, guessing her next question. "The sap will make her sleep, and in a large enough dose, it will paralyze her, and then finally kill her. Sekrine knows the right way to remove it."

"She's been removing thorns from silly children for as long as I've been here," Lily told Spear. "She'll be fine. Canin and Miriam treated the wound and the thorn."

Spear looked shocked. "I almost hurt her," she muttered. Canin embraced her, holding her to his chest.

"But you didn't. It's all right," he whispered.

"Now," Lily said, taking charge. "We must get home."

Aieren spoke up. "Spearhead. If you would indulge an old woman, allow Aurora to stay with me and Lily. She's asleep, and I don't want to wake her. And you two will want to be properly re-united." A giggle came from Sadie, who was at Heron's shoulder, looking at Stonefoot's wounds. "She will be safe in my house. We can introduce her to those who are teaching and caring for this season's children. There are many babies. They'll be her creche mates."

Canin felt Spear tense.

"I have plenty of Mother's Milk," Lily told her. "It would be good for her. I'll stay with Aieren tonight. She will be well cared for."

"As long as you do not leave her," Spear finally said, pulling out of Canin's embrace. "Thank you, Mum."

"She will never be far from my arms," Lily swore. "She is my granddaughter."

"So that's settled," Aieren said. "I expect the two of you at my house for breakfast. Then we will go before the Mother." She waved her hand, and the group set off. Lily took Heron's arm and prevented her from following.

"I need you to take Canin to my new house. He doesn't know where it is." She noted the girl's concerned look as Stonefoot was carried off with the others. "Maggie and the others will see to her. You'll only make her nervous." Heron opened her mouth to protest. "Her mother will be there," Lily said with finality. Heron's eyes dropped.

"Yes, Lily," she said low.

"I'm sure she'll be better by twilight," Lily assured her. "Then the two of you can be together. I hear there might be more falling stars." She patted Heron's arm.

"Yes. That would be nice. She loves to watch for those," Heron said, silently thanking her adoptive mother for understanding.

"I'll make sure she's alone," Lily promised. She went up to Canin and reached up to kiss him on the cheek. "I rejoice that you live another day to serve the Mother and the forest."

"Thank you, mother, for everything," Canin told her.

"I wish you had gotten over that long ago," she chided him. "It warms my heart to hear you call me that."

"I should have. I'm sorry."

"Not another word," she told him, kissing his cheek again. "I love you. Tell Coltsfoot to get Alexander to school, and then bring him to me at the end of the day." Lily gripped Spear's hand once more, then hurried to follow the group.

Spear stared after Lily. Canin wondered what had passed between them in the days he had been away. He was amazed that she had let them take Aurora out of her sight.

Spear answered his thoughts. "I trust them. Your mother is a wonder, and I could not have passed Aieren's test without her." Spear suddenly glared at Canin. She grabbed his arm and pulled him around to face her.

"Why didn't you tell me?" she demanded.

Canin, confused, replied slowly. "It's part of the test. If I had told you of Aieren's ability to sense lies, it would have tainted the test and made you more nervous. You're strong. I believed in you."

"Not that," Spear said, shaking him. "Her wings. Why didn't you tell me she had wings? Beautiful iridescent feathered wings. Small, but still beautiful. And she's an Elenite. Such a wonder. Why didn't you warn me?" She shook him harder.

"Spear, I don't understand," Canin told her, trying to break out of her grip, but she was too strong. Heron just stared at her. "Aieren doesn't have wings. She is a Child of the Mother, but none of them have had wings since the first."

"No Elenites have wings," Heron put in, her voice wistful.

"One did," Spear said so low Canin could barely hear her. "But she died." Spear let go of Canin. "I saw them. Bright wings. They brushed me, just now as she left. I saw them the first time I saw her. She asked me questions, and the wings covered me, held me. Made sure I spoke the truth."

"That's her ability," Canin told her. "She can sense truth and prevent lies." Canin turned to Heron. "What did you see when you first met her?"

"I was young," Heron said. "She came to Lily's house and stood in front of me. There was a large bird sitting on her head. It had a long beak, and its long legs draped over her shoulders." Heron smiled, waving her arms to mimic the long legs. "I asked Lily about it later and described the bird. 'That's a heron,' she told me. 'Heron,' I repeated, loving the sound. I had another name when I came here, but I started saying 'heron' so much, Lily started calling me Heron, and it stuck." She laughed. "I was all long legs and arms then. But I grew into them." She made a little step, sliding to the right, showing off her long legs.

Spear just stared at Canin and Heron.

"It's part of her ability," Canin explained. "All the Children have one. I don't know them all, but I always see Aieren in a red light. Red, like my mother wore." He stared off into the distance for a moment. "She appears as someone you love or respect, someone you would never lie to."

"Then it wasn't real," Spear said, shaken. "The lights? I was the only one to see them?"

"No," Heron said. "All of us saw those. That was something . . . else." She also appeared shaken.

Canin looked at them. "I don't understand. Lights?" Spear was lost in her thoughts and did not reply. Heron simply didn't have words for what she'd seen.

Maggie cut in. "You'll have to tell him the story later." She had returned, Spear's pack in her hand. "Here," she said, handing it to the Fairy. The motion broke Spear out of her contemplation. She took the pack and thanked Maggie.

"I just see her as an old blind woman who must be carried by others," Maggie put in.

"Maggie sees most things as they are," Canin noted.

Spear shook her head again. "I should have known," she said, taking Canin's hand. "There are no iridescent feather-wings. They're either white or grey. Should have known."

Canin leaned in and kissed her cheek. Heron looked at them wistfully, Maggie with annoyance.

"Come on, you two," she commanded. "I don't want to stand out here all day. I need to speak to Coltsfoot, so I'll walk with you."

"Lead the way," Canin told Maggie. "Lily has a new house?"

Heron fell in beside them, while Maggie walked ahead. "Yes. After she and Niel decided they wouldn't take in any more children, they gave the old one to the Maidens and took a house near Sekrine's ward. It's a small one, just for her and Alexander now. Coltsfoot stays there sometimes, but she also has a room in the old house. I still have my room there, too, and other Maidens come and go. Maggie hates it," Heron whispered to Canin. "But we have our privacy, and a place to gather." She noticed Maggie glancing back. "When we don't have duties," she said loudly.

Maggie sniffed and turned back around.

Canin laughed. "I must come and visit."

"We would welcome you." Heron glanced at Spear. "The others really want to meet you. We want to hear all about being a soldier in an all-woman group."

Spear nodded, but she looked even more uncomfortable. She squeezed Canin's hand for reassurance.

"Once we've had time to settle in," Canin told her.

Heron grinned and hustled over to Spear's side. She tried to take her arm, but Spear held it away from her.

"Heron," Maggie called. "Come walk with me."

Cowed, Heron went to join her Prime. Canin heard Spear sigh in relief.

Then she grabbed him and said, "Aieren was riding on a cart?"

Chapter 26
The Sanctuary Village

They descended the hill into the village. More people were about, running or walking from their houses toward the center of the village. Thorn-free trees grew between the houses and along the narrow paths, casting shadows in the morning sun. The houses were nearly all single-story. Most were small, but they got bigger the closer they were to the Sanctuary. Maggie led them away from the large path headed to the center of the village and the Sanctuary.

"There'll be crowds at the market at this time of the morning," she explained. They had already gotten strange looks from the people of the village. Most recognized Maggie and greeted her, but then stared at Spearhead and Canin. He would greet them with a friendly smile and their name, helpfully provided by Maggie. The villagers would smile warily at him, then hurry on. After the first few interactions, Spear lost her smile and began to stare at the ground, holding tight to Canin's hand.

As they passed one house, a Human woman and her Elenite children were coming out the door. She saw Spear — who was raising her hand in greeting, prompted by Canin and Maggie — turned white, shoved the children back into the house, and slammed the door.

Maggie called out to the woman, but she never came back out.

"It will just take time," Canin said as they moved on.

Spear nodded sadly.

"Now you know how I felt," Canin said, trying to make light of it. "I was alone among Fairies."

"But we accepted you," Spear shot back. "We didn't shun you and run away."

"Some did," Canin argued back. "You never saw how hard it was traveling alone in the Realm. I was lucky to find any place to sleep or eat."

"But you take in exiles here," Spear said with sorrow and anger. "I don't understand."

"It will take time," Maggie told her. "But you'll show them how powerful you are, and how much you can bring to the forest. It won't be today, but you will be welcomed."

Spear shuffled her feet. Canin moved to kiss her, but she turned away.

"How much further?" she asked.

"Just around the bend," Heron said, gesturing them on. Canin absorbed the hurt coming off Spear and felt helpless to do anything about it.

Finally, they stood before a small house. Across the hardpacked path stood a larger building with a large fenced area behind.

"That's Sekrine's home and ward," Canin explained. "It hasn't changed much. She lives upstairs, and there are many rooms. Most are devoted to birthing and care of the people of the forest, and she can expand out into that fenced-in area if needed."

"She has at least ten other midwives and healers," Heron filled in. "And others who can help out if needed."

"All of us," Maggie said with pride, "spend time with her and her healers. We may not be as good as she is, but we can save lives."

Spear nodded and continued examining the area, while Canin moved his eyes to the small house. It had short stairs leading to a small porch. There were two chairs by the door. Canin recognized one as Lily's. Niel had made it after they took in their first baby. The other — smaller — could only be for Alexander. Lily had always loved to sit and watch the people of the village. Canin recognized the curtains in the single window. He smiled, remembering how the blue fabric turned the sunlight strange colors.

Canin was climbing the top step when the door was flung open, and Alexander came barreling out. He collided with Canin's legs, and would have knocked them both off the porch if Spear hadn't held them up with a brush of her Power.

"Woah," Canin said, steadying the boy. "Where are you going in such a hurry?"

"School," he said, stumbling out of Canin's hands and down the steps to land on his knees. He picked himself up and brushed dirt off his pants.

"He's late," Coltsfoot said from the door. She looked tired and annoyed. "He cannot wake up on time." She looked at Canin and Spear with relief. "Where's Lily?"

"With Aieren, at her house," Maggie told her. "She wants you to bring him there after school."

Hearing Lily's name, Alexander gave a glad cry, and would have run off, if Heron hadn't grabbed his arm. His momentum swung her around and tangled her legs. She had to let him go or fall.

"School," he yelled again, and ran right into a tree.

"Oh, no," Coltsfoot said, with a long-suffering sigh. "Not again."

She bounded down the stairs and picked him up off the ground. His eyes were glazed, and he was unable to stand. There was a cut in the middle of his forehead that was just beginning to bleed. "Ow," he said as Coltsfoot kept him from trying to stand again.

Maggie hid a smile as Heron, with a similar sigh, pulled a cloth from her pocket and went to kneel before him. Canin just stared at the boy, remembering times when he had done something similar.

Spear began to laugh.

The sound pulled Alexander's attention, and he tried to focus in her direction. He seemed caught between crying and laughing. Coltsfoot frowned as she forced him to sit down.

"Stay still," she ordered. "Heron needs to clean it." He struggled under her hands.

Spear grabbed onto Canin. She was laughing so hard, she had to sit down on the porch. "I used to do that. But it was rocks I ran into," she finally gasped out.

"School, Auntie," Alexander managed to gasp out as Heron tried to clean the blood off to see the wound. Coltsfoot glared at Spear, who was still laughing.

"Spear," Canin begged, trying to get her to stop. He tried shaking her, but she was caught up in the laugh and could not stop. Alexander began to whimper.

Then a voice cut across all the noise. "What's going on?" Sekrine strode up the pathway and stooped in front of Alexander. "What did you do?" she asked, kneeling down and taking the cloth from Heron.

"Tree," Alexander said, Sekrine's calm voice heading off his tears.

"Yes, I see." She put both her hands on his head and closed her eyes.

Spear stopped laughing as she felt the surge of Sekrine's Power. She watched with wide eyes and Sight open as the old woman examined Alexander.

"Nothing cracked," Sekrine said, opening her eyes. She began to look at the wound. "But I will not waste my Healing on this little cut."

"Ow," Alexander said again, trying to back up, but Coltsfoot held him. "Hurts."

"Then stop running into trees, you silly child," Sekrine admonished him. She took the cloth away. She pulled out a vial and smeared clear goop on his forehead. "There. Should heal in a few days. I hope whoever you wind up with likes scars, because you sure will have a lot of them.

"Don't touch it," she told him as he raised his hand.

"What do you say?" Coltsfoot prompted.

"Thank you, Sek-rine," he said, saying her name with a pause in the middle.

"You are welcome," she told him. "If he feels dizzy or slurs, bring him back to me," she told Coltsfoot, who nodded, from long experience. "And you might want to carry him. At least for a little bit."

Coltsfoot stood and lifted him onto her hip.

"Back," he demanded.

"You're getting too heavy," she protested, but she began to try and shift him. He tried to help and only succeeded in almost knocking her over.

"Let me help," Canin offered, coming up behind them. He grabbed Alexander under his arms and lifted him so Coltsfoot could get her arms under him. "Arms around her neck," Canin instructed.

"Not too tight," Coltsfoot told him.

"Is that good?" Canin asked.

"Yes. Thank you."

"Come to the house after you deliver your burden," Maggie told her. She turned to Heron. "Spread the word. I want all the Maidens who can come at the house. As soon as possible."

Coltsfoot set off, Alexander bouncing on her back, yelling for her to go faster.

Heron looked anxiously at Sekrine, who was being helped to her feet by Canin.

"She's fine. I removed the thorn easily. I Healed it just enough. She should regain use of the arm in a few days. We'll have to watch for infection, but I see no reason she won't be up and around tonight." She looked at Canin. "You and Miriam did well. You remembered what I taught you. She was very lucky," she stressed.

"Thank you so much," Heron said, giving the small woman a hug. Sekrine patted her on the back lightly and winced at the tightness of the embrace.

"Heron," Maggie said after a moment. Heron pulled away and, after a quick glance at Canin, ran off.

Sekrine walked up to Spear. "I know you and your man want to be alone, but I could use your Healing." She crossed her arms. "I have a Brother who might lose his arm. I cannot Heal him enough. With your help, we might not have to remove it."

Canin felt Spear tense, and felt her rising anxiety and fear. He remembered what had happened to one of the Ladies. She looked at him, uncertain what to do.

"I could get some sleep," Canin told her. "I ran all night. Go help, and come back at midday." He took her pack. "The only thing keeping me going is Morning Leaves."

"You would just fall asleep," Spear said with a sigh. She took off her sword, bow, and quiver, and set them down beside Canin. "I will help you, Sekrine," she said, awkwardly saying the woman's name for the first time.

"Good," Sekrine said, taking Spear's arm. "I will have her back before midday," she promised Canin, and began to pull Spear away.

"Wait," Canin said, standing. He grabbed Spear in a hard embrace and an even harder kiss.

"Goodness," Sekrine said, after the kiss had gone on longer than she thought they had breath for. Maggie coughed uncomfortably.

Spear finally pulled away, smiling broadly, and took Sekrine's arm. "You'll have to explain your eye and cheek," she told him as they left.

Canin smiled and rubbed at the healing wound.

"Let me help you take your gear in," Maggie offered.

Together they entered Lily's house. It might have been smaller than the one Canin had grown up in, but it felt exactly the same. The same scent of roses filling the air. The neat, sparse furniture. A wood carving that Niel had made in the middle of the table. Canin took a deep breath.

"Feels like home," Maggie said.

"Yes," Canin agreed, setting his gear and weapons down on the floor. It was mostly a single room, with a large table in the middle, too large for the space. There was a wood-burning stove in the corner, surrounded by pots and other kitchen articles. In the back there were three doors.

"The one on the right is her bedroom," Maggie told him. "And the left one is Alexander's room. She moved him out and put in a larger bed and a crib for Aurora. The one in the middle has a bath and a chamber pot. There's a well over by Sekrine's fence."

Canin just looked around. Everything reminded him of his childhood. He had to sit down, overwhelmed by memories.

Maggie stood over him, silent for a while. Finally, she drew a loud breath. "I know you're tired, so I will only say this." She tapped his foot to get his attention. Looking up into her serious eyes, he pushed the fatigue away.

"I understand why," she started. "But put my Maidens in danger again for selfish reasons, and you and I will have a problem. They are my Maidens, and anyone who harms them will feel my wrath." She folded her arms. "Understood?"

"Yes, Prime," Canin said, rising. Telling her that both Miriam and Stonefoot had agreed to the plan, and even helped persuade Wolf, would do no good. She was their leader, and they were her responsibility.

"No matter who you are, and who your wife is."

"I understand, Maggie. It will not happen again."

Maggie sighed. "Yes, it will. I can feel things moving around you and Aurora. I'm afraid for the forest."

"I would never put them in needless danger," Canin protested.

"I know. I just want you to understand that your actions have consequences. Sometimes ones that you don't understand for a long time."

"Jessamine," Canin guessed.

"Jessamine," Maggie agreed.

Chapter 27
I Don't
Understand

It was dark when Spear returned.

She set a basket down on the table and surveyed the room. Their weapons and gear were stacked neatly by one of the chairs. She began to pull items out of the basket and set them on the table.

"I'm sorry," she called. "There were just so many to help. I understand Shield a little better now. It was a good feeling to help people. Sekrine sent me home with this as an apology. She says it's one of the best chickens in the village. She sent someone over to get you for the midday meal, but they said you never responded. Then Lily brought Aurora. She wanted her mother, she said. So, I took a break and nursed her and sat with her and some of the other children. There are so many babies and other children here. And not all are Elenite. Humans abandon their children, too. I was amazed. Sekrine told me of one woman who keeps bringing her newborns here. They can never speak to her, but she's brought three here now. Kick him in the manhood already! They call her the red woman. What is it with Human women and red? This chicken smells wonderful. Canin! Wolf and the others got back not long ago. I met River and Polly. What did you tell them? I'm not the greatest fighter in the Fairy Realm. They thought I would be ten feet tall, and move like a whirlwind. It was embarrassing when I tripped over a chamber pot. And Red Miriam. She's an interesting woman. Even if she hadn't told me, I would have known she was Wolf's daughter. I wanted to bring Aurora over here, but I got busy, and Lily wanted to let you sleep. She misses her father. Canin! It's getting cold! Miriam told me of your fight with Crow. That cursed bastard. Good thing he stayed behind. I would have ripped out his eyes. They described it, and it looks like you were paying more attention than Steel gave you credit for. She would be impressed. Why did you let him hit you? He was rejected by your wife. She picked you, and now I know why. He seems a Motherless. Am I using that right? There was one Brother, lost his leg, who just kept cursing Sekrine and all the other midwives. Such words he used! I finally sent him to sleep. They clapped for me. Then I watched her deliver a baby. I don't remember when she was born. It was terrifying and wonderful. I don't know if I can do that, but I understand why everyone looks up to Sekrine, even though she's short. She is a powerful woman. She's like Shatter and Flora: a small, strange-talking person. When she gets busy, she's even harder to understand. And she can talk so fast! It's lucky she's so easy to read, or I would have been so confused. Canin? Are you even here? She wants me back as soon as I can go. Then Maggie came, and wanted me to start a training plan for her Maidens. And more of them have cut their hair. I don't understand it. Some of them have beautiful hair. They're giving it to a rope maker. She says she can weave it all together and make a strong length. She promised me a good portion. Always good to have rope around. I can't decide if I want to grow my hair. What do you think? Then Lily brought Aurora again. This time Alexander was with her. I don't like him. It's horrible to say, but he kept dropping things and breaking things. Sekrine had to send him off. I don't know what I'll do if he stays here. But where would he go? We can't run your mother out, but I think I'll go mad with that little badger running around. Maybe we can find another house. You can't live in your old house; it's stuffed with Maidens. I'll have to ask Sekrine. Or Maggie. Then Stonefoot's mother came, and she is a horrible person. Glared at me. Glared at Maggie, and everyone but Sadie. She was there flirting with one of the wounded Brothers. I take back what I said about you sleeping with her. Stay away from her. I'm not that strong a Healer to cure what she might give you. Good thing you weren't there: Stonefoot's mother would have ripped your eyes out for getting her baby hurt. I tried to tell her it wasn't your fault, but she just ignored me. Then Heron came in, and ice formed on her. If it wasn't so horrible, it would be funny how she treated Heron. The girl just wanted to see how Stonefoot was, and the moment Heron came in, Stonefoot's mother pulled her out of bed and tried to take her home. I tried to tell her that women can give better pleasure. They just understand in ways men don't. She almost threw something at me. Everyone was trying not to laugh. Then Heron glared at me. I was just trying to help. But she told me to stay out of it. Then the mother took Stonefoot home. Heron made a brave face, but River and Miriam took her away to hit something. I hope she'll forgive me. I like her. If you need, you can sleep with her. Not now, but sometime. But she might not like you that way. Maybe I'll sleep with her. I'll have to talk to her. Maybe she'll need to hit me. You'll have to explain this, letting yourself get hit. I don't understand it. Canin! I will eat all of this if you don't come out now!"

Spear walked around the small room. Spotting the open door on the left, she looked in. Canin was asleep on the bed, fully clothed except for his boots.

"Canin," she called softly. He muttered and rolled over onto his side. Spear sighed. She went back and returned everything to the basket. After a moment of contemplation, she pulled out a roll and stuffed it into her mouth. Then she covered the basket with a cloth.

She returned to the small room. Squeezing around the end of the bed and the crib, she went to the other side. Then she remembered and looked out the door. She had left her bedroll with the Weave in the other room. She yawned, suddenly overcome with exhaustion. She sat on the bed and pulled off her boots.

"It's a good thing I love you," she told the sleeping man beside her. Carefully, she laid down on her side against his back and put her arm over his chest. He made a contented noise and gripped her hand.

"Love you, too," he muttered.

She kissed the back of his neck, and then she was asleep, too.

Canin opened his eyes to find Spear watching him in the dim light of the moon. She smiled and gave him a quick kiss.

"Feeling better?" she asked, pulling him closer.

"Yes," he replied, blinking the sleep out of his eyes. "I heard someone at the door earlier, but they went away, and I went back to sleep. Then I heard you, but I didn't know if it was a dream or real. It's dark. Is it almost morning?"

"No. The moon just rose. Dawn is still far away." She pulled him closer. "We have time," she muttered suggestively, nuzzling his face, her hands raking his back.

"Wait a moment," Canin said, scrambling up, and running first into the crib, and then the door frame. Spear watched him stumble toward the middle door. She thought about conjuring a Light for him, but then didn't. After a moment, he came back, shaking his foot.

"I forgot how strong her soap is," Canin remarked as he snuggled up to Spear. His hands began to caress her back as he kissed her.

"Don't touch my breasts," Spear told him around his kisses. "They're sore from nursing."

"Um," he said, moving to her neck.

"I don't want to move," she muttered as he tried to shift her on top of him. "I'll just stay on my side, and you can do the work."

"Like this?"

"Yes. A little higher." Gasp. "There!"

"Lift your leg a little more."

"Um, a little higher. Um, right there." She crushed him against her body, leg over his hips. "Don't move," she muttered into his neck. "I've missed you."

"Me, too."

There was a long moment of deep breaths from both of them, then, "Now you can move," she called.

The creaking of the bed rose to a crescendo, then fell away, as their breath rates began returning to normal, then leveled out as they both fell back asleep. In the other room, in a box under Lily's bed, a red light bloomed for a moment, pulsing to their inhalations, before fading away again unnoticed.

Chapter 28
Children of the
Mother

Breakfast — in Aieren's sprawling two-story, many-roomed home — made Spear feel better. She had woken hungry and anxious. Despite what the poets said, she needed more than just love to live on, but she couldn't eat the cold dinner from last night. Her work with Sekrine, and then her happiness to be back with Canin — which had led to their mutual exhaustion — had kept her worry about being separated from Aurora muted. Now it was back in full force. So she paced, and willed the sun to rise faster. Canin wouldn't let her go and beat on Aieren's door, waking the whole house. At the first hint of light, though, she was up and out the door, with Canin trailing behind, unable to keep up with her even at a full run. She went straight to Aieren's home, despite not knowing where it was.

Lily met them at the door, either her mother's intuition or a fussy Aurora having already forced her out of bed. Spear sighed with relief. Canin and Lily had to pull her inside, or she would have sat down in the dirt outside to nurse.

Then came the breakfast, prepared and served by Aieren's children. Spear ate more than her fill, finally calm, now that her baby was back by her side. Lily had even brought out a taller chair so Aurora could lay in her basket, but be high enough so Spear could see her and touch her during the meal.

Canin ate, too, but not as ravenously as Spear. His own worry was growing, knowing what was next.

Lily tried to keep the mood light and bantered with Canin. Alexander sat at her side, calm and still for once. He tried to eat as much as Spear, watching her with wide eyes.

Then they were introduced to all the Children of the Mother. Canin knew most of them, or was at least acquainted with them. He explained who each of these Elenites were, including their names and what positions they held in the forest. They were all, to varying degrees, polite and welcoming to Spear. Except the Commander of the Brothers and Maidens, Dornshen. While he wasn't openly hostile to her, he came very close to crossing that line. All of the others had smiled, shaken her hand in the Human way, and then moved on to greet Canin and briefly hold Aurora. Once they held her in their arms, any doubt or questioning of Spear and Canin's place in the forest fell away. Cobalt's polite smile became a beam of light. Even the hostility of the Commander became grudging respect. One, a tall skinny woman with dark black hair — who had grinned at Canin, calling him one of her best students — broke down in tears at the simple touch of Aurora's hand. She was so overcome, she had to be helped back to her seat. The other teachers, Tess and Edone-Reven, seemed similarly affected. Only Spindle, the Trade Master and close friend of Lightfoot, seemed unaffected by Aurora.

After meeting the first few, Spear began to watch Aieren. Now that she understood, she could See through Aieren's Weave, which seemed to be part conscious and part unconscious. She was old — maybe the oldest person Spear had ever seen — and blind. But she projected an aura not unlike the Queen or the Keeper. Every time one of the Children held Aurora and was changed, she wore an almost smug look. After the last one returned the now fussing baby to Canin, Aieren winked at Spear. Spear returned a nod of admiration for a captain who knew both her field and her troops.

"Let me take her," Spear said, pulling Aurora out of Canin's hands. She placed the baby under her chin and hummed to her, and she quieted.

"We are the Children of the Mother," Aieren pronounced, spreading her arms to take in the whole room. "We are the descendants of the Mother's First Children, when she walked alongside us in the grass and the woods. It has fallen upon to us to protect and nurture all those who come to the forest seeking sanctuary. We rebuild those who have been broken, making them stronger. We stand firm against all who would break us." She looked around at the gathered faces. "We are in agreement. Canin, our wayward Brother, and Spearhead the Fairy, you may go before the Mother and ask her for sanctuary." She turned in the direction of the youngest of the Children. "Yarrow, will you lead us to the Sanctuary?"

As the Children began to file out, Spear realized she had not even caught, let alone learned, all their names.

"It's all right," Canin reassured her. "It took me a while to learn them, too."

"Wait until Aieren has left," Lily advised them. "Then I'll lead you out." She smiled at Canin and touched Spear's arm. "She will see into your heart and know that you have a place here."

Spear felt Aurora's heart beat next to hers and could only smile with hope.

They followed Lily out into the midmorning sun, where they took a winding path toward the grass- and flower-covered mound in the center of the village. Spear felt a sudden reluctance as she saw that most of the people of the village were already gathered there. They stood in quiet rows, all around the path. Spear could see fear in many of their eyes. It was mixed with anger in others. A few faces were open and accepting, but most were not.

Spear stopped, grabbing Canin's arm and passing Aurora to him. She hated having all their eyes on her. Her hand itched for her sword.

"Don't worry," Lily soothed. "Once the Mother has accepted you, they will as well. And once you show them what you can teach them, their attitudes will change."

Spear wasn't so sure. She felt angry eyes from all sides. Her fear rose and she wanted to fly away, but her feet froze to the ground. Canin shifted Aurora to his other arm and took her hand. His simple touch calmed her, giving her the strength to start walking again. Aurora cooed as the motion of her parents calmed her. Spear took a deep breath and smiled.

"For her," she muttered.

The path took them around the front of the mound, where they stopped at the top of an incline leading down to the oak and steel doors of the Sanctuary. Spear blinked, suddenly reminded of a certain set of three doors within the Exile Queen's mountain. She opened her Sight and saw ancient Weaves binding and holding the doors. She wished Goldberry or Silidin were here to explain to her what she was seeing. In a burst of grief, she wished Silidin was anywhere.

The Children lined the sides of the incline. On chains of silver and steel, plain silver discs now hung around each of their necks. Surprised, Canin recognized the work as being similar to the ringmail he had been given by the Fairies.

Spear became even more nervous. She gripped Canin's hand. "What is down there?" she whispered.

"That is the Sanctuary of the Mother," he explained. "It's where She first lived. Before all of this was built. Before. . . ." He stopped.

"Before what?" Spear asked, hearing the hesitation in his voice.

"You'll see."

Spear's response was cut off by Aieren's voice. She was at the top of the incline, in a chair borne by two strong Thorn Brothers. She raised her arms. "Open the doors!" she called in a voice that somehow seemed both old and young.

The doors swung silently inward. The smell of earth and roses filled Spear's nose. She took a step forward.

Aieren's voice stopped her. "The mother should carry her child."

Spear turned and took Aurora back from Canin. She cradled the baby in her arms, and, with Canin beside her, they descended. Yarrow, her auburn hair aflame in the sun, waited for them at the bottom.

"I will take you to the Mother," she said, and turned on her heel, walking swiftly into the darkness. Canin and Spear hurried to keep up. After a few steps, the outside light began to dim, and Spear looked up and saw tiny Fairy Lanterns in the ceiling. As they passed, the light first increased, then dimmed as they moved on. Walking in a bubble of light, they followed Yarrow further. The corridor bent and twisted, turning back on itself till Spear was unsure what direction they were going in. As a soldier, she almost smiled, understanding how this would confuse and disorient an enemy. She thought she saw other corridors branching off from their path, and shallow alcoves where guards could wait. Knowing she was supposed to be confused and off balance, she let those emotions flow through her. They drowned some of her fear and left her feeling lighter.

Rounding another bend, they found themselves before a door of pure silksteel, its shine undulled by time. Spear could feel the Power coming off it, as strong as a forge fire. She let her Sight slip away, not wanting to be caught in any feedback from such a powerful Weave.

Yarrow held up her disk and used it to manipulate the Weave. The door opened, silently.

"I will wait here," she told them.

Canin nodded and drew Spear into the room beyond. Behind them, the door shut with a dull snap. Spear turned to see that all the lines of the door were gone, leaving nothing but a blank wall at their backs.

"It's all right," Canin said, trying to comfort her.

"I know," Spear said. Her eyes began to adjust to the dim light, like pale moonlight. "I've been in places like this." She adjusted Aurora on her hip. "The Shrine of the Goddess at Fae-Treval is much like this." She looked around the room. She couldn't see much in the near-darkness, and her Sight was blocked. "Now, do we wait for one of the Children to appear and speak with her voice? Or do we simply meditate and open ourselves to the Mother of Exiles?"

Canin was startled by Spear's flippant attitude. He drew in breath to speak, but a sudden light took the words from his mouth.

"No, Spearhead Trillium Jewel Luna Dark, Fairy soldier of the false Queen. You shall speak directly to me."

The light in the room was suddenly as bright as the full moon. A circle of nine pointed stars bloomed to life on the floor. In a swirl of magical energy, visible to even Canin's eyes, a globe rose into the air. It hovered in the center of the ring, spinning and sending off flashes of light. Inside, a triangle of silver stood still, its points gleaming in the light. Spots of color and sparks danced over the room.

229

"This is no foolish symbol. No dance to keep them in line. This is not an empty church of the Father. This is no abandoned Shrine of the Goddess. I am here. I am the one that you call the Exile Queen. I am She they call the Mother of Exiles. I was called The Dragon of All Time by my soldiers. I was Sarca to my lovers, and Thorn to my enemies. Starlight to the first ones I led here. I am a Servant of the Stars. I am the Queen of Thorns."

Chapter 29
The Mother of Exiles

Spear was alone again, the light cutting her off from the rest of the Realm. Canin's presence and touch were gone. Only Aurora's weight stayed, here in the blinding light of the Mother of Exiles.

"Why do you come before me, Servant of the Moon and Sun? Quondam protector of my betrayer's Heir, why do you come before me, a baby not of your womb in your arms?"

"She is my daughter!"

"You cannot tell lies here. Your evasions and half-truths may fool my children, but not me. I can see your mind. Everything you hide, everything you do not want to see. Everything you have worked so hard to forget. You may love her as your blood, but she is not your blood."

"She is the Returned spirit of my lost son. She is the chance to right my wrong. I must make up for what I did. I will protect her, where I failed him."

"That is not possible."

"Why was she brought to me, then? Why was I there, to save her from those horrible men? Why, if not to make up for what I did?"

"You cannot see the truth."

"I don't want to see it. She is my daughter, and I will protect her. From every Human, Fairy, or Elenite who would do her harm. Even from you. Whatever you've become."

"Then you will die."

"Any mother would die for her child. I will lay down my life now, if that is what will keep her safe. I will take his knife and plunge it into my heart, if that's what you want. If that is what will keep her safe."

"You are so quick to offer your death. Maybe she needs your life."

"Then I shall give my life. Whatever oath you need, I will give. Whatever tribute you need. Take it. Freely. Aurora is my life. Give her a place to grow. Give her a place to be safe."

"She will never be safe. Her path will be peril and hardship."

"Then I will stand by her side as she faces them."

"As you swore to stand beside the Heir? Beside Goldberry? How can I know you will not cast aside this oath, as you did those others?"

"I had no choice then. I was trying to return. Trying to get her to safety, but the lightning broke something in me. I couldn't concentrate. I couldn't hear the Song. He took us through. He got us lost. You! You must have rescued us. You brought us here. There was no Ring where we landed. Just grass and flowers. Why bring us here, then cast us out?"

"If you value your oath, why didn't you start walking back to the Fairy Realm? You gave an oath to your captain and your Heir. You betray it by standing here."

"She betrayed us first. She promised she would never throw our lives away. Then she did."

"A mother will do anything to protect or avenge her child."

"Exile Queen, Mother of Exiles, Queen of Thorns; whatever I must call you, tell me, what must I do? What must I say? What must I think? My child needs a home. Those men were either going to kill her or use her. She needs a place where she can be safe. Please! I beg you!"

"You do not hear me. She will never be safe. No matter where she is. There will always be danger, both real and in your mind. Danger you can fight, and danger you cannot. I do not know if you can tell the difference. I will not allow a wild, broken Fairy into my peaceful home."

"Your home isn't so peaceful. Your children fight in petty arguments. Men come here and are killed. Your Thorn Brothers and Thorn Maidens go off into danger every day. And some of them never come back. The Brothers greet one another, each glad that the other is not dead. I may be broken, and I may be wild, but I can defend her and your forest better than any of those women and men beyond that door."

"And what will be left when you're done? She thinks that way. She has acted. She will burn. You would burn down a house to save a cup."

"Aurora is my cup, and I will do anything to keep her whole."

"That's what I'm afraid of. That's what I see."

"Then I'll go. But let her stay. Let him stay. She needs a father, and he will be exceptional. I can feel it in his spirit. Everything I'm not, he will be. The mother I cannot be, he will be. Begging won't move you, so I'll demand it. On your honor as a Fairy Queen, keep her safe. I demand you fulfill your oath to your people."

"She is not one of my people. And I am not your Queen!"

"We're all your people now. Your children say it: 'We take in all that are broken. Make them whole. Stand firm against all who would break us.' Well, I stand firm. You would break me. I am broken. She will help me heal. He will help me heal."

"You ask too much. Too much danger follows you."

"Then abandon us. Abandon us like you did your people. But I will not abandon her."

Canin felt himself floating in Her presence. Only once before had he been here, had he heard Her voice speaking in his ears and mind. It felt so much like those moments with Min, when their spirits seemed to merge and they became one glowing entity for the space between breaths. 'Touching the Goddess,' Min had called it. Now, one was touching him.

"She seems surprised that I'm real, and not some hollow figure in the sky. One who asks much and gives nothing."

"Her Goddess gives her much. Her belief guides her and helps her, as it helps many of the Fairies."

"Does their Goddess speak to them? Does She guide them? Are Her words as clear as mine?"

"Sometimes, yes. To some, yes."

"Then why come back, if their Goddess has impressed you so? Why return here? You defied my commands. You left when I told you to stay. Your actions caused the deaths of five of my children. Five candles snuffed out. Five who cared about you and wanted to keep you safe."

"It was more than five. The woman I tried to help died as well. Others died, too. I made a mistake. I was impatient and arrogant. I admit that, and I will perform whatever penance you ask of me."

"What if that penance is to leave here and never return?"

"Then I will go. But I would beg you to allow Spear and Aurora to stay."

"But will she be safe here, without you? Would she leave this baby behind?"

"No. She would not."

"Then you would take your family away. Where would you go?"

"I don't know. This is the only home I've ever known."

"What do you bring to my forest? What threats do you invite here with this child that is not yours? Do you even know who she is?"

"No. I just know we rescued her from wingless Blood Cult members."

"She is covered in mystery and radiates potential. She has a profound effect on my Children. So much has led to her. From here I can see nothing clearly. All paths lead to sorrow. Darkness gathers. Whether you stay, or go. Again, what do you bring?"

"I bring my experience. My desire to keep the forest safe. All the people who live under its branches. All those who look to us for assistance. Helping to keep them safe will keep my family safe."

"But you do not simply wish to keep us safe. You would strike at others. Bring justice to the men who killed this woman and my children."

"I would."

"That has never been my way."

"Maybe it should be."

"Impertinence! Is this the same arrogance that led you to defy me? The same assurance that you are in the right that led to more deaths? Would you lead us to yet more death and suffering?"

"No. I have made mistakes in the past. But I know the clans and the King cannot let our community stand forever. One day, they will come, and we will be overwhelmed. Despite the bravery, strength, and tremendous skills of our Brothers and Maidens, fire and death will come for us."

"And you would bring it faster. You would strike out. Always I have protected this place. Always we have been careful. Never sticking our hands too far into the bee hives."

"Then why send us out to find others at all? Why not simply plant more trees and make a wall of thorns to keep the outside away? Keep us safe, and let the rest of the Realms burn? Let all those children who need our help cry in vain?"

"We cannot help everyone."

"But we can help many. Sometimes, it is better to strike first. We have long been the shield. Now, it is time to be the sword."

"You sound like your Fairy."

"She is not my Fairy. I am hers."

"What if your actions bring the clans here? Or the King sends his knights? What will you tell the mothers of the dead?"

"What will you tell the mothers who kill their infants because they're Elenite? The young girl married off to an old man? What will you tell the mother killed by her husband? What will you tell the children left alone in the hands of such a cruel, evil man? You can see what will be. It's a risk, but I will not stand by as more children like me are spit on by Humans and Fairies. I will not stand by as my people are used and killed as chattel. By the King, or the Queen. It doesn't matter. We have a responsibility to help. To rebuild those who are broken, and stand firm against those who would break us."

"You use my words against me."

"Why create all this, then? Just to hide?"

"You might bring disaster down on all of us. Then who will fight for our children? Who will defend those women and their Elenite babies? If the forest burns, who?"

"Others will come. We have more allies than you know. There are plenty of evil men out there, but there are also others who stand in defiance of such evil."

"You, Spearhead, and your child bring strange currents. I cannot tell which will lead us to a quiet lake and which will break us on the rocks."

"We will stand firm."

"You have the ambition, but do you have the courage?"

"I find my courage in the eyes of my wife and my child. I find it in the eyes of my Brothers and Sisters. I find courage in the eyes of the women who bring their children here for safety. I find hope in every man who can rise above his upbringing and be better than his father."

"And if I refuse to risk the security of my children?"

"I will leave, and I will take my family with me. We will find another place of refuge."

"What if there is no such place?"

"Then we will make one."

The voice of the Mother faded in their minds. Canin and Spear looked at each other, suddenly understanding that each had spoken with the Mother in the privacy of their own mind. The light in the room began to dim. They shared another look and the realization that this home would be denied them.

"I'm sorry," Canin said, to both Spear and the Mother. He gripped Spear's hand. Tears in his eyes, he pulled his Thorn Brother knife from his belt. "Someone dear to me repaired this. Not knowing our ways, she rebuilt it, and made it stronger. I would take it with me." The light in the room flickered. "If you demand it, I will leave it. Maybe the love she wove into it will serve to remind you of what you say you're fighting for." Canin moved to lay the knife on the floor before him.

The Mother spoke. "Wait. I have not heard from the child. Aurora," the voice commanded, "why did you come here?"

A blue-green light bloomed around Aurora, widening out to enclose her in a shimmering bubble. Spear let go of Canin's hand and held the baby tight to her breast as the light grew. It began to pulse, slowly at first, and then rapidly. The white light of the Mother pulsed in response and then counter to Aurora's light. It grew in intensity. Spear and Canin closed and shielded their eyes, but stood firm. Aurora's aura grew brighter in response.

The Mother spoke from the light. "Some things are sure, and others are in flux. I see echoes. I hear old tales in your voice. I remember memories not my own."

Both lights began to dim, but Canin and Spear were still held out of time for a moment.

"Yes. This will be too much for them. One day they will remember."

Canin and Spear opened their eyes to the dim white light. He held out his knife.

"You shall keep it," the Mother of Exiles commanded.

Canin and Spear looked at each other, not knowing what that meant.

"You will need it. If you are to lead the forest to a new way, you must prove yourself. Canin, Spearhead, I grant you a home in the Exile Forest."

Spear began to smile, grinning and bending to kiss Aurora on the head. Canin, looking relieved, returned the blade to its sheath.

"Canin," the Mother continued. "Seek your justice. Prove to me and my Children that this is not the path of disaster."

Chapter 30
Manzanita and His Apples

"Is it today?" Spear asked.

"I don't know. Maybe," Canin told her as he was getting his boots on.

Aurora was burbling in her chair beside Lily at the table, and Alexander, in a rare moment, was sitting quietly eating his breakfast.

"You said it would be today," Spear said, her voice rising.

"I said I thought it might," Canin stressed.

Spear looked at Lily, who just sighed and fed Aurora another spoon of thin porridge.

"Mum, you said." Spear spoke in a voice that was becoming more of a whine with every word.

Lily spoke in a firm tone, her voice that of both the stern mother and the veteran sergeant, which Spear seemed to respond to the best. "I said that this is about the time he usually comes down from his mountain orchards. He's fickle. You can never tell." She looked to Canin to confirm it. He nodded.

"Why can't we just go up there?" Spear asked.

"No," Canin and Lily said together, making Alexander jump and drop his spoon. Aurora laughed at the chime of the metal on the floor, and he glared at her.

"He's very . . . particular about his orchards," Canin said. "He'll only let a few people up there, mostly to help him harvest, but beyond that. . . ." He let his thoughts drift off.

"Wolf went up there once, to get apples for his latest woman, and Manzanita forbade him and the other Brothers from buying any apples for a moon," Lily said, waving her spoon in a pointed way at Spear.

"Oh," Spear said, her face dropping. "I guess I just better. . . ." She stopped, staring up at the ceiling. "But Sekrine said . . . ."

"Sekrine can't be trusted when it comes to that man," Lily said with a smile. "She's . . . bound up tighter than one of her bandages, but won't admit it. Neither of them will."

"Maybe we could go by the market before I have to meet Maggie, then?" Spear asked, her face pleading.

"I have to meet Sam and the apprentices," Canin reminded her. At her hurt face, he added, "I'll try to get away by midday. We'll go then. Maybe he'll come down today," he said with a smile. "Mother willing."

Spear sighed, then smiled her resigned smile. Then she bounded over and kissed Aurora on the cheek, ignored Alexander, and kissed Lily on the forehead.

"Well, come on," Spear said, already at the door. Her gear leapt into her hands as she crossed the threshold. "You don't want to be late."

Canin sighed, then went and kissed Aurora and Lily and gave Alexander a friendly pat on the shoulder before running to catch up with his Fairy bride.

Lily, watching them go, didn't see Alexander push his bowl of porridge onto the floor. At the clatter, Lily looked back, making a surprised face.

"She did it," Alexander said, pointing at Aurora.

Knowing full well that the bowl had been too far away, Lily frowned, but knelt to clean up the mess.

☾ 〜 ☀

"I've never seen such an amazing wound!" Spear exclaimed with excitement.

Sekrine paused in wrapping a bandage around the leg of the injured Thorn Maiden. The woman had been attacked by a hungry wolf in the far northern part of the forest. Just a moon ago, she would have lost the leg, if she had even survived the trip back to the Sanctuary village and Sekrine's ward. Now, with Spear's help, they were able to save the leg and Heal most of the damage. She'd still be unable to walk for a few days, or run till at least the next moon, but she would recover almost total use of her leg.

"What kind of scars would you like to keep?" Spear asked the woman. She was still woozy from the pain-killing paste her comrades had treated the wound with. Even so, her eyes went a little wide at Spear's question.

"A few nice marks of the teeth, all fierce and growling?" Spear suggested, holding up her hand, mimicking the snarling beast. "Or the rake of the claws down the leg? Or maybe both," Spear suggested brightly. She leaned in closer to the Maiden. "Women love scars." She gave her a saucy wink.

"I think we can worry about that later," Sekrine said as the Maiden looked ready to pass out again. "Just rest, child," she said, with a firm hand on the woman's chest, pushing her back into the bed. Sekrine glared over at Spear, but the Fairy wasn't watching. She had her eyes closed and was flowing Healing into the wound.

For the uncountable time, Sekrine thanked the Mother for the blessing of this not quite broken, but very bent, Fairy.

"Do you think he'll come down today?" Spear asked eagerly, opening her eyes.

'And then she says something like that,' Sekrine thought, letting out a sigh.

"That man will come down when he comes down," she said harshly. "He does what he will. I have no control over him."

240

Spear looked disappointed. "But you come from the same place, and you've known him a long time, or so everyone says."

Sekrine held in another sigh. Spear was like a child sometimes, unable to take subtle hints. "He's from the barrier islands beyond the Fan. I'm from further back on the delta, where the fresh and saltwater meet with the tides. Different to us, but not to most people here. Or you," she muttered.

"How did you come here?" Spear asked, her face smiling with wonder. "It's so far down the Diamond River. Past the southern Fairy cities and unmapped swampy wilderness."

"He was a wanderer," Sekrine said, her eyes losing focus as she looked up. "He was searching, planting his trees as he went. Always moving. Following stories." She shrugged. "I met him on the road through the Human Realm. We . . . got each other out of some . . . difficulty with the Priests and their Axes."

Spear frowned. She knew the Axes, the fighting arm of the Priests of the Father. Fanatical, they threw themselves into battle with the Fairies. They never gave — or asked for — mercy or quarter. At a battle before Brine Hill, Spear's position had been overrun by them. She had been the only one to survive. The twisted scar on her leg from the back spike of one of their axes ached as she remembered, but she brutally pushed the memory away.

"I was being . . . drawn here," Sekrine continued, her voice more dreamy, and full of memories. "I just knew I had to find something. And that turned out to be the Mother and this forest." She smiled slightly wickedly. "I . . . persuaded him to come with me." Then she lost her smile. "I'm not sure if he thinks that was a good decision or an ill one at this point." She shrugged, and looked over the bandaged wound to ensure it was secure.

"I'm sure you did," Spear teased. "But you must know something," Spear pressed. "I've seen you get baskets and bottles of his cider. That boy who helps him in the orchards brings one two days after every new moon."

Sekrine narrowed her eyes at the Fairy. "That is between me and him, and none of your concern."

"But. . . ."

"I think you'd better go," Sekrine said sharply. "I can handle the rest." She tugged at the bandage, making the Maiden start.

Spear just stared at her, hands hovering over the injured woman between them.

"Go," Sekrine ordered, her voice getting faster and her accent becoming more pronounced. "I have nothing more for you today. Go bother Canin and the apprentices. I'm sure one of them has gotten themselves hurt and needs you."

"I was just. . .," Spear started, but Sekrine's glare turned icy and her self-taught Wards came up, her aura glowing with anger. The Wards were weak, but strong enough to make Spear's head hurt.

"Curse you . . . you Motherless little . . . wolf," Spear spit, anger and puzzlement radiating out from her. She turned away, striding by the beds of the other recovering people of the forest. Her gear rattled and chimed as her Power jerked it off the wall and into her hands. She managed to avoid slamming the door, but shut it firmly.

"What's wrong, ma'am?" the Maiden slurred, trying to sit up.

"Nothing, child. Just sleep," Sekrine said, running her hand over the woman's forehead. A little something Spear had shown her — after many wrong turns and errors — sent the woman into a healing sleep. Sekrine sat down heavily, tired from using her limited Healing Power. One of the Maidens assigned to her ran over with a cup of water, but Sekrine waved her away.

"Just need to sit for a moment," she told her. "Get back to your charges. I'm fine."

The woman looked skeptical for a moment, but the rise of one of Sekrine's bushy eyebrows sent her running off.

"When will you come down?" Sekrine muttered to herself. "It's been a long season, Manzanita."

As they walked through the late afternoon market, Canin wondered at how, in just a short time, Spear had been accepted and even welcomed into the forest community. Some would never accept her, though, and their fearful reactions to her hurt Spear more than she admitted.

Yarrow, the youngest of the Children of the Mother, had told Spear, "They aren't afraid of you. They're afraid of what you represent. Their past trauma and experience. Some will never get past you being a Fairy. Most will get used to it. It all just takes time."

Spear had shrugged and grunted, but Canin could see her deep-seated frustration. Spear wanted to serve the people of her new home, as she had served the Fairy Realm.

"They will see you for who you are," Canin assured her with a smile. "Eventually. I was afraid of you, too, at first."

That brought a goofy grin to her face, and she kissed him with passion. "You should be," she said after he got his breath back.

One of the reasons for Spear's swift acceptance came via Maggie and her Maidens. Always pragmatic, the Prime of the Thorn Maidens saw an opportunity for her women to gain the upper hand over their enemies. Using Fairy fighting techniques, even without the benefit of Fairy Power, would give them an edge. Even the best fighters could learn from Spear and her Fairy Patterns. It could give them a vital advantage when their lives were at risk.

Canin noted the smiles and the good-natured waves as they walked through the crowded market. He saw men and women walking on two legs who, before their arrival, might not have been. To his mind, that was the tipping point. Spear helped save lives.

But it also put a strain on her fragile mental state. Spear didn't always want to be the focus of everyone's eyes. Her damaged wings stood out, and no matter how stoic she was about it, Canin could see and feel the pain every time she tried to move them unconsciously, and was reminded of the reality of their condition.

It seemed everyone was happy to see Spear and Canin today. They were offered fragrant spits of meat and vegetables at one tent. Spear took them with a smile, despite her impatience to get to the far side of the market. Fumbling with coins to pay the man, Canin almost lost track of her in the crowd. Hurrying up to her, he found her before the newest tent in the market.

Everyone was happy to see them, except, it seemed, Manzanita himself.

"So, you're her," he said in a dismissive tone. "I expect you want some apples?"

Manzanita was tall and bony, almost gaunt. His skin was dark brown, with an undertinge of red that Canin remembered very distinctly. His long, straight black hair hung down his back in a simple tail, the ends ratty like a broom. He was clean shaven, except for a bushy, untrimmed mustache that hung over his lips. Mustaches were rare among Humans and Elenites. They had been the symbol and pride of a clan who had displeased the old King and been destroyed, branch to root. Even here, where the people of the forest didn't care what the King wanted, they were seen as bad luck.

Except for Manzanita. He didn't care.

Spear looked at him, stunned to speechlessness by his brusque, cold manner.

"Well, speak up, Fairy," he urged, waving his gangly hands, making the silver bracelets on both wrists spark in the sun. "You've been pestering my boy since you got here. Now I'm here. Speak!"

Spear almost took a step back, but her spine stiffened and the wooden spit in her hand snapped as she clenched her fists.

"We're just glad to finally meet you," Canin said, stepping up to the table and getting between Manzanita and Spear. "We've been waiting for you to come down. Everyone has."

"I know you, Brother," Manzanita said levelly. "Renegade, returned with a Fairy wife and child."

Hurt, Canin held himself straighter, his hand going to his wooden knife.

Manzanita's voice and look softened. "You ran errands for me one season. When you wanted to be a spinner. You would always sit with me, and listen to me talk." He smiled, his mustache moving like a separate part of him. "I was always glad for someone to listen."

"I loved your stories of the Fan, where Humans, Fairies, and Elenites lived in almost harmony," Canin said with a cautious smile, his hand still ready to grab Spear.

"I'm glad you're back," Manzanita said with a shake of his head. "It was a horrible thing, your . . . wife."

"It was," Canin said tightly.

Spear stood, staring at them, her face still, but her hands busy, wiping the grease from the broken spit on her pants.

"Well, I guess you deserve some," Manzanita said begrudgingly. He reached under the table and pulled out two shiny red apples. He tossed them at Spear.

She caught them without a flinch and held them to her nose, breathing deeply of their scent.

"Ah." She sighed wistfully. "I've missed these." She took a bite, crunching into the fruit. Her face filled with wonder as she chewed and swallowed. Then she looked at him with a wary eye.

"These are Fairy Realm apples. I didn't think they grew outside the Realm."

"They do here," Manzanita said with a smile. "I collected many seeds and cuttings in my wanderings." He smiled, losing some of his antagonism as he talked. "It took some doing, but I got them to grow. They thrive up there on the mountain." He gestured to the tall, tree-covered hill rising behind them. "It took many years."

"And you have so many!" Spear exclaimed, leaning over the table and looking at all the bushels of apples arrayed behind him. There were so many colors: shades from dark red to pink, to orange and dull yellow. Two apprentice Brothers ran back and forth, filling baskets and taking coins from the excited people of the forest. A third man stood in one spot, doling out bottles of cider in exchange for wooden tokens. His right leg ended at the knee, and the rest was a dark peg of thorn wood from the deep forest. He pivoted easily, the end digging in the dirt.

"Good soil up there, but I had to experiment, too," Manzanita continued.

This was the voice Canin remembered, the accent of liquid vowels and run- together words. He felt like a child again, sitting at Manzanita's feet, listening to him pontificate about good dirt, and water and sun. Then the old man's voice would dip, to complain that he'd never see his home again.

Canin smiled, watching Spear fall under the spell of the cadence of the old apple grower's voice. She finished one apple, core and all, and bit into the next.

"Ah," Canin said when Manzanita took a breath, otherwise he'd never get a word in. "Do you have any of the . . . special apples?"

Manzanita gave him a sharp look. "You know those are just for the Children and certain others. Only one tree grows them. At the top, under the shade of the rock She stood on all those years ago." He shook his finger at Canin. "You know better than to ask for those."

Canin sighed, and Spear's eyes shot up.

"What special apples?" she asked, her mouth full.

"They are. . . .," Canin started, but Manzanita made a chopping motion with his hand and Canin stopped.

"Now I have to know," Spear said, biting off the end of the core of her second apple. She chewed, looking at them both. "Please. I love apples so. They remind me of home. I. . . ." She glanced at Canin. "I can pay. I have silver, or we can barter. I have many skills. I. . . ." She smiled in the way that made Canin nervous.

Manzanita looked her up and down. "You don't have anything I need," he stated. "A basket of Fairy Red as a. . . ." His voice seemed strained. "Present for you and your new family." He looked at Canin, eyes piercing. "But beyond that, no."

"Manzanita," Canin pleaded, glancing at Spear. "I'm not asking for a whole apple, just a sliver. It would mean so much to her." He laid his hand on Spear's arm in an affectionate manner.

"No," Manzanita repeated, his mustache quivering. "You're trying to manipulate me. Playing on. . . ." His voice drifted away as he looked up, over their shoulders. He swallowed, his throat jumping like a nervous foal.

Canin followed his eyes and saw Sekrine moving through the crowd, heading almost hesitantly toward Manzanita's tent.

Without another word to Canin, Manzanita left them for the corner of the tent where she was headed. Waiting for her there, he fiddled with his bracelets. For a moment, it looked as though Sekrine was going to change course at the last moment and go somewhere else, but then she straightened her back and strode up to him. Separated by only the table, they stared at each other.

He was much taller than her, but to Canin's eyes, they seemed to match. Each of them began to reach out, their right arms raising and twitching.

Then Sekrine folded her arms. "So, you're back. Old man."

"Looks that way," he said, also folding his arms.

"You have my special brew?" she demanded. "I've been running low. Many wounds need cleaned." Her dark eyes swept the crowd. People moved out of her eye line.

"I do," he stated, not moving.

They stared at each other. Neither of them twitched.

Spear crunched loudly into another apple. Sekrine turned and glared at her. Spear waved. Sekrine looked back at Manzanita, her stance softening a little.

"Well?" she asked.

"The case is in the wagon," Manzanita said, glancing over his shoulder. "I was going to bring it by after . . . the sun goes down. I brought a bottle of the bitter yellow as well. Mixed in some ginseng I dug up. You always liked that."

His face looked pleading, and Spear almost laughed, but the firm grip Canin had on her arm made her take another bite of her apple instead.

"I just need my bottles. I have many patients," Sekrine stated. She resumed her stiff and unyielding stance. "You've been up there so long, you forgot our deal."

"I did no such thing," he disagreed. His mustache bristled. "You're the one who forgot. Or was it deliberate?"

Anger flashed in Sekrine's eyes. "I just need my bottles," she said stiffly.

"The case is heavy," Manzanita said. "I'll have to pull one of the apprentices away." He glanced at the busy young men running back and forth with baskets of apples. A slight groan rose from the crowd of people waiting.

Spear spoke up. "I can carry them." She passed the half-eaten apple to Canin. "Just show me where they're at. I can take them back to the ward." She looked at Sekrine, a glint in her eye. "Just tell me where to put them."

Sekrine took a deep breath, looking like she was going to refuse, then nodded.

"I'll show you where they are," Manzanita said, turning away from Sekrine. "Be careful with them. They take longer to make than regular cider."

"Don't worry," Canin said with a smile. "Spear has a light touch. When she wants to."

A light laugh rose from the people who couldn't help but hear. Spear grinned and followed Manzanita around the back of the tent.

Canin slid over to Sekrine and offered her one of the red apples. She took it absently and dropped it into a pocket of her coat. In a moment, Spear came back, two large crates floating in front of her. There was a little gasping and muttering at her display of Power, but she smiled and waved.

"I'll go back with you," Sekrine said, falling into step with Spear. She glanced back and saw Manzanita. "But . . . I'll be back. When you aren't so busy."

They shared a little smile and a nod. Canin started to follow the two women, but a third stepped in front of him.

Chapter 31
A Gift for Good Advice

"Tymora!" he exclaimed. He started to hug her, but then hesitated.

The woman was tall, with long grey hair that hung around her like a crown of morning mist. There was a blue cloak draped around her shoulders. She smiled at Canin's hesitation and pulled him into a hug.

Relieved, Canin gripped her tight. He could smell wood shavings and the sharp tang of glue all around her.

"I wasn't sure," he said as they held each other at arm's length. "I haven't seen you since I got back. I. . . ."

She shushed him with a smile. "I've just been busy." Tymora held his upper arms. "You've grown. I still remember you as the boy who could barely pull a bow."

Canin smiled. She looked older than he remembered. There were deep lines around her Elenite eyes and up her cheeks from her smile. He only remembered her with grey hair, but now, she seemed more frail. He felt a sudden panic and worry about her.

Tymora tilted her head. "We all get old," she said.

"I know. I just. . . ." Canin stuttered.

She smiled and let him go. "But I can still pull a bow."

"Of course you can," Canin said, relief flooding him. "I never thought. . . ."

With a shake of her head, she took his arm and pulled him away from Manzanita's tent. They went over to the side where there were a couple of tables. She sat down, shifting her cloak around her. Canin sat across from her. A young woman who had been at Tymora's shoulder set a cup on the table beside her.

"Deneir, can you fetch us something warmer?"

"Yes, ma'am," she said quickly, and was off.

"I seem to feel the cold more lately," Tymora said, pulling her cloak tighter. "One of my fletchers. I brought her along to find more feathers. Dornshen has us working day and night." Her eyes narrowed. "Some news from the Realms worries him."

"It worries me, too," Canin said. "I'm sorry my return has created so much chaos."

Her eyes remained narrow as she contemplated him. Canin began to feel like the boy he had once been again and fidgeted. The young fletcher returned, breaking the tension by setting down two cups of steaming bitter. Tymora gripped her cup, smiling at its warmth. Deneir stayed for a breath, waiting to see if her mistress needed anything else. When Tymora didn't say anything, Deneir gave them both a nod and set off in the direction of the tent with the chickens.

"You shouldn't be sorry," Tymora said after taking a drink. "We needed to hear the news and start getting ready. I've been saying for years that we need to take a more active role." She set down her cup, reached under her collar, and pulled out a silver coin on a chain. The plain worn surface reflected the setting sunlight. She ran her finger over it as she looked at Canin. "Your news just put fresh wood on an already hot fire."

"Not everyone sees it that way," Canin said, also taking a sip. He grimaced a bit. After a long time away, getting used to the drink made from the bitter berries of the Green was difficult. He missed Flora's tea. Or maybe it was Min sitting beside him as he drank it.

"I thought Cobalt and Dornshen were supporting you?" Tymora asked with a look of worry.

"They are," Canin said, putting the cup down. "But I sense their anxiety. Dornshen's job is to worry."

"It is," Tymora agreed with a smile. "And it's my job to make sure you're prepared." She gave the disk another rub, then slipped it back under her shirt. "What you wanted is almost ready. We'll be able to test it by the next quarter."

Canin looked up into the sky and fresh anxiety bloomed on his face. "That's good. I'll go see her. Soon."

"This is your plan," Tymora said with a sharp look. "And from what little I've been told, it's a good one. Those men need to pay. And bringing Jessamine into it is. . . ." She paused, taking a drink. "Inspired."

"Someone taught me justice needs to be personal for it to mean something," Canin said with a grim smile.

Tymora nodded, but her smile was a little worried. She started to say something, but suddenly looked over Canin's head.

"Who's this?" Spear asked, sitting down heavily beside Canin. She had an apple in one hand and a bottle of cider in the other. This apple was a lighter red than the ones she had eaten earlier, and the skin looked rough.

"This is Tymora," Canin said.

"Ah, you make such wonderful bows and arrows!" Spear exclaimed, setting down the apple and extending her hand to the other woman. Tymora took it hesitantly.

"Almost as good as the long bows from Realms End. Those could punch right through a knight's plate." Spear leaned back and picked up her apple. She looked at it, then sighed and set it on the table.

"Mine can, too," Tymora said with pride. "That's what they're designed to do."

"Kill Humans," Spear said a little too brightly. A few eyes turned in her direction.

"What she means is. . .," Canin said with some embarrassment.

"I know what she means," Tymora interrupted. "My bows are used to defend the forest from its enemies." She gave a long look at Spear. "Whoever they may be."

"That's what I meant," Spear said with a smile. "Your bows pull so smoothly and release with so much power." She smacked her hands together. "Right through!"

Tymora looked a little puzzled, then smiled. "I'm glad you approve. I was thinking, since you're stronger than most, I could make you one with a stronger pull."

"But then it would be too heavy," Spear said. "I need to be quick."

"The wood from the deep forest is strong and light. I might. . . ." Tymora's eyes got a little unfocused. "I'd have to. . . ." She looked up, lost in thought.

Spear looked at her for a moment, then said, "I would be honored, ma'am."

"What?" Tymora said, her train of thought broken. "Oh, yes. I'll think on it." She got up. "I must go. It was good to meet you."

"And you, too," Spear said.

Canin smiled, watching the forest's chief fletcher and bow-builder walk away. He turned back to Spear.

"I expected you to be gone longer."

Spear shrugged.

After a moment, when Spear didn't say more, Canin asked, "So what happened with Sekrine?"

Spear got a secret smile and pulled him up. Canin scrambled, grabbing the basket of apples as he was pulled along. Back at Manzanita's tent, they found Sekrine, putting order to the line of people waiting for apples, while Manzanita and the apprentices loaded baskets. Sekrine glanced in their direction and gave a little nod.

Canin didn't have time to react before Spear pulled him around and headed toward the edge of the market.

"Lily wanted me to pick something up for dinner," Spear explained, hurrying him along.

Soon burdened both with the apples and a freshly killed chicken, Canin didn't have a chance to inquire further till they were back home and dinner was cooking.

"So, what did you do?" Canin asked as he bounced Aurora on his knee, making her laugh.

Spear said, "I simply told her, if she wants to win the battle, she must charge."

"Oh," Canin said.

Lily, who was busy trying to keep Alexander from burning himself on her freshly-baked bread, laughed.

"Niel was the same way," she said, pulling Alexander into her lap to keep him out of danger. "I had to practically grab him and shake him." She demonstrated with Alexander, and he laughed.

"Canin's still that way," Spear noted, sharing a look with Lily.

Canin felt his face go hot and sought refuge behind the giggling Aurora, while the two women shared knowing smiles.

Later, after Aurora and Alexander were in bed, there was a knock at the door. Canin answered it to find one of the apprentices who had been helping Manzanita.

"Setab," he said with indifference, handing Canin a small bag tied with string. "For your wife."

Confused, Canin accepted the bag, but before he could ask about its contents, the young man had run off into the dark. Shrugging, Canin shut the door and took the bag to Spear.

She unknotted the string and upended the bag. An object blacker than the deepest well tumbled into her hand.

"Mother Mercy!" Lily exclaimed.

"Is that?" Canin asked, his breath short in awe and shock.

Spear, unimpressed, turned the object in her hand. "It's an apple," she said finally. "A black apple." She looked at Canin and his mother, perplexed by their awe. "I've never seen something so black." She held it up. "It's like a piece of the sky."

"That's one of Starlight's apples," Lily said, holding her hands together tightly. "The Children of the Mother always claim those from the one tree Manzanita grows. Clawsister says they're like nothing she's ever tasted."

Spear looked at Canin. "Was this what you tried to get from him and were denied?" She beamed at him, her eyes full of love and desire.

"I. . . ." Canin coughed, suddenly feeling awkward in his entire body. "I just thought, since you've done so much . . . and you like apples. . . ."

He stopped as Spear came over and sat in his lap, making both him and the chair groan. Her kiss was firm and deep and went on for a long time.

Lily cleared her throat and Spear broke the kiss to look at her.

"If you two are going to be noisy, best to go." She made a 'get going' motion with her hand. "You'll wake the children."

"Yes," Spear said, standing. "But first we must taste this."

She brought the apple to the table and set it reluctantly down. It sat there like an irregular globe of night. They gathered around, staring at it in wonder.

With a flourish, Spear pulled her knife, and used the silksteel blade to cut through the black flesh of the apple. The halves fell apart, exposing an inner fruit as white as the skin was black. A sweet scent, unlike anything any of them had smelled before, filled the room.

"I. . ." was all Lily managed to say before she sat down, staring at the fruit. "I never thought I'd see something so beautiful."

"The stories say She was like that. Dark and beautiful," Canin said, his voice full of wonder. Then he shook his head. "Almost like. . . ."

Spear stopped his thoughts with a swift motion. "Not like that at all." She cut each of the halves again, yielding four pieces. The seeds inside were as dark as the skin. Spear took the tip of her knife and pulled one out.

"You're supposed to save those and give them back to Manzanita," Lily said, shaking herself out of the awe of the moment.

"I heard they cure women of childlessness," Canin said, reaching out but not quite touching one of the slices. Spear looked at the seed sharply, her eyebrows going up.

"They belong to Manzanita and his orchard," Lily said sharply. She picked up a small bowl and with respectful motions began to pick the seeds from the apple slices. They hit the bowl with a musical chime. Canin sat back, feeling the weight of the moment. It was like he was before the Mother again, listening to Her voice in his mind.

When she was finished, Lily pushed the bowl out of Spear's reach and gestured to the four quarters.

"One for each of us, and the fourth the children can share," she said.

"They're too young to understand," Spear said, grabbing one of the quarters. "And this was a gift for me."

"Trillium," Canin said with a touch of disapproval. "We shouldn't be selfish with this gift."

"I'm not being selfish; I just think they're too young. Alexander wouldn't understand," she said with a frown. Spear took the quarter and waved it under her nose. All her negative emotions fell away as the sweet scent surrounded her.

"Goddess," she muttered, resisting the urge to devour the whole slice in one bite. She licked the fruit and closed her eyes, quivering in ecstasy.

Canin found himself having to look away, his whole being overcome by strong feelings of desire for Spear, and also the pain that he couldn't share this with Min. The skin of the apple felt slick in his hand, like Fairysilk, or Min's slip as he'd pulled it over her head that first night at the inn in Bell-Oak. Pushing away the past, he closed his fist on the slice.

"Mother mercy!" Lily exclaimed, covering her mouth as she chewed. "That is the sweetest thing I've ever tasted. Even sweeter than honey." She took another bite. "I wish Niel could taste this." A tear ran down her face as she swallowed.

Spear put the whole slice in her mouth, but didn't chew. Her eyes were luminous and brimmed with joy.

"*Come on,*" she Sent to Canin, grabbing his arm and pulling him toward the door.

"We'll be back before dawn," Canin said, but he wasn't sure his mother heard him as Spear hurried him out the door.

"Now I understand why they say these cure childlessness," Canin said languidly.

Spear muttered something unintelligible into his chest.

They lay on the soft grass under a thorn tree steps into the forest at the edge of the Sanctuary village. Spear muttered again, her damaged wings moving as she gripped him tighter.

He ran a gentle finger down her neck and across one of her shoulder blades. Spear shivered, raising her head to look at him.

For a breath, his mind was assaulted by images of pain and loss and the emotions she had felt during those times. Grief and regret, deeper than anything she'd shared with him before. Anger and betrayal that made his blood freeze. He reached for his knife, laying under his cast-off clothes, afraid of what this Fairy soldier might do.

Then she smiled, wicked and full of lust.

"You cannot pierce my Ward that easily," she said. Spear grabbed his reaching hand and pinned it to the tree. "But I enjoy it when you try."

She kissed him, and Canin swooned. Her mouth and lips were sweet, both with the special apple and with their mutual love and desire. His free arm went around her waist and pulled her up his body.

Footsteps deliberately crunching in the undergrowth and fallen leaves made him open his eyes.

"Figured it was you two," Granite said with a smirk. "Somebody said bears were . . . fighting in the woods. Good thing I'm the one on night patrol. Called off a whole squad of Brothers."

Spear rolled off Canin, sitting up, unconcerned with her nakedness. "They wouldn't have been welcome." She stretched. "This time."

Granite's eyes went wide, and he looked away, after a long pause.

Canin wasn't self-conscious about his nakedness, either. For a moment, anyway; then he grabbed his shirt, covering himself.

Granite laughed, turning his back fully. "Come on. Wolf and Maggie want a full meeting over breakfast."

Canin knew what that meant and grabbed the rest of his clothes, struggling to put them on.

"Are you coming?" he asked Spear, trying to push both feet into one leg of his trousers.

"No," Spear said, her voice soft. "I'll bathe, then go home. You can tell me all about it later."

Her projected fear gave Canin pause.

"It's just to plan. I'm not leaving today," he reminded her, finally getting his trousers on the right legs.

"I know. But. . . ." Her fear turned to amusement. "You got me quite . . . dirty. I need to clean up before I can go home to your mother and our daughter."

Canin chuckled, then threw an annoyed look at Granite when he laughed, too.

"Go on, Setab," he said. "I'll catch up."

"I'm sure you will," Granite quipped, then jogged off into the woods.

Canin turned back to Spear. He felt a strong wave of love and desire for her wash over him, while he struggled into his shirt. She pulled it together at his chest and smiled.

"Go. I'll probably be with Sekrine." Spear kissed him, then pushed him away to fumble with his buttons.

"Unless she was out late, too," Canin said, buckling his belt.

"She'll be there. She's never late." Spear grinned, stretching again. "Even if she's a little bleary-eyed."

Canin laughed. He wanted to stay, but duty called, and, with one final kiss, he ran off after Granite.

Chapter 32
A Lesson of Forgiveness

The young thorn trees weren't as close together in this part of the forest. Cheerful sunlight washed over the soft grass of the clearing, setting the blades afire with emerald light. A faint breeze clacked the branches, a warm and welcoming sound.

Lily clung to Canin's arm, or maybe he clung to hers.

"This is where he's . . . resting?" Canin asked.

Lily nodded, her hand still tight on his arm.

Canin looked out over the green grass and the swaying trees before them and smiled. 'Yes. Niel would love it here,' he thought. Guilt and grief bubbled up within him and he forced back a tear.

"Where?" he asked, taking a step forward, but Lily didn't move.

"I don't know," she finally said. Her voice was strong and even. Her pain was only evident in the tightness of her grip.

Canin looked at her, surprised and a little shocked.

Lily smiled slightly.

"I said my goodbyes to him at home," she explained. "The other farmers and the members of his creche took him. . . . Took his. . . ." Her voice broke, and Canin stepped back, hugging her to his side.

Lily took a breath and continued. "I wanted to remember him as he was, not as the shell they buried." She took her arm from Canin's and stood up straighter. "He loved these trees. Always came out here when he needed wood to build a chair, or a table. He wanted to give himself back to the forest that had been his home." Lily smiled, brushing a stray hair away from her cheek. "Wolf was here, too, if you want to know exactly where he was buried."

Inside, Canin winced. Living so long among Fairies, that word had become a curse — a slur — in his mind. Now, here, it was just the end of most people's last journey. It was one of the things Spear feared the most. He had seen her whole body strain and her face wince when Sekrine had mentioned the final preparations for one of her patients.

"Mother," he said haltingly. "I'm sorry I wasn't here. That I wasn't. . . ."

"I know," Lily said. "I am, too. But what's done is done." She drew a long breath. "Some of his last words were wondering about you, and if you were safe and happy. I'm sure he knows now, but it still breaks my heart."

Canin wanted to embrace his mother, ask her again for her forgiveness, but her folded arms kept him still and silent at her side.

Lily took a small step, then knelt and brushed her hand over the grass.

"I love you," she said. Then she straightened and looked him in the eye.

"I have duties with Sekrine, and then I'm going with the Maidens to the Helenium fields." She smiled. "The flowers are blooming, and I love the smell." She patted his arm. "I will see you for dinner?"

Canin smiled, understanding. "Unless Wolf and the other Brothers have more duties for me."

Lily smiled back, then gave him a quick hug before walking quickly out of the clearing.

Canin stood there, absorbing the smell of the grass, the feel of the wind, and the sound of the trees. He took a few steps in and then stopped. He knelt, brushing his hand on the soft grass, remembering falling out of trees and being cushioned by grass just like this. He laughed and let a tear slide down his face.

Canin could feel Niel here. His good nature and strong will. He didn't understand all the debates about what happens to you after you die, but he knew a part of his father was still here. Not trapped, like the Fairies feared, but existing alongside the trees and the grass. Drifting at Canin's side. Happy, but still stern with his wayward son.

He might never let go of the guilt. It was part of him now. It was a lesson, hard in the learning, but necessary. Part of the path, as Flora might say.

Canin took out his wooden knife and laid it on the grass.

"I'm sorry, Niel. . . . Father," he said low. "I never called you that. I understand now. Forgive me, if you can. I'll never forget you."

Canin bowed his head, pressing his forehead into the grass. A breeze tickled his ear. In his memory, he could hear Niel's gentle voice saying, 'Sometimes it doesn't come out right the first time. But we can always try again.'

With a smile, he sat up. Behind him, he could hear Spear's footsteps and Aurora's soft babble.

"He's here?" Spear asked, standing by his side.

"Yes," Canin confirmed, retrieving his knife and standing. "His spirit is here. Returned to the forest."

A bit of fear passed behind Spear's Fairy eyes, quickly replaced by a smile.

"Good. Does he forgive you?"

"I think so," Canin said with a smile. "He kept grudges, but never against his family."

"I understand," Spear said. "If he's here, he should meet his granddaughter."

Spear gestured up and over and Aurora was lifted out of the carrier on her back. Cooing and smiling, Aurora drifted over to Canin and dropped into his arms.

"You love to fly, don't you, Little Wing?" Canin said, nuzzling his daughter's growing hair. She smelled like life and sunshine.

He set her down in the grass, then sat beside her. Spear plopped down on the other side. She grinned and pointed, drawing Aurora's attention.

"Look, one of those red birds with the black wings."

Aurora smiled, but Canin doubted that she could see the small bird high in the tree. Or maybe she could. Aurora was always surprising them.

She waved her arms, and the bird took wing, first flying over them, then disappearing into the trees. Aurora laughed and fell over, giggling and squirming in the soft grass. Spear did the same thing, laying down and laughing as she made patterns in the meadow.

Canin laughed out loud, and he knew Niel was laughing, too.

They stayed for a while, watching Aurora roll around in the field and attempt to crawl, but she kept flopping onto her face. Canin finally picked her up and held her in his arms. She kept squirming and reaching out away from him.

"What do you want, Little Wing?" he asked. She shook her hand toward the edge of the forest.

Spear was no help. She was lying on her stomach, making more waves in the grass. Knowing his stubborn daughter and her tendency to cry when she didn't get what she wanted, Canin stood up.

"Which way?" he asked her, and Aurora reached out toward a young, fast-growing tree on the edge of the woods.

"Okay," he said, and walked toward that tree.

It was a young tree, and its thorns were small and oddly spaced. But they were still sharp.

"Careful, Little Wing," Canin cautioned, as Aurora reached toward the bark. "You'll learn about those thorns one day, but not right now." He guided Aurora's little hand toward a portion of the bark that was free of danger.

Aurora cooed as her fingers touched the tree. Canin placed his hand beside hers. The tree swayed in the wind, and the branches above them clacked. Aurora's eyes were drawn up as a leaf drifted down toward them. The wide, spade-shaped leaf settled on Canin's outstretched arm.

Canin felt a moment of peace, of certainty not unlike the first time he had touched Aurora. He was home, and on the right path.

"Thank you," he said to the tree.

Aurora giggled and reached for the leaf. She grabbed it, holding it for a moment before moving to put it in her mouth.

"No, no," Canin said with a laugh, grabbing her arm before Aurora could begin gumming the leaf. "Mama doesn't want you eating leaves, Little Wing."

"Depends on the leaf," Spear quipped, leaping off the ground and landing in a soldier's ready crouch. Then she grinned and strode over to take Aurora.

"Time to go," Spear decreed, holding the baby before her. Aurora laughed as Spear's Power gently took her and floated her back to settle into the carrier on Spear's back. Canin leaned in to make sure the straps were secure and that the pad behind Aurora's head was in place.

"Wolf wants you at the meadow at the edge of the village," Spear said. "You're still not fast enough."

Canin shook his head. His legs burned from days of running back and forth across the sloping meadow. He had to get his endurance back. Every Thorn Brother had to be able to run the forest.

"I'm as fast as all the apprentices," he said defensively.

"But you have to be better than them," Spear stated, and Canin could hear the echo of Shatter and Steel in her command.

"Yes, ma'am," he said automatically.

Spear grinned and took his arm.

"What are you going to do?" he asked as they walked out of the clearing.

"Watch you, and eat all the purple berries I can," Spear said with a raised eyebrow and a wide grin.

"Pick some to take back with us. Lily can make tarts with them."

"Maybe," Spear said with a sly smile.

Canin shook his head and Aurora laughed, throwing herself around the carrier, making Spear first stumble, then laugh along with her as she recovered her footing.

Chapter 33
Giving Them to the Forest

Canin followed far enough behind the apprentice Thorn Brother and the Human father that he wasn't seen. The dim light under the close-growing thorn trees and his forest-woven silk cloak and hood of shifting green and brown also aided in the deception. Canin could have walked right on the heels of the Thorn Brother, and the father wouldn't have noticed. He had come looking for his runaway daughter, and was singularly focused on finding her.

This one was one of the quiet ones, silent in his anger and hurt pride. He only spoke a few words, certain that his bribe of silver was getting him taken via a secret pathway to where his daughter was living. He only spoke up when he was separated from the other men he had brought.

"The way in narrows, and we must move quietly," the apprentice had said. "I can cover your steps, but all the others. . . ." He smiled at the man with indifference.

"I'll bring the others by similar trails," Sam had said with the same smile. "We'll meet you there."

"Make sure of it," the father had said, looking down at his pouch of coins, which he jingled before handing over.

With the indulgent smile of a servant, the apprentice led him into the dark of the forest.

Canin was tired, but also full of nervous, ready energy. Many men had come to the forest in the last moon. It was wedding time in the Human Realm, and many women had decided they didn't want to be bound to cruel, heartless, demanding, or just careless men. Driven by shame and the loss of their investment, many fathers and deserted husbands had followed them.

They had all been given to the forest, in one way or another.

The angry ones were easy to manage. The arrogant, pompous ones, too. It was the quiet ones that Canin was always uneasy about. They might be smart enough to see through the deception, or devious enough in spirit that they assumed everyone was of the same mind. His hand hung gently on the crossbow at his side. It was light, easy to hide, and quick to aim and fire, thanks to Tymora's latest modifications.

Canin smiled, sure that even if the man tried something, he would still wind up being given to the forest. Maybe with a few bolts in him, before the thorns took him, but his blood would still feed the trees.

"It's getting dark," the father muttered, glancing over his shoulder.

"Best time," the apprentice said with a smile. "They'll be finished with the planting, and tired from the day's labor. We'll sneak up on them, grab her, and be gone before the alarm is raised."

The man grunted and kept moving forward. He brushed at the low-hanging leaves, shying away from the thorn-covered branches all around him. He was getting nervous, and suspicious, Canin could see, as the trail became narrower and the thorns pressed in.

They made a turn, and Canin stopped, letting the two of them go further into the narrowing tunnel of thorns.

The father fumed. "That way is blocked," he said, his hand on his long knife. "Did you make a wrong turn? Stupid half-breed! My dogs are better guides."

"No. This is the correct trail. I've guided you to your destiny," the young Elenite said, his voice full of conviction. "The Mother showed me the proper path for men like you."

Faster than most, the father recognized what was happening. He drew his blade and ran at the apprentice. Canin brought his crossbow to his shoulder, aiming.

The apprentice was faster. He blocked the father's downward thrust with one arm, and hit him in the shoulder with his other fist. The father grunted, and the blade fell from his hand to clatter in the groundcover. The apprentice brought his own hidden crossbow up and shoved the man back. The father's eyes widened when faced with a steel-tipped bolt right in his face. He stumbled back, crying out as thorns pierced his arm.

"I have more silver," he offered, trying to yank his arm away, but vines wrapped around him, holding him, pulling him back. He screamed as his back hit a tree trunk and tiny thorns pierced his back and legs. His other arm was still free, and he yanked at the vines holding his arm. Blood flowed as more thorns ripped into his hand.

"You have nothing I need," the apprentice said, getting closer. "But you're what the forest needs."

'Too close,' Canin thought, but he didn't call out.

The father grabbed at the apprentice, bloody hand on the stock of the crossbow, forcing it up. The wood smacked into the apprentice's face and the weapon fired, sending a bolt into the air. It made a sound like the fluttering of wings as it passed through the leaves.

Stumbling back, his hand going to his bloody nose, the apprentice let go of the crossbow. The father, his face lighting up with glee, tried to level the bow one handed. Canin kept a steady aim on the man's chest, ready to fire. This was one of the tests for new Thorn Brothers, and he wasn't ready to step in yet.

Muttering angrily, the apprentice straightened, shaking his body. He took his hand away from his face, letting the blood flow.

"Let me go!" the father demanded, waving the crossbow. "Free me! Or I'll shoot you!"

The apprentice grunted, spitting blood. Then he smiled. "How?" he asked, pointing at the crossbow.

The man looked down, finally seeing the empty weapon.

"It only holds one," the apprentice said, spitting more blood. With an angry gesture, he pointed at the man's arm. Thorny vines reached out, winding around the father's free arm and pulling it back.

The man screamed, dropping the crossbow. He whimpered as more vines wrapped around his body, holding him tight to the tree. He struggled, which only made the thorns sink deeper into his body.

"Damn you, you half-breed filth, and your foul Magic!" he yelled.

The apprentice wiped his face. The blood had stopped flowing. Still wary, he approached the thorn-bound man. Picking up his crossbow, he looked right into the father's eyes.

"You should have just let her go."

The father surged forward in his vine prison, grasping for the apprentice. Jumping back in fear, the apprentice gestured, and the vines tightened, jerking the father back. A thorn pierced his face, going through his right cheek, and filling his mouth with blood.

Mumbling in pain, his eyes filled with both tears and fear.

"Kill me, then," he said, his words garbled. "That's what you want."

"I don't want anything. The forest does." The apprentice folded his arms. "The Mother of Exiles does. Our Queen of Thorns defends us. We are but her arms and hands."

The father tried to laugh, but it came out in a gurgle, blood bubbling on his lips. "Then you're just going to leave me here?"

The apprentice glanced over his shoulder. Canin lowered his crossbow and nodded. A wordless understanding passed between the two men. The apprentice nodded back.

"No." The apprentice sat down, arraying his cloak around him. "I have to stay till you die. It's my last test."

The father's eyes widened. He tried to move, but the vines held him tight. Blood seeped from the hundreds of tiny holes where thorns had pierced his clothing and skin. Realization dawned on him.

"Kill me!" he begged. "Use my blade. Slit my throat." The apprentice just shook his head.

"It'll take days! I might starve first!" He lunged forward, maybe to drive the thorns deeper, but the vines held him still.

"Three days without water," the apprentice said with a shrug. "But the trees get hungry. Their thorns will grow into you. A day or two perhaps. One man lasted five. But most don't."

The man thrashed, but only succeeded in driving more tiny thorns into his face. He moaned, then let out a scream as more thorns pierced his back. He kept wailing and shrieking.

The apprentice sat still. Canin winced, remembering his own first man given to the forest. He had screamed himself hoarse, then begged and pleaded silently. It had taken two days for the thorns to do their work.

The apprentice looked at Canin. There was pain in his eyes, but also determination. If he ran, leaving his first victim to the forest, he would be demoted, and have to start his training all over again. Some did. The cries were too much. The eyes of the victim too cutting.

Many tried again. Others moved on to other tasks in the forest. Not everyone could be a Thorn Brother, and there was no shame in discovering you couldn't do this part of the role. Canin himself had almost run, fleeing the screams.

But he knew this one wouldn't. The sounds of the dying father would haunt him forever, but so would the knowledge that there was one less horrible man in the Realm. One less abuser, one less killer of children and women.

"We stand firm against all who would break us," Canin said, his voice low.

The apprentice nodded. He settled back against a tree trunk.

The father screamed again. The apprentice reflexively moved to cover his ears, but then, with resolute determination, he dropped his hands.

"Please, please, please!" came the begging.

"No."

Canin turned. His part of the test was over. He would leave the apprentice as Wolf had left him, so many seasons ago. He felt sympathy for the young man. This night would be long, but in the morning, he would emerge a Thorn Brother and take his place as a defender of the forest. A servant of the Mother of Exiles.

Another thorn in the armory of the Queen of Thorns.

Chapter 34
A New Thorn Brother

The morning crows were just beginning to flutter about, calling to their rook mates, when the man hanging in the thorns died.

The apprentice Thorn Brother, Griffin, looked up from his carving. He had been using the man's long knife to shape bits of wood into birds and wings. For as long as he could remember, he had been obsessed with a certain class of huge creatures. They were taller than a warhorse, with the body of a lion, and the head and wings of an eagle. They were the only thing he remembered from his life before the forest.

"A griffin," Aieren had said wisely on their first meeting. "Creatures of the far past, from the days of the First Fairies and Humans. One of the first Human kings tried to tame them. He wanted to use them as horses, flying on them in his war with the Fairies. One tore his head clean off and ate half his family."

The Maiden who had found him wandering lost and alone by the houses at the crossroads in the Human Realm and adopted him as her son had glared at Aieren for telling such a bloody story. But Griffin didn't care. He loved the beasts, and wanted to know more.

"So, there aren't any anymore?" he asked.

"Regrettably, no," Aieren confirmed. "If they could not be bound, they would be destroyed. The Humans hunted them to extinction. The Mother told tales of one bound by strong Wards, asleep under a forgotten tower somewhere to the far west of the Fairy Realm." She made a vague gesture in the general direction of west.

"Do you have any books? Pictures?" Griffin asked, turning to his Thorn Maiden mother.

"No, son, I don't," she told him. To his disappointed face, she added, "But the next time I go on a run to the Human Realm, I'll see what I can find."

Griffin either drew the beast or carved it every moment he could. So, of course, it also became his name, as he left behind the one his unremembered birth mother had given him. Most of the time, he couldn't remember that one anyway. All he had from that life was a torn bit of tapestry, with strange words on one side and the fading image of a griffin on the other.

Griffin stood. The man had stopped moaning a while ago. The rattling breaths had come slower and slower until their absence made the silence seem loud.

"How will I know?" Griffin had asked Wolf.

"You will know," Wolf had said simply.

"But. . . ."

Wolf made a dismissing motion, returning his attention to the sparring matches that all the other apprentices were engaged in.

And Griffin did know. It hadn't taken as long as some of the Brothers had told him it might. Maybe the forest and the Mother had taken pity on him and drained the life from this horrible man faster.

Or maybe the father hadn't been as strong as he'd boasted. Griffin smiled at that thought.

With a wet, ripping sound, a thorn burst out of the man's chest. Startled, Griffin dropped his knife and the half-completed wooden bird he'd held. The body made a sound like air leaving a waterskin. The smell of voided bowels made Griffin choke and pull his cloak up to cover his nose and mouth. The foul stench marched toward him, but Griffin stood his ground, breathing shallowly through the cloth. After a moment, the clean smell of water and new grass wafted from behind him, and the evil smell was pushed back.

Breathing in relief, Griffin let the cloak fall.

"What do I do? After?" Griffin had asked Wolf, Canin, and the other Thorn Brothers as they waited for the men they were giving to the forest.

"Leave them. Everything they carry goes as tribute to the forest." Wolf's serious face turned up in a grin. "We'll be sure to take all the coins they have in . . . payment."

A laugh ran through the gathering Brothers, quickly stilled.

"Even the bones?" Griffin asked. "Don't Humans want to be buried? Shouldn't we burn them? We're giving them want they want."

Wolf grumbled in annoyance. "You'll have to talk to Clawsister or Yarrow about all the different funeral rites, and all the mystical reasons behind them." He made a vague gesture in the air. "All I know is, we always leave the body to be consumed by the forest. More, I leave to others."

Griffin opened his mouth again, but Wolf stilled him with a glance. "They're coming."

"Leave everything," Griffin muttered, cautiously approaching the body. The scent of death was being rapidly absorbed by the trees and vines around him. The man's eyes were open, staring at him in dull accusation.

"You shouldn't. . . ." Griffin's voice broke in a sudden flood of emotions. Regret, revulsion, pride, and righteous anger all filled his heart. He stumbled, fighting the unexpected onslaught of sensations. Canin had tried to warn him, but he hadn't understood until now.

"You shouldn't have come back," Griffin said, his voice rising in confidence. "You should have let her go. Gone back to your life. But now you're dead, and good riddance to you. Curse you, and all other men like you."

He reached up and grabbed the thorn sticking out of the man's chest. Carefully avoiding the point, but not caring about the blood, he twisted. It resisted, slipping in his hand. Griffin frowned, worried about how he was going to get it out, but then, with a sudden snap, the thorn came free. Stumbling back, he stared at it, surprised and awed.

The thorn was longer than his arm, and black as night. Griffin started, almost dropping the piece of wood, afraid it was a deadly blackthorn. But the surface was smooth, almost warm in his hand. Griffin breathed a sigh of relief.

"Thank you, Mother of Exiles, for your faith in me," he said with reverence. "I will serve you as a faithful Thorn Brother." He bowed to the trees around him.

They seemed to bow back as a morning breeze wafted by him.

Drawing another fortifying breath, he wiped the blood and other bits from the thorn on the dead man's clothes. As he turned to leave, Griffen spied the man's knife on the ground. The silksteel of the blade reflected a dim light, rainbows in the steel.

"It can't hurt," Griffin whispered, kneeling and picking up the blade. "It's good steel. Rare. And he didn't really have it on him, because he dropped it before the thorns took him." Smiling at his reasoning, Griffin left his half-carved bird and tucked the blade into his belt.

He glanced back at the body. With a smile, he raised the thorn in mocking salute, then turned, leaving the dead man to the forest.

"Is he dead?" the Brother at the exit to the trail challenged.

"He is," Griffin confirmed, raising the thorn as proof.

The Thorn Brother looked at it with careful eyes, then smiled widely.

"Welcome, Brother!" he exclaimed, pulling Griffin into an unexpectedly strong hug. Griffin gasped at the sudden intensity, closing his eyes to unexpected tears.

"Sit," the Brother urged, finally letting him go. He motioned to another Brother standing a bit further away. "Sam, stay with him. I'll run to tell Wolf and the others." With a smile, the Thorn Brother ran off, disappearing into the new dawn.

Sam ambled over and offered Griffin a cup of water. He took it eagerly and drank greedily. Never had the spring water of the forest tasted so good.

With a grin, Sam sat down beside him.

"We didn't expect you out so soon," he admitted.

Griffin shrugged, and moved to give the cup back. The thorn felt suddenly heavy in his other hand, but he didn't want to put it down.

"He's really dead," he said with a worried edge. "I didn't kill him. I didn't. . . ."

Sam stopped him with a raised hand. "Don't worry. Sometimes it takes a long time. And sometimes." Sam snapped his fingers, and Griffin jumped, then smiled.

"How long was it for you?" Griffin asked.

Sam lost his smile. He poured himself a drink and sipped it before answering.

"More than two days."

Griffin gasped.

Sam chuckled. "Wolf was worried. Well, he didn't say so, but I could see it when I came out. Everyone was waiting."

Griffin smiled in understanding. "How did you. . . Didn't you get hungry? Or. . . ."

Sam pushed the cup back at him to still the questions.

"I didn't get hungry, really. Hard to, with someone hanging there."

"Sorry. I didn't . . .," Griffin muttered.

"No matter," Sam said with a faraway look. "She sent me water, and a few berries grew around where I was waiting." He took a deep breath. "He begged and cried almost till the end. I kept wishing the thorns would grow into his mouth, but. . . ." He stopped. "In the end, the forest took him." He patted his wooden knife.

"Yes, it did," Griffin said, with a glance at the thorn in his hand.

They stayed quiet till the others began to arrive.

Sam pulled Griffin to his feet as Wolf and a small crowd of Thorn Brothers walked out of the morning mist. They stood quietly, hands on their knives, till a running Canin appeared. He stopped, puffing and looking like he had been pulled out of bed. Wolf gave him a pointed stare and Canin adjusted his belt and stepped forward.

"Is he dead? Given to the forest?" Canin asked, standing before Griffin.

"He is. The forest took him," Griffin replied. He held out the thorn as proof.

A whistle of appreciation moved through the Brothers.

"A powerful thorn," Canin remarked. "For a strong Thorn Brother." He took the black thorn and held it up. Everyone fell silent.

"For the forest," Canin intoned. "And the Mother of Exiles. Our Queen of Thorns."

"For the forest," the others chorused. "For the Mother. For all."

Canin turned and looked at Wolf, who was smiling widely.

"Prime. Our brother has come out of the forest. He brings a token of his duty and commitment to defending the forest from all its enemies. Is he worthy?"

Wolf stepped up to Canin and Griffin, the smile fading into a look of serious responsibility. He took the thorn from Canin and looked at it, bringing it close to his eyes.

"What do you say, Brother?" he asked, looking at Griffin. "Are you worthy to join our brotherhood? These Thorn Brothers who stand before you? Are you ready to defend them, and all of the forest, to your last breath? To give your life to the Mother of Exiles, and all who live here?"

Griffin swallowed, suddenly faced with the reality of what he had been striving toward for so many seasons. All he had ever wanted was to bear the knife and help others.

"I don't know if I'm worthy," he said, voice breaking. "But I'm ready. The forest took me in. Gave me a home. A mother." His voice broke again. He shook his head to clear the emotions. "I serve the forest and the Mother of Exiles. That's all I've ever wanted to do."

Wolf smiled. "That's as good an answer as anyone has ever given. Welcome, Brother!"

A glad cry went up, and Griffin smiled so wide his face hurt. Wolf held up the thorn again, and an even stronger cry went up.

"Take it," Wolf said, holding it out to Griffin. "Take it as a symbol of all we do here. All we protect."

Griffin took the thorn. It felt warm in his hand. A tingle went up his arm and he let out a laugh.

Canin took the cup from Sam and filled it with more water. The glad talk stilled as Canin held up the cup. Griffin held out the thorn, parallel to the ground.

"Washed clean," Canin said, pouring the water over the thorn. "Out of death to defend life. May it serve you well."

He passed the cup to Wolf and stepped back.

"A strong thorn, Setab," Wolf said, pouring more water over it. "It will make a strong knife."

"I will carry it always," Griffin swore, pride in his eyes. "Nothing will break its bond."

Wolf pulled out a cloth and dried the thorn, wrapping it up. "Tomorrow we will go to Ankar, and we will begin the carving." He passed the wrapped bundle back to Griffin. "But now, we eat!" He flung his arm around Griffin, pulling him along.

As they walked, a bit of guilt began to eat at Griffin and he faltered. Wolf sensed his sudden reluctance and motioned for the rest of the Brothers to go on ahead.

Under a large tree, they stopped.

"Prime, I know we're supposed to leave everything, but." Griffin pulled out the long knife he had taken. "I can run it back. . . ." He started to turn, but Wolf grabbed his arm.

"A good blade," he commented, taking the knife. "And he dropped it," he said with a wink. "Canin told me. You got too close, but recovered. Well done."

"I. . . ," Griffin said, unsure under the eyes of his Prime. "I just reacted."

Wolf laughed "You did better than I did my first time." He passed the blade back to Giffin, hilt first. "Make this your only souvenir. Sometimes the spirits of those men cling to their things. They can . . . infect you." His face got stern. "I will not stand for you walking a dark path."

Griffin almost dropped the blade.

"But it's a good blade," Wolf said with a twisting smile. "Use it better than he did." Wolf clapped Griffin on the shoulder and strode off to catch up with the others.

Griffin wiped the blade and hilt on his arm, then put it away. He'd have to trade or barter for a new sheath. Or maybe, he thought with a smile, that handsome apprentice weaponsmith could make him one. It would be more expensive, but worth it. His hands were so deft.

Blushing, Griffin ran to catch up with his new Brothers.

Chapter 35
The Choosing

Wolf, who had been waiting at the head of the trail, gave Canin an understanding hug.

"It's been a difficult few days," Wolf had commented as the other Thorn Brothers returned from their trails. Fathers rarely came alone, and this one had brought many.

"The Queen of Thorns feasts tonight," Sam said, raising a cup.

Canin frowned, but he raised his cup, too. This was a necessary part of his life as a Thorn Brother.

"Go to Aieren's house in the morning," Wolf instructed him as the rest of the Brothers moved off. "Cobalt and Dornshen want to talk to you about your plan."

Canin nodded, falling into step with Wolf, but not without a backward glance down the trail. He saw the shadow of a Brother, waiting and guarding the exit. He was glad he didn't have to do that, too.

Wolf nudged him. "You've done well," he praised. "I know it's been hard, but. . . ."

"I had to prove myself again," Canin finished. "To assure the Children and the Mother that I'm still committed to being a Thorn Brother and remember my responsibilities."

Wolf raised an eyebrow in surprise.

"I'm not dim," Canin replied, more harshly than he'd meant. The days were wearing on him more than he realized. "I've been tested this last moon. In all possible ways." He counted on his fingers. "Fighting, building, more fighting, healing, identifying plants. Helping Sekrine. Watching the outer shrines. Taking the babies back.

Burning the dead ones." He took a deep breath. "It felt like I was your apprentice again. Only this time, I was everyone's apprentice." He took a breath. "I'm surprised I haven't been sent to weed the Wattle root fields and dry the Helenium leaves."

"You know Maggie and her Maidens take those responsibilities very seriously," Wolf said in a scolding, fatherly voice. "They're the women's responsibility, because those herbs are only used by women. Men's hands just get in the way." Then he smiled, showing the young man still present behind the grey. "Plus, I have too much for you to do here, and couldn't possibly spare you."

Sam overheard their conversation and gave an apologetic shrug as he walked by. Canin, smiling slightly, aimed to trip him, but Sam dodged away at the last instant.

"And you've been teaching us," Wolf went on, his Prime voice returning. "Those fancy Fairy Patterns. Everything you learned about Fairy tactics. You have been tested," he admitted, "but we have learned much from the tests."

Canin nodded and started to apologize to Wolf.

The older man waved the words away. "We do what we must for the forest and the Mother. We rebuild what has been broken."

Canin smiled and waved farewell as he turned to head toward home, leaving Wolf on his own path.

Canin walked slowly up to the door of Lily's little house.

He was physically tired and emotionally drained. This had been the sixth straight day in which they'd given a man to the forest.

The memories of his first time had been strong today: the screams, and the begging for mercy. Then the sobbing, and even more screams as the thorns had kept growing into the husband's body. He had sat and watched during the two days it had taken the man to die. He had been a horrible person, and this punishment was more than suitable, but his cries still woke Canin up out of dreams of blood and darkness on occasion.

Canin opened the door slowly. He had learned it was perilous to open it without warning. Alexander always seemed to be too close to it, and the sound of his head hitting the solid wood was well known.

Nothing happened as Canin stepped into the small room. Hanging his gear on the pegs by the door, he looked around. Lily was in her chair, sewing something. She saw him and raised a finger to her mouth, signaling him to be quiet. Looking around, Canin saw Aurora sitting upright on the floor, in the middle of her favorite blanket. She didn't seem to notice Canin's entrance; she was entranced by Spear.

Spear was also sitting on the floor, bent over and carving something. She looked up and acknowledged Canin, but went right back to her carving. Wood shavings littered the floor around her.

Puzzled, Canin went over to Lily and gave her a quick kiss. "What's going on?" he asked in a whisper.

Lily only shook her head. "Aurora crawled across the floor today." She gestured for Canin not to react when he would have run to pick up his child and hug her. "When Spear came back from her time with Sekrine, and I told her, she became very serious and began doing. . . ." She waved her hands vaguely in Spear's direction. "Some Fairy things."

Spear set down what she had been carving and put her knife away. "When a Fairy child crawls a long distance for the first time," she explained to them, "the Choosing must be done." She tapped the piece of wood on the floor. Canin saw that it was a small carving of a sword.

"I need a coin," Spear announced, holding out her hand to Canin.

"I have one," Lily said, digging in her pocket.

"No," Spear said. "It must be from the father," she said harshly, but then smiled at Canin's disapproving look. Lily nodded, used to Spear's fluctuating moods.

"I think I have one," Canin said, moving toward their room. He stopped and reached to caress Aurora's head as he passed.

"Don't touch her," Spear snapped.

Canin drew his hand back. Aurora was oddly still. She just looked up at him with her green eyes.

"It's part of the ceremony," Spear explained.

Forcing a smile, Canin continued into their small room. He took down his satchel. It wasn't as good as the one he had left in the Fairy

Realm, but it was adequate for what he needed. He wondered if Min still had his old one, or if it had been lost. He pulled a silver coin from a pocket.

"It has the face of the old King," he said apologetically, returning to the main room.

"Doesn't matter," Spear remarked, waving for him to set the coin on the floor beside the small wooden sword. Then she waved Canin back.

Still puzzled, Canin returned to stand beside his mother's chair.

"Now we need a crystal of some kind," Spear muttered, more to herself than to the others. She patted her top and pants, looking for something. Then she looked up at them, clearly expecting them to reply.

"I don't know, dear," Lily said. "I might have a bit of glass."

Spear shook her head. "No. It has to be crystal." She looked with begging eyes at Canin.

He looked around the room. He didn't know if there was anything here. "I might have to go looking," he finally said.

"No," Spear grunted, angry and frustrated. "It must be now."

"Spear," Canin began, moving to comfort her.

She waved him back, her hand shaking. "It must be right," she mumbled.

"I might have something," Lily said into the tense silence. She handed Canin her sewing and got up. Stepping carefully around Aurora and Spear, she went to her room. Canin heard something being dragged across the floor. After a moment, Lily emerged and handed Spear a small object.

Spear held it up. A blue-green crystal, about as long as a small finger, shone in the light. Spear smiled, all the worry draining from her face.

"This is perfect," she declared. She ran her finger over the facets and frowned slightly. She looked up at Lily, who was sitting back down. "Where did you get this? It's from the Fairy Realm."

Lily didn't answer right away. She took back her sewing and arranged it in her lap. "Someone traded it for some blankets a long time ago," Lily finally told her. "I was younger then, and thought it was pretty. It didn't know it was from the Fairy Realm." She looked up at Canin.

He shrugged.

Spear smiled again and put the crystal on the floor. She waved her hand over the three items.

"Now," she said seriously, looking at Aurora. "These are three possible paths for you. Magic." She pointed at the crystal. "Merchant." The coin. "And soldier." She pointed at the wooden sword. "These aren't the only paths that the Goddess could open for you, but this will show us where you should begin." Spear looked up at Canin and Lily's questioning eyes. "She won't be bound to one path," she explained. "It's just the beginning."

Canin nodded slowly. He felt something building in the air, a swirl of possibilities and potentialities. He gripped his carefully carved wooden knife, so much like the one Spear had made. He remembered pulling the longest thorn from the first man he had given to the forest, and how long it had taken to make it into this knife.

Aurora swayed slightly, staring at the three items on the floor in front of her. She raised her little arms, her fingers moving. Spear gestured again at the three items.

"Choose one," she urged. Aurora just sat, her head moving side to side.

Lily held her breath.

The sun glinted on the coin and the crystal.

Canin cleared his throat, the tension getting to him.

Spear glared at Canin, and then looked back at Aurora.

"Choose one," she urged again, a bit of desperation creeping into her voice. Her damaged wings fluttered nervously. Canin wanted to go to her, but he knew it would only make things worse.

Lily muttered something Canin couldn't hear.

"Goddess and Mother mercy," Spear swore, thumping the floor. "Just choose one. You're making me look the fool."

"Trillium," Canin started.

Then Aurora leaned forward, and began to crawl toward the items. Canin, caught up in the moment, marveled at how she moved. She stopped in front of the items and looked down.

Spear held her breath as Aurora looked up at her.

"Yes, Little Wing," she said quietly. "There is a path for you."

Aurora moved forward, her little hands hovering over the three items. Spear's eyes went to the sword at the end. Canin tried to push aside the tension building throughout his body. Lily gripped his arm.

With a quick motion, Aurora pushed all three items aside and crawled into Spear's arms. Spear picked her up, suddenly crying. Aurora nuzzled into her chest.

"Mama," she said, gripping the front of Spear's shirt.

Canin felt tears come as Lily began to cry and laugh, too, letting go of Canin and holding her hands in front of her face.

"Papa," Aurora said, turning in Spear's arms and reaching for him.

Canin laughed and went to them. He carefully put his arm around Spear, and together they held Aurora. He felt that something important had just happened, but he couldn't get past his giddy happiness to figure out what.

Chapter 36
A Cat and a Crystal

Later that night, after their meal, Aurora was back on the floor. She was playing with the coin and crystal, waving them around, watching the points of light reflected from the Fairy Lantern play across the floor and the adults in the room.

Lily's cat, Anina, had taken the wooden sword and was alternately chewing on it and rubbing it on her face. Aurora had been waving it around earlier, but Anina had sunk her teeth into the wood and pulled it from her grasp before she could do any damage to herself or others.

"Very good, Auntie," Spear praised, looking up from her meal and tossing the cat a bit of meat.

Anina was the third of her name, a grey and white cat of the forest. She and her litter mates and extended family had defended Lily's former, larger, house, from rats, mice, and other creeping pests. When Lily and Niel moved into this smaller house, Anina had followed her, leaving the duty of protecting the Maidens' house to the younger generation.

Anina was getting old, and spent most of her time lounging in or on one of the many wooden boxes and ledges Niel had built into the little house. Before their arrival, she had mostly watched the sun all day, but she'd still kept a sharp feline eye for potential intruders.

Spear had been wary of the cat at first. Her experience with the sea cats at the cliffs had colored her reactions, though the cats of the forest weren't as large, and lacked prehensile tails. Their relationship had begun badly on their first morning , when Spear had woken to find Anina snuggled up with the sleeping Aurora in her crib. Only Canin's quick observation that the cat was keeping her body away from Aurora's head had prevented Spear from hurling Anina out of the room. She had settled for picking the cat up and unceremoniously dropping her to the floor.

Unperturbed, Anina had sauntered away and settled into a box to groom herself.

Thus began the battle of wills between the Fairy and the cat. No matter how many times Spear threw her out of the crib, Anina always came back. Only when Aurora cried, deprived of her purring, warm blanket, did Spear relent. Anina took to waiting till Spear was asleep to jump up into the crib, and took care to be gone before Spear woke up.

Most evenings, Spear and Anina stared at each other across the small main room. The set of their similar eyes stood as proof that they were locked in a battle of wills.

Lily found the whole thing silly, maintaining that no baby had ever been smothered by one of her cats, and none ever would be.

Alexander was jealous, because Anina no longer wanted to sleep with him. He took to taking bits of fish to bed to try and lure her back. Lily had put a stop to that after the smell forced her to wash all of Alexander's blankets.

Remembering one of Niel's favorite sayings about women and cats, Canin had stayed out of the whole thing. Though he did try to wake up before Spear, to give Anina time to find another place to appear to have slept the night away.

He understood Spear's feelings toward the cat, remembering Min's tale of the sea cats' tragic ends. Canin had tried to explain it to Lily, but, as with many things about Spear, she did not understand, and simply accepted it as a Fairy thing.

Tension between the cat and the Fairy remained high, till one night, in the darkest hour, the house was woken by the sound of fighting. Anina's high-pitched growls were mixed with another, sharper cry.

Spear and Canin had rushed into the main room just in time to see Anina breaking the neck of a rat almost as big as she was with a sharp shake of her head. Spear grudgingly praised Anina as a good soldier and checked her for wounds as Canin disposed of the dead rat and Lily went to calm the crying Alexander. Aurora slept through the whole thing. Anina took the praise as her due and retreated to her favorite box by the fireplace to bathe her paws.

Spear went back to bed, her feelings for the cat unchanged, till the morning, when they discovered the rat's claw and tooth marks on the legs and railings of Aurora's crib. From then on, Spear and Anina were sisters in arms, each committed to defending their baby in their own ways. Spear took to slipping bits of food and milk to Anina, despite knowing the milk made Anina throw up. Neither of them cared. Lily had other thoughts on the matter. Canin, as usual, stayed clear, and cleaned up the messes. He did take to bringing a little more Mother's Milk than Aurora needed back with him each evening. Anina accepted it all with feline grace.

"So how many bastards did you feed to the thorns today?" Spear asked conversationally. She set aside the fletching of her arrows and picked up the Fairy Lantern she was working on. She seemed to have more patience today, and the Weave went smoothly.

"A large group," Canin answered. "A father and several other men who came looking for the woman and her sisters who came here last moon." He looked at Spear, but she was no longer listening. She was trying to place the small piece of crystal that was the heart of the Fairy Lantern in the right spot. She frowned, moving it around.

Canin shifted his attention to Lily. She nodded. "It was a large group," she remembered. "Five children with those three women. Looked to me like all of them were from the same father."

Canin nodded. "I got that impression from the leader, too. He was an arrogant and cruel man. I thought there might be a fight, but we got them all separated." He paused. "It was the first time for one of the new Brothers. I was his backup. Brought back memories." He stopped, lost in thought.

"The Mother guides us," Lily reminded him. Her eyes drifted to the floor. Aurora was crawling toward Spear, the piece of blue-green crystal still in her hand. It began to glow as she got closer to Spear and her work. Jolted out of her Weaving, Spear looked down at the crawling baby. She grabbed the crystal, but the light went out as she touched it.

Looking up at Lily, she asked, "Where did you get this?"

"I've had it a long time," Lily said, sounding defensive. "It never glowed before."

Spear examined it closer with her Sight. "This was part of a Fairy Lantern. A large one." She shook the crystal in her hand. "But I can't get it to work." She frowned.

"I don't remember where it came from," Lily said again. "I just thought it was pretty."

Canin gave Lily a strange look. "That's odd," he said slowly. "Usually, you only take things we need in trade."

"Well, this time I did," Lily stressed. "I can have pretty things around." She looked hard at Canin, wanting the discussion to end. "What about your plan?"

Canin frowned. "I'm going to talk to Cobalt tomorrow. Crow and Sadie should be back before the new moon. Then. . . ." He looked at Spear. "We can set things in motion."

Spear snorted in disgust at Sadie's name. Then she handed the crystal back to Aurora, who was reaching for it. She settled back, and promptly put the crystal in her mouth.

"No, no, no," Lily said, rising and grabbing the crystal from the baby's hand. As she started to cry, Lily picked up Aurora's favorite toy — a stuffed raven — and pressed it into her hands. Aurora stopped crying and happily began chewing on the toy's wing.

Lily sat back down, relieved, and slipped the crystal into her pocket. Spear noticed, but didn't comment, returning to the Fairy Lantern's Weave.

"Where's Alexander?" Canin asked suddenly, looking around.

"He was getting in the way," Lily told him, taking back her sewing. "He kept reaching for the sword Spear was carving."

Canin winced.

"So," Lily continued, "I sent him off with Coltsfoot. He's going to spend the night with her at the Maidens' house. They love him, and he's always so good when he's with them."

Canin smiled and glanced at Spear, wondering how she was reacting to all this talk about Alexander. The two of them had started off even more badly than she and Anina had, and living in the small house with his rambunctious clumsiness was trying at the very least.

Spear was concentrating on the Weave and didn't notice Canin's look. She frowned, her hands clenching. Canin felt a surge of Power around Spear, and sparks leapt between her fingers. She jerked her hands back. Anger filled her face, and she balled her fists.

Lily dropped her thimble, which hit the floor with a musical chime.

Spear heard it and, with obvious effort, controlled her anger and opened her hands. She looked up at Canin.

"You can try again later," he told her.

She looked down at the half-completed Lantern. An old friend of Wolf's had offered to make wooden boxes with a glass lid for Spear to use. The wood was a warm brown, and when the Fairy Lantern was active, it glowed with a light that made the room feel more like a home. Inside the box was a small crystal. The crystals came from Starlight's Shield. Manzanita had found them in the mountain's streams. They were mostly milky white, but some were clear, and rare ones were blue. He had picked them up for the simple reason that he liked how they looked. He kept them in a basket by his side when he sold his apples. Sometimes he sold or bartered the crystals, but mostly he just kept them. Good luck tokens, he claimed.

Spear, with her love of apples, was always first in line at his tent in the marketplace when he came down from the mountain. At some point after his first few visits, now that she knew she could reliably get the apples she craved, Spear had noticed the crystals and, with an absent wave, had made some of them light up.

Canin had noticed many of the people of the forest reacting with fear. But many more had looked at the glowing crystals with interest. Fairy Lanterns had always been rare and expensive, and now that the border with the Fairy Realm was closed, they were almost unobtainable. When he saw many of the people who had at first given Spear a wide berth approach her and ask about how she had made the crystals glow, Canin had had an idea.

It took some convincing to get her to try it, though. "I'm not one of the Ladies," she'd complained as she tried to anchor the Light Weave into the crystal. She knew the basic theory, but it took concentration, something she didn't always have. With trial and much error, she was eventually able to make a few Lanterns. Canin had wanted to sell them, but Spear was stubborn and simply gave them away. This act of generosity helped many of the forest people accept her and stop looking at her as someone who might kill them.

Dealing with Manzanita to get the crystals had taken a little more doing. He was protective of his mountain and wouldn't tell Spear — or anyone — where he found the crystals. After a few failed negotiations, Spear, in a raw moment of making connections, offered to help him get back into Sekrine's good graces, since she knew they had been having a very fiery off and on affair for many, many seasons. It worked, and Spear was now able to get all the crystals and apples she needed and wanted. Manzanita began to spend more time in town, and Sekrine smiled a little more.

Spear sighed and closed the little lid. "I promised Wren that I would have this ready before Crow came back."

"Maybe in the morning," Canin suggested. "When you're rested."

Spear gave her head a tilt. Then she went and picked up Aurora, flying her through the air. Aurora's laughter filled the room, as Canin and Lily watched. Then, with a whoosh, Spear settled into her chair with Aurora in her lap.

"Hungry, Little Wing?" Spear asked.

Aurora shook her head and settled into Spear's lap. She had her stuffed toy in one hand and Canin's coin in the other. She made flapping noises and flew the two things around. Spear watched her intently.

Lily watched, smiling contentedly, enjoying her family.

Aieren sat up in bed. There was only a sliver of moonlight coming through the curtains, but she couldn't shake the sudden feeling that something had changed.

There was movement to her left.

"Grandmother," a voice whispered. "Are you all right?"

"Yes, Wren, I am. Just a dream." She frowned as she felt the heavily pregnant woman stand and come to her bedside. "You shouldn't still be up. It's late."

"More like early," the younger woman commented, pulling a chair closer and sitting down. She took Aieren's hand. "And you know I can't sleep when Crow is away."

"Yes," Aieren replied, touching her granddaughter's face. "I was like that once. He should be back soon." She fussed with the blankets over her chest. Wren helped her.

"Or maybe it's who he's off with," Aieren suggested.

Now Wren was frowning. "Do you think it was more than what he told me?"

"I don't know," Aieren said honestly. "It's just my intuition as a mother and a woman. I do not trust Sadie."

"Maggie does," Wren noted.

"She does, and Sadie is a very good archer and a quality Maiden. But." She paused, gathering her thoughts. "She came here late, and I can sense. . . ." She paused again. "Something." She shook her head. "Maybe it's just that I'm worried about her flirting with all the men."

Wren's hand went to her belly. "Crow would never betray me and our child," she stated, but with a tinge of doubt.

Aieren shrugged. "I trust your judgment of your man. He's a good Thorn Brother. He needs to grow as a leader, but one day." She trailed off, looking toward the window. She pulled back the covers. "Climb in bed with me," she offered. "Like you used to do. We'll comfort each other."

"She'll kick," Wren warned as she climbed into the bed.

"I don't mind," Aieren said, putting her arm around her granddaughter. "I'm old, and your warmth keeps the cold away."

"Maybe I'll dream of my daughter," Wren said hopefully as she settled in.

"Dream of the peace of the forest," Aieren urged as they both drifted off.

Chapter 37
Learning to Cope

The creation of the Light Weave for the Fairy Lanterns was taxing and took more concentration than Spear had today. As the Weave slipped out of her fingers and fizzled in a buzz of sparks, Spear smashed the half-completed Lantern.

Alexander jumped, dropping his cup and splashing Aurora. She began to cry, both from the cold and from the anger coming off Spear. Alexander began to cry as well, as he watched the water he had begged for drain away through the floorboards.

"Quiet!" Spear snapped, crushing the wood of the Lantern in her fist.

"Calm yourself!" Lily snapped as Canin picked up Aurora.

Spear glared across the room, her eyes blazing. Lily did not back down, repeating her demand for Spear to be calm.

"Look," she said, pointing to the crying Aurora in Canin's arms. "You've scared your baby. You cannot continue these outbursts. I will have a calm house. Aurora needs a peaceful home. I've seen children grown in angry houses, and I will not have that happen to my granddaughter."

At first, Spear only glared back. Then she stormed out.

Canin rose, Aurora fussing in his arms as he tried to pass her to Lily.

"No," Lily said firmly. "You can't go after her every time. She must learn to control herself. She's a soldier, or so you said. Where is her discipline?"

"I'm just afraid," Canin started. Then a cry from the floor interrupted them. Alexander had cut his hand on one of the pieces of the broken Lantern. He was sitting on the floor, whimpering and staring at the blood oozing down his hand.

Lily got up quickly and took his hand. "It's not that bad," she soothed. She wrapped the cut and took him to the back room to wash it off.

There was nothing for Canin to do but sit back down and comfort Aurora. She fretted and cried for a while, before finally accepting a bottle of Mother's Milk. Canin sighed, worried, but his concern was lessened by the look of contentment on his daughter's face as she drank.

Lily returned without Alexander. She motioned to the mess on the floor and held out her arms for Aurora. Canin passed the baby over and went to sweep up the wooden shards.

"She'll go to Maggie," Lily said after some time. "She understands Spear and will direct her anger someplace else."

"I just hope you're right," Canin said, picking through the debris, looking for anything that was salvageable. He shook his head. There was nothing. Spear's blow had ruined even the small crystal that was the heart of the Lantern. She would have to start over.

"I am," Lily said with confidence. "I didn't raise angry and hurt children for seasons without learning something about how to deal with them. She'll find a way to channel her anger into something better. Healing with Sekrine, training with the Maidens. Loving you," she said with a raised eyebrow. Canin blushed, and he swore Aurora laughed, too, or maybe it was just a burp.

Lily shifted Aurora to her shoulder and went on. "But understand me, Canin. I'm serious. If she cannot control herself, or she becomes a danger to this child or anyone in the forest."

"I know, mother," Canin said. "I must protect everyone, even her. Even from herself."

Lily frowned at how he said 'mother.' "I did not wish to hear you call me 'mother' for so many seasons for you to use it as a curse," she said severely.

Canin, contrite, went immediately to her side. "I'm sorry, mother," he said softly. "Forgive me."

Lily smiled and took his hand. "Of course," she said brightly. "Just talk to her. Make sure she understands. Our Jewel is fragile, and I don't want her to break. We must find her strength and help her see it."

"You were always good at that, mother," Canin said, kissing her on the forehead.

"I had a good teacher, and good students," she replied wistfully. "So many children passed through my house. So many hurt and traumatized little ones. But we found a way through all of that and made them better."

"We rebuild what has been broken," Canin stated, stroking Aurora's back. She burped and spit up on Lily's shoulder.

Spear returned later, smelling of dirt, sweat, and blood. A lot of sweat, and just a little blood, thankfully. She looked around the room. Canin was mending a pair of boots, and Lily was reading to Alexander.

"I just put her down for a nap," Canin informed her.

She moved toward their room, but Canin blocked her. "I just got her to sleep," he stressed. He gently took her arm. "She's been fussy since you left," he said with a tinge of reproach. "I don't want you to wake her."

Spear started to push through him, but then her face changed, and she looked down at her hands, covered in dirt. She sniffed the air. "Yes, I'm dirty," she said with a laugh. She turned, pulling Canin. "Come on. Take me to the baths." She gave him a quick kiss and headed for the door.

"Take Alexander," Lily called, setting the boy on the ground.

"But, Auntie," Alexander whined.

Spear's face echoed his emotions.

"No. You're filthy," Lily told him. "You've been rubbing your head in the dirt again." Her face softened as she turned to Spear and Canin. "I'll send Coltsfoot to get him, so you two can have some private time."

Spear nodded, still frowning. Canin pulled his boots on and then motioned for Alexander to take his hand. He did, but he was still pouty. Spear hurried them out the door.

With her racing ahead of them, practically running, Canin had to pick up Alexander, so he wouldn't trip and cut or break something. The boy rode awkwardly on his hip, arms and legs flailing.

"Grab my shirt," Canin urged him.

"Don't like baths," Alexander complained, gripping him too hard.

"I know," Canin sympathized, walking through the pain. "But Lily wants you clean." He looked down at the boy with a serious eye. "We must be good for her and do as she says."

"Don't like baths," he repeated, lowering his eyes.

Canin smiled as he turned his own eyes ahead and saw Spear looking at him. She smiled in her confusing way, somehow happy, sad, and puzzled all at once. "Yes, we must," she agreed, rubbing her face.

They passed the Sanctuary and headed toward the low buildings beyond, where natural hot springs bubbled up. They descended the stairs and met one of the spring-keepers. He smiled warmly at Canin and Alexander and with caution at Spear, and gestured them toward one of the back rooms.

"A smaller one, just for your family," he muttered.

"Coltsfoot will be coming by soon," Canin informed him. "Make sure she's directed to the right room this time."

"That was a mistake, Brother," the spring-keeper muttered. "I got confused."

"And she got an eyeful," Spear said with humor.

"If the two of you would keep it in your home," he shot back. "That's not what these rooms are for."

"I like water," Spear replied, bordering on anger. "And so does he."

The spring-keeper huffed and led them on. Canin set Alexander down and glanced at Spear. She was smiling and humming.

At the door to one of the bathing pools, the spring-keeper handed them some towels and made marks on the door with a piece of chalk. "There," he stressed. "I will send her here when she comes." He looked in Spear's direction. "Are you and she going to be. . . ."

He began to make an obscene gesture, but Canin stopped him with a sharp gesture of his own.

"With the boy in the room?" he replied angrily. "What do you take us for? I will speak to Mortise. You might be in the wrong place."

At the mention of Mortise, the Child of the Mother who was in charge of making sure everyone one had a place to live and work, the spring-keeper blanched and lowered his head. He sputtered through an apology. "Leave your clothes outside the door. I'll make sure they're cleaned and ready for you."

Canin gave the man another dark look before he turned and left.

Spear was eyeing him with a crooked smile. "He might wind up pulling weeds in the Wattle root fields."

Canin grunted and opened the door. "I just don't like how he looked at you."

"I'm used to it," Spear said easily as she entered the room.

"You shouldn't be," Canin said, following, pulling Alexander with him. He shut the door firmly before the boy could bolt.

Spear shrugged and began to take off her clothes, already walking into the water.

It was a small room, with a short staircase going down into the deep, steaming pool. The water stretched back into the rock, narrowing to a point at the farthest edge, where bubbles rose.

Alexander was staring at Spear as she disrobed, her back to him. Canin pulled him around and began to help him out of his clothes. It was more — probably — a fixation with Spear's wings and how they moved than any desire to see her naked at his age, but after the conversation with the keeper, Canin felt strange about bringing the boy. Spear had a soldier's lack of modesty and displayed it often.

Spear's dripping garments floated over to them as Canin took his clothes and Alexander's back toward the door. Alexander laughed as an arm of Spear's shirt batted playfully at Canin. Spear made the shirt dance around the boy, making him grin.

Canin grabbed the flying clothes, added them to the pile he was carrying, and set them all outside the door, making sure it was securely closed and locked again afterward. Then he took Alexander to the first step, sat him down, and began to scrub him.

"Stop fidgeting," Canin complained, working soap into the boy's hair. It was full of dirt and other little bits he had somehow picked up.

"You got water in my eyes," Alexander complained as Canin bent him back to rinse the soap out.

"Just dunk him," Spear said, watching the two of them bend and contort. She was in the deepest part of the pool, with only her head above the water.

"No," Canin said, but Alexander heard her and twisted out of his grasp to try and go up the stairs. He slipped, and went under the water with a cry.

Canin pulled him out and held him firmly as the boy rubbed soap and water out of his eyes.

"Here," Canin said, pouring water over his head. "This will help. Stop struggling. You're not going to drown."

Spear laughed, watching the two of them. "Soon," she taunted, "you'll have to learn how to swim." She gestured, her hands coming out of the water. "We'll just throw you in and let you float or sink."

Alexander, scared and wet, twisted out of Canin's grasp and made it to the door. He grabbed one of the towels and frantically rubbed at his face.

"Stop it," Canin scolded Spear. "You're just making him worse."

"You're just making him more afraid," Spear shot back. "He's picking up on your fear of being underwater. He has to learn. It might mean his survival one day."

Canin twisted his mouth, aware that she had a point. "Alexander," he said, trying to make his voice calm. "Come back here. We have to finish washing your hair."

The boy shook his head, not moving.

Spear laughed, and ducked under the water.

Canin sighed. "You said you would be good," he reminded Alexander. "Lily needs you to be good. I can't take you back with dirty hair." A thought occurred to him. "She might not read you more of the tales of the Mother, if you aren't clean."

Visibly torn, Alexander twisted the towel in his hands. Then, having made a decision, he put it down and came back to the stairs.

"I'll do it," he told Canin, taking the soap. Canin smiled as the boy rubbed the soap through his hair.

"Let me," Spear offered, appearing behind him and helping him rub the suds around. "It's nothing to be scared of," Spear told him. "Just take a deep breath and go under the water. Keep your eyes and mouth shut. And hold your nose," she instructed, demonstrating.

He looked scared, but did as she asked. With a great intake of breath, he dipped under the water, with Spear's hands in his hair, rubbing away the soap. She pulled him up, sputtering but smiling.

"Again!" he cried.

Spear looked at Canin as the boy dipped back under the water. He folded his arms at her look of superiority. With a huff, he began to unbraid his hair. Spear shook her head and smiled at him. Then she reached under the water and pulled Alexander out, after realizing he had been under too long. He burst out of the water, flailing and splashing all of them, but he was laughing, too.

As Canin washed his own hair, Spear tried to teach Alexander how to float. He sank like a stone every time, but Spear kept hauling him up. Canin was amazed at her sudden patience with the boy. She was always short with him, and complained about his tendency to break things. Canin didn't know what had caused the change, but he was glad for it. Maybe it was simply the water.

A knock at the door made Canin start. He climbed out of the pool, grabbed a towel, and wrapped it around himself, ignoring Spear's laugh.

He opened the door a crack. Coltsfoot was there, holding Alexander's clothes.

"I'm here for Alexander," she said, glancing through the door. Canin opened the door wider and let her in.

"I'm swimming," Alexander called from the deep end, before promptly disappearing under the water. Spear hauled him out and pushed him toward the stairs.

"Join us," Spear invited, rising out of the water.

Coltsfoot looked uncomfortable. "I think I should just take him back." She held out a towel for Alexander. "Ready."

The boy ran to her and let her wrap him in the towel. "Thank you," he called back to Spear.

Spear waved in reply, the stubs of her wings moving slowly in the water. She smiled, and then lost it as the boy turned away.

"Your clothes are outside," Coltsfoot informed Canin. She hurried Alexander out the door with a quick backward glance at Spear. She shut the door quickly.

"It's like she never saw two people giving each other pleasure before," Spear commented from the water. "And you were giving me so much," she remembered, grinning. She motioned for him to join her in the water.

"You shouldn't tease her like that," Canin said, but he moved quickly to return to the pool. But not before making sure the door was locked again.

Spear put her arms on his shoulders. "This is not the Fairy Realm," Canin told her after they kissed.

"No," Spear agreed, wrapping her legs around him and pulling him closer. "But I will not be embarrassed that I love you and want you. That is one way we praise the Goddess: giving and receiving pleasure." She bit her lip as he lifted her into a better position.

"Then we must praise Her," Canin muttered into her neck.

Chapter 38
The Field of
Wellcomb Trees

The sun was moving toward midday over the Maidens' training field. Spear stood in the middle of it all and felt at home. The sounds of women all around her training and fighting filled her with joy and purpose.

To her left, Heron was running the apprentice Maidens through the new Fairy fighting Patterns. Since the four elemental morning exercises of the forest seemed to be related to the Fairy Patterns somehow, most of the women and girls were picking them up quickly.

Heron, with her long limbs and graceful steps, had learned all the Patterns remarkably fast, and could now teach them with the proficiency of any Fairy Pattern master. She also had much more patience with the young ones than Spear did.

"Take a closer stance," Heron corrected one apprentice. "The parry must be a full movement," she called to another. "Bring it all the way round," she told the whole group. "And back to the ready position." She demonstrated, bringing her fists up in front of her body.

"Good," she called, looking over the huffing and puffing women. "Again!"

Spear laughed at the low groans, but smiled as the students moved together like tall grass in the wind.

Motion to the right caught her eye and she turned to see Stonefoot come out of the forest at a dead run, leading five older apprentices. They loped around a stump, and then headed back into the forest. A woman at the end stumbled at the turn, but got her feet back under her and sprinted to catch up.

"Run faster!" Spear called after them.

The twang of bowstrings and the thunk of arrows hitting targets pulled Spear's focus to the far end of the field, where Sadie was leading target practice.

"You've got the wrong stance," she barked. Sadie used her bow to bump the girl's feet. "Can't you remember anything I've shown you?" Her anger rose, and she hit the girl again.

"But, Sister, you said it was this way," the girl protested, stepping away from the blow.

"No. No. No," Sadie growled, stepping to the next girl in line. "You've got it all wrong! Elbow in. Feet apart."

The frustrated girl, on the verge of tears, bumped into the apprentice beside her. Both of them turned pleading eyes toward Spear.

Spear sighed and started across the field. Sadie wasn't a good teacher. She was an amazing archer, but when she tried to explain things to others, she just expected them to know how to do everything.

"Again," Sadie snapped. "Hit the target, or no midday meal."

Spear increased her speed. These were young girls, barely out of the creche school. Anger filled Spear as she remembered another instructor with a stern voice and a swift switch.

"I think that's good for now," another Maiden said, stepping to Sadie's side. She looked over the exhausted and frustrated children. She was older, weathered and lined, but her Elenite eyes were still sharp. She gestured with her left arm; her right one was missing. "Go join Polly at the bathing pool. Get cleaned up. All of you will be serving tonight." She swept the group with stern eyes as they all groaned.

"This is my class, and I say when they're done," Sadie decreed, turning on the older Maiden. She reached out with her bow as though she were going to tap the woman like she'd been tapping the girls. The woman's arm came up and Sadie pulled back.

"You forget yourself, Thorn Maiden," the older woman said. "I've been teaching since before you or your mother were even born."

Spear stopped, watching the Human and Elenite stare at one another. The girls went quiet, captivated by the conflict between their teachers.

"That just means you're old," Sadie muttered quietly, but Spear's Fairy ears heard it, and by the curl of her lip, the older Maiden did, too.

"I gave all of you an order," she said to the girls. "Go find Maiden Polly."

"Yes, Maiden Dinah," one of the girls said.

"She was over there," Spear offered, gesturing toward the woods.

Sadie glared at Spear, but took another step away from Dinah. The girls neatly stacked their bows and quivers, then ran off in the direction Spear had indicated.

"You push them too hard," Dinah scolded as Sadie scowled.

"I have to, or they'll get themselves and others killed," Sadie shot back.

"I know, but there are ways to teach without hitting them," Dinah said, resting her hand on the wooden hilt of her sword.

Sadie's face began to twist into a sneer, but then flattened out. She stepped closer to Dinah.

"Do not talk about my mother. You know nothing of her." Sadie's hand tightened on the grip of her bow.

"I know more than you think," Dinah said calmly. "And I can guess even more."

Now Sadie did sneer. "You know all about getting people killed, don't you?" Her eyes went to Dinah's missing arm.

Spear let out a breath of shock and watched carefully, thinking she might soon have to deflect blows between the women.

Dinah's only reaction was a slight narrowing of her eyes and the tightening of her hand.

"I take my responsibility to the young ones very seriously. Do you?" Dinah challenged.

"Of course I do," Sadie huffed. "I just want them to be ready."

"So do I," Dinah said more calmly. "But they are still children."

"They won't be for long," Sadie remarked. She looked at Spear. "She understands. She pushes us harder than anyone."

Spear held up her hands, surprised at being dragged into the argument.

Dinah's reply was cut off by a yell from the forest. Miriam came running out, waving a red scarf.

"She's coming down! They're headed for the field!"

A feeling of anticipation and happiness broke over the women.

"Gather the apprentices," Dinah ordered. Her eyes swept over the Maidens. "Meet us there."

Heron nodded, but her apprentices were already moving toward the eastern woods.

"Someone needs to tell Stonefoot," Heron remembered.

"I saw her on the trail," Miriam said, catching her breath and leaning on Spear. "She's leading her group there now."

"Take these inside," Sadie ordered one of the lingering apprentices, gesturing to the pile of bows and quivers. The young woman paused, but at a nod from Heron, began to gather them up.

"Where are we going?" Spear asked, falling into step with Miriam and Heron. She was confused, but could see the joy on the Maidens' faces.

"To the field of Wellcomb trees," Miriam answered with a smile. "A new Maiden has passed her test. She's looking for her hilt."

"I don't understand," Spear said. Her eyes were drawn to the wooden hilts of all the various Maidens' swords.

"You will," Heron assured her, clapping Spear on the shoulder. "Hurry! We don't want to miss this!"

It was a short run out of the Sanctuary village, past the fields of Wattle root and the late-flowering Helenium plants. All the Maidens they encountered noted Miriam's red scarf and fell in with them, muttering happily. The growing group climbed a small rise to a wall of thorn trees. As they got closer, everyone fell silent.

"This is one of our sacred places," Heron whispered to Spear, but the information was unnecessary. Spear could already feel the pulse of the earth, the memories of the grass, the steadfast guardianship of the trees. It felt like one of the groves — Shrines to the Goddess — that she had visited in the Fairy Realm. Spear took a deep breath, drinking in the fragrant air. She made the Sign of the Three, whispering, "Mother Goddess, I honor you."

They passed through a break in the trees, moving in single file. As they entered, the women ran their hands over the thorny bark of the trees, leaving their blood behind.

Spear felt a sudden anxiety, afraid the trees would reject her Fairy blood, but nothing happened as the thorns pricked her hand and drew out a few drops. She smiled, rubbing the cut, and leaving it to heal naturally.

Through the canopy of trees they went, emerging onto a wide field that sloped down toward even more trees. Spear looked around, noting that they stood in a bowl. The press of the Maidens forced her forward as she took in the surroundings.

The field was populated by spindly, multi-limbed trees. On average, each was maybe as tall as two Fairies, but some were shorter. They grew in uneven rows, scattered around the field. Some grew in clumps that formed loose circles, others in wavy, snaking lines.

As they moved through the knee-high grass, Spear began to see cairns, short standing stones, and carved wooden markers scattered beside and amongst the trees. To the right, a large cluster of trees grew out of a grassy mound marked with weathered grey stones. With the grass brushing past her boots, Spear began to feel something coming up through the ground. A feeling nibbled at her senses and brushed against her Wards.

Primal fear — arising from the memories of lives before this one and stories heard long ago in childhood — anchored her to the spot.

"What is this place?" she demanded of Heron. Spear gripped the Maiden's arm, forcing her to stop.

"It's one of the fields of Wellcomb trees," Heron explained, as she pulled Spear out of the way of the other Maidens coming through the trees. Polly, leading the girls, glanced at her, asking if she was all right. Heron nodded and drew Spear closer to one of the trees.

"This is a special one," Heron said, gently slipping out of Spear's grasp. "Many Maidens are laid to rest here." She gestured toward the markers and cairns. "Not all, though. Some wanted to be burned, and have their ashes either scattered or brought here.

Others were . . . lost." Emotions flickered over Heron's face: grief, sorrow, inevitable loss. She took a breath. "Their loved ones and family can bring tokens here, too. Some hang them in the trees, to bring them closer to the flowers."

Spear breathed in the scent. The branches were heavy with white, four-petaled flowers. Each petal had a notch at the end. In the center grew a dome of red buds. Spear reached out, her fingers stopping just short of touching one.

"So, this is a . . . burial site?" she asked, the foul word heavy on her tongue.

"Oh." Heron exhaled in understanding. "Fairies don't bury their dead."

"No. We burn them, releasing their spirits to Return to the Cycle," Spear said. Now that she understood this place, she knew why she was feeling this way. Why confusing tendrils were reaching out to her.

'I am not your enemy,' she thought, pressing the statement through her Wards. 'I am a defender, like you. I am a friend. Please, accept me.'

Some retreated, while others sniffed at her like cats.

'Rest,' Spear pleaded. 'Others are here to take up your fight. I serve the Mother. I'm making a home here. My daughter is one of you.'

Spear concentrated, filling her mind with memories of Aurora. The scent of her, her laugh, her cries. The peace when she nursed and fell asleep on Spear's chest. She projected these memories out. The tendrils sniffed at them, then slipped back into their cairns and markers. Spear felt a touch, not unlike her baby's hand, on her face as the last one retreated.

"I understand," Spear said out loud.

Heron tilted her head. "I guess I do, too. Their spirits come back?" she asked. "Find other bodies? Lead new lives?"

"Finish unfinished deeds," Spear confirmed. "Find forgiveness for our wrongs."

Heron nodded. "I think I'd like to do that. Come back after I die. See my loved ones again."

"I don't know if you can," Spear stated.

Heron gave her a dark look.

"I'm no Keeper, but I don't know if Elenites can. Maybe their spirits are too entangled with their Human souls. It holds them down. Or at least that's what I was taught." Spear stopped. She touched the branch before her. "Or at least that's what one Keeper said. But he hated Humans and Elenites." She turned to smile at Heron. "Goddess only knows."

Heron gave her a deep look. "Come on," she finally said. "We're going to miss it."

Spear smiled and followed her down into the field of trees.

"These are Wellcomb trees?" Spear asked.

"Yes," Heron replied. "After the flowers fall off, the center is harvested. Dried and ground up, it makes a paste that kills pain and heals."

Spear nodded. "Sekrine uses it all the time. Saves many lives."

"Given in time, it can cure fevers and sickness. Fight off infections." Heron patted a pocket at her side. "Every Maiden carries several vials and pouches." She smiled widely. "It even soothes the cramps when we bleed."

"Oh," Spear said casually. "I don't do that. My Ward takes care of that."

"Lucky," Heron said with a wistful look.

They reached the center of the field, facing a dense stand of Wellcomb trees. The Maidens and apprentices formed a loose circle, all of them quiet, and standing at attention. Spear fell easily into the habit, hands at her side. Heron nudged her and gestured over to the east.

A young Elenite woman was walking slowly toward the grove. She was escorted by Maggie and River, who had their hands on her arms. The young woman looked tired; her eyes bore dark circles. Her long black hair hung around her face, blowing in the wind.

"Who is that?" Spear whispered.

"Marie," Heron whispered back. "She just passed the final test. She's been in the north of the forest for the past few moons."

"What test?" Spear asked, but Heron shook her head. Other Maidens around them looked at Spear with distrust. One glared, pressing a finger to her mouth for them to be quiet.

Spear smiled and turned her attention back to Marie and the other Maidens.

Marie stumbled, but was held up by Maggie and River.

"I'm all right," Marie said, her voice cracking. She shook herself and brushed her hair back from her face. "I can stand."

Maggie nodded, and she and River stepped back. Marie straightened her back, and Spear could see her push the exhaustion away by force of will. Marie smiled at the crowd of women all watching her.

"You know what to do," Maggie prompted.

Marie nodded. With precise steps, she walked up to the grove. She reached out, brushing the trunks and limbs of the trees. She walked around, a look of contemplation on her face. She made it all the way around the stand without stopping. Spear found herself holding her breath, waiting for something, but she didn't know what.

Marie looked at Maggie, confusion on her face.

"It's not always here," Maggie said. "Listen for Her voice, and you'll find it."

"I believe in you," River said.

Marie nodded and stood still, her hand hovering over the flowers.

A cloak of silent anticipation settled over the assembled Maidens again.

Then, Marie looked up and out across the field. Her eyes fixed on a point in front of her, she set off across the grass. Maggie and River followed, with the others behind.

Marie walked right up to a single standing tree. It was more twisted than the others, with three separate thin trunks twined around each other. A weather-broken stone stood before it, while other smaller stones radiated out from it in a swirl.

"This is it," Marie announced, grasping the closest branch.

The sense of waiting flowed out of the crowd and a small chuckle replaced it.

"A strong tree," Maggie agreed, stepping up beside Marie. She glanced down at the stone. "She was a Prime, and all her daughters were Maidens. She held back the Briar clan when they wanted to burn out the families of the Boundary Wood so they could cut down the trees to build their Briar Line."

"Brought them here," another voice called out.

"Gave them sanctuary," another voice added.

"Killed the clan chief!" yelled a voice off to Spear's right.

Laughter rippled through the crowd, and Maggie smiled.

"Died to save them," River said, and the laughter died, transforming into reverent silence.

"A strong tree," Maggie said again. She looked at Marie, who nodded.

"Marie of the Islands," Maggie called out in a strong voice. "Who came to us fleeing slaughter, brought to us by strong Brothers and Maidens. You have passed all our tests, and now stand before us as a Thorn Maiden. Do you accept the responsibility of defending the forest and its people from all their enemies?"

"I do," Marie said in an equally strong voice.

"Will you go out and find others like yourself and defend them from violence, guide them on the path to the Mother of Exiles?"

"I will."

"Bring to them the tools they require to defend their own lives? Teach them to avoid being the toys of men's desires? Give them choices they've never had before?"

Maggie's voice rose, echoing around the valley.

"I swear!" Marie called back.

"Sisters!" Maggie cried. "Do you accept Marie as a Thorn Maiden? Will you teach her, and learn from her?"

"Yes," came the resounding reply from all throats.

Spear looked around and saw tears on the faces of both young and old Maidens. The apprentices gripped each other tight, caught up in their emotions.

"In the name of our Queen of Thorns, I bring you into our sisterhood." Maggie embraced Marie.

"Marie!" came the cry all around. Spear found herself shouting, too.

Maggie turned the openly weeping Marie to face her new sisters, who yelled and clapped for her. Maggie let it go on for a moment, then raised her hand, and the crowd fell silent.

"Thorn Maiden Marie," Maggie instructed. "Cut your hilt." She reached behind her, and River passed her a wide weapon with a saw-toothed blade.

It took a moment for Marie to wipe her eyes and accept the blade. She nodded to Maggie and River, then grasped the branch she had been holding. With a sure hand, she drew the blade across the wood. After only three strokes, the branch came off in her hand. Another shout rose from the crowd as she held it above her head. Petals fell, catching in her black hair.

When the shouting had settled, Maggie said, "In the morning, we'll take the branch to the swordsmith, and she will make you your sword." A mischievous smile played over Maggie's face. "I think I know just the blade, too."

Laughter flowed as everyone went to embrace and congratulate Marie. After a moment, Maggie waved everyone back.

"Now, we have a celebration feast to prepare," she called out.

"Back to your duties!" Dinah added. "Everyone knows where they should be. Apprentices! With me."

A lighthearted groan rose, but the young women and girls fell in behind her as she led them out of the field. Soon, it was only Maggie, River, Marie, Spear, and Heron standing before the single Wellcomb tree.

"You should go back to the house and rest," Maggie urged Marie.

"I'm not tired," Marie said with enthusiasm, gripping the branch tight. "I feel great!"

"You will be soon," Maggie said with the voice of experience.

"Come on, Sutab," River said with a smile, gently taking Marie's arm. "There's a room ready for you at the house. You can sleep, so you'll be ready for the feast tonight."

"But I want to see Balete!" Marie exclaimed. "He's been alone with little Narra for so long while I've been away and training."

"He's waiting for you," River informed her. "And he hasn't been alone. Lily and the others saw to that."

With a wide smile, Marie finally let herself be led away.

"You're wearing your broach today, Prime," Heron noted with a sly grin.

Maggie's hand went to the silver broach at her throat. Spear looked closer and saw that it was a Wellcomb flower, but the center was purple instead of red.

Maggie smiled ruefully and pulled it off, slipping the silver flower into a pocket. "I'm always afraid of losing it, running through the forest. But I have to wear it sometimes."

Heron smiled, and Spear tilted her head in confusion. She'd only seen Maggie wear the broach a few times, always when she was meeting with Dornshen and the other Children on official forest business. Wolf wore his broach whenever he was in town, the green center always looking bright.

Maggie glanced at the tree Marie had chosen for a moment, then, with a nod to Heron and Spear, walked toward another clump of trees. Spear tried to follow, but Heron shook her head. So Spear pulled one of the flowers down and sniffed it.

"It has a clean smell," she observed.

Heron nodded. "I guess it does. I'd never thought about it before."

"So, all Maidens are . . . buried here?" Spear asked.

"No, not all," Heron said. "Those who want to be are. Some families have their own places, or keep the ashes. One family wants to be given back to the forest. They leave their bodies in hidden places and let them nourish the trees." Heron frowned a little.

"I can understand that," Spear said, brushing her hand over the tree's bark.

"But all hilts come back here," Heron continued, tapping the hilt of her sword.

Spear looked confused.

"Here, let me show you."

Heron led her across the field to a place where the grass was low.

"A moon before you and Canin arrived, one of my teachers died. She was Human, but she believed what the Fairies do about the cycle of life, death, and rebirth." Heron smiled. "She was a hard woman. She fought all her life so her daughters and sons could have a better life. She helped me through my tests, and stood beside me when I found my hilt." She touched her sword. Heron took a deep breath.

"After her pyre, we brought the ashes out here and buried them, along with the hilt of her sword, all wrapped in a paste of Wellcomb seeds." Heron knelt, touching the ground. "Soon, with the Mother's blessing, a new tree will grow here, and the cycle will begin again."

Spear nodded, looking down at the ground. "I understand," she said. "She Returned to the Cycle in her own way. May she Return swiftly."

Spear made the Sign of the Three, and Heron awkwardly mirrored it.

306

"She had such stories," Heron continued with a grin, standing and brushing off her knees. "One time. . . ."

"What is she doing here?" a rude voice broke in.

Heron and Spear turned to see an older woman limping across the field toward them. She leaned on a walking stick of white oak, and a Thorn Maiden's sword swung at her side. A silver broach of a Wellcomb flower was pinned over her heart, but unlike Maggie's, one of the petals was broken off.

"Maiden Dala." Heron greeted her with a nod. "This is Spear."

"I know who she is," Dala said with contempt. She stopped, pointing her stick at Spear. "Why is a Fairy here, in one of our most sacred places?"

Spear's damaged wings twitched, their phantom pain shooting through her like lightning. Her left hand went to her sword, gripping the sheath, while her right hand clenched.

"She came here with me," Heron explained firmly, stepping a little between them. "To witness the raising of a new Sister. Maggie has. . . ."

"She's the reason many are here." Dala's stick swept over the field. "Fairies killed many of them! And now she stands here!"

Heron tensed, her hand jerking toward her sword, but she held back in respect for this former Prime.

Spear, on the other hand, relaxed. Her hands fell to her side. "I didn't kill them."

At Dala's shocked and angry look, she continued, "Or at least I don't think I did. Unless they fought at Brine Hill. I killed a lot of Humans that day." She frowned in apology. "Forgive me. I was just defending myself and my squad. Doing my duty to Captain and Queen." Spear put her hand over her heart and bowed slightly.

Dala ground her teeth as Heron covered a smile. "Do not play the fool with me, Fairy," she spat. "My people — our people — were forced to fight that day, and all the days before and after." She glared at Heron, who smoothed the amusement from her face.

"We refused to fight when the King declared war — again — on the Fairies," Dala said. "It was not our fight. Elenites refused, all up and down the border." She folded her arms. "And the King's men came, the Priests and their Axes. Took us from our homes, killing the loud ones, and forcing our men to the front lines. They starved them, and fed them herbs till they were no better than animals." She spat on the ground. "Then they used them as chattel, throwing them at the Fairies to be slaughtered."

"I know," Spear said calmly. "We would have given them mercy, but they were like rabid dogs." She shrugged.

"Fairies were no better. You used them to gather spent arrows and rescue downed flyers." Dala's face was red.

"We never did," Spear disagreed. She clarified. "My squads never did. We treated them with honor."

"Honor!" Dala snapped, stepping closer, her stick waving erratically at Spear. "Don't speak to me of Fairy honor. Soldiers took my sisters, my brothers. Used them."

She took a step closer, and Spear stepped back, pain from the woman's anger clear on her face.

Heron stepped between them again. "Maiden Dala," she said firmly. "Spear has been given rights and responsibilities as a Maiden. She's taught us. She's been accepted by the Mother. She respects our ways."

Dala scoffed. "Respects?! If I were still Prime. . . ."

"Then it's a good thing you aren't." Maggie broke in, shouldering her way between Heron and Dala. She folded her arms, giving Dala a firm look.

"Prime," Dala said with thin respect. She pushed her stick into the ground and leaned on it.

"Spear is a valuable member of the forest community and my Maidens. I made the decision for her to train them." Maggie glared, but Dala didn't back down. "Her skills and knowledge will help them better defend our home. Your home."

Dala let out a contemptuous breath. "As you say, Prime. It was your decision."

"Many would have died, or been maimed, if not for her," Heron said.

"I could look at your leg," Spear offered. "Maybe Heal that limp."

"You will not touch me, Fairy," Dala replied. "I received this wound in defense of the Mother. You will not defile it with your . . . Magic." She pulled her stick free from the ground.

"Prime," she said through clenched teeth.

"Maiden," Maggie said with a nod.

Dala glared again at Spear, then turned and walked off, limping, but with her back straight.

"I'm sorry," Heron apologized, turning to Spear.

"No," Spear said with a smile. "I understand. I'll just have to work harder."

"You work hard enough as it is," Heron argued.

Spear just shook her head and ran a hand over her bare skull.

"But. . .," Heron started, before Maggie interrupted.

"Maidens, we have duties."

"Yes, Prime," Heron said with a sigh. "Come on, Sister," she said to Spear. "You can show me that multi kick again. I'm close to getting it."

"Not that close," Spear commented with a smile.

The two of them walked off, leaving Maggie alone.

"Mother help me," she muttered, then jogged after them.

Chapter 39
Under the Stars

The red of the sunset had faded away, leaving a dark sky, speckled with stars. Clouds piled up in the east, but at the top — as though the Goddess had drawn a blade across the sky — they ended in an almost perfect line. Bright moonlight peeked over the trees below them, making Spear's Fairy eyes glint.

Canin sat up, the Power-infused bedroll moving underneath him. Spear made a small sound and ran her hand up his bare back. Her touch made him shiver.

The small fire had burned down to just coals, glowing faintly. He reached out toward them, as the fading heat of their passion made the night air bite his skin.

"Is there someone else out here?" Spear asked, also sitting up. She gestured across the dark field to another faint glowing light.

Canin looked in the direction she pointed. Here, on the eastern edge of the Exile Forest, the land rolled, sloping down toward the farmlands of the Human Realm. Beyond his sight lay a river, the understood boundary of the forest. It was a line Maidens and Brothers had long fought to enforce.

"It's one of the Shrines to the Mother," Canin said after a moment. "There's always a light, so people seeking Her can find it." He reached forward, stirring up the coals. Bits of wood caught fire, and flames flickered.

"So, we're not alone," Spear said with a grin.

"We never really are here," Canin admitted. "There's a Treetower somewhere behind us, and watchers and scouts moving through the forest. There's a Maiden and a Brother at the Shrine." He shrugged. "They're far enough away." He shrugged again.

"But I do feel like we're alone." He took her hand. "We haven't really been alone since we got here. We've both been so busy."

Spear nodded.

"What with Aurora, you teaching the Maidens. Me rejoining the Brothers." Canin sighed. "Feels like we've been running for what . . . how many moons?"

Spear shrugged. "I've lost count. Maybe four? Your mother would know."

Canin laughed. The days since he had returned to the Exile Forest with Spear and Aurora had sped by, leaving him feeling bewildered. But every day brought a new challenge, an old friendship rekindled, a new Brother made.

Aurora was growing like a sapling. It must be the combination of the Mother's Milk and Spear's own milk that made her grow faster than the other babies. Sekrine would just shrug, and say that all babies are different.

"Regardless, I'm glad we took this time," Canin said, looking warmly at Spear. She smiled back, love and passion in her luminous eyes. She pulled him closer and pressed him back down on the bedroll. Their lips met, and their bodies melted together.

☾ ⌇⌇ ☼

The clouds had fled, leaving the sky above them clear.

"The Dancer," Canin noted, pointing to a line of three stars. "There's something about seeing those three stars. I would stare up at her for hours. I used to wonder if my mother was seeing them, too. I hoped she was."

His voice dropped and he took a deep breath. "Now, I wonder if she's seeing them."

"I'm sure she is," Spear said casually. "Min has very sharp eyes."

"That's not what I mean." Canin sighed, rolling to his side to look at her.

Spear raised her hand, tracing the curve of the stars that formed the sash of the Dancer, below the bright line of three stars. "So graceful, like she was when we danced under the full moon. You don't do that here." Spear turned her eyes to Canin, "I miss that."

"Maybe we could," Canin said carefully. "Just us. Or maybe some of the Maidens. They'd like that. Maybe."

Spear shook her head. "No. Too Fairy. People would talk and complain." She sat up. "It's better to forget." She pointed to the bright star just below the Dancer. "I'll be like the Old Man, always watching, but never touching."

Hearing the sorrow in her voice, Canin slid closer, putting his arm around her.

"I always hated the Old Man," he confessed. "Always watching her dance. Now, I understand. He stays close, but is never able to touch her." His voice trailed off.

"You can touch me," Spear offered, pulling his other hand into her lap. "I'm not the graceful Dancer, but I'm here. I need you. I'd never be able to live here alone."

Canin smiled, feeling the warmth of her skin. They leaned together, kissing long and passionately. Canin was about to pull her back down, when Spear pulled away.

"When are you leaving for this mission?" she asked.

Canin sighed. "Two days. We can't leave too early, or the harvest celebrations won't have started. That's the best time to catch his eye."

"What if Sadie doesn't grab his attention?" Spear asked, all trace of romance gone from her voice.

"She will. I trust in her skills."

Spear snorted. "But what if she doesn't?"

"She will."

Spear's eyes turned cold. "What if she doesn't? You're the leader! You have to be prepared for anything. It's a good plan, but what if everything goes wrong? What will you do then?"

Canin took a breath. "Then we'll figure out another way to trap him. I trust in the Mother to lead us."

"Trust in the Mother, but keep your knife sharp," Spear counseled, poking him in the chest.

"I will," he swore.

"And you'll be gone a long time," Spear said, her eyes becoming wide and full of tears at the sudden realization. "What will I do till you come back? What if you never come back?"

Canin gripped her hand. "It will only be a few moons. Enough time to make sure we have the right man, and then for Sadie to ensnare him. We won't be gone too long. I promise."

Spear took a long breath. "But. . . ."

"No," Canin said firmly. "Nothing will go wrong. I trust in everyone who's going with me. I'm not going alone this time."

"But you're leaving me alone," Spear accused.

"You won't be alone," Canin stressed. "Lily will be here. Maggie and the other Maidens will keep you busy. And Aurora needs you."

Spear nodded slowly.

"I'm going to miss her," Canin admitted. "She's growing so fast. I'll miss a lot of things."

"Then don't go," Spear cajoled.

"I have to," Canin said. "I have to do this. I have to make up for the mistakes I've made. All the people I've hurt. I. . . ."

He stopped.

"I understand," Spear said, sitting up straight. "I know all about regrets. My heart is full of them. They rattle in my mind. Their voices keep me up at night." She took a long breath. "But with you and Aurora, the voices are quieter. Even Lily keeps them away sometimes."

"Then everything will be fine," Canin said, putting on a brave face. Inside, though, he was still torn between these two conflicting duties.

"She needs her father, so if you don't come back. . . ." Spear grabbed his face and pulled him close. "I will never forgive you."

"I'll be back," Canin promised, pulling her palm to his lips. "I swear it. On my love for you and our child."

"Good," Spear said, grabbing him and pushing him down onto the bedroll. "Now show me your love."

Canin tried to swear again, but she was on top of him, and kissing him with such intensity that words failed him. Actions were required.

The rising call of a forest bird woke Canin.

'They shouldn't be singing so early,' he thought, snuggling closer to Spear.

When the call came again, Canin sat up.

In the dim, pre-dawn light, he could see a figure moving across the field, headed toward the flickering light of the Shrine. The call came a third time, rising, then falling. Canin threw his blanket aside and concentrated on the figure still walking toward the Shrine. He strained, trying to see in the dim light combining from the almost-set moon and the not-yet-risen sun. His stomach knotted, knowing what his eyes could not yet confirm.

Spear was sitting up beside him, laying her hand on his arm, but he could barely feel it. The figure was getting closer to the Shrine, and the light of the lamp now showed it was cloaked and hooded in red.

Canin stopped breathing as the woman stopped just inside the circle of light. And he knew it was a woman; no one else would come to a Shrine cloaked in red. Overcome by memories and dreams, he shrugged off Spear's insistent hand.

The Shrine was a simple structure with three walls, open on the side facing east. Inside were a simple straw-lined crib and a chair. The woman stared at the crib, her arms hidden under the red cloak's fabric. She stood there for what seemed a long time, then, with a straight back, she stepped inside the Shrine. Quickly, she took a bundle from under her cloak and placed it in the crib.

The weak cry of a baby broke Canin out of his paralysis. Tears blurred his vison, but he could clearly see the woman in red turn from the baby and walk away from the Shrine.

"She's just. . .," Spear breathed.

"Leaving," Canin said.

Appearing out of the dark, her brown hood cast back, a Thorn Maiden caught up with the woman in red. She spoke for a moment with the woman, who barely paused. Moving quickly, her crimson cloak billowing behind her, the mystery woman walked away.

The baby issued another weak cry. The light of the lamp was eclipsed for a moment as the Thorn Brother went to check on the child.

Canin knew he should get up and go help, but the voice of memory kept him rooted to the ground. "Mama! I'll be good. Please, Mama!" He could see her walking away, disappearing into the dark as a man with a beard loomed over him, huge and scary.

"It's all right, my boy. You're home now."

Tears filled his eyes, and all he could see was a blur of red.

Spear was shaking him, and Canin dug his nails into his hand to banish the memories.

"I'm okay," he said.

"I saw her leave you. All in red. Was that your mother?" she asked, still shaking him.

"Yes. Please, I'm all right." He pulled his arm free of her grasp and struggled to his feet. "We have to go."

Not waiting for her, Canin walked across the field toward the Shrine. Inside, the Thorn Brother — an older Human with a scar across his forehead — was trying to feed the baby. He looked at Canin, resigned fear in his eyes.

"She's starved and neglected, and she won't take the bottle." He pressed the nipple to the little girl's mouth, but there was no response. His eyes lit up with hope as Spear joined them.

"Can you try?" he asked.

"Because I'm a woman?" Spear asked.

"No. Because of your Magic," the man said, offering the baby to Spear.

Spear took the wrapped infant. Her eyes glazed a little as she reached out with her Healing Power. "I can Heal her a little, but it won't do any good if she won't drink. Abandoned. . . ." Spear's eyes closed, and her hold on the baby loosened. Canin reached out, feeling the sudden despair radiating off Spear. The baby's pale hair shone in the light of the lamp hanging above them.

"No," Spear said. "I won't let you. Not again." She sat down in the chair, ripped her shirt open, and pressed her breast into the mouth of the Human child. For a moment, nothing happened, but then the baby latched on and began to suckle. Spear sighed, and a silver glow covered them both for a moment.

"Mother Mercy!" the Thorn Brother breathed. "I didn't mean. . . ."

"Brother Marsh, why don't you make sure no one else is around?" Canin asked with a pointed look.

The man nodded, and stepped out of the Shrine.

"I thought you were done making milk?" Canin said softly.

"Fairies can control their bodies," Spear said. "I thought you knew that."

"I guess I did."

"But I'm not going to be everyone's wet-nurse," she said with a tinge of anger. "This was just . . . for her. I wasn't letting another baby die because they were abandoned."

"I know," Canin said, leaning in and kissing her. He still felt both his and Spear's raging emotions as he watched the baby suckle. He felt her gain strength. Felt her come back from the brink.

Felt himself come back. He drew in a breath, taking in all the pain of his own abandonment. All the blurry memories of his mother — in red — walking away. All his begging for her to come back.

And let them go. Canin forgave his mother. Forgave her for doing the hardest thing she ever had to do, giving him this life. He kissed Spear again and felt her joy and determination.

"Another friend for Aurora," he pronounced with a smile.

Spear smiled back and looked down at the baby.

The sun was up by the time the Maiden returned. The baby was sated and sleeping in Canin's arms. He sat while Spear investigated all the crannies of the simple Shrine. The Thorn Brother, Marsh, sat just outside, waiting for their morning relief.

"Raphaella?" he asked with a raised eyebrow.

The Maiden shook her head. "I followed her to the river. She met some Humans on horseback there. Three women and two men. She mounted up behind one of the women, and they all rode off to the south."

"She never spoke to you?" Canin asked.

"No. I tried," Raphaella said with a frown, "but she just shook her head and drew a red veil across her face. So, I just followed her."

"No one else?" Marsh asked.

"No. I waited, but it's all quiet this morning." The young woman smiled. "Can I hold her?" she asked Canin.

Canin smiled, too, and held the baby out to her. The Maiden took her and held her gently. The baby fussed a little, but went back to sleep.

"Didn't even give a name for the babe?" Marsh asked.

Raphaella shook her head, but didn't otherwise respond. She was gazing down at the baby.

"I guess we'll have to call her something till she's old enough to choose her own name." Marsh stood up and went to look over the woman's shoulder. He, too, gazed in wonder at the sleeping child.

"Red veil?" Spear asked, her eyebrows raised in question.

Raphaella smiled, pulling her gaze away from the baby. "Red, for sorrow at the loss of a loved one or baby."

Spear nodded, still not quite understanding.

"The family will tell everyone the baby died," Marsh said with an angry edge. "They'll mourn. Then, after a decent amount of time, she'll get pregnant again. Everyone will pray to the Father that it's a boy this time." His face darkened. "Motherless bastards, all of 'em."

Raphaella gave him a look, and his frown softened.

"Sorry, Sutab," he said low.

Canin tilted his head, guessing there was more there than he knew. Spear just shrugged and tapped him on the shoulder.

"We'll take her back with us," he said, standing. "Sekrine will want to see her right away." At Spear's grunt, he added, "And I'm sure she can find a wet-nurse for the babe."

Raphaella reluctantly gave the baby back to Canin. "She should have a name."

Marsh and Canin looked at each other blankly. Even though she had suggested it, Raphaella looked puzzled, too. Spear looked from one to the next, reading their thinking faces. Finally, she spoke up.

"Izi."

All of them looked at her, baffled.

"It means 'fire' in Old Fairy."

"I don't understand," Raphaella said.

Spear rolled her eyes. She pointed to the oil lamp above them. "The mother was guided by the fire. The baby had a fire in her. She should have died, but something kept her alive. Fire." Spear shrugged. "We have to go," she said, tugging Canin outside.

Canin nodded, allowing himself to be led away.

"Maybe I can come with you?" Raphaella asked softly, following them.

"We have duties here, Maiden," Marsh reminded her firmly. "At least till the half moon."

Raphaella looked at Canin, almost pleading. Surprised, Canin wondered why she was looking to him for support. Marsh was the most senior Brother or Maiden on the night watch for this part of the forest, and thus, the leader.

"He's right. You have important work here, Maiden Raphaella," Canin said with a smile to her disappointed frown. "I'll tell Sekrine of your interest, and I'm sure she'll keep you informed of the baby's . . . Izi's progress. Maybe you can ask to adopt her, or be one of her guides?"

Raphaella's eyes lit up at the prospect, but dimmed when Spear added, "If Maggie and the Children approve."

"It's a big responsibility," Marsh said with a good-natured slap to her back. "Sure you're up to it?"

"They let you have a child," Raphaella shot back, giving him an elbow to the stomach.

He laughed, waving to the group of Maidens and Brothers coming out of the forest from the direction of the Treetower. One waved back and hurried toward them.

"Come on," Spear said, impatiently dragging Canin toward their little campsite. "Aurora and Lily expect us back."

Raphaella and Marsh laughed openly as Canin followed his wife, baby in his arms.

Chapter 40
Warriors of the
Queen of Thorns

They met on the hill above the Sanctuary village, intending to take the Pine Haven trail as far as they could before turning east. Canin arrived first. He set down his pack and looked out over the village. The rising sun painted shadows and light over the trees and houses below. He could just see the tree that grew beside his mother's house.

Canin touched his wooden knife and remembered the vow he had made to all of them — even Alexander! — that he would come back. Doubts married to determination rolled in his mind, and he might have descended deeper into that battle, but he heard footsteps on the trail.

Heron and Stonefoot came around the bend, saw him, and waved. The shorter Stonefoot had to take two steps to match each one of Heron's, but somehow they stayed side by side.

"Don't let it bother you," Heron was saying.

Stonefoot frowned, shaking her head. "She won't even say good-bye. All she did was complain because I was going with you."

"Your mother?" Canin asked as the two Maidens stopped beside him.

"Of course," Heron said, adjusting the long bow and quiver slung over her shoulder.

Stonefoot just frowned, picking at the strap of her own quiver.

"She's going to have to get used to us," Heron declared, laying a hand on Stonefoot's shoulder. "My feelings aren't going to change."

Stonefoot smiled slightly, her hand brushing Heron's. "Mine aren't either, but I don't want to talk about it anymore." She looked at Canin. "We have an important task to do."

"We do," Canin agreed.

Heron nodded and stepped back.

"I thought Jessamine was going to be with you?" Canin asked with a sudden frown.

"She has a favorite bathing pool she wanted to visit first," Heron said. "She'll meet us at the eastern edge."

Canin frowned more deeply, worried — not for the first time — that all of this would be too much for the former Maiden.

"Marie and Raphaella are with her," Stonefoot explained. "They'll make sure she makes it to the meeting place."

Canin pushed aside his worry, trusting in the others to keep Jessamine safe. Even though both were newly raised Maidens.

'Trust in your people.' Wolf's words echoed in his mind.

"Where are the boys?" Heron asked, looking out over the village.

As if on cue, they saw Maggie — with Sam on her heels, and Granite behind — come around the bend. She stopped in front of them, hands on her hips. Everyone but Granite straightened under her gaze. He just leaned on a tree, absently running a hand over his scar.

"Where's Sadie?" Maggie asked.

Canin looked at the Maidens and Brothers, but none of them made a sound.

"I thought she would be with you," he said to Heron.

"She just got back from a run a few days ago," Granite said casually. "Maybe she's just sleeping late."

"We were supposed to meet at dawn," Maggie said. "With Wolf on another run, it's up to me to make sure you all leave on time."

"She'll be here, Prime," Granite said. "Don't worry."

Maggie shot him a look, and Sam gave Granite a nudge.

"It's my job to worry," Maggie said. "Thorn Brother Granite."

Realizing he might have pushed things too far, Granite straightened and gave an apologetic nod to Maggie.

"If she's not here soon, I'll go looking for her," Sam offered.

Maggie gave him a look usually reserved for overenthusiastic puppies. Granite and Stonefoot stifled a laugh, while Heron looked up at the sky, pretending she hadn't heard.

More worries tightened Canin's stomach. Crow had been leading that run, and he had been opposed to this mission from the very beginning. If he had persuaded Sadie to back out, then everything would be delayed. Neither Heron nor Stonefoot could fill Sadie's role. Granite could, but he wasn't the kind of bait this plan needed. Maybe. . . .

"I'm here!" Sadie's voice rang out clearly over the sound of her running feet. She skidded to a stop in front of Maggie. "I had to deliver a message to Lightfoot's wife."

Maggie didn't move, but just stared at Sadie, her arms folded.

"Prime," Sadie said with more deference. "I'm sorry I'm late. But you know how Meredith loves to talk. Even this early."

Maggie nodded, her stance relaxing some. "Who was the message from?"

"Chana," Sadie said with a smile.

Heron, Stonefoot, and Granite stood straighter and turned to listen.

"How is she?" Maggie asked slowly. "She's not been home in many seasons."

"I didn't speak to her," Sadie said with a frown. "She left the message in one of the caches by the crossroads. She wrote that she and her brother were on a mission, and might be out of touch for a while."

"Her brother?" Canin asked. Then his face lit up in recognition. "Mathias. I remember them. He taught me to ride a horse. He was always so good with the horses. And she was always at his side. I couldn't help but notice her. . . ." He stopped, getting red.

Heron and Granite looked at each other with a smile. "Neither could we," they said together.

The others laughed, except for Sadie, who frowned for just a moment, then smiled.

"She left no message for me?" Maggie asked. She coughed. "Her Prime?"

"No," Sadie said with a shrug. "Just for Meredith."

"Why just for her?" Sam wondered.

321

Maggie looked at him coldly, and Granite rolled his eyes.

"I thought Spear would be here to see you off," Maggie said, turning to Canin.

He shook his head sadly. "She couldn't take seeing me walk away. And Aurora was crying, so we said, 'I'll return' at the door." Canin pushed down the sorrow. "You'll watch out for her, won't you, Prime?"

"As much as I can," Maggie promised. "Sekrine will keep her busy, and we also have a new crop of apprentices to train."

"That will keep her focused," Heron said.

Granite grinned. "Those poor ladies!"

Maggie nodded. "No more delay." She swept a look over the group.

Heron, Stonefoot, and Sadie moved closer together, drawing their swords and offering them, hilt first, to Maggie. With a nod, Maggie touched each of the offered hilts and said, "Brings these back to us with victory."

Each woman nodded, kissed their hilt, and slid it back into its scabbard. Maggie turned to the three Thorn Brothers. They offered their knives to her in the same manner.

"I stand for your Prime," Maggie said. "Bring these back to us with victory." Sam and Granite nodded, kissing their blades before re-sheathing them. Maggie lingered, her hand still on Canin's knife.

"Take care of my Maidens," she said.

"I will," Canin swore with a nod.

Maggie's serious face turned into a smile. "Or Spear will have words with you."

Canin chuckled and kissed the wooden blade. "I made the same vow to her."

"What about his Brothers?" Sam asked.

"You two can take care of yourselves," Maggie replied, with a smile at Sam and Granite. They smiled back, Sam with barely hidden emotion. He started to speak, but Maggie drew her sword.

She stood with her back to the Sanctuary village. The sun glinted on her blade.

"In the name of our Mother of Exiles," Maggie pronounced. "As warriors of our Queen of Thorns, go forth and bring justice." She paused, looking at them over the edge of her blade, this blade that had been wielded by so many other Maidens before her. "And come back to us."

"For the Mother of Exiles!" they all shouted back.

"Our Queen of Thorns!" Canin said with dark determination.

"Let her guide you," Maggie counseled, sheathing her sword with a click.

The group gathered their gear and set off down the trail. Sam and Stonefoot led, with Granite and Sadie in the middle, and Heron behind. She glanced back at Canin, who waved for her to go on.

He would have said something, but Maggie held up her hand and motioned for him to go.

"I'll take care of our family here. You go and take care of yours."

Canin nodded, and ran to catch up with Heron.

Maggie watched them disappear into the dark forest.

She wondered how many of them she wouldn't see again.

 ## End of Book Four

If you've enjoyed the adventures of the characters in this book, please remember to sign up for my news and updates list at https://www.ServantsoftheMoonandSun.com and review this book on Amazon.com or your preferred platform to help others find my work. Thanks!

Also, if you haven't already, please read the earlier books in this series, which are all available at Amazon and wherever books are sold, in hardcover, paperback, e-book, and audiobook formats!

And be on the lookout for Book Five: coming Fall 2025!

Also By

Joel C. Flanagan-Grannemann

The Servants of the Moon and Sun Series:

Talia: Heir to the Fairy Realm
Talia: On the Shore of the Sea
Fairy Court in Exile: An Epic Fantasy Novel of Civil War
Mother of Exiles: The Epic Fantasy Adventure of a Prodigal Son
Returning to the Exile Forest

Short Story Set in the Servants of the Moon and Sun World:

The Fairy Soldier's Last Request, from Tales Untold: Mythos from
Around the World

About the Author

Joel C. Flanagan-Grannemann has been writing since childhood, and has a B.A. in writing from the University of Pittsburgh at Bradford in Bradford, PA. He has lived in Columbia, SC for more than twenty years with his wife and editor, Jay-Jay Flanagan-Grannemann, and a coterie of cats. Joel has a day job in back room operations at a major national retail chain where he has worked in various capacities since 1995. For more information, please visit www.ServantsoftheMoonandSun.com.

www.ingramcontent.com/pod-product-compliance
Lightning Source LLC
Chambersburg PA
CBHW070044030726
47506CB00002B/331